KW-222-997

Slate

Rebel Wayfarers MC

MariaLisa deMora

Danniellei
Thank you!
MariaLisa
de Mora
♥

Edited by Hot Tree Editing

Melissa Gill @ MGBookcovers and Designs

Copyright © 2014 MariaLisa deMora

All rights reserved. This book or any portion thereof may not
be reproduced or used in any manner whatsoever without the
express written permission of the publisher except for the use of
brief quotations in a book review. This is a work of fiction. Names,
characters, places and incidents are either the product of the
author's imagination, or are used in a fictitious manner. Any
resemblance to actual persons, living or dead, or actual events is
entirely coincidental.

First Published 2014

ISBN 13: 978-0990447320

DEDICATION

To my best friend, Hollie. Thank you.

Contents

ACKNOWLEDGMENTS

Slate brought different challenges to the table than the first book in this series. Because I can be taught, I shined and polished the story even more before I passed it off to family and friends, and as a result, they fell more deeply in love with the characters, which was hugely gratifying.

To my daughters Stephanie and Tobyhanna, thank you for your support. You are amazing women! My dear, bestie Hollie, you offer an unflappable faith and confidence in my dreams, you crazy woman. You help me believe. Brenda, you were the voice of sanity that never let me lose sight of what a gift the response was to *Mica*. Again, I tell you beautiful, strong women—tequila (or drinks of your choice) all around!

Kayla and the folks at Hot Tree Editing, you rock hard for continuing to edit under challenging circumstances, and for sending me photos of your goose bumps as encouragement. What's not to love! Melissa Gill, woman, you did a phenom job on the cover, you just *got* what I wanted. Thank you.

Woofully yours,
~ML

1 - Wyoming

Twenty years ago

Andrew Jones sat on the floor in front of the fireplace, his half-hooded eyes looking into the flames. He was leaning back against the front of his mother's tired leather couch, letting the warmth seep into his bones. At this time of year, the heat of the fire was welcomed after a day of working the cattle. He tipped his head back and let it rest on the flattened cushions, closing his eyes. He felt a tug at his boot and automatically lifted up his leg, allowing his little brother to begin the process of removing it from his foot. Benjamin was only five, but he tried to take care of everyone as if he was a grown man.

Even though his brother was ten years his junior, he let Benny do as much as he could and thought it was funny the things the shrimp took on himself, such as undressing his big brother like this. On the ranch proper, the hard, outside work was falling more and more on Andy's shoulders. Their dad had been sick for a couple of years now, and for this last stretch of several months, he'd been unable to do anything physical. Andy knew the ranch could only afford to hire so many hands before it was a losing proposition, so he absorbed as much of the load as he could.

Feeling a hand on his head, he looked up to see Ben's face only inches away, his pale blue eyes staring at him while he tugged on the bandana wrapped around Andy's head. He claimed it was there to soak up the sweat, but honestly, it helped keep his too-big hat on his head in the relentless Wyoming winds. Lifting his head so the kid didn't pull his hair out along with the bandana, he grinned up at his brother. "Put that in my hat; don't forget. Did ya get the other boot yet, shrimp?" he asked, closing his eyes again. "Nawp, willth now, though," Ben said with his lingering lisp.

Andy sighed and shifted his shoulders against the couch, stretching his back and sliding his ass down a little more on the rug, asking, "We need wood?" He knew his brother brought in wood as was needed during the day, but he liked to leave the box beside the fire full before bed.

"Yep. I can help," Ben responded, tugging at the toe of Andy's other boot.

"'Kay, shrimp." He picked up that leg, letting him pull the second boot off his foot. Eyes still closed, he reminded Ben, "Not too close to the fire...don't ruin 'em," and heard the boots being shifted a couple feet further away from the hearth.

"Boys, come to the kitchen and eat," Andy heard his mother call from another room. She must have stuck her head around the doorframe, because her voice was closer when she said, "Soon, please, while it's still warm."

"Yes'um," he replied, climbing to his stocking feet, feeling the chill of the floor through his thin socks. Picking up Ben, he slung him onto his back, feeling his brother's little arms and legs wrap around his neck and waist. "Let's go, little man," he said, and walked them into the kitchen.

His mother was standing in front of the sink, leaning back against the countertop. She had one hand on her hip, with her other arm folded across her stomach, and she was looking at Andy with an intense gaze. He thought something must have happened; she only looked like this when there was bad news, or if she was ticked at something he'd done. Cocking one eyebrow, he threw a non-verbal question at her as he settled Ben into his chair at the table.

She didn't respond, so seeing there were only three places set at the table, he asked, "Need me to take a tray up, Mom?" His dad had been making the trip down the stairs less frequently, and his Mom usually took dinner upstairs to him when he wasn't mobile enough to come down.

Not answering him, she asked, "What time did you hit that door this morning, Andy?"

He shook his head; it had been before sunup, and he didn't think he had been late, but maybe he had shorted doing something that was needed. "Um, prolly about five this morning, why? Did I forget to do something?"

She sighed at him, "No, I was wondering what time you started your day, was all." He had looked in the wood box in the kitchen before he sat down, making a mental note she needed some small wood and kindling in here. Sitting in his place across from his brother, he reached out his hands to either side, holding their hands with a bowed head as she said Grace over their meal.

He and Ben both echoed her, "Amen," and then he reached across and began filling her and Ben's plates with the food. Putting ample servings of the roasted chicken and green beans on each plate, he gathered up a slice of bread and buttered one for each of them. He passed those plates along the table at their places, and then stopped for a second. "Did you already make Daddy a plate?" He waited for her nod before he served himself.

Shoveling food into his mouth, he realized how hungry he was. It had been a long day, and he hadn't been able to take a break for lunch. The veterinarian had been scheduled out all day, and they'd had to shift and sift a bunch of cattle through the corrals and catch pens in order to get the calves out for shots, drenches, branding, and cutting. They'd gone through about two-hundred head today, and had that many to go tomorrow before they were done.

He'd been in the bunkhouse at about five that morning to start the cowboy coffee, and to throw biscuits in the stove out there. He fed the horses while the biscuits were baking, and got back in time to fry sausage and bacon, and to scramble some eggs. Preparing enough food for the ranch hands to eat breakfast and then make wax paper-wrapped lunches for later had taken up a chunk of time, so then he had to rush through his chores in the horse barn before they got started on the day's work. He'd gotten most of the horses saddled and ready to go before the hands rolled out of their bunks, and Nash, his favorite ranch hand, had helped him with the rest.

Standing up from the table, he stretched his back to the left and right, straightening some of the kinks out of it from being in the saddle all day. With a yawn, he picked up his empty plate and dirty silverware and dropped them in the wash pan next to the sink. "Gotta get some wood in before it gets too much colder," he said over his shoulder as he walked back to the main room. His full, generous mouth smiled at his mother. "Good food, Mom. Thanks for supper."

Slipping his boots back on, he struggled to force his feet into the just-too-small leather. He straightened his jeans over the boot tops, and then raised the lid on the wood box to check and see how much was needed in here. Pulling his hat on over his unruly brown hair, he swept the room with his green-eyed gaze, looking for anything out of place. Stepping to the door, he lifted the latch as he grabbed his coat and headed into the darkness surrounding their home.

Standing on the porch in the dark, he listened to the lowing of the cattle; quiet music came from a guitar and harmonica in the bunkhouse. He heard the trill of the wind in the stay lines of the windmill and was quiet, taking in the music of the plains that had been his home his whole life.

Smiling, he walked the path to the woodpile by memory, not needing even the bright light of the moon to find his way. He knew this place like the back of his hand, and was glad each day to wake up and see the sunrise coming across from the eastern hills. He detoured a little by the windmill and patted the seat of his dirt bike, promising himself he'd ride the bike tomorrow instead of his gelding. He missed it when he went too long between rides.

After his third trip back into the house with firewood for the fireplace and woodstove, he grabbed the ax and chopped up enough kindling to get them through tomorrow. He had turned to go back, but stopped short when he saw his mother on the porch. She was standing there with her arms wrapped around her body, but no coat or shoes on.

"Mom, get back inside; I'm done here," he yelled across the yard to her, watching as she raised a hand to sweep her hair back from her face.

"Andrew, we need to have a chat. Come in, son," she called out to him and turned to go back into the house.

Sitting down on the couch after he dropped the kindling off in the kitchen, he looked around and asked, "Where's Benny?"

"I sent him on to bed; he doesn't need to hear this," she said with a hiccup in her voice. Andy sat still, afraid to move or say anything, thoughts racing through his head about the ranch and how broke they were. He thought about his dad and how sick he was, and about how skinny his mom had gotten...and how all of those things frightened him.

"Andrew, we heard from the doctors today. Your daddy isn't going to get better." Her voice hitched again. "He's only going to get worse." Andy nodded at her, because that didn't surprise him; he'd seen livestock sicken and waste away, like Daddy had been doing for months. Once they reached a certain point, they never came back from it, and he'd been thinking Daddy had gotten to that point a few weeks ago.

"We're considering selling the property and moving into town, where we can be closer to the hospital and doctors," she said, "closer to help." She continued speaking, but he couldn't hear anything over the noise in his head. It sounded louder than anything he'd ever heard, blocking out everything else. They were going to sell the ranch. It was his dad's legacy to him; it had been his grandparents' home.

His mouth dropped open because he was panting for breath, but he couldn't get enough air inside him anymore. He was hurting, in agony, and his mom *just kept talking* at him. They were going to sell the ranch; it was part of him. That dirt flowed through his veins sure as it was blood, and it was what kept him going each day. *They were going to sell his ranch.*

He knifed up, pushing away from the couch and leaned his arm against the fireplace mantle, feeling the roaring heat of the fire against his legs, welcoming that pain. Tall for fifteen, he knew he was thin, but he was strong; all the hands said so. He could run this place; he knew it in his bones. He could make it okay for the people he loved; he could make it all okay. He wasn't a kid anymore, and he thought he'd been proving it.

"Mom, I got this," he said softly. "You don't gotta sell. We don't…we don't gotta sell." Please, God, let her see what this meant to him. Let her take it back with a laugh and an apology. She was sorry, and she'd misunderstood. "I got this."

"Andrew, it's not about what you can or cannot do, son. It's about your daddy," she snapped, apparently not having expected any resistance. "He can't be out here, when the help we'll need is in Enoch."

"Mom, this was GeePa's daddy's place. We've had family living here for nearly a hundred years." He was in tears now, fighting to keep them from his voice. Standing with his back to her, he asked, "What about renting a place in town for you, Dad, and Benny?"

"Andrew, you know we don't have the extra money for that. We have to be realistic about what options there are, and your dad and I have decided that selling the ranch is probably the best one we have," she replied, her voice growing steely.

"You can't sell it, Mom. You can't," he pleaded, repeating, "I got this. I swear." He turned to look at her and saw how tense she was, sitting on the edge of the couch, her arms around her middle and holding herself together by digging her fingernails into her sides. If he was honest, it looked like this was killing her, too. He saw her pain and fear for his father in her face, clear as a summer's sky.

She opened her mouth again, and he cut her off, "No, it's okay, Mom. I get it." With a big sigh, he toed off his boots, set them to the side of the hearth, and asked, "What do you need me to do?"

***

The next months were busy as they entertained offers for the place. Andy sorted cattle and horses, sending the culls to the feedlots and auctions. One by one, the ranch hands left as they secured permanent employment at neighboring ranches until they were down to just him and Nash. They'd keep running the ranch until it sold, caring for the remaining cattle and horses.

Standing on the front porch of the house, Andy was holding a cup of hot coffee and sipping carefully. His sixteenth birthday had come and gone a month back; Nash was gonna take him in for his final driving test today. He'd had a hardship license for over a year, but that expired when he came of legal driving age, so he had to retake the test. He felt an arm circle his thigh, and without looking, dropped a hand down onto the tousled blond head beside his hip. "Hey, Benny, whatchu doin' up, shrimp?"

"GeeMa ith comin' to pick me up today." Ben rubbed his head against Andy's leg. "Mamma sayth I'ma stay with GeeMa and GeePa a while."

Andy rubbed his brother's head absently, ruffling the too-long hair, noticing he needed a haircut. "Did ya pack yet? Don't forget the bathroom stuff." Squatting down to Ben's height, he told him, "I'll be there in three days. Can you hold out that long? Three days."

"Yeth, and I got the toofbruth," came a considered answer.

"Good man," he told him proudly, standing back up, and keeping his hand on Ben's head, he repeated, "good man."

Andy heard his mother come rattling down the stairs in a hurry. "Andy," she called loudly, then she saw him on the porch and veered that way, "Andy, I need your help with Daddy." He took another drink of the coffee, dashed the dregs into the yard, and handed the cup to Ben. "Put that in the sink for me," he said, and followed his mother up the stairs.

Entering the sick room was like being transported to a different planet. Not only didn't it smell like the rest of the house, most things looked different too. Even the light coming through the windowpanes was different, as if it was a different wavelength than the sun's rays shining on the yard. His dad was in a hospital bed with the head cranked up a little, but not too much, because he didn't have the strength to hold his position in the bed. If it was cranked up too high, he would scoot down with his knees rucked up, and his back bent like a pretzel.

Medical equipment surrounded the head of the bed, each wavering control screen adding a green or blue hue to the light in the room. The oxygen machine created a humming noise, not unlike the slushy machine in the Stop-n-Go in town. The cannula—he'd been learning all the right words to describe the equipment, so he could more easily explain to someone over the phone when something was malfunctioning—was in position on Daddy's face. His eyes swept to the next machine and he saw the problem; the IV had stopped dripping.

Picking up his dad's arm, he saw the large, swollen spot that told him the intravenous needle had slipped free of the vein in his arm, depositing the necessary medicines and fluid into the muscle, instead of the more readily absorbed blood vein. "Mom, can you get another IV kit? This vein has blown," he said over his shoulder as he approached the bed. Picking up a small notebook that had a pen attached by a string, he made a note of the problem in their logbook.

Peeling back the tape from the existing needle site, he shut off the medicine and carefully removed the needle from his dad's arm. Dropping the used tubing into the trash, he put the needle part into the special container—

the Sharps container—which protected them from accidently getting stuck by used needles. After seeing what hepatitis had done to his dad, he sure didn't want it, and was always careful with things that needed to go in that container.

"Hey, Daddy, how you doin' this mornin'?" he asked as he worked. "You gonna let me know if I hurt you, right?" He always asked that and Daddy never said 'boo', so like every other time, he kept working on the task at hand. "Sunrise was pretty today; the sky was all pinks and oranges. Sure was nice. We've got a dozen head that went up the hill to old Mr. Jenison's place, so we'll have to be bringing them back home." He continued quietly, "Nash and I will go. We're gonna have to take the rifles; there have been varmints around lately, and I don't want to mess with them."

He paused, and then asked, "Mom, can you open— thanks." Interrupting himself, he'd looked over mid-statement and saw she'd opened the package and had everything he needed ready. Looking for a better place to start the next IV, Andy ran his fingers gently up and down his dad's arms, pausing at a place on the back of his wrist. "We haven't used this spot for more than a week, Daddy." He checked the logbook to make sure, with a quick-spoken, "Whacha think?"

When it came, the response was in a voice so gravelly with disuse it startled him, "Looks good, son."

Making quick work of cleaning the spot with an alcohol pad, Andy tenderly used the rubber tourniquet like the nurses had showed him, and deftly inserted the needle. He set it at the proper depth, anchoring it with strips of tape his mom had already torn off. Using a syringe of sterile liquid to flush the line, Andy made sure he had a good stick—that's what the nurses called it, a 'good stick'—and then he connected the tubing. Checking the logbook again, he set the machine to the correct dosage, made a note of what he'd done, and put the logbook back down on the table.

"Mom, what time is the ambulance coming to pick you guys up today?" he asked over his shoulder. Watching his dad's face, he asked, "Need to go pot, Daddy?" When his dad nodded, he moved the bedpan into position and effortlessly lifted his dad's wasted body onto it. "Pee, too?" His dad shook his head. "Dokies, I'm right here," he said, and he turned his back on his dad, giving him the illusion of privacy.

Andy realized his mom hadn't answered him, and he looked into her face, "What time, Mom? I want to make sure I'll be back before you leave." She shook her head at him, whispering, "No ambulance, Andy. We're staying here. Doctor said it won't be long enough to warrant the pain he would feel if we moved him."

His knees went weak and he took in a deep breath, blowing it out in a quavering rush. Another deep breath, he held it for a second or two as his eyes closed then blew it out steadily. Opening his eyes, he looked at his mother standing helplessly in the middle of the room. "What do you need me to do, Mom?"

***

Andy stood with his head bowed against the wind, his hand securing his hat in place. His other hand was cradling Ben's head against his hip, holding him tightly. The wind was fierce today, gusting across the open spaces; the clouds were gray and dense, streamers of darkness crawling across the sky.

Benny's form was swallowed up by an old suit of Andy's, the shoulders of the jacket draping across his body and the arms way too long. Andy had on one of his father's suits; the cuffs showed inches of sleeve, and were frayed and worn, while the shoulders were too tight across his back, causing the lapels to gape.

His mom stood on his other side, her arms wrapping around herself, fingernails clutching at her dark dress. Some of her hair had escaped the pins that held it in a bun at the back of her head, and wisps and strands whipped around her face wildly in the wind. She never looked at the preacher who was reading his dad's obituary, but stared stoically at the casket sitting in front of them.

Andy looked around, seeing the ranchers who had come to pay respect to Allen Jones and his widow, Susan. All their old hands were there too, hats in hand, listening to the preacher talk. Andy reached up and took off his hat, belatedly taking his cue from Nash, who was standing right behind him. Nash had been running things for the past couple of days since Daddy passed.

Ben's shoulders started to hitch, and Andy pulled him in front of him, turning him against his legs so Ben couldn't see the coffin any longer. He held him like that for the rest of the service, and then helped him pick up a handful of wet dirt to drop it into the hole after the funeral home people had lowered the casket.

Nash was there with a damp bandana to help clean up Ben's hands. Andy shook his head; he hadn't thought about that, but what kid wants to keep his daddy's funeral dirt on their hands? He needed to take better care of his brother.

Andy waited for his mom by the truck, letting her say her 'goodbyes' and 'thank yous' to the folks standing around in the cemetery. He'd boosted Ben up into the seat and was watching the shrimp lose his battle with sleep. His brother's eyes were drooping, and his head had nearly fallen over on his slender neck stalk, like a flower in heavy rain.

A warm hand clamped down on his shoulder, and Andy turned to see Nash holding him at arm's length. "You doin' okay, Andy?" he asked.

Andy nodded. "Well, as can be expected, I think. Momma coming?"

Nash shook his head. "She's headed over to your GeeMa and GeePa's place with them. I came to help get you home, but we need to drop Benny off with them first."

Andy nodded and opened the door to clamber across Ben and into the cab, leaving the keys in the ignition. "Would you drive, Nash? I don't wanna today." Sitting with his arm around his brother, looking out the window past the mirror, Andy bounced and swayed easily with the motion of the vehicle as they jounced through the ruts in the road.

"Nash, you gonna stay on with the new owners of the ranch?" Andy asked, turning and looking at him. He'd asked this question every day for two weeks, and the answer had been noncommittal each time. "I just wanna know if you're gonna be there, if you can stay."

Nash nodded. "Yeah, Andy, I'm staying."

Turning back to the window, Andy replied absently, "Good. That's good, Nash. I'm glad you'll still be on the place."

They pulled up in front of his dad's parents' house, and he saw GeeMa was waiting on the porch. Opening the door, he slid out of the truck, reaching back in for Ben. Draping his little brother's sleeping body across his chest, he had one arm around Ben's back and one around his hips, carrying the child like a sack of potatoes. GeeMa looked past him to Nash, asking, "Where is she, son?"

Andy looked from his grandmother to his mentor; something was going on, and he was pretty sure he wasn't going to be happy about it. "Where is who, GeeMa?"

"Your momma, Andy, she was supposed to ride with you," she said tartly.

"Nash said she was riding with you and GeePa," he said. He hitched Ben's body up because he'd lost his hold a little; his arms were beginning to get tired. "Let me lay Benny down; I'll be right back out."

He came out and the truck was gone, Nash with it. Standing in the front yard, he looked left and then right, thinking maybe Nash had parked the truck somewhere. Nope, Nash was gone. "GeeMa, where did Nash go? I have chores to get done before dark."

She came up behind him, rubbing his shoulders lightly. "Nash is taking care of your chores tonight; he'll be back in the morning to pick you up."

"Oh, okay." He chewed on his lip, looking at the ground. "Where's Momma?"

"She's visiting with some friends, Andy; she'll be along directly," his grandmother said as she turned away from him.

He stayed like that for a minute, looking down at the rocky soil of the yard. Nodding his head, he took one stiff step, and then another unbending one towards the house. Slowly following his grandmother inside, he looked around, and then lifted his head to ask, "GeeMa, what do you need me to do?"

2 - Susan's journey

Eighteen years ago

"Andy, I'm dropping her off in ten minutes, son," came through the phone as soon as he answered.

"Thanks," was all he said in response, severing the connection quickly. A few minutes later, Andy walked outside and stood on the small back stoop of their rental house, watching his mom weave her way up the driveway. Her shoes were in one hand, her purse in the other, and Andy could see the smeared lipstick on her face. He waved at Nash idling in the street, and watched him drive away.

Andy stepped off the stoop and met her halfway, holding up his hand to halt her progress towards the house. "Benny's sleeping, Mom. You're gonna need to keep it quiet so he can sleep. He's got a test tomorrow," he said, shaking his head.

Susan Jones stood swaying in the driveway, her feet betraying her with a sideways step occasionally, trying to find an elusive balance, even though she was no longer walking. "Benny won't mind if I wake him up for a kiss," she said with a smile. "He loves his Momma."

Andy closed his eyes, blowing his breath out through tensed lips. "Mom, he's sleeping and needs his rest. Here, gimme your shoes and I'll carry 'em." Looking down and chewing on his lip, he asked, "Who'd you go out with tonight?"

She gave another one of those little sideways steps, and he reached out to grip her arm and keep her upright. "Nash took me home, Andy." Frustrated, he shook his head. "Yeah, he called; I know he brought you home, but who were you with?"

She looked at him puzzled and he shook his head. "You know what? It doesn't matter. Is Nash still working on the ranch?"

"I think so. We don't talk much about that," she muttered, continuing her weaving walk towards the house.

"I picked up a job at the feed mill, second shift." He had her shoes now, and tucked her hand into his elbow, helping her walk more confidently.

"That's good, Andy," she replied, but she seemed puzzled. "I thought you worked at the school and the grocery store?" Looking into his face, she asked, "You quitting one of those?"

"Naw, the other two are just part-time. I can work their hours around what's needed at the feed mill," he lied, knowing that he'd get caught out eventually, but she was pretty blotto tonight, so she might not even remember.

He guided her through the house, attempting to reduce the noise she made. Once in her bedroom, Andy undressed his mother and pulled a nightshirt over her head. He got her into bed, and then tucked her in, kissing her forehead before he turned off the light. Seven-year-old Ben slept through it all, thankfully.

Andy's alarm went off to wake Ben for breakfast and school, and he had started the coffee and oatmeal before he roused his brother. Up and awake, they chatted through their morning ritual, Andy reminding him to gather his homework as he finished packing his book bag for the bus. Walking to the bus stop, Andy looked over at the tarp-covered dirt bike leaning against the shed in the backyard. He hadn't been able to ride it for a long time, and he wondered if maybe it was finally time to sell the bike. They could use the money, for sure.

Not long before his shift at the grocery store, Nash and GeeMa showed up at the house. It felt like an ambush, because they said they didn't want to see his mom—they wanted to talk to Andy. This scared him, because he thought he'd been doing a great job of keeping everything together. The house was clean, there was food in the pantry, and it had been months since their electricity had been turned off. He was taking care of his family, even if he'd had to quit high school so he could work and bring in money to keep them fed and clothed. He sat anxiously, waiting to find out what they wanted.

Nash pulled up a chair to the kitchen table and sat silently, tapping on the tabletop nervously. "Andy, you understand what a tough time your momma's having," GeeMa began, "but she's crossed a line now. I don't want you to be mad, but I think your brother should come live with me and GeePa."

"What did she do, GeeMa?" he looked at her, but she pursed her lips and looked away, so he turned to look at the man sitting at the table, "Nash, what happened?"

"Betty, the boy deserves to know," Nash growled, and Andy watched his grandmother nod sadly. Nash said, "Son, you stopped giving her money for drinking like we talked about, didn't you?"

Andy looked at him. "Yeah, why?"

"Have you wondered how she's still getting money?" He shook his head. "She's in the alley behind the bar, Andy. With men. You don't want Ben around those men, and she'll start bringing them home next. A bed makes more money than standing against a wall."

"You take that back, Nash Fowler. That's a foul thing to say, and you take it back right now. That's my momma, and you *take it back*!" He stood in a rush and pulled back one fist, his face twisting in fury.

"Son, I would take it back if it weren't true," Nash said in response. He didn't move to defend himself, seemingly willing to let Andy pound him if he needed to.

"GeeMa, don't listen to Nash; he's been sweet on her since Daddy died. He's just mad she wants nothin' to do with him. He's a liar," Andy shouted.

Her head was bowed over the table, and she shook it back and forth. "Andy, she was a good wife and mother before my Allen died. You know she was. She's hit a hard patch and won't let any of us help her. I don't want to talk about my daughter-in-law anymore right now, but Ben is too important to leave to chance. I want you both to come live with GeePa and me. Susan already agreed to this yesterday, so it's a done deal, baby boy."

Andy looked from Nash to his grandmother, his face twisting from anger to sorrow. "You'll be taking Benny away from me. He's my shrimp, GeeMa. I do right by him; I do. I can't do more than I'm doing, and I don't know what you all want from me. Don't take Benny away, please." The tears started trailing down his cheeks. "Please, GeeMa, I got this. I swear...I got this." He stopped talking, his chest hitching with unreleased sobs. He whispered, "Nash, don't let her take Benny; he's all I got." Shaking his head, he sat down hard in the chair. "I got this. I swear."

"Andy, you're coming with him, son," Nash said, looking carefully at his face. Andy shook his head violently back and forth. "I can't," he said shrilly. "You don't understand. *I can't.* I can't leave her alone; she wouldn't be able to take care of herself and things. I can't go, Nash. I'll lose one either way...I lose either way."

His chin dropped to his chest, tears dripping off his nose and onto his blue jean-clad legs. His shoulders were shuddering with the emotions he was keeping tightly held inside, shaking with such force that the chair legs were squeaking where they were loose. He picked up his head and looked at the two of them again, seeing sad resolve on their faces, and he knew this was over. It was just...over. He'd lost before he even got to fight. They'd take Ben, and he'd lose his little brother.

Looking around the room, he saw for the first time how the room wasn't comfortable. It lacked the touches that made a house a home. It wasn't bright or cheerful; it looked like pain lived there. It would only get worse, if what Nash said was true about Momma. There were so many nights he silently carried her to bed so Ben wouldn't wake up.

He thought about all the times that his brother had woken up, and then not been able to get back to sleep. He remembered the shadows he'd seen in Ben's eyes this morning when their mom's door stayed closed through breakfast.

He pulled his bandana from his back pocket, sniffling and wiping his nose on it. Twisting it in his hands, he took one deep breath in through his nose, blowing out through his mouth, and then another, willing himself back under control. Lips still trembling, he looked between them again, then facing his grandmother, asked, "GeeMa, what do you need me to do?"

3 - Where I work

Fourteen years ago

"Hey, AJ, you picking up that extra shift tomorrow?" his supervisor called questioningly after him as he went to clock out.

Andy stood still, feeling his weariness come over him like a smothering fog. "Yeah, I can if you need me. Can always use the money, boss, thanks. See you bright and early then."

He walked on out to the truck, sitting behind the wheel for a minute before he jabbed the key into the ignition and started it. Putting his hands on top of the steering wheel, he rested his forehead against the backs of his hands, closing his eyes for just a moment. Between the exhaustion and the stress of taking care of his family, he felt far older than his twenty-one years. He was listening to the men he worked with as they walked through the parking lot shouting and joking with each other; they were off for the weekend and ready to party.

Andy picked his head up, waving at the guys still in the lot as he pulled out onto the road. Automatically shifting up through the gears, he drove into town, pulling up behind the grocery store in the employee parking spaces. Reaching over into the bag lying beside him, he pulled his uniform shirt out and changed while sitting in the driver's seat. He looked down at his jeans; this pair was still okay, so they would do today. He'd have to wash both pairs of his jeans tomorrow, and get his laundry done for the week.

He needed to get Ben down to the store in Cheyenne to get him some new school clothes. The kid was outgrowing everything he owned, and when Andy saw him last weekend, he needed new boots too. If Andy could get a full week in at both jobs, he'd have a good payday coming and would be able to take care of Ben. He could even gas up the dirt bike and take him out to play at the old ranch. The bike was too small for Andy now, but his little brother was the right size and loved the thrill.

Cheyenne's Frontier Days would be coming up soon too, and Ben always enjoyed going to watch the cowboys and cowgirls compete at the rodeo. Andy'd have to plan for that, because it was a couple nights, which meant staying in a cheap motel; it never made sense driving all the way back home for only a half-dozen hours of sleep. Maybe he could get a job at the Days to help out, with a bunk for pay, or he could load or unload trailers of stock for cash.

Ruffling his hands through his hair, he tried to smooth it down, but like normal, it persisted in sticking up from his head every which way. He padded across the parking lot, jumping up onto the little porch the daytime employees used as a lunch area. Punching his timecard at the machine inside the door, he grabbed an apron off a hook and slung it over his head, walking and tying the strings around his waist.

"Truck should be here any minute, Andy," said a pretty, blonde cashier, looking him up and down while twirling her hair around her finger, "but I can think of ways we can pass the time."

"Hey, Carlee. Thanks, but I need to front some shelves while I'm waiting." He pushed through the swinging doors that separated the warehouse area from the customers' domain. God, he regretted sleeping with her now. He'd held out against her for months, but she'd brushed up against him one too many times. Three weeks ago, he'd followed her home. Her tits were nice, but her mouth...he couldn't stand her talking. She'd been excruciatingly flirty since, but it wasn't in his nature to sleep with that again. He'd yet to find a piece of tail he wanted seconds from.

This one had laid there like a lump, not joining in at all. He'd about exhausted himself trying to make it good for her. After a half-hour of absolutely nothing, he'd simply taken care of things and rolled off her, snagging his jeans as he walked to the bathroom to flush the condom. Probably made him a dick...he probably didn't care.

He worked quickly and efficiently up and down the aisles, straightening and making note of items that needed restocking later tonight. Eventually, the call came over the intercom that the truck had arrived, and he made his way back to the dock. He and the driver had become friendly, and they cheerily chatted while they worked together to unload the store's order from the back of the truck.

Pulling the last half-pallet from the trailer with the pallet jack, Andy parked it along the wall. He used the interoffice phone and called the manager to come verify the order before the driver left for his next stop. Leaning against the wall as he waited, Andy saw a cute brunette walk past outside, more than likely using the parking lot as a shortcut.

He stuck his head out to get a better look, and when he scanned the parking lot, his eyes stopped on a familiar car parked along the back row. Closing his eyes for a second in disbelief, he opened them and then really looked at the car, noting the steamy windows and the single silhouette in the passenger's seat. Jumping down from the dock, he called over his shoulder at the driver, "Mitch, tell Mr. Hawthorn I'll be right back, okay?"

Stalking up to the driver's side of the car, he pounded on the window, using what he thought of as a 'cop knock' to get the attention of the couple in the car. The window rolled down a couple of inches at first, and then all the way, as he heard, "Andy, fuck, you scared the shit out of me."

Andy sniffed and then made a face, smelling the sweet smoke wafting from the car's interior. "Mom, what are you doing sitting in the parking lot where I work?"

She looked at him, her lips puffy and red, with her lipstick smeared across her chin. In the passenger seat, the man was trying to stuff his still-hard dick back into his pants. "Andy, I didn't think—" she started, but he cut her off.

"No, you never think, do you? Never once do you think how this makes me feel, finding my mother giving some random guy a blowjob in the parking lot where I work. Oh, and smoking a joint too. You don't think, Mom. You never have. You simply do what you want, without regard for how it impacts other people, even your own fucking kids. What would Daddy think, Mom, huh? What would he say if he could see you now?"

He ran both hands through his hair, shaking his head frantically back and forth. "I'm done. You're on your own from here on out. Time to be the grownup for a change." Leaning down to the car window, he yelled at her, "I am done cleaning up your shit, Susan Jones."

Turning on his heel, he walked back to the dock, pausing for a moment as he saw the faces turned his way. He suspected the entire thing had been witnessed by his boss and co-workers. *Great, just great.* Course, it's not like they didn't already know what kind of mother he had, but this was the cherry on top of his shit sundae today. Using the ICC bar on the trailer to get a step up onto the dock, he looked his boss in the face, daring him to say anything about what he'd just watched. "Mr. Hawthorn, is the order okay to sort out and put away?"

"Yes, Andy, everything's in order." Holding out the paperwork towards him, Hawthorn said, "Here's the list. Let me know if you need anything, okay? Anything."

Anguished, Andy stared him in the face, "Will do, Mr. Hawthorn. I got this."

It was nearly midnight, and he was exhausted by the time he finally had everything put away on shelves or in storage. The last one in the store, he headed out the backdoor and used his key to lock the employee entrance.

Walking towards his truck, he saw a couple of kids standing next to it and narrowed his eyes in a hard squint. What were those punks doing next to his truck? One of them looked up to see him coming and took off running, slapping the arm of his friend in alarm. The second boy waited a moment too long, and Andy's hand wrapped around his arm, holding him in place. The kid squealed, "Mr. Jones, I'm sorry. I'm sorry!"

Looking at the side of his truck, he saw words spray-painted on the fender. "What the fuck did you do?" he asked, leaning closer. "Does that say *whore* on my fucking truck, kid? Does it?" Kicking his tire in frustration, he turned to face the boy he was holding onto tightly. "You wrote *whore* on my fucking truck? Who's your daddy, kid? We're going to go have a chat with him."

Pulling him into the truck cab, he shoved him across the seat and then sat there, still holding his arm, waiting for him to begin talking. Looking at the boy, Andy realized he was about the same age as Ben, probably only ten or eleven. That made him angrier, because now he suspected that Ben had to deal with this kind of shit too. "Fuck me. Who's your daddy, kid? Or, I can take you to the courthouse...and we can talk to the sheriff. I'm good either way."

He rattled off a name that Andy recognized, a local businessman who'd been known to frequent the bars where his mom hung out. He was also known to have a painfully free nature with his hands when it came to his family. "Fuck me," he muttered, dropping his head back and thumping the window a couple of times, thinking. "Son, you ever do anything like this before?"

In his eagerness to answer, the kid stuttered over his words, "Nuh-uh, no, Mr. Jones. N-never."

"You know my little brother?"

Less stressed now, he got a clearer answer from the boy. "Yes, sir, I know Ben."

"You ever grief him about this shit? Don't lie to me; I'll ask him." Andy waited for his answer.

"No, sir, Ben's nice."

"Fuck. Am *I* not nice? So *I'm* not nice, and I deserve to have my truck painted up like this?" It had been a rhetorical question, and the kid seemed to know that, staying quiet. "Your daddy hit you?" As far as Andy was concerned, this was the most important question tonight.

Ducking his head, the boy answered, "Not often."

"Not often still says sometimes, kiddo, right?" Andy probed.

"Yes, sir," came the quiet response.

Andy took in a deep breath, he didn't want to be the reason this boy had any more pain in his life than he already did. "Who was that with you?" Without additional prompting, the boy offered up his accomplice in crime, whose father was another jerk of a guy who Andy knew from the mill. "All right, if I let you go, you gotta promise me something," Andy said, still leaning his head against the back glass of the truck.

"Yes, sir, anything," and that response was genuinely eager.

"You gotta be nice to Ben. He don't deserve the momma he got, like you don't deserve your daddy. Be his friend, if you can." Picking his head up, he looked the kid in the face as he let his arm go.

Sitting for a second, the boy nodded his head vigorously up and down. "Yes, sir. I need friends, too."

Leaning across him, Andy pushed the door open. He waggled his fingers at him. "Go on, get. Go call your friend and let him know the deal. If I find out you've gone back on your word...I *will* come get ya." He watched with a little grin as the kid skedaddled out of the lot and into the trees, headed home in the dark as fast as he could run.

Andy got out of the truck, and went back into the store for some paint thinner and rags to clean the still-wet paint off his truck. He came back out with a weary sigh and squatted down to start the job that would take up most of his sleeping time. Work at the feed mill would start at seven in the morning, but it wasn't the first time he'd worked a shift with no sleep. He was wrong earlier—*this* was the chocolate drizzle on top of the cherry sittin' on his shit sundae this week.

4 - Motorcycle

Eleven years ago

Standing across the street from the Harley Davidson showroom in Cheyenne, Andy was almost drooling at the sight of the motorcycles lined up across the front of the store. He wanted a bike in the worst way, and he could almost feel the wind on his face just looking at them. Things in Enoch had gotten hard, with lots of changes over the years. Work at the feed mill had dried up months ago, because it was cheaper for them to make the products in Mexico somewhere. He'd quit the grocery store last week when Mr. Hawthorn told him that the store was being sold.

Thank God, he'd been saving his money for years now, in two bank accounts. Every penny went into one of those two accounts, if it wasn't spent on bills, food, or clothes for him or Ben.

The first account was for Ben's college, and it was finally reaching a respectable balance. Andy worked with an investment manager at the bank to get the money into a high-return account, which would mature right when

Ben'd need it for school. His grandparents knew about the money, and were proud of what Andy had done to provide for his brother in only a handful of years.

Andy's living arrangements had been back and forth for a while, between his grandparents and his mom, and then he'd moved out on his own several years ago. Recently, he'd taken a job at a ranch, taking care of their windmill equipment, and part of the pay was room and board. It was an ideal arrangement, since it meant he didn't have any rent to pay, which was especially important now since he wasn't working anywhere else.

That second bank account was nearly as healthy as Ben's college fund, and it had long been earmarked for a motorcycle for Andy. When he was thirteen, his dad had driven the two of them down to Cheyenne for Frontier Days, while his mom and three-year-old Ben stayed home. His dad had run into some old friends, and one of them had taken Andy on a couple of short rides on a bike. And, just as simple as that, he was hooked.

Not long after that, his dad bought him a cheap dirt bike, and Andy rode it all over the ranch. It had freed him, and fed his imagination too. On the bike, he had pretended he was a famous daredevil jumping river canyons, a Hollywood actor living the bad-boy life, or a lawman hunting criminals. He could be anything, and everything.

Asking himself again why he wanted a bike so badly, he leaned back against his truck fender. He knew the answer, of course, but it was a mental exercise he felt the need to complete again. He wanted a bike, because in the truck— even driving a hundred miles an hour—he felt caged. Only on a bike did he really feel free, and the carefree lifestyle of riding the road appealed to him. He'd been the responsible one for so much of his life, holding everything together with willpower alone; he couldn't imagine if all that pressure was simply gone...*poof*.

He loved his GeeMa and GeePa, and God knew he loved Benny. He even loved his mom, but he didn't like her. He loved these people in his life, but he wanted to be more than...anything he'd been so far, more than they expected.

He'd stood in this spot at least once a year for the past three years, and every time he'd talked himself out of the purchase, because in his heart, he knew that it was more than purely buying a motorcycle. He'd also be buying himself a departure, an exit strategy. Once he bought a bike, he knew he wouldn't want to stick around Enoch any longer, especially now, when there was hardly anything holding him here.

Looking both ways for traffic, he strode across the road, pausing for a second to look at the bikes parked in a line in front of the building again. These were all owned by employees or customers, and it was amazing to see the many different kinds people rode. He'd been promising himself a Harley and had saved enough to pay cash for a used one, which was saying—he'd saved a lot.

Stepping into the store, he was straightaway at ease; the smells and sounds were like coming home. He listened to the rumble of pipes from the garage behind the counter, taking note of the singing from a bike being revved. Strolling towards the counter, he caught the eye of an older man with a full beard and the required black Harley t-shirt. The old guy came over and stuck out his hand, introducing himself, "Harddrive, man," and they shook. "What brings you in today?"

"Andy," he replied, "and I think I want to buy a bike today."

Harddrive shook with laughter. "Kid, you've walked into the wrong candy store." He chortled some more. "These aren't cheap, man."

Andy nodded. "I know, but I want to see what's available today before I go to the bank."

Harddrive scrutinized his face for a minute, then nodded and threw back his head, roaring, "Man wants to see some fucking bikes. We got bikes, motherfuckers?"

There were answering shouts in the affirmative from workers and customers alike, and Harddrive put his arm around Andy's shoulders. Steering him outside, they made their way to the end of the row of bikes parked out front. One by one, he patiently explained about each one: what the engine was capable of, what the style felt like when taking an extended ride versus a short one, the history of the make or model, the climate needs of some bikes, and a dozen other facts that came so fast it was hard for Andy to process.

Walking through the building to the back, they looked at used bikes for sale, and Harddrive continued the commentary, telling him about every one they looked at. Andy saw there was a pretty red and white number coming up, and he was looking forward to learning about that one, but listening to Harddrive explain about an inline shifter on one of the bikes, Andy realized he'd skipped the one he liked.

"Um...what about that one there, the red and white one?" he asked, barely stopping himself from saying the bike was pretty.

"That's an Indian, and a pain in the ass to fix," Harddrive explained. "It's a nice bike, good for both town and touring, beautiful, classic style with large fairings on the wheels to capture or deflect rain or dirt. The seat's comfortable, nice and wide, with a brace to keep your ass from sliding off. Pain to repair, though." He moved on to the next bike in the row.

"Who makes the Indian?" Andy asked, and his tour guide guffawed at his naivety.

"Indian makes the Indian. That, son, is a Roadmaster, an Indian Chief Roadmaster."

Andy kicked the gravel for a minute, and then asked, "Is that one...is it...is *she* for sale?"

Harddrive focused on him. "She speakin' to you, son? Tell me what you're thinking."

"I'm thinking that's a pretty bike. It looks like it has enough heft to feel comfortable going up and down mountain roads, but not so heavy as to bog down on a high hill. It looks like someone needs to take care of her." Andy cut his eyes over to the old man. "I'd like to hear her run, see what she feels like. Is she for sale?"

Harddrive nodded slowly, "She's a good bike, man. Let's get the key."

5 - Good news

Driving back to Enoch, Andy couldn't keep his eyes off the rearview mirror. He was looking at the beautiful red and white motorcycle strapped into the bed of his truck. Harddrive had helped him load the bike, and showed him the best way to secure it so it wouldn't wobble or dump over on turns or bumps.

He'd been in love with the Indian since he caught sight of it, half-hidden behind all the used Harleys at the shop. The distinctive lines of the bike were arresting; it looked hardcore and sexy as hell, and the look of the fringe on the seat was the topper. Harddrive had thrown in a pair of saddlebags for the bike; he said it was the least he could do, since Andy's new bike would be a bitch to repair if she broke down in a remote place.

Andy'd been surprised at the price; it was less than half what he had expected to spend, so when Harddrive told him the figure, he had jumped into his truck to go to the bank right away. The guys in the store had laughed when Harddrive had to drag him back out of the truck in order to take the bike on a test drive. But *man,* he'd been glad that old guy was so stubborn, because when he rode her, it was amazing.

Getting on the Indian was nothing like his dirt bike, it was much heavier and harder to hold upright. Bigger between his thighs, there was no mistaking the potential for power in the size of the engine. Turning on the key and kicking it to life, that was a thrill he wouldn't soon forget, and the sweet rumble of the pipes up through the soft leather seat had him rock-hard in seconds. She was definitely his new baby.

Driving out of the parking lot on the bike was exhilarating as he turned up the highway and let the throttle out a little, listening to the motor. She was smooth as glass, and he only went about five miles before he pulled a U-turn to head back. Back at the shop, he'd really wanted to be cagey and bargain the price down, but honestly, he'd been so excited he didn't think he could stand the wait and had agreed to the first price Harddrive wrote down.

When he got back from the bank, he paid in cash and Harddrive handed over the slip for the bike. He also talked Andy into a pair of leather chaps like some of the people in the store were wearing, along with a durable leather jacket. If he could have, Andy would have left the truck there and ridden the bike home, but he knew he would need the truck for a couple more weeks anyway. So here he was, nearly home with the bike in the back of the truck.

Pulling up in front of the house he'd shared with his grandparents and little brother in past years, Andy climbed out of the truck, stretching his lean form's tight and sore muscles. GeeMa came to the door, and seeing it was him, she raised a hand with a smile, turning back into the house. Andy tipped his head, glaring at his boot toes for a minute, kicking the dry dirt of the driveway. He hated thinking about leaving Ben, but he couldn't contribute without working, and jobs had dried up here.

He lifted his head and looked at the house; Ben would be home from school soon, and he wanted to talk to his grandparents first. He'd heard about some good jobs in Colorado, and that was the first place he'd be headed once he set out on the bike.

6 - Goodbyes

"Andrew, why would you do such a foolish thing?" scolded GeeMa about his purchase of the bike. "How much of Ben's college money did you throw away on that motorcycle?" She leaned against the kitchen cabinet and cocked one hip, frowning at him. "Where you think you're going to go? Why do you have to leave to get work?"

Andy folded his arms across his chest, waiting for her to wind down. There was a pause, and she quirked an eyebrow at him, waiting for his answers to her barrage of questions. "First of all, I didn't spend any of the money for Ben's school. That's tied up nice and tight until the year he graduates high school. Not even Mom can get at it, so you can stop worrying about that.

"I've been saving money from other jobs too, so I had a little bit put aside for a rainy day; GeeMa, this is a freakin' downpour. There aren't any jobs around here that will pay enough to help cover expenses for Ben after bills. Everything is barely enough to live paycheck-to-paycheck, and not ever enough to get ahead.

"There're good jobs down in the Denver area, oilfield jobs, and I know someone who's hiring. I got the bike, because the truck sucks oil faster than it does gas, which is pretty fast. I can't afford to take the truck down, or if I did, I'd never be able to afford to get back up here to visit you guys. Right now, I'm planning to stay in Enoch until the weekend, giving the Michaels' time to find someone else to help with the windmill, and then I'll be headed down to Denver.

"I'll let you know an address as soon as I have one, and I picked up a cell phone today. I'll write the number down, but it's for emergencies, not visiting. I have this figured out, GeeMa. It's not forever, but for now, it's what I need to do."

"I hate the thought of you being by yourself like that, Andy," she said, and he knew she was convinced since she'd shifted from calling him Andrew to Andy. "What are you going to tell Ben?"

He bit his lip. "Ben's going to understand. He's only a child in years, not experience, and we both know that. He's been taking care of other people for most of his life, and he knows this is how families work. We do what we have to."

She crossed the room, pulling him into her arms. "Andy, are you sure about this? I don't want to lose you, too."

He hugged her tightly. "I know, GeeMa, but I'm not sick; I'm just gonna be working in Denver. It's only a couple hours away, and I can come back at least one weekend a month. You're not losing me." He felt his shoulder dampen. "GeeMa, stop it. I got this, and you know it. The bike is a good one, and it's as safe as the truck—that's for sure. Don't cry; Ben will worry more if he sees you like this. I love you guys so much, but this is what I need to do. I'm going to miss you like crazy, but I got this."

* * *

Waiting on the school bus, Andy stood in the front yard like he'd done so many times over the years. Ben's bus always stopped at the bottom of the hill and disgorged the dozens of children who lived in this neighborhood. With their age difference, the brothers always attended different campuses within the school district, so they never rode the same bus.

Andy was comfortable, with his elbows hooked over the truck tailgate and ass resting on the bumper. No stress, no strain…just waiting. He wasn't worried about this conversation, because he knew Ben would understand his reasons for leaving. But, he really wanted their talk to go well, since regardless of what he'd told his grandmother, it might be a few months before he could come back.

Listening, he heard the rackety clank of the bus making its way up the highway and looked down the road, seeing the roof of the bus coming into and out of view on the rolling hills. The bus pulled into the residential road fronting the neighborhood and stopped where it always did, halfway between the road they lived on and the next one. Kids began pouring off the bus as soon as the driver opened the accordion doors, and he watched for Ben's yellow head. Once, one of their grandmother's friends had called Ben *Goldie Locks*; fortunately for him since he'd hated the nickname, it hadn't stuck.

The flood of kids slowed to a trickle and then stopped; the bus driver closed her doors and began to pull away. Ben hadn't gotten off the bus, and Andy narrowed his eyes, thinking. Pulling himself upright, he walked to the kitchen door quickly. "Hey, GeeMa, did the school call?"

She yelled back, "No, nobody called, Andy. Why?"

He growled out a string of inventive curses, "He wasn't on the bus. Ideas?"

Listening closely, he heard her sigh before she responded, "He doesn't ride the bus anymore. He rides with one of the older kids from school."

Andy thought for a second, paying attention to what she hadn't said. "Do you know who this kid is? Ben's only fourteen, in junior high. This kid must be in high school. What's his name?"

She stuck her head around the doorframe to look at him. "*She* is Benita Owens, and yes, she's a sophomore at Enoch High." Ducking back out, she left him standing there with his mouth gaping open in surprise.

"Owens? Darren Owens' girl?" he asked. "How did Ben meet her?"

The too-casual answer came quickly, raising his hackles again. "He said they met in church; isn't that sweet?"

"The question is whether he's sweet on her, and if he knows what Darren would do to him if he left her less sweet than she is now," he retorted. "Church, my ass— that girl is dangerous for him. Hell, her daddy owns half the town."

He walked back outside, sitting on the edge of the porch and watching the road. Nearly two hours later, he saw a gray sports car turning towards the house. It pulled up in front, and Ben stepped out of the passenger side. He moved to the back of the car and took several bags from the trunk, and then walked to the driver's window. It buzzed down, and he leaned in for a few moments, pulling back with reddened lips and color in his cheeks.

"Love ya, Nita." He leaned back down for a second, and then stood back up. "See ya, baby," he spoke to the driver of the BMW. Stepping back, he walked out of the way. as the car made a U-turn in the street and quickly drove back down the hill to the highway.

Strolling up towards the house, he saw Andy sitting on the porch and his face broke into a huge smile. "My favorite brother, Andy, my man, whacha doing here?" He stepped up onto the porch and set the bags by the wall; squatting on the edge of the porch for a second, he dropped his feet and legs over the edge, slapping his ass down.

"I'm your only brother, asshat," Andy responded.

Ben turned with an affectionate fist bump to the shoulder for Andy and grinned devilishly. "Hope you weren't waiting long; I had to take care of my girl before I came home."

Andy looked hard at Ben, trying to see past the tousle-headed little boy he used to be, who had always-worried eyes and a soft spot for strays of any kind. Looking at his brother now, he saw a young man taller than most fourteen-year-olds, with light blond hair long enough to style and ice blue eyes that seemed to smile all the time.

He was fit and defined, and walked with an easy grace. He honestly looked closer to seventeen than fourteen. In his face, you could see the man he would grow into, with a strong jaw and slightly upturned, straight nose. Ben was going to be a lady-killer, for sure, but he was starting too young, and with the wrong girl.

"Ben, you are fourteen. Ain't nobody taking care of their girl at that age," Andy drawled. He was a little put out with Ben, but couldn't put his finger on why.

"I might be fourteen, but I at least *have* a girl," Ben teased Andy. "I'm not sitting home every night with Rosie Palm and her five sisters, man."

"Goddammit, Ben, do you know what her daddy'd do if he heard you talking like that about his little girl?" Andy twisted to look at the bags, zeroing in on what bothered him. "And what's up with the shopping? You come into money I don't know about?"

Ben had the grace to look a little sheepish. "She bought me a few clothes, is all. She wants me to look nice when we go out with her friends." He shrugged. "It's not a big deal; it's only a couple of things."

Andy looked at him and ran one hand through his hair. "If you needed new clothes, why didn't you tell me, Benny? Have I ever said no?"

"It's not that, Andy. My school clothes are all fine. These are for going out in, and they aren't practical."

Shaking his head, Andy looked at Ben and decided to change the subject. "Benny, you know I lost the mill job, yeah?" Ben nodded. "There aren't any other jobs around here, so I'm headed to Denver in a couple of days; there's oilfield work there. I'll be back as I can, and I'm gonna send money to GeeMa for you."

Ben sat and looked at him for a second, then leaned forward to put his elbows on his legs and dropped his head into his hands. With a strangled voice, he asked, "You're leaving, Andy?" His fingers clenched in his hair and he rocked back and forth for a second.

Slinging an arm around his shoulders, Andy pulled him into his side in a one-armed hug. "It'll be okay, shrimp. I'll be back for a visit in a few weeks." He could feel Ben's muscles tense and tighten all over his body; he was holding himself stiff and eventually pulled away from Andy's grip.

"Okay, Andy. Whacha need me to do?" Ben asked softly.

"Don't need you to do anything, shrimp. Just keep going to school, learn lots, and do good things." Andy pulled him back into a full hug, folding Ben against his chest and resting his chin on his little brother's head. "I got this."

Releasing Ben, Andy cut his eyes over to see his reaction. Pleased with his calm aspect, he laughed. "Hey, I bought a bike. Wanna see her?" he asked, and then laughed louder when Ben's face shone with shock and awe. They slid off the edge of the porch, both of them slapping their ass to get any dust or dirt off and grinning at each other like crazy people. They'd always liked it when they did things in sync; it emphasized the fact they were family.

As they walked over to Andy's truck, Ben was making all of the appropriate noises of appreciation for the bike.

Andy looked proudly at her again, loving the sleek lines of the fairings and the tank; running his hands over the leather seat, he flicked his fingertips against the fringe underneath. "She was a good price, an Indian Chief Roadmaster. She'll be lots cheaper on gas than the truck, and powerful enough to take pretty much anywhere."

"Oh my God, Andy, this bike is awesome. Red, white, black, and chrome. Can we unload it? I want to watch you...hell, I want to drive it." Ben was suddenly looking and sounding fourteen, overly enthused about a motorcycle.

"No way you're going to drive her," Andy shook his head, "but we can unload her. You can see me ride for a minute, and then I'll show you how to check the oil and stuff. It's a little different from the dirt bike."

Putting down the truck's tailgate, Andy dragged out the planks he and Harddrive had used to push the bike up into the bed of the truck. Wedging them into place, he climbed up and straddled the bike, loosening the straps that held it upright. Slowly, he began backing the bike down the makeshift ramp and breathed a deep sigh of relief when he got to the ground without falling off or turning the bike over.

Turning the key, he kicked the bike into life, watching Ben's face as the engine revved. It grew louder and then backed off, the pipes burbling with power. Nodding his head, he pulled out of the driveway slowly, letting his feet drift inches off the ground until he was safely turned to go down the hill. Pulling away faster, he picked his feet up and started shifting through the gears as he reached the main road. In the mirror, he saw Ben still standing beside the pickup, so he raised one hand and waved before he goosed the bike.

The wind teased tears from his eyes as his mouth froze in the widest smile he'd ever felt on his face. He instinctively crouched down over the gas tank, streamlining his profile for speed. When he realized how fast the vegetation was flashing by in the ditches on either side of the road, he glanced down at the speedometer and saw he was going over one-hundred-miles per hour. Backing off on the throttle, he slowed down to highway speed and sat upright on the bike. After slowing even more, he pulled to the shoulder and looked up and down the highway, turning around to head home.

Driving back up to the house, he saw Ben had remained in the same place beside the truck, and he lifted a hand to wave at him as he drove up. He killed the engine, and put down the kickstand; tilting the bike, he couldn't get the grin off his face.

"Brother, that bike is awesome," Ben growled out, and Andy grinned some more.

"I know, right? It's just so good; it feels like this is what I'm supposed to be doing."

***

He sat on the bike in a parking lot two blocks from her house. He'd already put the truck in storage, and had the few things he was taking packed in a backpack and the pannier bags on the bike. This was the last stop on his way out of town, and he was contemplating simply leaving without seeing her.

Leaning his elbows on the handlebars, he rubbed his face in his hands briskly, twisting his neck back and forth. Adjusting the backpack on his shoulders, he kicked the bike to life and idled out of the parking lot.

Pulling into her driveway, he saw the car was parked in the back and knew that it was likely she was home. He hoped this visit wouldn't last long, but he wanted to let her know he wouldn't be around, that she had to take care of her own shit. Parking, he put the kickstand down, angling the bike over as he stepped off, and onto the driveway. He dropped the backpack on the ground beside the bike and walked up to the backdoor of the house. He raised his hand to knock at the door, and then dropped his hand silently back down to his side, still not sure he wanted to do this.

Before he could walk away, the door opened, and a tall, scrawny man with an unbuttoned, stained shirt free from his waistband stood in the doorframe with a lit cigarette in his fingers. His fingernails were long and yellow, and his skin looked dingy, like it had been some time since he had showered. They stared at each other for a minute, the guy giving him time to speak first, but Andy stood silently.

"The hell you want here, boy?" was the guy's even greeting as he lifted his cigarette to his mouth, taking a long drag. Andy looked at him steadily. "Susan here?"

"Yeah, she's here, but you ain't gonna get anything; she's passed out," the man said with the same even tone, no animosity, dragging hard on his smoke again.

Andy's eyes closed for a second. "Susan's my mother."

"Oh, man, you do *not* want to see this, then," the man said, his voice animated for the first time as he moved slightly over into Andy's way. He blocked the entrance and lowered his head to look at his bare feet.

Shaking his head at him, Andy sighed, "I've seen it all, man," and stepped around him, headed into the house through the doorway.

The backdoor opened into the kitchen, and he looked around the small room but didn't see her, so he continued into the living room and pulled to a stop barely inside the doorway. "I told ya that you did not want to see her like this," the man said from behind him.

He was right, thought Andy; *I could have lived my entire life without seeing my mom like this.* She was on a stained and discolored couch, lying sprawled on top of a man. They were both naked, and even passed out, his dick was still inside her.

There was a second man, kneeling between their legs. Propping himself with one hand on the back of the couch, he was moving back and forth, in and out; his dick was in her, too. Andy could see blood on his mother's ass, but her face gave lie to any discomfort. In her passed-out state, she was as placid-featured as any bored debutante at a party.

Andy moved. He reached out and dragged the man off her by his neck, carelessly tossing him to the floor. "Get dressed and get out," he said without emotion. Pointing to the man who had met him at the door, he mumbled, "You too, okay? Just get dressed and get out."

He pulled his mother off the couch and laid her on the floor. Briefly checking the amount and source of the blood, he quickly covered her with a dirty shirt from the floor. "This dude a friend of yours?" he asked over his shoulder as he slapped the passed out guy awake.

"Yeah, that's Terry." The door guy threw a pair of sweats their way and Andy handed them to Terry.

"You know what she took last night?" Andy asked the room in general. "Is she simply passed out, or do I need to take her to the ER?"

Door guy bobbed his head. "She's just passed out, mixed liquor and E. She went mellow and horizontal."

Lifting a hand to acknowledge the statement, he watched as the men left the house by the front door, not looking at him or his mom; they carelessly vacated the house as if this was a regular morning in their world.

He picked her up and carried her down the short hallway to her room. Toeing the door open, he found a mattress on the floor, with empty bottles surrounding the edges. He put her in the middle of it, pulling a blanket up to cover her.

Gathering up the empties, he took them into the kitchen and found a roll of garbage bags in the cabinets. Taking one, he began going through the house to clear the obvious trash. He wound up back in her bedroom, picking up and throwing away drug paraphernalia along with the trash.

Andy looked down where she lay curled on the mattress, and saw age in her face for the first time. She was barely in her forties, but looked much older, worn and beaten down by life. She seemed past the point of caring about herself; for a moment, Andy tried to imagine how he would feel if this was the last time he saw her alive. He slowly nodded to himself; he didn't feel anything, no sadness and no glee, just a void where his love for her had lived.

"What would Daddy say, Mom?" he asked with disgust thick in his voice. Turning to walk out of the house, he took three trash bags with him to the dumpster down the street.

7 - Riding south

Sitting on the bike, Andy watched the tractor-trailer rigs drive in and out of the truck stop outside Colorado Springs. It was an ever-moving kaleidoscope of truck types, logos, and colors, the big vehicles weaving up and down the aisles between parking spaces.

He'd been on the road for a dozen weeks, and was back to looking for work. If he could find a safe place to park the bike, he could probably pick up a few bucks unloading trucks. He'd been doing lots of different odd jobs since leaving Wyoming; nothing paid great individually, but if you did enough jobs, the money piled up. He simply had to work harder to get the cash than he'd expected.

He'd found that the oilfields weren't hiring inexperienced hands, and since you couldn't get that experience without working—which you couldn't do without experience—well, that severely limited the opportunities to break into that area.

So, Denver had been a bust, but he'd talked to some ranch hands and backtracked north by a couple hours to a small town off the interstate. Sitting on a bucket in a feed store there, he had introduced himself to several ranchers in the area, and was able to pick up a variety of jobs. Those ran the gamut: fixing a bunkhouse roof, stretching five miles of fencing, seining a stock pond for turtles, digging irrigation ditches, and stacking tons of square hay bales into a hayloft.

He'd been a sheepherder for a day on a ranch northwest of Denver, which wasn't a bad gig. That had lasted until the second day, when they were supposed to dip the sheep prior to shearing in order to kill any parasitic hitchhikers they'd picked up in their wool.

A deep channel with cement walls and a fence served for the dipping process. The fence ran along the inner edges of the structure to create a funnel. The ranch hands filled up the channel with the potent dip solution as if it was an artificial pond, and then began driving the sheep between the fences and into the dip.

Andy had watched the sheep wading into the chemicals and realized that a few of them were climbing on the backs of the herd to escape it. "Hey," he shouted at the lead hand and pointed.

The guy nodded and rode his four-wheeler over. "See the railing? Stand on the cement inside that, and walk on top of the sheep to push them under," he yelled and roared off on the equipment.

Andy looked after him like he was crazy, but he wanted the job, so he edged closer. Swinging one leg over the railing, he held it in a white-knuckled grip, sliding his other leg over and leaning back against the rail. Tentatively reaching out with one foot, he shoved down on the back of one floating sheep. It went under quickly, and he gave himself a little air punch of victory.

That was his first undoing, because he lost his grip and his feet slid off the cement into the dip. His legs were pushed against the wall by the bodies of the sheep, and he felt his boots filling with dip. Pulling them back up, he grabbed the railing with both hands again, disturbed by the smell now coming from his lower legs.

Cold, wet, and smelly—that sounded like an ad for his last girlfriend back home, he thought and snorted. Seeing a brave sheep moving his way, one that had almost totally gotten itself out of the dip by climbing onto the back of fellow sheep, he primed his pushing foot. Just as the sheep got to him, it launched itself sideways onto the back of yet another sheep.

"Walk across there and push them all under," he heard from behind. He looked around in disbelief, but it was the lead hand again. "Walk them sheep, boy." Holding the railing with one hand, he shook his head but stepped out onto the back of a sheep, pushing it down into the dip.

He took a soggy step, and then another one, his footsteps absorbed by a combination of more than a half-dozen inches of saturated wool and bodies of the individual sheep trying desperately to get away from his weight on their backs.

Looking back, it was probably an inevitable conclusion to the exercise, and maybe even laughable that he hadn't seen it coming. Maybe at some point in the future he could tell the story humorously. Maybe.

He'd taken a step outward, and the sheep simply wasn't there. It had juked on him and avoided his big platter-sized foot. His foot and leg went down into the dip, and continued to go down. His other leg bent double and found no resistance to push against in order to help keep him upright.

Then suddenly, there were hooves climbing his back, pushing him underneath the dip. His hand was ripped away from the railing, and he barely had the presence of mind to take a big breath before he went under, closing his eyes and mouth tightly.

Those sheep and their hooves pushed him to the bottom of the channel, but his knees hitting cement reminded him that it was not deep, so he unfolded to stand upright. Reaching out blindly to find the railing again, he pulled himself up to the cement ledge.

Holding onto the railing with one tight hand, he tried to shake the dip from his hair and use the side of one hand to scrape the thick liquid off his face. *Oh God*, he couldn't open his eyes yet; this shit would surely blind him. He couldn't open his mouth either; he'd die if he swallowed this crap.

He pulled himself over the railing, getting away from the dip channel entirely. He was bent over, shaking his head violently back and forth when he heard the four-wheeler driving closer. "Goddammit, boy, did you fall in the dip?" came the terse question.

He nodded, still unwilling to open his mouth. Struck from behind, it felt like the man had rammed him with the four-wheeler. He was scooped up, with his butt up near the storage shelf on the front of the vehicle and his back wedged tightly against the handlebars. Andy held on to the metal mesh of the shelf with his fingers, nearly losing his grip a dozen times, only saving himself from falling off by sheer determination.

The four-wheeler came to an abrupt stop, and he tumbled forward into the dirt. Raising his head, he strained his eyes open a hairsbreadth to squint through his lashes just in time to see a hand reaching down to grab his collar. Dragging him ignominiously across the open area in front of the bunkhouse, the man dropped him into the cement gutter of the outside shower and cranked the water on full.

Andy scrambled to his feet, pushing his face up into the water, sputtering it out of his nose and mouth as he scrubbed frantically at his face, trying to get the cloying dip off him.

"Here, take this, son," came a gruff order, and he automatically reached out his hand to feel a bar of soap being pushed into it. He grunted in appreciation and raised the bar to his face, only realizing that it was a rough, scrubbing detergent soap after it had scratched his face raw and started burning. He squinted through his lashes again, making a thick lather to attack his hair.

He was rinsing out his hair when he heard, "Strip, son. Get those clothes off before it burns your tender bits crispy." Nodding his head and squinting out of eyes that were only slightly more open than before, he toed off his soaked boots and then stripped off his shirt, socks, and jeans, standing naked in the water now.

After an additional ten minutes or so of lathering and rinsing his whole body several times, he realized the water was—and had been all along—colder than fuck, and he stepped out of the shower, turning off the faucet.

Goddamn, his balls were trying to crawl up into his belly; he was *that* cold. He hoped he'd gotten all the dip off, but the smell was up in his nose so badly that he wouldn't be able to tell by smell.

Covered in goose bumps, his eyes tearing, he looked at the man who had helped him. "Never had anyone fall all the way in before," the man said, shaking his head. "You gonna be sick, boy? That's some powerful stuff; I've seen it burn through leather gloves."

"Not gonna be sick, but I don't think I want this job anymore," was Andy's retort through chattering teeth as he gathered up his wet and smelly clothes and footwear. "I'm pretty sure that's the last time I want to do that job."

The man had laughed as he watched Andy walk to the bunkhouse. "Good idea, son."

Sitting at the truck stop now, Andy swore he could *still* catch whiffs of the chemicals every time he moved. Wait a minute...*there*...his patience had paid off; one of the trucks pulling in had to be fully loaded by the way it moved on its springs, and the driver had looked his way—a clear sign he was hoping to hire a helper. Andy half-waved a question at him and received a chin lift in return. Now he needed to find a safe place to park the Indian for a few hours.

Later that evening, he checked in with Jen, a waitress, to thank her for helping him. She had let him park the bike in a locked storage shed out back of the truck stop. Smiling coquettishly, she asked him if he'd give her a ride when she got off her shift, and he shook his head and said, "I don't have a second seat, baby, sorry."

She grinned at him. "Who said I was talking about the bike? I'm off in ten minutes; meet me by the truckers' showers." She patted his cheek, turned, and walked away, her ass swishing with every step.

He was waiting by the showers in five minutes with a towel and a key, because whether she showed or not, he needed a shower. Hearing the *clip-clop* of heels on the tile hallway, he looked up to see her sauntering towards him, taking off her apron. She squealed a little as he reached out to grab her by the waist, and then he quickly unlocked the door and pulled her inside.

Wrapping his arm around her, he held her tightly, her breasts crushing against his chest. He dropped the towel and key on the bench inside the door, and raked one hand through her hair; he used that grip to angle her head back, which allowed easy access to her throat as she gasped and groaned. Sliding his other hand up the column of her throat, he wrapped his fingers around her neck, and then moved to cup her jaw, rubbing his thumb across her lips. Nibbling and lightly biting along her throat, he used his grip on her hair to control her movements, twisting her head back and forth to ease his access.

He leaned her hard against the wall and pushed her skirt up to her waist. Angling himself into her, he bent his knees and rubbed his erection against the thin fabric covering her cunt, pushing and stretching her panties. Her hands were wandering over his body, and it was distracting, because he didn't know if she was going to pinch, scratch, or stroke, so he caught her hands in his and pulled them to the wall above her head. "Leave 'em there, baby," he growled out.

He moved one hand to stroke up the back of her thigh, flirting with the elastic edge of her underwear. Slipping a finger underneath, he dragged his hand around her leg to the inside of her thigh and his goal. She wasn't wet yet, so he was careful as he slid his fingers along her folds. He flicked her clit with one fingertip and heard a quick intake of breath, then a groan when he grasped it lightly between thumb and finger, rubbing and pinching.

He focused back on her neck, kissing and pressing his body against her. His hand left her hair, sliding down her side, where his thumb brushed the underside of her breast and found her hardened nipple. Putting his mouth over her breast and on top of her clothes, he mouthed and sucked, nipping and biting. Finally feeling her slicken below, he slipped one finger deep inside her, capturing her groan in his mouth and eating it down.

He added a second finger and stroked slow and long, allowing the heel of his hand to press hard against her clit with every movement. Her kisses were more frantic now, and he was waiting for her to break the honor bondage position in which he'd placed her. *Just another minute or two*, he thought, and then smiled when he felt her fingers run through his hair and down his back.

He froze in place, quickly pulling his fingers out of her and his mouth off her breast. "Baby, I told you to leave your fucking hands where I put them," he snarled at her, forcing himself not to smile when she quickly put her hands back up against the wall.

"I'm sorry," was her breathless reply. "I wanted to touch you."

He nodded, putting his mouth back down beside her nipple, saying, "I know." He took her breast back into his mouth as he pushed three fingers deep into her cunt. She seemed open and trainable, and if he was going to be around here for any time, it would be good to have someone who was willing.

⁎

Andy fell over onto his back, breathing heavily. He reached down casually and stripped off the condom, tied a knot in it, and dropped it onto the floor beside the bed. He closed his eyes, forcing his breath into regular rhythms, bringing his racing heart rate down. Sighing, he jumped when he felt fingernails trailing up the inside of his thigh. "Jen, baby," he used an intentionally discouraging tone, "I'm done for now."

He refused to let his lips twitch when he felt the hand remove itself hastily. He had a private policy of no cuddling after fucking; it kept the emotional bullshit to a minimum. No cuddling included those slow, sensual touches that women liked after sex. He didn't like to be touched period outside of actual fucking; it made him feel too vulnerable and he couldn't afford that, ever. Look what vulnerable had done to his mother, for fuck's sake.

Opening his eyes, he looked around the efficiency apartment and scoffed at himself. Efficiency was a stretch, because what it really meant was a weekly-rated, one-roomed hole with a hotplate. The bathroom was down the hall, shared with nine other apartments. It was still better than camping out in the field behind the truck stop, with a side bonus of keeping the truck stop hooker visits to a minimum. Once the lot lizards found out he was the one with the tent, they kept him awake almost every night trying to crawl into his sleeping bag.

He'd been gone from home for months now, but when he talked to GeeMa a couple days ago, it sounded like

Benny was still doing okay. Andy sent home as much money as he could every month, and she had said that everything she didn't spend on Ben was going into a savings account. Andy wondered to himself if she was simply socking everything away, but he couldn't *make* her spend the money, at least, not from here.

Unloading trucks was hard, physical labor, but it paid well. Unfortunately, it wasn't steady work, and was only available as long as there were trucks that needed unloading. He could manage five or six loads a day, and depending on the piece count and the weight, he could make between fifty and a hundred dollars per load. Working like this had kept his body in shape, and his arms and back were better defined than ever in his life; he silently flexed his arms as he laced his fingers together behind his head.

The apartment cost seventy-five a week, but he felt that a locking door and sleeping surface that wasn't covered by rocks or sticks was worth it. *For now*, he thought, and acknowledged he was starting to itch for the road again. It was that way every time; he'd find something that seemed semi-permanent, and then he'd want the wind in his face and new sights to see.

He'd need to change the oil in the Indian, and pack his pannier bags with some food and water. If he headed into southern Colorado, it wouldn't do to get caught without water. Maybe he'd go west from here, into the mountains proper. He'd like to see the scenery, and imagined the roads would be perfect for a bike. Musing, he thought he should pick up some kind of map so he could figure out his gas stops.

Might as well get it over with, he realized. The way his mind was leaning, he'd be leaving in the morning, and he didn't want Jen to look for him. He wasn't a total dick; at least, he hoped he wasn't. "Baby, we've had a fun time," he started, "but I'm headed west in the morning." He rolled onto his side to face her in time to see relief wash across her face, and thought, *what the fuck*?

She swallowed. "Okay, Andy, be careful." She sat up on the edge of the bed, reaching down for her panties and skirt.

"Jen, what the fuck? Am I an asshole or something?" he asked. Breaking his own rule, he raised his hand to trail his fingers down her back, watching as the shivers and goose bumps hit her at the same time. "Huh? Am I?" he prodded.

She took a deep breath before standing to pull her clothes on. "No, Andy, you aren't an asshole. You are a capable lover, but—"

"Fuck me...*capable*?" he interrupted her. "Capable? Is that right? How many times did you come today, Jen? Was it three, or four times?"

She looked down at him as she continued dressing. "Oh, you are an exceptional fuck, Andy, but you aren't ever here emotionally. As a lover, there is a lack of connection. Orgasms are great—don't get me wrong—I like a good, big O like the next woman, but I also want the tactile sensations of running my hands over my lover's body, during and after sex."

She shrugged, amused at his open-mouthed surprise. "I don't mind a little dominance in bed, but there should be some give and take. I want to know my lover is thinking of me, not counting my orgasms in order to notch some stick." She leaned over the bed, kissing his forehead. "Sometimes, it needs to be about the build, you know? It should be about the back and forth of the journey, not just the final destination. If life is only ever about the ultimate result, then it can be exhausting instead of invigorating." She touched his cheek, cupping his jaw in her hand to kiss his lips briefly, chastely. "Be safe, Andy." Then she was gone, the door closing softly behind her.

"Fuck me," he muttered, getting up to lock the door. Shaking his head, he flopped back on the bed, but tossed and turned for a time before sleep rose to claim him. His dreams were filled with unending roads, trees casting shadows and letting light through in turns, with something always just out of sight around the next bend.

Getting up the next morning, he was ready in minutes, letting the front desk know he was leaving. He gassed and serviced the Indian, making one final stop prior to hitting the road. He pulled into the parking lot at the tattoo place and took a deep breath before walking inside. He'd wanted a tattoo for a while, but had been afraid he'd wimp out. Several hours later, he walked out with plastic adhered to his shoulder and his ribs, feeling pretty good about his decision to leave Colorado Springs, and also his choice to permanently remember the most important lessons he'd learned so far in life.

Pulling up his shirt, he looked at the block-lettered words on the ribs on his left side, *The journey is the reward,* in stark black. He thought for a second about going by the truck stop and showing Jen, but then laughed viciously at himself, remembering she had been relieved he was leaving. He'd take her lesson to heart, and the tat would always remind him there was more to learn, and he needed to slow down and take it all in.

Dropping the hem of his shirt, he pulled up his left sleeve, seeing the angel with the bowed head, naked sword in one hand, gun in the other, arms and body flexed and tense. Wrapped tightly in its own gossamer wings, the sentinel was looking down at the words under its feet, which were supporting it, *My Brother's Keeper*.

Andy nodded to himself, pulling his sleeve down and shrugging on his jacket. Slinging a leg over the bike, he quickly took stock and decided he was as ready as he could get—late start or not, he was headed for Durango.

***

Three months later, Andy pushed a bar rag across a tabletop in Las Cruces, picking up the coasters and stacking them back into the middle of the empty table. He stood, rolling his shoulders to work tension out of his neck and looked around the bar, thinking, *Thank God, only a couple diehards are still here for last call on a Tuesday night.*

Walking behind the bar, he picked up his water bottle and took a long drink, running through his closing checklist in his head. He needed to stage the next kegs of draft for the day shift gal, pre-chilling them and making it easy for her to tap them when needed.

Then, there was the cleaning. Bathroom cleaning was a fucking constant when you worked in a bar. He swore if he never had to clean up man-puke again, he would be fucking *ecstatic*. Chicks nearly always hit the toilet with their vomit, but men simply spewed where they stood...and they didn't fucking chew their food. *Fuck*. He'd finally begged Arlon, the owner, to buy a long-handled brush to scrub the back of the toilet tank. It was too hard to clean otherwise, but he couldn't stand the smell if he left the puke back there.

Okay, back on track—kegs, bathroom, chairs on tables to make it easier on the cleaning crew, stock the well bottles, cut up fruit garnishes for the day gal, stack the empty liquor bottles for inventory, fill up condiment bottles, run the dishes, do a load of bar rags, and finish wiping down the tables. Easy breezy.

With his hands busy with the work he had outlined in his head, he let his mind drift to the last conversation he'd had with Ben. It was his fifteenth birthday, and Andy was pretty sure the kid was drunk when they were talking on the phone. He was still seeing that Owens girl, and GeeMa said nineteen-year-old Benita gave Ben a car to drive. Kid wasn't old enough to get his license, but he was driving a loaned car around town. *Fuck.*

GeeMa'd cried on the phone, telling Andy about the language Ben used when talking to her and it seriously pissed him off. Physically, Ben might be a young man, but he was turning into a dick to his grandmother. They'd decided months ago that she needed to stop giving Ben money, which would prod him to find a job, because they thought working would probably help him mature. But, he hadn't gotten a job; he hadn't even looked for one from how it sounded. Instead, Benita simply gave him more money when he asked for it.

GeeMa had asked Andy to come home, but he was in southern New Mexico now; the bar job was good, steady work, and in air conditioning. He made decent tips, and was able to live off those pretty much exclusively, sending nearly all his paychecks home. He explained to her that he'd have to take a week off work to come visit; it would be three days up and back, leaving only one day to be in Enoch. She seemed to understand, and stopped asking him.

With only fifteen minutes until last call, he looked up, startled when the door banged open and saw nearly a half-dozen men stroll in. Bikers, they had on leather vests with back patches showing the American flag, staged with empty boots and a rifle. These were Southern Soldiers; he'd seen them around town some.

Andy'd gotten used to chatting with bikers wherever he went. It seemed like simply owning and riding a bike made him a small part of a large brotherhood. He loved the low, underhand waves and two-fingered gestures bikers gave each other as they passed on the road. More than once, he had ridden alongside strangers for long miles, never stopping and meeting, just waving goodbye as their ways parted, brothers in spirit.

These men looked the room over, and the man in front made a motion to the bar, so they all pulled up stools instead of going to a table. Good, that would be easier on him, because it meant he could keep working on his list in-between serving them.

Wiping his hands on a bar rag, he approached them. "What can I getcha? Fair warning, we're only fifteen minutes from last call, so you need to order heavy and fast." He grinned at them, seeing a white smile parting the leader's dark beard in return.

"Shot of Jack and a draft," he said.

"All around?" Andy asked, his hands already pulling up iced mugs for the beer and a stack of shot glasses for the whiskey.

Nodding, the tall biker slapped a fifty onto the bar and Andy acknowledged it with a return nod. He set up a mug under the tap, starting it on the tilted side of the glass first to reduce the head, and then picked up a bottle of Jack, pouring it up and down the sides of the stacked shot glasses, getting an overflow start on filling them. Alternating between the beer and the shots, he served the men quickly, taking the money and returning the change to the bar in front of the dark-haired man.

Walking away from the group, he cleared empty glasses and bottles from the rest of the bar, realizing the remaining patrons had vacated while he was serving the bikers. At least everyone had already cashed out their tab, and several of them had left tips. He collected those along with the empties, and pushed the money into the jar on the bar back. The jukebox did its random thing, and started playing *Ladies and Gentlemen* by Saliva. Andy grinned down at the tabletop he was wiping; that song was an anthem for his life recently.

"Whose Indian is that out back?" The question came from down the bar and Andy looked up, wiping down the inside of the ice bucket.

"She's mine," he smiled proudly.

"Nice ride, man," came from the man closest to him, a blond beast with a nonexistent neck.

"Thanks, I try to keep her spiffy," he nodded, and turned back to his work.

"Who do you ride with?" That came from the far end of the group, a dude with brown hair and swirling tattoos on his face.

"I'm not affiliated, man, just moving through. Here for a few months." Andy tensed up, wondering if this would be a problem here, like it was in Durango.

He'd been jumped there by some bikers who thought he was a nomad scouting their territory. The beating wasn't that bad; they stopped once they stripped his shirt and couldn't find any tats of colors or club brands. He hated that vulnerable feeling though, because he knew they didn't *have* to stop...and there was nothing he could have done either way.

Standing upright behind the bar, Andy mentally ran through the motions it would take him to reach the shotgun under the countertop at the other end of the bar. "That a problem?" he asked the group.

"Nah, ain't no big thang," said the leader, taking a long drink of his beer.

Nodding, Andy pointed at their empty shot glasses and almost empty beer mugs, asking, "Want another round?"

Flipping out a twenty to add to the money on the bar, the leader answered him wordlessly, and Andy nodded. He moved back down the bar and started the process again, serving the men their drinks and ringing up the sale.

Seeing sudden movement in the mirror, he watched as four of the men descended on one of their own, taking him down to the bar top and holding him there. Spinning around, Andy saw the gun in the man's hand in the same moment it was plucked from his fingers.

Tucking the gun into the back waistband of his jeans, the dark-haired leader grinned over at Andy. "Looks like Spider *thought* he had a problem with that, but he was wrong," he said, sitting back down on his stool.

Spider was sitting upright again, sandwiched between the blond and the leader; he spit out, "Ain't right and you know it, Watcher. We don't need a nomad gettin' in our business."

"Shut up, Spider," said the blond.

"You shut up, Opie. You know it too," came the retort.

Andy's head was spinning; he...that guy might have been going to shoot him. "You might want to sit down a minute, kid," Watcher said, looking at him closely. "You look a little green." Andy immediately plopped his ass on top of the beer cooler, scooting away from the group and glancing under the counter towards the shotgun.

"Awww, naw, kid. Don't do that," Watcher tisked and shook his head, pointing at the tattooed man and saying, "Pops, grab that scatter gun, wouldja? Devil, why doncha give your Jack to the kid."

Watching, Andy saw the tattooed man, Pops, reach over and pull the shotgun from the rack underneath the bar. Andy laughed weakly. Opie, Spider, Watcher, Devil, and Pops—he was about to be killed by a group of men with comic book names.

Something bumped his hand, and he looked up to see Devil's face inches from his own; he was pushing his still-full shot glass into Andy's hand. Narrowing his eyes, Andy took the glass and brought it up between their faces, drank it down, and then set the glass carefully on top of the cooler next to his leg, staring into Devil's eyes the whole time.

Devil laughed loudly and reached out a tattooed hand, ruffling Andy's hair. Moving to sit back on his stool, he said, "He's a keeper, Watcher. Look at this fucker; he's not even sweating." Andy's eyes flickered between Watcher and Spider, believing there would be another test, but not knowing where it would come from. He glanced at the clock on the wall across the room and took a breath.

Pushing to his feet, he grabbed a bar rag, saying, "Last call, gentlemen." His hand scrubbed his jaw hard and he ran one hand through his hair, even though he knew attempting to straighten it was a futile effort.

All five men hooted with laughter, slapping the bar and each other's backs in amusement. Spider stopped laughing and abruptly launched himself across the bar towards Andy. His moves had been telegraphed long before he acted on them, and Andy smiled grimly at how easy it was to sidestep him, knocking him onto his face into the narrow aisle behind the bar.

He dropped a knee hard onto the man's tailbone, knowing how bad it hurt to have your dick smashed into the floor like this. He used his hands and legs to secure the man on the floor, leveraging the limited space to his advantage, hearing the liquor bottles in the well rattle together with the force of Spider's efforts to get up. Looking up, he saw four interested faces peering over the bar at them. "You dropped something, Watcher," he said dryly.

"Let the fucker up, kid," Watcher drawled, looking hard into Spider's face. "He's done." Andy looked down in time to see Spider's face go gray. Gazing back up at Watcher, he stood quickly and stepped out of reach, keeping Spider trapped in one corner of the bar. "Let's have one more round." Watcher flipped another fifty onto the bar. Looking at Andy, he grinned through his dark beard again. "Let Spider serve and you come sit. Got a name, kid?"

"Name's Andy, and I got this," he said as he backed up to the middle of the bar, flipping up the pass through for Spider. He let him walk through and closed it behind him, but remained tense and strung tight as a wire as he approached the group again.

Going through the actions one last time, he poured the shots and handed them out along with the beer. Turning sideways this time, he rang up the transaction while keeping an unsubtle eye on the group of men. "Well, that's a shit road name, Andy," Opie laughed. "We should call you Ice Man."

"Yeah, Ice Man, because you are cool under pressure," said Watcher. "Pour yourself a shot, Ice Man. Drink with the Southern Soldiers before you close up."

There was no more drama before the men left, and Andy locked the doors behind them with a huge sigh of relief. Watcher had left all the change on the bar, and Andy set it aside in case he came back for it tomorrow, he wasn't sure he wanted to assume it was a tip.

He secured the shotgun back in its place under the bar and finished up his list of duties quickly, ready to head out for an early breakfast and then bed. Exiting through the bar's backdoor, he locked up using his key and turned to his bike, only then realizing he wasn't alone in the back alley. "Fuck me," he muttered underneath his breath, recognizing the two men sitting on their bikes parked next to his.

He pulled his jacket from the pannier bag, yanking it on as he straddled the bike. "Watcher, Devil." He nodded as he kicked the bike to life. He wasn't sure what the protocol was in a situation like this, but when they started their bikes too, Watcher made a motion for him to proceed them, so he pulled out.

Headed down the main drag towards the diner he frequented, he pulled into the parking lot, not surprised when they pulled in behind him. He waited on his bike while they backed theirs into spots next to him, and sat for a second after they killed their engines. "Can I help you, gentlemen?" he asked, finally.

Devil laughed hard. "You gotta quit bein' so fucking funny, Ice Man." Andy cocked his head, looking at him. "We ain't no fucking gentlemen. That's twice tonight you've made that joke."

Devil laughed again, and Watcher said, "Just wanna have a chat, Ice Man. That's all. Public place is good for this," and he stood up off his bike.

8 - Scars

Nearly a month later, Andy leaned against the edge of the doorway, blocking the men outside from coming into the adobe building. He casually held a length of iron pipe in his hand and scowled starkly at the crowd gathered in the street. He yelled over his shoulder into the house, "Watcher, we got a fuckuva lotta company out here."

There was a meaty thud from behind him, and he risked a glance backward into the main room, seeing several men gathered around someone sitting in a chair.

"Keep 'em outside, Ice Man," Watcher said tightly. "We don't have our money yet." Andy took a breath and stood up straight, bringing the pipe to rest on his shoulder as if it were a baseball bat. He took one long step forward and saw nearly the entire crowd step back by at least three feet. "*Vamonos. No hace falta que te quedes,*" he said to the crowd in general, tapping his shoulder lightly with the pipe. "Get the fuck out of here, bastards," he muttered to himself. "Nothing to see."

A large portion of the group broke off, wandering up streets and away from the house. Their departure exposed the people he'd been set to watch for. "Watch, I got green patches," he called over his shoulder again, muttering, "Fuck me," when those patches didn't turn and leave like the citizens did. The Soldiers had said to watch for the rival club colors, and here they fucking were. Jesus fucking Christ, what was he doing here in Mexico, getting into a fucking biker gang war? "*Fuck me*," he muttered again.

"Fucking Machos," Watcher swore from behind him. "Watch 'em, Ice." There was another thud, and then he felt a presence at his back, knowing it was Watcher and his club members. He stepped out into the sunshine and off to the side, allowing the Soldiers to take the lead.

Watcher had brought a full dozen of his patch brothers with him to Mexico; they were trying to find out where the money had gone for one of their last shipments. Either a full case of handguns had gone missing, or the tens of thousands of dollars in payment had. Machos or cartel, either way, the Soldiers wanted payment or restitution, and they'd come hunting one or the other.

There was a roar coming from the right, and Andy turned to see an old convertible sedan driving quickly up the dirt road. It was lurching back and forth in the ruts between the adobe and cardboard houses. As if they were in a movie, he saw a man pop up from the backseat like a jack-in-a-box. But this version of the children's toy had its own plaything, and what looked like an AR-15 was pointing at the center of their group. Andy watched as the men around him hit the ground, and either got behind cover or retreated into the house.

He heard a loud bang and knew it had to be gunfire, so he started to crouch down to make himself a smaller target. Before he could move far, there was a ripping pain in his leg. His left leg gave out, and he found himself sprawled in the dirt. Turning his head to look right then left, he saw Soldiers returning fire; Opie was down, bleeding from a wound in his shoulder. The car vanished around a curve in the street. Everyone except the Soldiers had also faded away, leaving the street strangely empty as silence descended in the wake of the car.

Andy tried to stand, but his leg wasn't cooperating; he looked down and saw a round hole in his thigh, and his jeans were saturated with blood. Forcing himself to stand, he pulled the bandana off his neck and tied it tightly above the bullet wound in his leg. He felt around the back and found an exit wound. The bleeding had already slowed, so it probably hadn't hit anything major. His leg felt numb, but he knew it wouldn't stay like that long, so he had to figure out what he was going to do before the hurt hit.

He saw one Soldier down behind a barrel and headed over there. The hole in the guy's shoulder was still bleeding heavily, so Andy got down on his good knee to put pressure on the wound. He pulled the guy's—*fuck*...he realized he didn't even know this guy's name—vest off, and then used his pocket knife to rip a strip of fabric from the bottom of his t-shirt. "Gonna hurt," he told the guy.

Squinting up at him in pain, the man responded, "Just fucking do it."

He made two pads, tied them into place in front, and then behind where the bullet had gone through, pulling the guy's vest back onto him. It would help keep the makeshift bandage in place.

Grabbing the edges of the guy's cut, he dragged him into a sitting position, leaning against the barrel, ignoring a gritted, *"Fuck."* Andy looked around again, seeing that Opie didn't need any help; his wound was a shallow groove from a glancing bullet. It didn't look like anyone else was injured, thank God.

Struggling to a standing position, Andy shook his head. *Fuck,* but his leg was starting to hurt. He reached down and released the makeshift tourniquet, watching to see if the blood flow would start again and was pleased when it did not. He wadded the bandana up and shoved it into his pocket; he didn't want the blood-soaked thing around his neck. He had heard yelling for the past few minutes and realized it was coming from inside the house, where Watcher and Devil had gone.

Limping over to the doorway, he saw the guy still tied to the chair was now lying on his side, his face an unrecognizable pulp of blood and bits of bone. "Watcher, got a dude hit out here," he called, leaning heavily on the doorframe.

"Saw you patching him up, Ice Man, thanks," Watcher said quietly, reaching into the shadows of an interior room and pulling a young woman in demure clothing out through the doorway.

He gently brought her around the edge of the room to where Andy was standing, and prevented her from looking at the man on the floor. *"Donde esta tu tio?"* he asked her, turning to explain to Andy, "Her uncle is the President of the Machos. He'll want her back. I need to know how to get in contact with him."

Hearing Andy's intake of breath, Watcher looked at him. "Unharmed, I'm not a fucking monster," he growled, shaking his head. Seeing the blood on Andy's leg, Watcher asked, "You okay, man? Looks like you were hit too."

"Yeah, through and through, muscle only. It'll hurt like a bitch tomorrow," Andy said, grimacing.

The girl looked at them with trembling lips. "I speak English."

"Thank fuck," Watcher exclaimed, "I need to talk to your uncle, little one. We have some shit to get straight before I can leave."

She nodded and reached into her pants pocket to pull out a phone. She dialed and said one word, "*Tio*?" before Watcher took the phone away. He stalked off, speaking rapidly to someone who Andy supposed was her uncle.

She gestured to his leg. "Do you need anything, *senor*?" He shook his head at her, not trusting himself to speak. He was wondering again how the hell he wound up here in Juarez, Mexico with a biker gang in the middle of a war over weapons.

"Please, *senor*, do not let them hurt me," she pleaded in a whisper, grasping his hand. "My uncle, *mi tio,* Estavez, he will not bargain for my life. I am worthless to him."

Andy soothed her with a gesture, patting the air with his palm down. "Easy, shrimp, nothing bad will happen to you."

Without turning, she gestured behind her towards the man on the floor. "You see that man? That is who my *tio* gave me to. He is dead, and I am now of no worth."

Andy's eyes widened in disbelief; the man had to be fifty. "Your uncle *gave* you to that man?" She nodded. "Fuck me." He closed his eyes, shaking his head slowly from side to side as he reached out and pulled her into a tight hold. He rocked her back and forth gently, feeling a profound tension that had to be fear radiating from her small body.

"I promise you are safe now. You'll be okay. All right, shrimp? Do you understand? You won't be hurt again. I promise you on my life." Andy was crazy with fear that Watcher might have different plans, but he wouldn't let anything happen to her. He couldn't. No way. No fucking way. She was just a girl.

Andy made soothing noises as he rocked her, stroking her hair as she slowly relaxed into him; he kept her tucked tightly against him so she couldn't turn and see the dead man again, repeating, "You'll be fine. You're okay now. I'll make sure of it. It's okay."

Watcher came back into the room and handed Andy the girl's phone. "Spider, Opie," he said, lifting his voice. Half a dozen Soldiers walked into the room, including the two he had called. "Clear out that trash; use his car out back." He pointed to the dead man in the floor. He reached out, motioning with his hands that Andy should release the girl. He turned her, but kept his hands on her shoulders.

"Little one," Watcher stooped down, putting his face on a level with hers as Andy steadied her, "where do you go?"

She shook her head, tears pooling in her dark eyes as she pressed back against Andy. "I have nowhere, *senor*."

Watcher nodded slowly, scrubbing at his cheeks with one hand. "Devil, I want you to put her on your bike, nice-like." He was still looking into her eyes; it seemed as if he was asking permission. She craned her neck to look up at Andy, waiting for his response. Only after he nodded did she reach out to take Devil's outstretched hand, walking outside with him while keeping her eyes locked on Andy.

Andy shook his head. "I promised her safety, Watch. Don't make me sorry I trusted you."

Watcher bowed his head, teeth clenched tightly, muscles popping in his jaw. Andy opened his mouth again, and Watcher stopped him with a slashing motion of his hand. "It's not like that, fucker. Her uncle told me to bury her with her *patron*, Ice Man. I can't do that. We'll get her safe, hear me?"

"Soldiers," he shouted, striding from the house into the street. "Five minutes, we ride home." Andy limped after him, seeing that the only thing remaining in the room was a pool of blood and a splintered chair. He walked to his Indian and slung his injured leg over her, waiting for the rest of the men to return. Watcher went to where the injured Soldier was sitting still propped against the barrel, and helped him up and onto his bike, speaking quietly to him.

Devil waited on his Harley, the girl seated in front of him between his arms. He saw Andy's questioning glance and quietly said, "With little ones, it's easier to hold them secure like this. They can sleep if needed without us having to worry they'll fall off. Carmela is safe with me, Ice Man. No worries, brother. I have a daughter her age."

Andy mouthed *Carmela* to himself and nodded. Watcher walked over. "Are you sure you're okay to ride, Ice Man?"

"Yeah, it's good. I got this," he responded. Watcher nodded, looked down at his bloody left leg, and laughed; he kicked the Indian to life for him, and gave him a chin lift. "You did good with Diamond, thanks." Andy offered his knuckles for a fist bump and nodded, mouthing *Diamond* to himself.

The rest of the men returned, and the group roared off northward, headed back to Las Cruces. Andy and Devil were safely sandwiched in the middle of a double line of motorcycles ridden by Southern Soldiers members, surrounded by their brothers.

***

Several weeks later, Andy gave notice at the bar and packed up his bike. He looked down at his right forearm, seeing the new tattoo there in pretty script, *We live with the scars we choose*. He'd gotten the tat to remind himself of Carmela, because she no longer acted like a girl traumatized by life's experiences, but like a young girl. She'd discarded the scars of her past, and he knew there was a lesson to hold on to there.

Now, he was headed over to Watcher's house. He wanted to let him know that he appreciated the offer to prospect into the Southern Soldiers, but he wasn't done with the wind in his face yet. Pulling into the man's driveway and around to the big shop behind the house, he saw Devil was there with his old lady and their kids. Parking the bike, he looked around and saw Carmela running and playing with the rest of the kids as if her life had never been hell.

"Fucking kids are resilient, Ice," Watcher said from behind him, walking out of the shop with Devil.

"You look packed for travel, man," Devil said. "Headed out somewhere on a run?"

Andy stood and got off the bike, sticking out his hand. "I wanted to thank you for what you've done for me, Watcher. You too, Devil."

They stood there unmoving, and he lowered his hand to his side, suddenly much more nervous. "I'm going to go east; the heat here isn't working for me. Love and respect for your colors, man. Southern Soldiers are good men." He wondered if he should shut up now, but forged on, "I hope we can part as friends, if not brothers." There, he'd said what he wanted, and now he waited anxiously for their response.

"What the fuck, Ice Man? Do you think we kill people who turn down a chance to prospect with us?" Watcher laughed. "You look jumpy as dick." He pulled Andy into a one-armed hug, pounding his back before thrusting him away. "I respect you, Ice. You *are* my Brother." Andy heard the capital B on that word, and he warmed. Watcher continued, "Call on us...anytime, man. The Soldiers won't forget your help in Juarez."

Devil grabbed his wrist and shook his arm like a warrior. "You should say goodbye to Carmela, Ice. She'll miss you."

Andy nodded, his throat full of emotion and relief. He really hadn't thought they would hurt him, but he knew how prickly the men were about the honor of their MC, and he wanted to make sure they didn't feel he was disrespecting them. They'd shown him a depth of connection he now longed for, that sense of belonging and brotherhood. Now that he knew what he wanted, he would keep searching until he found the right home for himself.

Turning with a jerk, he yelled, "Carmela, come give your Uncle Andy a hug goodbye," and smiled when she came pelting full speed over to him.

"Andy, you are going away? Will you come back?" she asked him, wrapping her arms around his waist and laying her cheek against his chest.

"Hard to say, shrimp, but I'll think of you." He tightened his arms for a minute. "Be safe, little one." He kissed the top of her head, then released her and turned away. "I gots to go; I'm burning daylight," Andy climbed back on his bike, kicked it to life, and rode away waving.

9 - My life's story

Andy had been looking for a rest area with a picnic table for about two hours. He was beat and wanted to go to bed, but *really* didn't want to sleep on the ground. He'd woken up two nights ago with a snake not two feet away from him, and he was pretty much against having any kind of a repeat show. Maybe he could sleep on the bike; he'd done that before for short periods of time, bent over the tank with his head pillowed on the handlebars.

Pulling off at a wide spot in the highway, Andy grabbed a map out of his bag. He was nearly to Odessa; he could keep it together that far and stay in a motel tonight. He'd been alone on the highway so long he didn't look before he pulled out, and wasn't prepared for the wild honking of a horn right behind him. Ripping the bike back over to the narrow shoulder, he looked and saw a pickup shuddering to a stop barely feet from him.

"Fuck me," he breathed, "that was close."

The driver's door popped open and a little blonde head shot up over the windshield. "You okay, mister?" Her face was small and narrow, but her blue eyes were bright and brilliant, and he smiled in reflex.

"I am now," he teased, "but I don't know which is worse on my heart." She cocked her head questioningly. "Nearly getting run over, or seeing such a pretty face." He grinned and she responded in kind. He killed the bike, putting down the kickstand and making sure it was stable before sliding off. His legs were shaky as he walked over to the truck, and he leaned across the hood, angling towards her. "Are you okay?" he asked quietly.

She squinted at him, nodding, "I nearly hit you. Were you not even looking before you pulled out and started driving? That scared the doo out of me."

"Me too," he admitted. Standing quietly for a minute, he thumped the hood of the truck with his palms. "I'm headed to Odessa. Do you know of a good, cheap motel?"

She looked at him, an attractive pink to her cheeks and a shine to her eyes. "There's a nice motel on the other end of town, with a diner attached, mister. You can't miss it."

"Andy," he said, looking into her eyes. "My name is Andy."

"Andy," she repeated, looking pleased.

He waited a beat and then lifted an eyebrow at her. "And you are?"

"Oh, I'm Chelsie, sorry, Chelsie Transom." She smiled at him. "You passing through Odessa, Andy?"

"Looking for work, actually. Hoping to get on with a stock company or something similar. I grew up working ranches in Wyoming, so I'm suited to it," he patted the hood of her truck again, backing up, "and I gotta get to it.

Won't find work talking to a pretty girl on the side of the road. Chelsie, it's been a pleasure. I promise I'll be more careful in the future to watch out for pretty girls driving pickup trucks," he teased, straddling the bike again. He almost started the bike, but then realized she was still standing on the running board of the truck, looking at him over the windshield.

"Mister Andy, you're looking for ranch work?" she asked. He nodded. She took in a short breath and blew it out. "Daddy's looking for a short-term hand. We have several miles of fence that needs replacing, and it's nearly haying time." Frowning at him, she added, "It pays, and there's room and board with it. I'm a dab cook, and none of the hands complain."

He nodded slowly. "Lead the way, Chelsie. I'll follow you and speak with your daddy."

He realized that last part must have sounded like a question when she replied, "Yeah, he's the last say." Kick starting the bike, he motioned her ahead of him with a bow from the waist, pulling out to follow her after she moved past him.

***

Andy used his forearm to wipe the sweat off his face. He adjusted his gloves and reached down, reattaching the wire stretcher to the strand of barbed wire he was stringing along the fencerow.

Using the ratchet, he pulled the wire taut, and then used staples and a hammer to nail it to the wooden fence posts already in the ground. In some places, there were metal posts; he also had a pocketful of fasteners and a pair of pliers to bend them into place as needed.

Amos Transom had initially taken one look at his daughter's face that day and started shaking his head no before Andy had even opened his mouth. Smiling ruefully, Andy had nodded wordlessly at the man, and got back on his bike to leave. Chelsie ran over to her dad, and while Andy couldn't hear what she said, it looked like Mr. Transom was surprised; his eyes cut back up to meet Andy's and he motioned him over.

"Chelsie says you are a ranch hand?" He held out his hand and Andy gripped it, ready for a crush match, but was surprised when it was simply a good, firm handshake.

"Yes, sir. I was raised on a beef ranch in Wyoming. I also worked sheep in Colorado a few months ago, but don't hold that against me," he joked.

Mr. Transom laughed and motioned him up the steps to the front porch. "Come in and have some coffee; let's talk."

As easy as that, Andy was hired. Like Chelsie had told him, it wasn't long term, but that was okay with him. He wanted to keep moving, and knew he'd get that itch sooner or later. He was now about halfway through their fence repair project. It was around fifteen miles total, and he'd completed nearly eight of them. At this rate, he'd be done with this in another couple of weeks.

Gauging the time by the angle of the sun in the sky, he walked over and grabbed his glass, filling it from the water cooler strapped to the fender of the truck. He'd only forgotten to fill it one day, and by quitting time, he was one thirsty fucker. This heat was killer.

The rattlesnakes were too, of which he'd seen far too many for comfort. They were masters of camouflage, hiding in the brush and scrub until he approached too close. The leather gaiters he wore were hot as hell over his boots and jeans, but it was a fuckload better than being bitten. He finished his water and put the cup in the post brace hole in the fender, turning to walk back to the fence.

By quitting time, he'd finished another half-mile of fence. Picking up the roll of wire, he slung it, the stretcher, and his tool belt into the back of the truck. They rattled around on top of the metal and wooden replacement posts, posthole diggers, post setter, and various other supplies and things already there.

Pouring another glass of water, he leaned against the truck drinking it down, eyes closed. He was listening to the music of the land. It was different from where he grew up, but just as beautiful. Owls, coyotes, hawks—all were sounding their evening calls, either waking or readying for sleep. He heard the lowing of cattle in the distance, and closer, there was a rapid beat of hooves coming his way. Opening his eyes, he stood straight and looked down the fencerow to see a big man on a bigger horse riding towards him.

He grabbed another glass and poured some water, standing and waiting patiently until the man on the horse was within comfortable hailing distance. "How are ya?" he asked, lifting the glass towards him. "Water?"

"Obliged, man, thanks," he pulled the horse to a stop and took the water, introducing himself, "Reuben Nelms. You working for Mister Transom?" He took a drink.

"Yeah, about halfway through a fencing project. Andy Jones, the Transom's temporary hand." He laughed and shook Reuben's hand in greeting.

Reuben stepped down from the horse, automatically loosening the girth on the saddle and slipping the bit from its mouth. Andy reached into the back of the truck and pulled out a canvas bucket; filling it with about a half-gallon of water, he handed it to the big man. Startled, Nelms thanked him and took the bucket, positioning it for the horse to lower its muzzle into.

"You from around here?" Andy asked.

"Yeah, my family owns a rodeo stock company. I compete for a living—rope and wrestle—but I'm off the circuit for a while to help Daddy," Reuben said as an odd emotion waved across his face. Andy thought it looked like regret or fear, and wondered what could scare this imposing guy. Reuben shook it off and asked in return, "Where are you from? That ain't no Texas accent."

Andy laughed out loud. "Nah, I'm from Wyoming. My family had a beef ranch there for a lotta years, so I can turn my hand to most any ranch work." He turned and refilled his cup, stepping back and offering with his hand for Reuben to refill his if he wanted. "I've been riding my bike around for a while now, working job to job, meeting people, and seeing the country."

Reuben perked up at that. "I've always wanted to buy a bike to ride. We use dirt bikes to work the cattle in some places where it's hard on the horses, but I think I'd like the open road a lot."

Andy nodded. "It's been an education in people, that's for sure."

"You can get that lots of places." Reuben shifted from foot to foot for a minute. "I'm going into Lamesa tonight, to the Mexican restaurant. Want to meet me there and we can talk bikes? I got to get going if I'm gonna make it home while it's still daylight, and Rosie here sucks for night riding." He thumbed back at the mare standing with her eyes sleepily at half-mast.

"Sure, man," Andy answered. "Okay if I bring Chelsie if she wants?"

Reuben nodded, laughing, "Yeah, if you can get her out of her kitchen...and if the other hands will let her go." Andy nodded; her cooking was good, and she seemed to enjoy the work. He'd heard her singing most mornings as she made an early breakfast.

He had her body singing at night, too, when she crept into his bunk, but that was not something to share with Reuben.

"Okay, I'll see you there." Andy gathered up the cups and bucket to stow them. He got into the truck as Reuben secured his saddle and bridle, and swung onto the horse. Both men lifted a hand in farewell, each turning towards home.

***

He shook Mr. Transom's hand, grinning when the man pulled him into a brief hug. "Be careful out there, son," he muttered into Andy's ear.

Andy smiled. "I will, Mr. Transom. I appreciate the job, and hope you've been happy with the work. I like helping out, but I guess you already figured that out." Transom nodded, stepping back into the shade of the porch. Andy swung down the steps and straddled his bike, starting it. He saw Chelsie in the kitchen window and raised a hand to wave at her, but she ducked out of sight.

He sighed; that was the one thing he didn't like about leaving today. He'd hurt Chelsie's feelings a few days ago and hadn't been able to apologize to her as he wanted. It made him feel like an asshole. He killed the bike and Transom turned to look. "I gotta tell Chelsie bye. I haven't been able to catch her out of the kitchen for the past couple of days. Okay if I go into the house, sir?"

"Sure, Andy," he said with a puzzled look on his face.

"Thanks," Andy tossed out as he took the steps two at a time, heading into the house. Finding Chelsie in the kitchen, he stood between her and the doors, waiting patiently until she turned around. "Chelsie, I wanted to say goodbye before I left. I'm sorry, but I can't stay. This isn't the place for me."

Looking steadily into his face, she said, "I know, Andy. I...well, I don't understand, actually, but I know that's how you feel."

He pulled the door closed behind him, walking slowly across the room to her. Reaching up a hand to touch her face, he skimmed her cheekbone with his knuckles, pushing his fingers into the hair at the back of her head. Slowly pulling her close, he gave her every chance to push away or say no. He paused with his lips right over hers, mingling their breath for a moment before softly kissing her.

"I *will* miss you, Chelsie," he murmured, kissing her again. She pulled back fractionally and he released her, his fingers trailing down her throat as he stepped back.

"I'll miss you too, Andy," she said. He started to smile, but she continued, "I would never have guessed that we would have so much fun, and that it was okay to be funny, especially in bed." She blushed. "I know I wasn't very experienced, but you were patient and kind." She leaned forward and kissed him softly on the cheek. "I'll see ya, Andy. Be careful, okay?"

Riding down the driveway, he thought about her goodbye and felt his heart clench a little, but he'd known she was not for him. He stopped in Lamesa at a tattoo place, walking in and talking to the resident artist. He'd started the outline of a dragon on his chest when he got into town; they'd worked on it over the weeks and now needed to put scales on the wings to finish it out.

Andy sat in the chair, thinking about Chelsie. "Hey, man, when you get done with the dragon, let's do a band on my left bicep. I want it to say 'the past is practice'."

Admiring his chest later that night in a motel mirror, he loved the way the wings stretched from collarbone to collarbone, dipping at his throat to the dragon's neck. The tail hung sinuously down his chest and belly, with the last half-inch dropping to the waistband of his jeans. The hind legs were drawn up tightly, coiled as if to strike. He liked this ink a lot; it was an original, drawn just for him. *Expensive as fuck, but worth it,* he thought.

Turning, he looked at the plastic wrap on his bicep covering the tribal band that held the new saying. Everything tattooed on his body had meaning, even if he was the only one who knew it. It made the ink profound, as if it were telling his life's story through the pictures on his skin.

10 - Lessons everywhere

Ten years ago

"Fuck me, this state is fucking wide," Andy muttered as he realized there was nearly another hundred miles to Louisiana. After five days, he was *still* in Texas. He'd stopped in Dallas for a day, hanging out at a local bike shop and begging use of some tools to tune up his Indian.

He'd been able to purchase a tool roll bag a while back he had strapped under his seat, but he did not yet have all the tools needed. Buying them one at a time was harder than it sounded, because sometimes shops didn't have tools available when he needed it, or when he had the cash.

His girl was humming along today, though; she was happy, and so was he. Now, he simply needed to find a place to stay. Pulling over, he drew out his well-worn map, deciding to detour north of old highway 80 for a bit, turning onto some smaller country roads.

Going north out of Gladewater, he came to a small town called Gilmer. Pulling into a gas station, he filled up his tank and walked to the window to pay. Picking up a pop and a candy bar from the slide-top cooler beside the building, he looked into the glassed-in office and saw a pretty brunette.

That was his first impression of her, and his second impression was, *Holy shit, she's pregnant...like, very fucking pregnant*. She was so round she had to be miserable, but was looking at him pleasantly. He glanced and didn't see a ring, and wondered about her circumstances for a bare second. "Hey, beautiful, how are you today?"

Her smile lit up her face. "I'm doin' okay, thanks. You?"

He nodded. "It's a gorgeous day, I have a good bike, and a beautiful woman just smiled at me. It doesn't get any better."

She blushed and looked down. "Gas, pop, and candy— $15.50, sir." She marked something on a piece of paper; there was only one other mark there, and he wondered what she was counting.

"What's that?" He pointed through the glass at the marks.

She blushed deeper, keeping her eyes off his face. "Just a tally, sir."

"Andy," he said.

She frowned and looked up at him. "Excuse me?"

"That's my name...Andy."

Her smile broke through again. "Hi, Andy, I'm Charlotte." He passed cash through the little tray, and she sent back his change.

"Nice to meet you. Would you like a pop, Charlotte?" he asked, startling himself. *What the fuck was he doing talking to this preggo gal?*

"No, thanks, carbonation isn't my friend lately." She laughed silently.

"When are you due, beautiful?" He raised an eyebrow.

"Another month," she sighed.

He frowned. "That's not very far away. Your doc says you are okay to keep working?" Leaning against the cooler with his hip, he settled into the conversation.

"I have to," she replied and shrugged.

"Dad's not in the picture?" he guessed, and she shook her head no, her dark, heavy curls swinging across her back. "Ever ridden on a bike?" he asked, thinking to himself, *Fucker, shut your mouth now.*

She grinned at him, nodding. "Yeah, I'm friends with folks in a motor club in Longview. It's been a while, but I love bikes and riding."

He frowned, because the clubs he'd met so far would have treasured any baby born to one of their members. The brothers always seemed to love babies and kids, and the old ladies sure did too. All the clubs had been family-friendly for at least a portion of their gatherings.

He looked at her and saw she had tucked that chin again, looking down at her hands clasped on the counter with her hair hiding her face.

"Is the baby one of the members'?" he quizzed her. She shook her head, not looking up. "No?" he pressed.

"No, it's not a member's. Their Sergeant at Arms would have killed anyone that tried anything." She smiled fondly. "He was my first friend there."

He changed the subject, "Charlotte, can you recommend a good place for dinner in Gilmer?" He'd made a decision without trying to understand it; he was just gonna go with it.

"Sure, there's a great Mexican place, *La Finca;* it's the best sit-down food in Gilmer after dark," she said.

"What time do you get off?" He raised his eyebrow at her again, watching as her eyes flew up to meet his in alarm. He said, "It's nothing more than dinner. I don't know anyone in town, and I don't like eating alone. You'd be doing me a favor, really."

Watching her face, he saw she was looking down again, but her finger was tracing that mark she'd made on the paper. "Six," she said quietly.

He nodded and rapped gently on the glass to get her to raise her eyes again. "I'll be here at five-thirty." He smiled and walked over to his bike.

He was back and waiting at the promised time, sitting behind the gas station office. About ten minutes until six, a pickup drove up and parked, with a little blonde woman inside. Then, right at six, another pickup drove up, and a tall gal with crazy hair got out and knocked at the back door of the office.

Charlotte came out, talking to the tall gal and pointing towards a storage shed. They both nodded and laughed, and the tall woman bent down and put her hands on either side of Charlotte's belly, looking like she was talking to it. They smiled, and she stepped into the office, closing the door.

Charlotte waved at him, and walked to stand between him and the other truck. "Andy, I wasn't sure if you were serious," she said quietly.

"Can you ride with me?" he asked. "Is it safe for the baby?"

She nodded. "Yes, it's okay. Let me tell my cousin what I'm doing. What time should she pick me up?"

He looked at her. "I can take you home, beautiful." He smiled widely. "I'd like to."

Her eyes cut down to the ground and then back up, her hair swinging into her face. "Okay."

Turning, she addressed the blonde in the truck. "Lissa, this is Andy." She took a deep breath, looking down. "I'm going out to dinner with him." Her shoulders drew in on themselves like she was readying for an attack, and almost immediately, it came.

"What? Are you crazy, Charlotte? You can't go out like that. You know how people will talk. I know you know better." The blonde was hanging halfway out the window of the truck, yelling at her.

Andy got off the bike and went to stand behind Charlotte. "I'm a very safe driver, Lissa. I'm also a nice guy." He smiled at her. "I promise." Putting his hands on Charlotte's shoulders, he turned her and said, "But, I don't want to cause problems you don't need. You can say no to dinner, beautiful."

She shook her head, whispering, "I'd like to go. I want to."

"Well then, let's go." He looped an arm around her waist, turning her towards the bike. Waving at Lissa, he shouted a goodbye over his shoulder, hearing her sputter in surprise. Pulling a helmet from his bag, he handed it to Charlotte and waited for her to put it on, glancing over to see Lissa staring at them.

"Okay, how do you think will be the easiest way to mount the bike, beautiful? I can pick you up and put you on it, or you can stand on the pegs and swing a leg over the back. I don't want you to hurt yourself, and I'm kinda clueless here about," he gestured to her belly, "all of that."

Grinning, she gestured towards her belly with her hands. "I confess, it's the first time for me, too." He laughed at her joke and raised both eyebrows at her.

"I was riding horses up until a couple weeks ago, so I can stand on the peg and swing over, if you can hold the bike nice and steady," she offered. He straddled the bike, leaning down and flipping the pegs into position. Holding out his hand, he smiled when she put hers trustingly into his to step up onto the peg.

He heard the truck drive away, and was glad that Lissa had finally given up her hateful staring. Charlotte settled into place behind him, her round belly pressed against his back. She laughed. "I can't put my arms around your waist very well," she told him, and placed her hands on his shoulders instead.

He leaned his head back, turning to see her face; she'd pulled her hair into a ponytail before putting on the helmet. For the first time, her features were clearly visible, no more hiding behind a screen of dark hair, and he could see that she *was* pretty, "Alrighty, which way, beautiful?"

"Turn right onto the highway out of the lot, then right at the courthouse square. Straight through two stop signs. It's bumpy and downhill, so be aware. We'll turn left at the stop sign by the feed store, and you'll see the place on the left." She took in a breath and he thought she would continue, but she sat back a little.

"Okay, right, right, bumpy, left—got it, but if I mess up, tap the shoulder that's the right direction, okay?" He saw her nod.

Starting the bike, he glanced back at her face again, pleased to see a wide smile. He grinned, guessing she must have missed riding. Pulling out of the gas station carefully, he softly throttled up through a couple of gears, and then held steady to the courthouse square. He was ready for her to lean the wrong way, but was surprised when he nearly went out of position because she leaned *into* the turn instead. "Whoa," he called back, "sorry about that." She nodded and rubbed his shoulders lightly with her thumbs, her fingertips softly touching his collarbones.

She leaned up close, repeating her instructions from before, "Straight through two stop signs, but don't roll them; the cop shop is down that street." She pointed to the right. Andy caught his breath as she pressed up against him, saying, "Then go left at the third stop." Sitting back, she put her hands lightly on his shoulders again.

Goddammit, he'd gotten hard from her belly and breasts pressing tight against his back. Thank God her arms weren't around his waist, or she'd feel more than she'd counted on. Rolling slowly down the hill—she was right; it was full of potholes—he got to the last stop sign. Looking to the left, he saw the restaurant like she'd said, and the highway just beyond.

He had an idea, and turning his head to catch her eyes, offered, "Want to go up the highway for a couple miles? I won't go too far or too fast, but you seem to like riding..." he trailed off as she nodded furiously. "Alrighty, then off we go. Hold on, beautiful."

Stopping before he pulled onto the main road, he asked, "North or south, right or left?"

Her hand went to her waist, and she pulled a quarter out of her pocket. "Okay, heads we go left, tails we go right," she said as she flipped the coin and caught it deftly, calling out, "Heads." He grinned at her quirky navigation, waited for her to slip the coin back into her pocket, and then pulled out to the left headed north.

They rolled northward on the highway for nearly thirty minutes. Every time he glanced back, she still had that big, shit-eating grin on her face. When he figured it was time to turn around, he pulled into an empty parking lot, slowing to a stop. He felt her hands tense on his shoulders, and when he looked back, the grin was gone and she was looking down. "Ready for food, Charlotte?" he called back, watching her nod.

Riding back towards town, he caught glimpses of that gorgeous grin occasionally. Most often though, he saw her eyes were closed, chin lifted into the wind with a soft, contented smile as if she wanted to keep this as a memory to save for later. If her cousin was any indication, her pregnancy and this baby were not celebrated, and that had to be tough. She didn't look older than eighteen, and disapproval could be harsh to deal with at any age.

He pulled into a parking space at the restaurant, and carefully handed her off the bike. She waited and seemed puzzled when he killed the engine. "Aren't you going to back it in?" she asked. He'd been around a lot of bikers and had noticed that some of them backed into a parking space, but a lot of them did not. It always seemed like too much trouble to him, so he usually just pulled in.

"Nah, I'll back it out when we're ready to go."

"Okay," she murmured.

Clearly missing something, he asked, "You think I should I back it in, beautiful?"

She cut her eyes up at him, saying softly, "Here, it doesn't matter, because they aren't busy, but it makes it easier for a passenger to get on the bike out of traffic."

He nodded. It made perfect sense; you didn't back the bike up with someone riding pillion, so he started the bike again, maneuvering to back it into the space. "Thanks, I learn something new every day."

She put the helmet into the bag without being asked, and then stepped back to let him precede her. He looked at her baffled, then reached out and gripped her shoulder. Turning her, he moved her in front of him, placing his hand on her lower back. Moving them towards the building, he reached out and opened the door, holding it so she could enter first.

The hostess smiled at her with genuine pleasure. "Hey, Lottie, good to see you. Two for dinner?"

She nodded and smiled. "Hi, Erica, yeah, two." Taking the ponytail tie out of her hair, she used her fingers to comb and smooth her rucked-up curls.

They followed Erica to a booth, and he waited for Charlotte to sit down before sliding in beside her on the bench. She looked startled and shifted over quickly, putting distance between their legs on the seat. He lounged back, stretching his legs out across the space between the benches.

He started tapping on the table and she threw him a quizzical look. He pointed up at the speakers, saying, "Maroon 5...*Harder to Breathe*, I love this song!" She laughed at him, playing along by bobbing her head. "So, what's good here?" he asked, looking down at one of the menus the hostess had left on the table. Their waitress approached before she could answer, bringing glasses of water and bowls of tortilla chips and red salsa.

"Hey, Barbara, can I get some verde sauce?" Charlotte asked.

"Lottie!" the waitress exclaimed, leaning across Andy to hug her. "I'll be right back with that green sauce, girl. What about drinks?"

He indicated the water. "This is fine for me," and turning to Charlotte asked, "Beautiful?"

"Water is fine," she replied and her eyes dropped. "Everything," she said quietly once the waitress had left. He looked at her, confused. "You asked what was good. Everything here is good. In fact, I'd go so far as to say I've never had anything here that I didn't like." She grinned. "I say that, but I'm a creature of habit, so I always have the beef burrito, so maybe it's best?"

God, her grin was adorable, and he smiled back at her. "Burritos all around, then?" he asked, and she nodded.

He gave their order to the waitress when she returned with a full bowl of a nearly neon green sauce. It seriously looked like pea soup mixed with crayons, and was of a particularly thick, dense consistency. He looked dubiously at it, picking up a chip and gingerly poking at it with one corner.

Charlotte laughed out loud at him, reaching into the basket for a chip of her own, breaking it in half and dipping one end into the sauce. Putting the coated chip in her mouth, she closed her eyes and moaned. She fucking *moaned* at the taste of the food, and he was hard again. Grinning, he watched her open her eyes and blush when he asked, "Is it that good, beautiful?"

She nodded. "Their green sauce is made fresh each day. They use it mostly for cooking, but it's made from peppers, spices, and avocado, with onions cooked in. It's so good." She looked down. "I don't like the red sauce as much, because there's usually too much cilantro, and that can make it taste kinda bitter." She glanced at him, took the other half of her chip, and dipped it in, putting the smeared chip into her mouth. "But, green sauce, oh my...this is just goodness," she whispered around the food in her mouth, putting her hand in front of her lips with her eyes smiling.

He picked up another chip. "Why do you break your chips in half?" he asked.

"So I won't double-dip, because—trust me—you'll want to," she answered with enthusiasm, still from behind her hand.

He hadn't even considered there was etiquette like that for chips and dip. Dipping his chip into the green sauce, he brought it to his mouth, surprised by the spice and fire; then his taste buds pulled individual flavors out of the mix, and he deliberately moaned loudly. "That *is* goodness," he agreed, and she laughed at him.

The meal continued that way, with Andy teasing conversation out of Charlotte. He would talk until he found a topic she was passionate about, and then she would take off. That was only until she *realized* she was talking, then she'd drop her eyes and get quiet again, and he'd have to look for another subject to draw her out.

She laughed at him when he didn't recognize the country songs that played over the speakers, pointing out that not knowing Toby Keith was virtually un-American, especially if you didn't recognize his *Courtesy of the Red, White, and Blue*, which she called an 'anthem'.

He found out the father of her baby was not involved. They'd broken up, and he'd moved four states away right before they found out she was expecting. She lived with her parents to save money, but planned to move out on her own soon after the baby was born.

She hadn't told the bikers in Longview about her pregnancy. It sounded like she was afraid they would be disappointed in her, so she dropped out of their lives several months ago. He sensed there was something else working there, but couldn't put his finger on it.

Her eyes were the greenest-green he'd ever seen, but she thought they were common and plain. She was divorced, but that predated her pregnancy by a couple of years; he was not in the picture either. She seemed oddly reticent about her ex, but Andy supposed most folks were.

She was nearly twenty-two, so a little older than he had originally guessed. She was working two part-time jobs, getting in about fifty hours a week between them. That was only when she could get her schedules to line up, which seemed a struggle. She was funny, smart, and beautiful. She was also very pregnant, and virtually alone.

They sat there for nearly three hours, until the hostess came by and told them the restaurant would be closing in about thirty minutes, which they took as their cue to leave. Charlotte argued about the bill, and insisted on leaving the tip when he wouldn't let her pay for her meal. He liked that she was independent and wanted to carry her own weight, but he hated that she seemed to be waiting for a punishing response all the time. He wanted to find whoever had made her feel that way and deal with them.

Strolling out towards the bike, she shivered in the cooler night air. He frowned; her shirt had been fine during the day, but it left her arms bare, and she would be frozen by the time he got her home. He walked to the bike and grabbed his backpack, digging into it until he found a clean, long-sleeved thermal shirt.

She looked at him, and he motioned her over, gathering the material of the shirt in his hands. "You don't have a jacket, Charlotte. Put this on." He pulled it over her head and held it while she tucked her arms down into the sleeves. Once she was settled into it, he pulled the hem down, stretching it tightly around her belly. He gave it a last tug and smiled at her.

"Thanks, Andy," she said softly, looking down.

He lifted her chin with one finger, bringing her eyes up to meet his. "You are more than welcome." He packed his bag again, asking her casually, "What were those tally marks you were making at work?"

Occupied with putting her hair up and then fastening the helmet under her chin, she answered without thinking, "The number of times people were nice to me today." Her hand shot up to cover her mouth, and she shook her head. "Oh my God, that sounds pitiful, doesn't it?"

"Well, I think I should return tomorrow, and we can put more marks down," he replied, ignoring her last statement and urging her gently towards the rear of bike. He straddled it, making sure the pegs were down for her. She stepped up behind him, hands on his shoulders again. "Where to, beautiful? Your carriage requires direction."

She giggled brightly. He hadn't heard that often enough tonight; she needed to laugh more. "Out to the highway, left, then turn left at the first light. We'll go until it seems like we're headed out of town, and then turn left on the first county road." Shaking her head, she added, "It's several miles out on that highway, but I'll let you know about a mile before we need to turn right onto my road."

The bike's headlamp illuminated the parking lot; he was amused they were the last customer vehicle. "Charlotte, I want you to know I've enjoyed this a lot, and the food was delicious, as promised," he said, smiling, "but the company was even better than the food. You have been a very nice surprise." He turned his head to see her reaction, and saw her eyes glittering with what looked like tears. Twisting his torso, he looked her fully in the face. "Baby, what's wrong?"

"You are so nice, Andy. I enjoyed tonight, too. Thank you for this." Her voice hitched. "You don't know what it meant to me. Just...thank you."

"No, Charlotte, thank you. I don't often have company for my meals, and I can't remember the last time I've laughed so often, or so hard. I needed this, and the food was good, so bonus." He leaned in and kissed her cheek.

Her lashes drifted down to her cheek as she blinked slowly, and then she smiled at him...for him, nodding. He started the bike, holding the thought of that smile tightly as he rolled out and they were on their way.

He expected the lean now, and followed her shoulder taps for the turns onto the country highway. He took it slow; the highway wound through woods and fields, and the moonlight made everything gleam and glow beautifully. Before he knew it, she was tapping his right shoulder and holding up one finger, one mile for the road to her house...her parents' house.

He turned onto the narrow, dark road; it wasn't dirt, but some other material, firm beneath his wheels, *thank fuck*. She tapped his left shoulder, holding up one finger on that side. They were close to the house.

He idled down the road, pulling into the driveway of the house she indicated, a modest two-story ranch. There was a porch light on, and a dog barking in the distance; he saw a figure moving in the house, and it looked like someone was waiting up for her.

Rolling to a stop, he killed the engine and held his hand out; he liked how her grip was trusting as she allowed him to help her off. He put down the kickstand and leaned the bike, making sure it was stable.

Standing up off the bike, he turned, taking the helmet and putting it away as she pulled his shirt off over her head. It mussed up her hair, and she looked incredibly sexy like that. He could imagine seeing her laying on pillows after they had made love, looking exactly like that. *What the fuck?* he thought again. *What was his deal with this chick?*

He reached out and gently took out her hair tie, smoothing her hair down in the back. She ducked her head and stepped back, looking over his shoulder at the house. He'd heard the door open, but wasn't going to pay attention to anything but her until he absolutely had to.

"Charlotte, did you eat yet, baby girl?" came a man's voice, pleasant and full of care for her.

"Yes, Daddy, I ate in town," she responded, and Andy heard the smile in her voice.

"Bring your friend in, sweetie. The skeeters are getting bad," her dad called, and the door closed gently.

"Andy, would you like to come inside?" she asked, already stepping away and seeming to assume he would rather be anywhere than here.

He said, "Yes, I'd like to meet your dad," and saw the shock in her face.

He reached down and took her hand in his, winding his fingers between hers. "If that's okay with you, Charlotte. I don't want to intrude if I'm unwanted."

Her eyes glanced up at his. "I want you...I mean, you are welcome, Andy. Please, come in."

He nodded and smiled at her blush he could see even in the dark, and they walked to the house hand-in-hand. A man he assumed her father was sitting in a recliner watching TV. He saw Andy and stood, walking over with his hand out. "Randall," he introduced himself, "Randall Stevens."

"Andy Jones," he replied, and they shook hands carefully.

"Come in, sit down," Randall invited. "Would you like anything to drink?"

Andy shook his head. "I'm good, thanks." He looked at Charlotte, letting her lead him into the room; she moved towards the couch against the wall, perching along the cushion's edge on one side. He settled into the seat beside her, and his movements unbalanced her, tipping her over backward with a squeal and flail of her arms.

Her head was wedged tightly where the back of the couch met the seat cushion, and she was flat on her back. Sighing defeatedly, she laughed at herself. "I will never be able to get up again." Then, slowly rubbing her stomach in small circles, she smiled softly, privately.

She was looking down at her belly and had pulled the fabric of her shirt tight across it. Andy watched her and saw movement under the clothing. He asked softly, "Is the baby moving?" She nodded, not taking her eyes off her belly. Even more softly, he asked, "Can I feel it? Can I touch you?"

She glanced over at him startled, and then slowly nodded, directing him, "Here, put a hand on either side; she's stretching all over right now."

He carefully put his hands on her belly, extremely conscious of how intimate a moment this was, and his eyes were on her face as he touched her. She smiled softly again, and Andy felt the languid movements underneath his hands. It felt like there were feet on one side and hands on the other, and the baby was slowly and lazily pushing itself back and forth. Then, there was a quick twisting movement, and the shape of her belly changed entirely, pushing up towards her full breasts, becoming longer than it was wide, and the movements stilled.

"Oh my God," he whispered, "I felt her move. Her, right? You said her?"

She nodded at him, grinning. "She moves around a lot. I think she has too much room in there right now, but she's growing into it every day." His eyes flicked towards her father, and Randall was looking at them with a thoughtful expression on his face.

Her dad cleared his throat. "Andy, looked like some bags on that bike. You traveling through?"

Andy straightened, leaving his hands on Charlotte's stomach in case the baby started moving again. "Yes, sir, I've been making my way across the country for more than a year now, picking up work where I can." He looked down at her face, not wanting any mistakes or misunderstandings. "I've not found my place yet, so I simply keep moving. I don't aim to stay in any one place over long."

She nodded soberly, but Randall frowned. "What kind of work, son?"

"Oh, pretty much anything I can get. I grew up on a ranch in Wyoming, but along the way, I've learned some mechanicing, some carpentry, how to tend bar...I've been a short order cook, and a garbage separator," he grinned at them, "but don't ask about that one, sir. I've worked at loading and unloading trucks, and of course, anything to do with ranching or stock." He laughed. "Typical Jack of all trades, master of none."

Randall smiled at him. "Sounds like fun, actually."

Andy grinned back at him. "It's been exciting. I've met a lot of good people, interesting people, with stories all their own."

He leaned over Charlotte, looking down into her face with a soft smile. "I've seen the sun come up more than four hundred different ways, and seen it disappear beyond the horizon the same. I've lived, with my bike to point the way."

He looked up, and Randall was still smiling at him. "Sounds like a blast."

Andy pulled his eyes back to her belly; the baby was moving again. He closed his eyes, feeling the movements of the vulnerable little life, separated from entering the world too soon by a narrow membrane and thin flesh.

"Charlotte, I think you are amazing," he said impulsively. "What a gift to carry life in your body like this." She smiled shyly, and started struggling on the couch. He realized she was trying to regain an upright position, so he stood, took her hands, and pulled her effortlessly back to her seat on the edge of the cushions. "I see now why you sit on the edge like that," he teased.

Looking at her dad, Andy asked, "Is there a decent motel in town, Mr. Stevens?"

Randall glanced up at the clock on the fireplace mantle before replying, "Yeah, there is, but their office is closed at this time of night. Do you need a place to stay, son?"

Andy nodded. "Definitely. I learned that camping around here is somewhat treacherous, and setting up a tent at night doesn't give you a chance to look for ant mounds." They both laughed with him, nodding their heads.

He grimaced. "I found that one out the hard way two nights ago." He pulled up his left sleeve, exposing the angry red and white marks of ant stings. "Guy at a bike shop in Tyler said they are fire ant bites. I can attest they certainly burned like fire. Now they just hurt."

Charlotte looked at his arm, and then climbed laboriously to her feet; without speaking, she walked away and disappeared deeper into the house. Andy watched her leave, disappointed; she hadn't even told him goodbye.

Frowning, he took a breath and turned back to her dad. "I'll find a place, sir. Thank you for your hospitality." He moved quickly towards the door, hand outstretched for the knob.

Randall got there ahead of him, placing a hand softly to hold it closed. "We have a spare room since Charlotte's sister moved out. You're welcome to stay here tonight, son."

Andy looked at him, holding his gaze for a minute. "I don't know what to say, except thank you." He nodded and saw Charlotte coming back in with a jar and a towel. She motioned to him, and then pointed at the couch, simply saying, "Sit."

She was clearly more comfortable here in her home than anywhere else; he hadn't seen her with downcast eyes since they walked in. Sitting on the couch, he watched her push his sleeve up. The stings went far up his arm, and he had quite a few on his torso, too.

She frowned. "You're staying the night." It came out more as a statement than a question, but he nodded. "Okay, go get your stuff and bring it in. I'll need your shirt off to get this on all the stings." She struggled again to stand. "Let me show you the room." Putting her supplies into one hand, she unselfconsciously reached out and snagged his hand with her other one, pulling him up the hallway.

She passed one door, muttering, "Mine," and then stopped at the next one, simply saying, "Here," as she pushed that door open. Reaching inside, she flipped on the wall switch, turning on the overhead light. There was a double bed covered with a faded quilt, and the bed had a bookshelf headboard filled with paperbacks. The room also had a dresser, and a nightstand with a lamp.

"I'll wait here," she said, walking inside.

He nodded. "Okay," he replied, smiling to himself over her refreshing self-confidence as he turned to go back to the living room.

Randall held the outside door for him, and waited with a smile as Andy walked back to the house with his backpack. "Sleep well, I'm headed up to bed; my room is on the second floor at the back of the house."

"Sir?" Andy started and then paused. "Charlotte said she lived with her parents." He left it like that, not quite a question.

"My wife has a room upstairs," Randall said curtly. "She's not well."

"I'm sorry," Andy said, and meant it; this must be a difficult subject from the look on his face.

Randall nodded edgily. "G'night." Andy turned and went the other way, down the hall to the room where Charlotte waited for him.

She was sitting on the bed, watching the doorway when he walked in. He tossed his bags on the floor next to the wall, and pulled his shirt off over his head, throwing it on top of his bags. He held out his arm to her. "There are stings on my arm," he gestured to his shoulder and ribs, "and all over here."

Her tongue darted out to lick her lips, and he had to close his eyes. God, that was so sexy his cock had half-risen again, and he felt the buttons of his jeans impress themselves against his hard-on.

"Sit down, Andy." She casually patted the bed beside her. He sat down carefully and slowly, not wanting to tip her over as he had earlier on the couch. She opened the jar, tilted it cautiously onto the cloth, and then closed the jar tightly once she was satisfied with the saturation.

"What is that stuff?" he asked. "It smells a little like liniment and kerosene."

"My Granny's salve," she said absently, picking up his arm and turning it this way and that to see underneath and on the back. "She makes it only once a year, so I am careful to conserve it as needed." Frustrated, she shook her head. "I can't get to all the bites and stings from here, can you stand back up?"

He complied, and she pulled him over between her knees by his belt loops. "Hold your arm out, please."

His thigh was touching her belly, and if she looked, she'd see the outline of his hard cock in the crotch of his jeans. He breathed slowly and raised his arm. "How's that, Lottie?"

She looked at his ribs, and he watched her mouth move as she read his tattoo on that side. "What does that mean, Andy? *The journey is the reward.*"

He looked down at her face, which was turned up to wait for his answer. "It's something a woman told me once, that journeying without enjoying the trip along the way is a waste of everyone's time."

She reached up a fingertip, and his breath caught as she ran it along the script, raising goose bumps all over his body. Picking up the cloth, she dragged it roughly across the infected marks from the ant stings, telling him belatedly, "This will smart a bit."

He swore and tried to jerk back, but she had a firm grip on his arm and kept him tight between her knees. "It helps the stings heal a whole lot faster and with no scarring; otherwise, you'll wind up with a little round scar from each sting," she said, running the cloth up underneath his arm, scrubbing at the marks there. She slowed when she worked across the tattoo on his bicep on that side, raising her face to him again with a questioning look.

"It's a reminder to not repeat mistakes, but to build on what we learn and move forward with greater purpose."

She mouthed, *The past is practice,* and nodded her head. There were a few marks on his chest, and she first used her fingertip to trace the wing of the dragon on that side, and then the cloth to cleanse the stings of their infection.

"Do you have more tattoos?" she asked. He turned to show her the script on his right forearm, telling her without prompting, "It means that we can decide what events we carry with us, and what emotional baggage we leave behind." She nodded again, and he saw her lips move, knowing she was reading the words for herself— *We live with the scars we choose.*

He turned again, putting his left shoulder towards her, and she smiled at the angelic look of the tattoo. Then, her eyes darkened, and he knew she'd seen the implements of risk and death that the angel carried, the unsheathed sword and pistol. "My brother is in Wyoming. I haven't seen him since I left. He's nearly sixteen now, but no matter how far apart we are, or how old he gets, I'll always be there for him if he needs me."

She flattened her lips between her teeth, biting down gently, and then told him, "I get this one; I worry about my little sister all the time. I guess that makes me 'My Sister's Keeper', huh?"

He laughed gently at her. "You are about to become a little momma. I think you will be keeper for lots of people by the time you are done."

She laughed. "It's funny. I forget sometimes—you know...that I'm pregnant—when she's being still and I'm not focused on how ungraceful and ungainly I've become." Shaking her head at her own silliness, she continued, "Then I breathe, move, have to pee, or do pretty much anything, and I'm reminded again."

He stepped back, sinking to a crouch between her legs. Placing his hands on her stomach, one on either side, he leaned quickly forward and kissed between his hands. His forehead touching her, he closed his eyes and breathed deeply. She was so beautiful and soft, and smelled wonderful, a sweet musk overlaid with floral perfume. Smiling, he kissed her baby again. "Lottie, I'd like to hold you. Would you lay with me for a while?" he asked.

She nodded shyly. "I'd like that, Andy. Let's go to my room, though. My bed is bigger; plus, I have my belly pillow...wait 'til you see it." She laughed and shifted forward to the edge of the bed.

"I'll change and meet you there." He smiled up at her, then stood and helped her regain her feet. Taking the jar and cloth with her, she turned up the hallway. He grabbed his sleep shorts and changed swiftly out of his jeans, sighing with relief when he tugged off his clothes and boots. He was exhausted, but wanted to clean up, so he grabbed the bag with his bathroom stuff off the floor.

In the hallway, he turned the opposite direction from her bedroom, anticipating that the bathroom was probably this way. Opening the door at the end of the hallway, he saw Lottie reflected in a mirror, standing naked except for a small pair of panties.

Her areolas were large, covering half her breasts, which were full and looked painfully weighted. She had a thin, dark mark down the middle of her belly, widening below her bellybutton, where it led into her panties. Holding a lacy wad of material in one hand, her other rested on top of her belly.

He smiled slowly at her reflection, allowing her to see the desire he felt for her. She looked back at him with a quiet confidence tempered by shyness, but made no move to cover herself. He had been aroused by her every time he turned around today, and this was no different. Within seconds, his cock was tenting his sleep shorts, and he reached down to adjust himself.

"Lottie," he started, his voice low and shaky, "God, you are beautiful." He began backing out of the bathroom, watching as she pulled that lacy material over her head, the gown covering from her shoulders to her knees.

She stopped him with a soft, "It's okay. I'm done in here. I'll be in my bedroom, Andy," and she lowered her eyes as she moved to walk past him.

He reached out and gently stopped her. "Don't do that, Charlotte. Don't hide your eyes from me. Give me your eyes, baby; let me see what you're thinking." He raised her chin with one finger again. "You are so beautiful," he said. "I don't know why you won't look at me. I can't figure it out. You have to tell me if I've done something wrong."

She shook her chin free of his touch, saying somewhat sharply, "It's not you, Andy. You've done nothing." She turned, repeating in a softer tone, "It's not you," and walked to her bedroom, leaving her door slightly open, a soft light seeping into the darkened hallway.

He washed up quickly, and then left his bag in his room, taking the two steps to Lottie's doorway. She was lying on the bed, covered only by a sheet. She had the largest pillow in the history of man wedged underneath her belly, with one leg and arm wrapped around it. "Holy smokes," he chortled, "is that the belly pillow?"

She snorted her laughter. "Yes, and it's comfortable and exactly the right size. It took me three tries to get the perfect one. Do not laugh at me."

He grinned. "I wouldn't dream of it, baby," he assured her and walked around the bed. Lifting the covers, he slid into bed behind her, wrapping her up in his arms. Snuggling his nose into the hair at the back of her head, he cradled one of her hands in his, resting their joined hands between her breasts.

Sighing deeply, he let go of her hand as she made a disappointed noise and reached over to turn out the light. Closing his eyes, he murmured, "Shhhh, baby," and recaptured her hand, threading their fingers together. He listened as her breathing evened out and deepened as she slowly folded into sleep. Andy shook his head, bemused; this had been an unexpected kind of day.

Waking in the morning, he was lying on his back, and he felt an arm across his chest. There was a weight on his hip, and then he realized a leg was thrown across his thighs. He shifted slowly, opening his eyes to look down to see Lottie sleeping, draped across him. Her belly was wedged into his side, propped on his hip, and she'd pressed her body as tight to him as she could manage with the baby in the way.

Andy gently pushed her hair back from her face, kissing her temple softly. Stroking her cheekbone with his fingers, he teased little breathy whispers and moans from her. His other arm was wrapped around her back, and he moved his hand to anchor hers to his belly, where he struggled with himself a little not to drag her hand down lower. She moved restlessly, her knee sliding up to nudge his erection lightly, and he groaned. "Fuck me," he said on a breath, biting his bottom lip hard.

She moved restlessly again, scrubbing her face into his shoulder. Her hand tensed, pulling loose from his grip and wandering southward. Capturing it again, he drew her hand higher on his stomach into neutral territory as her leg slid back down, her knee pressing on his again.

Rolling his hip outward, he bent his knee a little, giving her a better place to lay her leg. Her head rocked backward, mouth opening slightly as she gasped. He felt her hips move forward once, and then back and forth again, and realized his leg had slid between hers, his thigh pressing against her.

Loving her unconscious sensuality, he stroked her cheek again, sliding his hand to cup her jaw. Looking down into her face, he was witness to the moment when she awakened and became aware of her arousal. Her eyes fluttered and opened, her green gaze lifted to his eyes as she licked her lips, catching her bottom one between her teeth. "Hey beautiful," he greeted her with a smile. "Good morning."

Pulling her hips back, she disengaged from him, and he reluctantly released her hand. Then, shaking his head, he reached over and slid his hand down her back to her ass, pulling her tight against his hip and leg. Caressing the curve of her ass, he slipped his hand further down along her leg to the back of her knee, and tugged it up onto his legs. He flexed his thigh, rubbing lightly against her core while her leg brushed his cock.

"Andy," she whispered, "what are you doing?"

He whispered back, "Taking care of you, beautiful." Stroking slowly up the back of her thigh to her pussy, his fingers dragged and gathered the fabric of her short nightgown as he went. Pressing a finger against the satin of her panties, he skimmed over her clit back and forth. "Baby, go ahead. I want to watch you come. I want to see you," he said quietly, licking the shell of her ear as she trembled.

Andy lifted her chin and captured her lips in a soft, sweet kiss, working gently for entry, stroking her tongue with his own. She groaned into his mouth, and he felt her hips begin to move again, pressing herself against his hard thigh.

His eyes closed, listening to her breathing catch and release, feeling the shuddering that started deep between her legs. "Baby, come for me," he urged, stroking her firmly through her panties, relishing the heavy wetness there.

Her hand clutched at his stomach, fingers closing and opening restlessly. His fingers on her face slid down and stroked the column of her throat, then down to her breast, cupping gently through the fabric. She shook, and her breath became jagged and quick, her hand moving more urgently against his muscles. Moaning softly into his mouth as she climaxed, her lips grasped at his, kissing him hard. He gently stroked up and down her back, rubbing smoothly but firmly down to her ass and back up again.

As the wave of sensation began to recede, she lay her head back on his chest, and her hand went to her belly, rubbing the mounded side. She laughed a little breathlessly, and he asked, "What?" Reaching over, she took his hand and laid it on her belly. It was hard...very hard, and round, not at all like it had been last night when he touched her. "What happened?" he asked curiously, not sure if this was a good or a bad thing, but she was laughing, so maybe it was okay.

"It's these little contractions, a way for the body to prepare itself for the real show. I've gotten them all the time these past few weeks, but this is one of the strongest I've felt. My belly is like a basketball or something. Feel how hard it is." She pressed his hand down, putting her fingers between his as they covered her belly.

"Does it hurt you when it does this?" He wanted to make a joke about her saying how hard it was, but couldn't bring himself to ruin the moment.

"No, it just feels odd, like my body is doing things I can't control, but it doesn't hurt." She giggled. "I totally told you to feel how hard it is, didn't I?" She rolled onto her back, away from him, laughing. "That was nearly funny."

"It *was* funny." He laughed as he tugged her back into him, skimming her gown up again so he could rub a path from the satin covering her ass to the bare skin of her hip and belly, and back again. "Did you sleep okay?" He kissed her temple, smiling into her hair.

She nodded against his chest. "I slept really well; it felt so good, too. I don't remember the last time I've slept like that."

Touching her slowly, stroking wherever his hand could reach, Andy closed his eyes and explored her body leisurely. He listened to the sounds coming from outside, and he realized there was an odd absence of noise from within the house. "I hear dogs outside, cows, and horses. Sounds like things are up early around here," he laughed, "but I don't hear your dad moving around."

"He's probably already in town; it's got to be nearly eight, and he'll have coffee at Swanner's with the other ranchers," she mumbled, scrubbing her face against him again.

"Your mom?" he asked quietly.

"Her caregiver will be in her room with her. She can't come downstairs anymore," she said casually, rolling away from him to arch and stretch her back.

He pushed her hip, positioning her facing away from him; turning onto his side, he propped his head on his hand. Slipping his other hand underneath her nightgown, he rubbed her lower back firmly, circling with his thumb slowly from hip to hip. "Why doesn't she come down?" he asked.

Charlotte was rounding her back, pushing hard into his fingers. "Alzheimer's, she doesn't really remember how to walk anymore, and it's too hard to get her downstairs and then back up."

"Oh, baby, I'm so sorry," he muttered, kissing the side of her neck.

She made a tiny shrugging motion. "I know, and thanks. It's not fair, but it happened. I feel sorry for Daddy more than anyone, because with all else she's lost in the past months, she's forgotten him. So now, he's lost her too." They were silent for a minute, and she murmured, "God that feels sooooo good, Andy. I rub and rub at my back, digging my fingers in, trying to work it all out, but nothing I do feels like this."

He smiled, and quiet descended into the room again as he continued to rub her back slowly and with care. Feeling the knots loosen, he stroked them away from her muscles as he massaged and kneaded her back. Her breathing evened out, and Andy grinned; he was pleased she'd relaxed enough to have gone back to sleep. Maybe this could be her sleep catch-up day.

Sliding out of bed carefully, he brought the sheet up and tucked her in, kissing her temple softly. Headed first to the bathroom, and then into the kitchen, he found a carafe of hot coffee waiting on the countertop. Looking through the cabinets for a cup, he poured himself a mug full, taking it to the backdoor.

Stepping out onto the porch and into the morning, he took in the view, which encompassed several fields and a pond framed in on two sides by thick, dense woods.

A curious, red-colored brindle dog ran up the porch steps, stopping several feet away from him to look at him cautiously. Andy patted his leg, but that didn't entice the dog closer; it stood with its head slung low and tense. Putting itself between him and the door, the dog was now lifting a lip and snarling at him silently.

He took a step towards the door, and the dog took an aggressive step towards him, keeping one front leg lifted, ready to move again. *Fuck, this dog wasn't kidding around.* How was he supposed to get back into the house?

The dog's head swiveled towards the door, ears perking up and stubby tail wagging. A few seconds later, Charlotte stepped out onto the porch wrapped in a terrycloth robe. She absently reached down and rubbed the dog's head. Her fingers scratched down along the cheek and underneath the edge of its chin, while the dog's squinted eyes and tilted head gave proof of its enjoyment.

"What kind of dog is that?" He took a step towards Charlotte, and the dog was on full alert again; it whipped around to face him and backed into her legs. Turning sideways, the dog pushed her two steps back towards the door, lifting that silently snarling lip at him again.

"Dammit Dog, knock it off," she scolded it. Looking up at Andy, she grinned, "We think she's a red heeler, mixed with Catahoula, mixed with no-one-knows."

The dog's animosity had faded again, and it was staring up at Charlotte's face, waiting on a command, an acknowledgement, or something. He held his hand out, palm down, letting the dog decide to introduce herself or not. "What's her name?" he asked and Lottie laughed.

"Dammit Dog," she replied.

He lifted an eyebrow at her. "Is this like a Three Stooges skit, where I'm never going to understand what to call the dog?" Jerking at a cold touch, he looked down as the dog pushed herself under his hand for scratches.

Charlotte laughed again. "It could be a funny skit, I guess. She was a stray; we get a lot of dogs dumped on these country roads. She decided this was her home and we were her family, but Mom didn't want another dog, so she tried to run her off. About a dozen times a day you'd hear, 'Dammit dog, get out of there', or 'Dammit dog, knock it off', or sometimes just 'Dammit dog'." She shrugged. "The name stuck."

"So you have a dog named Dog, but not just Dog...she's named Dammit Dog?" He laughed hard at that, grabbing onto the column at the corner of the porch to steady himself. "That is a fucking awesome name for a dog, and she is this awesome reddish color. What a great story, Charlotte. Your mom sounds fun."

She nodded, flattening her lips. "She is...was."

Andy finished his coffee and carried the mug back into the kitchen, washing it in the sink. Lottie followed him in, leaning against the countertop. "What does your day look like, beautiful?" he asked, moving closer to her, sliding the back of one finger down her neck into the folds of her robe and slowly back up again.

Her breath caught in her chest, and her chin lifted so her eyes met his. "I'm off today, unless one of my jobs calls me in."

He deliberately brushed the inside swell of her breast with his fingertip. "What do you want to do today, then?"

She bit down on her bottom lip hard, closing her eyes. "I don't know, Andy," she whispered, bringing her hand to her mouth, covering it tightly. She turned her head away from him, but didn't move her body.

Something didn't feel right to Andy, and he slowly dropped his hand, stepping away. As he moved, he saw the tears begin to flow down her cheeks. He reached out and pulled her into a gentle hug. "Hey, hey. Hey now...stop that...baby, don't cry. Everything's going to be okay." He stroked her back softly. "Beautiful, baby, don't cry. What did I do?"

She shook her head silently, pressing hard into him. *Fuck me*, he said inaudibly as he tipped his body back at the waist, keeping her belly in contact with his hip, but trying to give her space. "Charlotte, what the fuck have I done wrong?"

"Andy, you didn't do anything wrong. I'm pregnant," she laughed at herself through her tears, pulling away, "so my hormones are crazy." He frowned at her, sensing she was hiding something and had been all along. He was on the fence about what to do, from the basics of stay or leave, to a more advanced notion like pressure her to tell him what she was hiding from. He chose something simpler, something he was sure she would really like. "Charlotte, would you like to go for a bike ride?"

***

They sat down to dinner around the table in the kitchen; Randall asked about their day and listened with interest as Charlotte described the ride they'd gone on. Andy saw real joy on her face as she talked about the places she'd shared with him, and he knew her father saw it too. After they were finished eating, Andy gathered their dishes and washed them in the sink, using his damp rag to wipe down the table too.

Hearing Randall call a goodnight from the living room, Andy wondered again at their easy acceptance of his presence in their home. Neither of them had questioned whether he would be staying another night; it seemed to be a given. Leaning one hip against the countertop, he closed his eyes for a minute; he was tired again, and ready for bed.

There was a feather-light touch on his hand a split second before fingers wrapped themselves around his palm. Without opening his eyes, he brought her hand up to his mouth, running his tongue boldly across the knuckles followed by a kiss. "Charlotte, what are you up to, beautiful?" Opening his eyes, he saw her shy smile and pulled her into a loose hug, rocking back and forth with her in his arms.

"Are you wanting company in bed again tonight, Andy?" she mumbled against his chest.

His sigh was big, but happy sounding; he was sure of it. "I'd love your company again, beautiful. We both slept well last night, so here's hoping for a repeat." Her terrycloth robe was gaping open a little, and it looked natural and unconscious. He didn't think she had a premeditated bone in her body; she was honest and real.

Reaching over and turning out the lights, he tucked her underneath his arm, holding her close to his side. They walked up the hallway like that, turning in when they got to the door that lead to her room. "I need the room down the hall for a minute," he said. Kissing her temple, he released her and walked down to the room where his things were stored.

He grabbed his bathroom stuff, and headed down the hall. Looking in the mirror, he saw an unfamiliar uncertainty and fear reflected in his eyes. He didn't know what Charlotte was expecting, and that was unsettling. Hell, the whole past couple of days were unsettling. He didn't know why he had come here...or why he was *still* here.

Finishing up his bathroom routine, he dropped his stuff off and then walked into Charlotte's room, again dressed in his sleep shorts. Scanning the bedroom, he saw a puddle of fabric beside the bed, and noted her shoulders were bare above the sheet. She had to be naked under the covers, giving him an idea what her expectations might be.

"Lottie, are you ready for lights out, beautiful?" He paused in the doorway. She nodded, adjusting her belly pillow and pushing her face into the arm folded underneath her head.

Turning out the overhead light, Andy slipped under the covers behind her and found that she was indeed nude, except for her panties. Pressing his chest against her bare back, he gently stroked from her ribs, down to the back of her knee, and back up. Pushing with his leg to bend hers, he slid his groin tightly against her ass, gripping her hip to pull her curves back into him.

"Beautiful," he murmured against her neck, "you've got to tell me what you want...or tell me if you don't want anything other than this, to be held. I need some direction, baby, because I know what I want, but this needs to be about you." Hand sliding down her side again, his fingertips dragged over her ass and down between her legs. "Baby," he kissed her shoulder, "talk to me."

"Andy, this feels amazing," her whisper floated over her shoulder, "but I don't know what to ask for. That seems so greedy, and you've been so nice already."

"Shhhh," he said, "tell me what you want. Show me."

Her fingers wrapped around his hand, tugging it forward and up to her breasts. She wound her fingers into his, pressing his palm against one breast, cupping and molding it gently. "I like that, a lot," she said, her breath hitching as he pinched her nipple lightly, rolling it between his finger and thumb.

"God, yes. Talk to me, baby," he whispered, trailing kisses over her shoulder and down her arm. Andy licked firmly back up to her neck, nibbling and biting a trail to her ear. Flexing his hips and pressing his hard cock against her ass, he gently licked the shell of her ear, remembering she had liked that last night.

Her body was shivering, shaking all over, and her breath was coming erratically. He whispered in a rough voice, "I want you, Charlotte. So much. I want to be inside you. Tell me if this is what you want too. I need to stop now if it's not. The choice is always yours...always, always yours," he kissed her shoulder again, "but know that I want you very much."

He knew he had to be honest with her and remind her of something before she made a mistake in the heat of the moment. Taking a deep breath, he growled low, "Baby, Charlotte...you need to remember I'm only here for now, not forever. I won't be staying long, so please, don't do anything you'll regret. I want you, but I won't leave you sad and lonely."

Reaching back, she stroked his cock through the fabric of his shorts. "I want you too, Andy." Turning her face for a kiss, her tongue stroked against his, licking along the edges of his teeth and then letting him dive into her mouth. "I want you," she repeated, kissing him deeply, and then she pulled back and whispered, "but I don't have any protection."

Pressing his mouth against hers desperately, he ate at her for a minute, angling his lips across hers again and again, bringing his hand up to cup her jaw. "I'll be right back." He pulled back enough to speak. Standing, he was taking in great gasps of air as he tried to control his desire. Gathering a couple of condoms from his things, he returned to her room and found her waiting, covers thrown back.

Kneeling beside the bed, Andy worked her panties off her body, dropping them on top of her nightgown already on the floor. He tugged her legs towards him, leaving her heels on the bed; his hands pressing her knees apart, and opened her legs further with the width of his shoulders.

Stroking up her legs with both hands, he let his thumbs lightly rub across her labia, pressing barely inside with the tips and then withdrawing. Finding her clit with his fingertips, he slid them in circles around it, never quite touching as it stiffened and came out of its hood.

Dropping his head, he kissed up the inside of one thigh, and then transferred his attention to the other. Keeping the rhythm of his stroking fingers and thumbs, he licked and kissed her legs alternately until he reached his hands.

Lowering his mouth to her, he used the broad surface of his tongue to lick her from bottom to top again and again. God, he'd known she would taste sweet; it felt like he'd been waiting for this all day.

Thumbs pressing into her entrance farther with each successive penetration, he used them to spread the wetness through her folds and up to where his fingers teased her nub. He slid and thrust his tongue into her, stiffening it and using it to replace his thumbs while he continued rubbing gently. He murmured against her, "So good, Lottie. Goddamn, you taste so good."

Sitting back on his heels, his mouth hovering above her, breath whispering out across her hot wetness, he asked, "Baby, is this good for you? Do you like this, beautiful?" He was rewarded by a low "yes" on an outrushing breath.

Dipping his head back down, he pulled her clit into his mouth; he sucked and nibbled at the bundle of nerves, then flicked it hard with the tip of his tongue. Her hands were in his hair now, tugging his face tighter against her pussy, her hips were pumping in time with his touch.

She was making little noises deep in her throat as he stroked and licked faster. Separating her folds, he carefully pushed one thick finger deep inside her, thrusting and withdrawing in time with the movement of his mouth and tongue. She twisted on the bed, tugging firmly on his hair.

He withdrew his finger, lined up a second one with the first, and slid them both deep inside her. Thrusting in and out smoothly, he was finger-fucking her hard while sucking sharply on her clit, listening to her cries of passion.

Her thighs tightened alongside his head as she shattered, and he kept eating at her as she came. She called his name breathlessly as she came powerfully, and then quieted, stroking across his head with the palms of her hands. Curling her fingers under his jaw, she pulled him gently upwards until she could reach his shoulders. Urging him up on the bed, she guided him to her face, and kissed him deeply once he was within reach.

"I taste myself on your lips," she whispered against his mouth. He felt her lips curve up, and knew she was smiling. She lifted against him, pulling him into another kiss as she arched and stretched.

Andy was counting from one to ten over and over, trying to rein himself in. God, he wanted to bury himself inside her, letting her walls that had felt so silky against his fingers wrap themselves tight around his cock. *Fuck. One, two, three...so soft...Fuck.*

He kissed her deeply, his mouth slanting over hers hard as their tongues slid and thrust against each other. Pulling back a little to catch his breath, he raised his hand, stroking his fingers across her cheek. Deliberately, he slowed down the kiss, making it less deep, less frantic.

She moved, and he felt her fingers slip into the waistband of his shorts. "Baby," he started but had to stop when she wrapped her hand around him, taking his breath away. Her fingers didn't reach all the way around the girth of his cock, but she gripped him tightly. He tried again, "Ahhh...beautiful, you should..." and stopped again as she stroked him firmly, pumping up to the rim and then down to the root twice.

Charlotte rolled, facing away from him, shifting her grip on his cock and wiggling her ass backwards. She positioned him against her opening, wiggling again and dipping the head of his cock inside her.

"Baby, stop. Stop. Let me put a condom on." Shifting his hips away, he slipped out of her. He ripped the foil and quickly rolled the sheath down the length of his cock, looking over at her waiting on him so impatiently. Moving back into position behind her, he let her grip him again with her little hand, thrusting firmly through her fingers and then stilling, letting her set the pace.

Arching her back, she pushed her ass backwards again, tipping her hips to line them up. Andy gripped her hip and slowly began sliding into her, feeling her heat engulf him.

Pausing when he was inside a few inches, he struggled to speak, "Ba—" sigh, "Baby, tell me if it's too much. You have to tell me; I don't want to hurt you. God, you feel goo—"

She pushed back, taking him inside to the root, grinding her hips down into his crotch as she stole his breath and voice away. She groaned out loud, and tucked her chin down to her chest. Sliding her hand down and around her belly, she reached between her legs and stroked him where they were joined.

"Beautiful, I'm going to move. You ready?" he growled, listening for her approval. When it came, he slowly slid out of her to the very tip, then stroked back into her deeply. He focused on the welcomed additional pressure of her fingertips touching his cock between her legs.

Establishing an even, smooth rhythm, he leaned his forehead against her back as his fingers wrapped around her hip, pulling and pushing her against the movements of his thrusting. He was deep inside her when he felt her inner walls begin to tighten and clamp hard around him.

"Andy. Oh, Andy, I'm going to come again," she cried, tipping her head back into his shoulder. He kissed her cheek, then pressed his forehead against her back again. His climax was so close; the tingling deep in his belly was growing, moving down, lifting his sac tight against his body. He was moving faster in response, but he needed to wait for her, thinking, *God, please, go now. Soon, please.*

"Come for me, oh God...please." Abandoning his deep thrusts for shorter, faster pumps of his hips, he called out, "Come for me, Lottie." The new rhythm pushed her over into another orgasm, and he felt her clamp tightly around him as the muscles in her whole body tightened. She grew still, pushing back firmly against his cock and holding there.

A few short, frantic thrusts later, he groaned his release into her ear, growling her name as he stiffened and came, emptying himself inside her.

They settled down into the bed, muscles slowly relaxing and loosening. She moved a little and his cock twitched, his stomach muscles jerking. She gasped, and he heard the smile in her voice. "Andy, that's naughty." He tightened his muscles again, deliberately moving his cock inside her as she squeezed down on him.

"Point made," she said with a laugh, and he shifted, slipping slowly out of her. She made a little sound of disappointment, then turned onto her back so she could reach his face. Stroking down his cheek with the backs of her fingers, she turned her hand to let her fingertips play across his lips. Tugging on his bottom lip, she pulled him down for a kiss.

"Thank you," she sighed against his mouth, "that was wonderful."

"Oh, beautiful, it was wonderful for me too." He kissed her again. "I didn't hurt you, did I? I tried to be careful, but you were so hungry and ready." He chuckled darkly.

"I know, and no, you didn't hurt me," she yawned, "but you did wear me out, sir."

He kissed her one more time, smiling. "Wait here, baby. I'll be back in a minute. Let me clean up."

He slipped out of bed, taking care of the condom and coming back with a warm, wet washrag. Gently and carefully, he cleaned between her legs, depositing a lingering kiss there before he covered her up with the sheet. By the time he returned to her bed, she was nearly asleep, turning drowsily in his arms and snuggling into him.

He lay next to her, listening to her breathing far into the night. He smiled softly when she made noises in her throat and wrapped herself around him tightly, wedging her baby belly into his hip. She was so sweet, and desperately in need of a support system, and he had an idea where they could find one for her. As he dozed off to sleep, he was still making plans in his head.

***

"Let's go for a ride again today, beautiful," he said idly, looking out from the porch and taking a drink from his coffee. He glanced over at Lottie, seeing her smile as she anticipated the wind in her face again.

He'd already made a couple of calls that morning, waiting for her to wake up. He knew she didn't have to work today; she'd mentioned that yesterday evening at dinner. Now, he just needed to get her on the bike, and that meant they needed to get out the door.

"Go get dressed; let's hit the road for a couple hours," he told her as he tossed the rest of his coffee into the yard, and then took his cup inside, washing it in the sink. He straightened his things in the guest bedroom, not quite packing, but readying everything. He'd probably be on his way tomorrow; it was time to get moving again.

Andy worked their way south on country highways, gradually angling towards the town of Longview. He'd gotten directions earlier, and was waiting to feel her hands tighten on his shoulders when she realized where they were headed.

Anytime now, he thought. They were close enough now that she might...her fingers gripped him like vises, and her breasts and belly pressed into his back suddenly. "Andy don't go this way. Let's head home, okay?" she called to him.

He shook his head, making the last turn that would bring them to a house on the corner, a house with dozens of motorcycles parked in the margins of the yard and in the wide driveway. Idling into that driveway, he pulled about a bike's length in before rolling to a stop.

"Andy, this is *not* a good idea," she spoke firmly into his ear, her hands tight on his shoulders. "In fact, this is a *terrible* idea."

He shook his head, seeing the faces in the windows and shadows approaching the doorway from inside of the house. "It's a great idea," he said, shutting off the bike's engine. He put down the kickstand, but remained sitting on the bike, keeping it balanced.

A gruff voice called from the porch, "You in the right place, man?"

Andy grinned. "I think so. Is Blackie here? I'm told he's around most days."

"You don't fucking know me, motherfucker," the same gruff voice called. "Don't have my name in your mouth if you don't know me."

"Sorry, man, I didn't mean to offend," Andy called towards the house. "I brought a friend to visit you." Andy leaned his head to one side as a tall, stocky man stepped to the edge of the porch.

The man ran his hands through his hair, disheveling it as he peered down the driveway to where they sat. He froze for a second, squinting, and then he shouted with pleasure, "Peaches! Fuck me running, baby girl. Where the hell have you been?" Blackie jumped off the porch, and his long legs ate up the distance between the porch and the bike.

Lottie reached out her hand and Andy gripped it, steadying her as she dismounted. She turned her back to the approaching man, taking off her helmet and setting it down. Andy tilted the bike over, resting it on the kickstand as he grinned back towards her.

He didn't see Blackie's face when she turned around and he recognized her condition, so Andy was totally blindsided when a huge fist landed on the side of his head, knocking him sideways and off the bike.

His head was buzzing loudly, and he couldn't get his bearings as he lay on the gravel of the driveway. He tried to slap the hits away as they came, pounding into his ribs and his head. Dimly, from far away, he heard shouting, and gradually the beating ceased, and then hands were helping him up.

He brushed the hands away, taking an unsteady step backwards, tripping, and being pulled back upright by hands under his arms. The men released him again and stepped to the side, out of reach.

Shaking his head sharply, he squinted to focus on the man in front of him. Blackie was holding Lottie carefully, like she was china and about to break. He was smiling joyfully down at her face, running his hands over her shoulders and arms, and then back up again to cup her cheek. It looked like he was memorizing her, or remembering her. Either way, it was an indescribably sweet and tender moment. He cared for her a great deal; that much was obvious.

"Fuck me," Andy groaned. "Was that fucking necessary?"

Blackie had the grace to look a little sheepish and apologized, "Awww, sorry, brother. All I saw was Peaches knocked up, and I saw red, man. That shit caught me totally off-guard—first, seeing her after so long, and then like this." He placed a large hand over her belly, and looked down into her face as his tone softened again. "Missed you, babe. Missed you a fuckuva lot."

He scowled back over at Andy, his face darkening alarmingly. "Is this your baby, you son of a bitch? I don't see no fucking ring on her finger. You ashamed of your woman? She your old lady, motherfucker, and you're ashamed of her?"

Andy put up his palms. "Whoa, whoa, whoa. Let Lottie talk, man. It's not my kid; I'm a friend. It's all good."

Lottie was grinning up at Blackie, waiting on him to look at her again before she spoke. "Hey you," she said, and snuggled her face into his chest, "Andy was my ride here to see you; he's not the baby's daddy, Blackie. Don't hit him anymore, okay?"

Andy echoed, "Yeah, don't hit me anymore."

Blackie tipped her chin up with his fingertips, his eyes searching her face for something. He must have found it, because his face darkened again as he said, "Come inside, Peaches. Let's go have a chat with your friend, *Andy*. You were riding tail on his fucking Indian, goddammit." Frowning, he reached a hand out and grabbed Andy's shirt, half-dragging him towards the house with them. "That needs a chat."

They swept through the door and through the front room, where a dozen bikers lounged around on couches and chairs, and a few women scattered among them. Blackie kept going beyond what looked like a meeting room with a bar in the back, and into a kitchen on the backside of the house. He carefully sat Lottie down in a chair, and then dropped a kettle on the stove, pulling out a mug and teabag. Glancing at Andy, he asked, "Beer, coffee?"

Andy gave him a chin lift. "Beer."

Voice soft, Lottie asked, "You still have my tea, Blackie?" The big man looked at her and nodded, not speaking. He reached into the refrigerator, bringing out two dark brown bottles of beer, opening them one at a time with a sharp rap of the lid against the countertop. Handing one to Andy, he laughed. "You got balls—I'll give you that, brother—riding up to the clubhouse without an invitation like that." He took a long drink. "You're lucky we were in an obliging mood; otherwise, it could have gone sideways for you."

Andy nodded, curled the corners of his mouth down indifferently, and muttered, "Fuck me, that in the driveway wasn't sideways, then? Seriously, not sideways?" He joined Blackie in a short round of laughter, holding his ribs.

The kettle started to whistle and Blackie gestured to a chair. "Sit." Turning around and making tea for Lottie, he brought her cup to the table and sat down across from Andy. He was close enough beside her that their thighs were pressed together.

Sighing deeply, Blackie looked at her. "Peaches, talk to me, baby girl. If it's not this guy, then who? It's not your fucking ex; I know that for dead certain."

Andy saw her blanch as she swallowed hard. Lifting her chin, she held Blackie's gaze. "The father isn't in the picture. He's in Ohio. It wasn't anything bad, simply failed birth control. Neither of us wanted this, but here it is, and here he's not. Blackie, I've missed you, but I was ashamed to come back after how I left the last time. I know what Sarge's old lady said about me, and she was right. I didn't want the same things you did. Me turning you down wasn't disrespectful, but it was near enough to make it hard to come back once I realized I'd made a mistake."

An outside observer, Andy took small sips of his beer as the two of them talked. Blackie moved restlessly as he listened to her. He stood, turned his chair around, and crossed his arms on the back of it, leaning forward to rest his chin on his arms. She continued, "Then, when I knew I was pregnant, I had nothing to offer you anymore. I couldn't saddle you with some other man's baby, and I won't give it up. I may not have wanted the pregnancy, but I want this child—"

"What do you mean nothing to offer me, Peaches? Are you fucking nuts, baby?" Picking up his head, Blackie interrupted her, waving off her disagreement with a swipe of his hand. "You think that because you had some other guy's dick in you that you wouldn't matter to me? You think for one minute I'd turn you away, because you are growing a little one in your belly? Baby girl, you know me better than that, and I fucking know you do. I fucking love kids, and I fucking love *you*." He tipped his head sideways, looking strangely boyish as he held that position. "*I fucking love you.*" His eyes closed and he reached out a hand blindly. Lottie gripped it tightly, bringing the back of his hand to her lips and kissing it softly. "It's not your baby, Blackie. I can't ask you to take that on."

"Well, it's fucking fortunate for me you can't tell me *not* to take it on, either." He grinned and used their joined hands to pull her closer. "If you want them, my arms are right here waiting on you and your babe. Right here, always. From your belly to the breakfast table, I want everything you'll give me. Every fucking thing." He kissed her softly, curling one hand around the back of her neck, and Andy felt like a voyeur. Blackie's love was written so plainly on his face.

"Reena was jealous, baby," he spoke quietly, his hand tight on her neck. "I knew you weren't trying to play with me like that. You weren't ready for what I wanted, but I was willing to wait. I *was* waiting. I would have waited for-fucking-ever. Your ex fucked up a lot of things, including anything we could have had back then. We both know he's not around anymore though, so we can make up lost time, if you aren't against it." He slid his hand down her shoulder and over her arm, holding onto her.

"Blackie, I need to talk to Daddy. Mom is so much worse now; I don't want to leave him if he needs me." She looked at Andy, and then back to Blackie. "Andy can take me back to my parents' house. You'll need to talk to the chapter about me; I know that. I'm nearly full-term too, so consider what that means. I've messed things up so badly, but, oh...I missed you so much."

"Any of that is doable, baby girl. It's *all* doable. I promise you." He looked at her for a minute. "You got anything to say, Rabbit?" Blackie's head swiveled to Andy.

"Umm...Peaches? That's an interesting road name."

Shouting with laughter, Blackie reached over and swiped the empty bottle out of Andy's hand. "You get a look at her, brother? That skin, soft as a baby's butt. So...Peaches."

Andy nodded. "Ah, gotcha. Um...Rabbit?"

Laughing again, Blackie explained, "Motherfucker, you took a hell of a beating and kept on going, like that battery bunny."

"Yeah, I guess better Rabbit than Bunny. *Ugh*, but...I like Rocky better," he said and grinned.

The afternoon wore on, filled with pleasant conversations as club members drifted in and out of the house and kitchen. It was clear Lottie had been a favorite with the folks here, and she was genuinely happy to reacquaint herself with them. As the sunlight slanted steeply across the sky, Andy realized they probably needed to head back soon.

Lottie was busy talking with a couple of women, so he stood and gestured at Blackie to follow. They stepped out of the house onto the porch, and stood looking at the bikes gathered in the yard. Andy stuck out his hand. "I'll be taking her home soon, but won't be back here, Blackie. I'm headed out tomorrow; I haven't found my spot yet, so I'll keep going east for a while." Clasping hands, Blackie pulled him into a one-shouldered hug, pounding his back with his free fist.

"Motherfucker, I'm glad you brought her. I am truly sorry for the pounding, but you have no idea what it was like to have her drop out of the world for months, and then to show up on the back of another fucker's bike and pregnant. Goddammit, Rocky, that shit pissed me off," he shook his head, "*really* pissed me off. Sorry again, brother. No hard feelings, yeah?"

Andy laughed quietly. "No hard feelings, Blackie, honestly. I do have a question for you," Andy started, and Blackie looked at him. "What happened to Lottie? She gets lost in herself sometimes and won't speak up, won't meet your eyes."

Blackie shook his head. "Her fucking ex was an asshole of giant proportions. Married her when she was sixteen, divorced by seventeen, but he wouldn't leave her alone. That's how I met her; she started working in our bar as an emancipated adult at seventeen...a fucking biker bar at seventeen. First time I saw her, she looked like a fucking raccoon, goddamn black eyes and busted nose.

"We settled her into the bar and the club, and I made it my fucking mission to find out what was happening with her." Blackie growled, "She'd flinch if you looked at her. Fucking *flinch*, man. And talking to her? Nearly impossible to keep her eyes. It took me two fucking years to get her to trust me."

Andy shook his head. He'd thought the story was probably like this, but it sounded more brutal than he'd expected. "What happened? Where is the ex now?" he asked.

Blackie turned to look at him, his face stony and rigid with anger. "Put the motherfucker in the ground. He came in the bar one night; I was there. Took care of business."

Andy nodded. "Good fucking deal."

They stood in silence for a minute, looking back out at the bikes until Blackie broke the quiet. "Ever think about patching into a club, man? It's lonely riding the road by yourself. When you're in an MC, you always have your brothers to back you up. They're your family."

"Thought about it, but haven't found my spot yet, like I said. It'll come I'm sure, but I've not found it yet." Andy stretched his arms over his head, wincing as his ribs argued with the movement.

Blackie nodded at him. "Keep it in mind, brother. If you need anything, you can always call on me until you have your own rocker and patch. Happy to help, man. Happy to."

***

Andy and Lottie were riding back to her parents' house. She seemed quietly nervous, but her smile was still a mile wide. "Andy, how did you know there was still a place for me there?" She leaned up as close as she could, talking into his ear, her hands holding tight to his shoulders.

He shrugged. "It was something you said about Blackie when I first met you, that he would have killed anyone that touched you. One thing I've learned is that bikers don't let their fear drive their lives, and they are loyal to a fault. He could not have turned that off and on at will, no matter what you thought," he glanced back at her, "and you simply needed someone to point the way."

Andy sat outside for a long time that night, letting Lottie speak privately with her dad. Dammit Dog had finally warmed up to him, and she lay down next to his chair, letting him trail his fingers up and down her spine. Creaking, the door opened behind him, and the dog abandoned him with a lurch, going over to rub against Randall's legs. Scuffing the porch with its legs, he dragged a chair noisily over beside Andy, sitting heavily into it. "She needs this," he said, leaning forward and scrubbing his cheeks with one hand.

It seemed as much a question as a statement, and Andy nodded. "I think she does."

Randall leaned back in the chair, folding his hands across his stomach. "You think he'll be good to her and the baby girl?" He was seeking reassurance for something he already knew.

"Yeah, I do," Andy said. "You should have seen him today when he thought she had been disrespected by me." Rubbing his ribs, he told her dad, "He's protective of her, and his love shines through everything he does. He'll do right by her, yeah."

Sitting in silence for a time, Randall shifted. "I'm headed up to bed, Andy." He stood and reached out a hand. "I'll say goodbye now; I don't think I'll see you tomorrow."

Andy stood, accepting the handshake. "It's been a pleasure, sir. Thank you again for your hospitality and trust."

Randall looked at him. "I think I need to thank you, son. She hasn't smiled like that for months."

Settling back into his chair, Andy made a quick call, and then stayed on the porch until he was fairly sure Lottie would have already gone to bed. Walking quietly up the hallway, he saw her door was closed and smiled ruefully, knowing it was for the best. He pushed his door open, and was surprised by a sleeping Charlotte curled up on his bed.

Smiling down at her for a minute, he snuggled in behind her, lifting her heavy hair off her neck to kiss her softly. Andy wrapped one arm around her, laying his hand tenderly on her round belly, and fell asleep feeling her baby girl move languidly inside her.

Up early the next morning, Andy had his now usual coffee on the back porch, and Lottie came to sit with him. They spoke about yesterday, her hopes for the future, and a little bit about her fears.

When they were finished, he packed his things carefully, taking them out to the bike. Charlotte and Dammit Dog were standing, watching him closely. While he was tightening the straps on the bags, he heard the unmistakable sound of several motorcycles approaching from up the road.

Straightening and stretching, he watched as Blackie led five other bikes into the driveway. The bikers were a mix of individuals and couples, and they all stepped off their rides to stand beside them, looking around. Charlotte had a puzzled look on her face, and she reached for Blackie's hand.

Blackie wrapped her up in his arms. "Baby girl, how's my baby girl?"

"Hey, you," she said softly, lifting her face for a kiss, "I'm good, Blackie—so good, now." She waved at the others as he turned her to face them.

"We all want you, Peaches...not one nay vote, baby. If you want us, you have us."

Andy watched the tension leave her body; she seemed to sag for a minute, and then that bright smile lit up her face. She looked from one person to the next, giving them her thanks wordlessly and honestly. He cleared his throat.

"Y'all riding with me for a bit, or headed back to Longview right away?"

Blackie chuckled. "Brother, we gotta escort you out of our territory. We'll ride with you to Mount Pleasant, and then from there, you are on your own, my friend. You ready to ride?" He looked down at Lottie. "How about you, baby girl? You ready to ride tail with me for a while?"

Reaching out to grab a helmet from Blackie's bike, she strapped it on and looked up at him laughing. "What are you waiting for, baby?"

The grin on his face said it all, and they all began mounting bikes and getting ready to ride.

Thirty minutes later, Blackie slowed down beside Andy, waving low. Lottie blew him a kiss, waving broadly, and Andy returned the wave, knowing they were about to leave him. Blackie raised one hand and made a turning gesture, and the group of bikes pulled off onto the shoulder, turning back down the highway towards their clubhouse and homes. Andy lifted one hand, watching them in his mirrors for a minute, and then turning his eyes forward again, he headed up the road.

That night, he stopped in Texarkana and found the tattoo artist Blackie had recommended. Walking in, he explained what he wanted and sat back in the chair for the now familiar routine. In the motel that night, he took off his shirt, seeing the compass drawn on the inside of his left wrist and forearm. It was classy looking, black, styled almost like a dream catcher, and it had a detailed feather tied to the south vane. Beside the longest arm of the compass was the saying 'Never let your fear decide your fate', and looking at it, he nodded. There were lessons everywhere he looked, each and every single fucking day.

11 - Clarity

After nearly six months in Memphis, you'd think he'd be used to the pilgrims. It seemed that every week there was some Elvis anniversary they flocked to. Each time he saw the lines waiting to get into Graceland—or the plane, or the cemetery—it still took him by surprise. There were conspiracy theory nuts, who would try and convince you the government had killed off The King, or the alien abduction theorists, among a dozen others, but he couldn't bring himself to give any of them the time of day.

Beale Street was chaos tonight, but that was nothing new. The street and clubs were all filled with tourists, and local celebrities who wanted to be seen and recognized.

Andy stood near one of the entrances to the bar, observing the patrons and keeping his back tightly to the wall. He'd learned to keep his eyes open when working security, and tonight was no different. He'd been lucky to get this job soon after pulling into town, and he had Watcher to thank. He called and talked to the man about once a month since he left Las Cruces, checking up on Carmela and making sure everyone was okay. When he mentioned he was going to Memphis, Watcher only had to make one call and he'd had a short-term security job lined up. One thing led to another, and after working a half-dozen events, he was hired on permanently.

The music crashed and peaked as the house band wound their set down. They were the warm-up for the night; there'd be about an hour break, and then the headline group would play. Andy didn't remember who they were, but Ben had asked him to get an autograph when they last spoke. The kid was nearly seventeen, and music crazy. He thought Andy was the shit since he was not only in Memphis, but worked in a famous bar on Beale Street.

Still skimming his gaze over the crowd, he locked onto a face he recognized and groaned. *Dammit*, she wasn't supposed to come here anymore; she had promised him the last time he saw her that she would stay clear of this bar. "Fuck me," he muttered, because the bad vibe had just ratcheted up a dozen notches. He slipped through the crowd, weaving his way between the clumps and groups of people, taking care to stay in what should be her blind spot.

Stepping close behind her, his hand darted forward and clamped tightly on her bicep, pulling her away from her goal and leaving her intended victim unaware that his wallet had nearly been pickpocketed. "Edith, I'm so disappointed in you," he said quietly in her ear, wrapping his other hand around her wrist and pulling it away from another patron's pocket. Shaking his head at her and holding her firmly in his grasp, Andy started easing them back towards the door.

One of the few women he had never been tempted to sleep with, Edith Khole was a professional thief. She was damn good at her job, which was a problem for Andy, since his job was pretty much to prevent her from doing hers.

Short and thin, she sagged bonelessly into his arms, tilting her blonde head up to look at his face. He could see the blackbirds tattooed on her collarbone and neck, winging delicately up towards her hairline behind her ear. They were incredibly detailed; he could identify individual feathers on each wing.

She was having a good time, laughing soundlessly at his efforts to get her out the door unobtrusively. Dressed in a denim jacket, with a bright, flowery sundress over capri-length tights and flat ballet shoes, it looked like she should have about two places, tops, where she could tuck her stolen prizes. You wouldn't ever think she had a dozen places to hide the things she lifted from her marks.

"Andrew, it's good to see you," she drawled, trailing the fingertips of one hand across the edge of his jaw. He reached down and pulled her other hand out of his front pocket. "Edith, stop it, dammit. You want me to call the cops in here, sweet pea?" He scolded her, knowing she avoided the cops like the plague. As far as Andy knew, she'd never been arrested, and her evasive moves were legendary when it came to killing a tail or investigation.

Stretching her arm up, she trailed her fingers through his hair, pausing at his ears. "These are new," she purred, fingering one of his earrings.

"Fuck me," he complained; he'd forgotten to take them out before starting work. Nothing like breaking up a fight and having one of the combatants rip jewelry out of your earlobe. Pushing her body to the exit with his, they finally made it outside, and he first checked for his wallet and keys before letting her go, stepping quickly away.

"Awww, Andrew, don't you trust me?" She laughed. Her eyes flashed, and her gaze shifted quickly as he watched her determine the course of her remaining evening. "Ta, Andrew, be safe, baby," she trilled, and then she was strolling down the Beale, bopping sideways into a group of German tourists. Apologizing to them as they helped set her upright again, she flashed him a quick glimpse of her white teeth in a grin. He knew they'd just lost passports, wallets, phones, cash, or something else of value. Damn, she was good.

Walking back into the bar, Andy gestured to one of the other security guys that he was taking a quick break. He headed into the employee-only area, needing to call GeeMa to check on Ben. Standing in the bathroom, he looked in the mirror while he waited for her to answer the phone. His hair was a couple inches too long again; it was time for a haircut. His green eyes gazed back peacefully, and he was stunned for a minute at how much older he looked than the last time he'd studied himself.

A combination of road life, where the wind and sun played havoc with his skin, and the weight of all the things he'd seen and experienced had aged him. He'd been gone from home for about two years, but it seemed like he'd matured a decade more than that. Leaving a voicemail, he clicked off the phone, sliding it into his pants pocket. He removed his earrings, zipping them into one of the smaller cargo pockets; now he was ready to go back to work.

Exiting the bathroom, he entered the hallway in the middle of a group of musicians on their way to the stage. Caught up in the flow of people who were all acting either drunk, high, or both, he moved along with them until he reached a door that gave access back to the bar, turning and cutting out of the group there. Covertly acknowledging the other security personnel, Andy walked into the back of the main performance room. He watched as the band moved on stage to warm up and tweak the set-up done by their roadies.

He knew from talking to GeeMa that Ben had started playing guitar, and wondered if he was any good. He'd heard him singing in the background a couple of times, and the boy could carry a tune, but what kind of job would that get him in the long run? Especially in Wyoming, forget for a minute that they lived in Enoch, think about just fucking Wyoming. He worried about Ben, and was glad he'd gotten the money set aside for college for the kid.

Scanning the room, he caught sight of a familiar blonde head for the second time tonight and cussed under his breath. Edith was back, and he was sure she was up to no good. Pressing his way through the crowd as the band began their set, he pushed between patrons as he angled towards her, watching as she worked the room. There was a sudden roiling in the crowd near her, and then she was gone from sight. She'd probably clocked him the minute he'd come into the room, and had used the crowd's movement as a distraction. She was good and smart, a deadly combination. Still, something felt off to him.

About halfway through the first set of songs, the band sounded pretty good. They had a loyal, local following too, and the room was packed with kids all rocking out. He shook his head, feeling so much older than these kids out partying like their life depended on the next exciting adrenaline high. Life was so much more than this; they simply didn't know it yet.

Restless without knowing why, Andy stood near the door to the back alleyway he thought Edith might have exited through, and he decided to check it out and make sure everything was okay. Pushing open the door, he looked left and right without seeing Edith or anyone else. There were dumpsters pushed up against the far wall of the alley at intervals, and someone could easily use them for cover, but he didn't see anything moving.

Listening as much as he was able with the raw sound pouring around him from the bar, he wasn't able to pull anything from the night. About to let the door swing closed, he glanced down beside one of the dumpsters and saw a red pile of rags. Lifting his eyes to the newest addition of graffiti on the wall, he jerked his gaze back to the pile of fabric, recognizing the floral pattern of Edith's dress.

"Fuck me," he muttered. He strode quickly across the alley and stooped down; gently touching her neck, he felt for a pulse. It was faint, but there as he pulled out his phone and dialed 911. His hands were shaking as he waited for an answer. After giving the operator instructions, he hung up and called Darryl, the head of security for the bar. He stayed on the phone with him, talking through the events of the night as Darryl and a couple other security team members rushed through the winding warrens of employee hallways, and Andy slowly stroked Edith's contorted limbs.

Sirens were getting closer, echoing oddly in the winding alleyways that ran between the buildings on the Beale. Andy saw the flashing lights reflecting on the brick as Darryl squatted down beside him. "How is she?" His eyes took in the devastating injuries that had been dealt to the woman lying on the cobblestones in front of them.

"It's not good," Andy replied as he moved around to the top of her head. "She's bleeding internally I think; her arms and legs are getting cold too fast. She's also broken all to shit and back. Look at her fucking face, man. She's gonna take a long time to heal."

Darryl stood and stepped back, getting out of the way of the emergency medical team from the ambulance. He said dispassionately, "*If* she lives, Andy. This shit is bad."

Sweating from the heat of the night, he watched the EMTs look her over and then bundle her up for transport to a hospital. "She wasn't out here more than five minutes, D. This was vicious and fast." Andy scrubbed his face into the crook of his arm; his hands were too bloody to touch his face. "She was in the bar earlier, and I tossed her like we normally do. I wonder why the fuck she came back; that's not her normal MO." He shook his head helplessly. "She had to have pissed off the wrong person, D."

Darryl cleared his throat. "Ling," he named one of the biggest drug dealers in Memphis, "Edith owes him big for blow." He turned to walk back towards the bar's back entrance, sidestepping Andy's hand as he tried to catch his arm. "She's a thief and a drug addict, Andy; don't romanticize this shit. She will live and pay Ling off with some non-existent wad of miracle cash she has somewhere, or she will die—either at the hospital tonight or in another alley on another night. This shit don't wash off, man, and it leaks. Be careful where you step."

Andy stood in the alleyway, watching Darryl walk through the door back into the darkened halls as the ambulance's flashing lights pulled away, disappearing down the alley. Clenching and unclenching his bloody fists, head bowed in anger, he realized he was staring at the smears of blood on the bricks where Edith had lain. He couldn't conceive how such a beautiful, vibrant woman had come to this, looking like a discarded pile of rags in a dirty alley behind a bar. She was likely going to die, and would die alone. "No one will give a shit," he muttered. "Fuck me."

***

Darryl slapped the door closed before Andy could walk back out. "What the hell, Andy? Are you quitting on me? No warning, no notice, no fucking howdy-do?"

Andy scrubbed his hands over his face exhaustedly, and ran his fingers through his just-cut hair, rucking it up every which way. It had been over a month since Edith died on the way to the hospital, and he hadn't been able to sleep much since then.

Andy's apartment lease was terminated as of this morning; hell, he'd even remembered to have the utilities cut off. It had been bizarre to have to consider such mundane things, since he'd never had his own place before. He'd liked the space, but wasn't sad to be leaving it. He needed to be in the wind, and there was no way Darryl would ever understand. "Sorry, D, I just...I just gotta go, man. Time for me to be moving on. This is the longest I've stayed in one place since leaving Wyoming, and I have itchy feet." He shrugged, turning to face his former boss.

Darryl stared at him for a long moment, neither of them speaking or moving. "Sit down for a minute, Andy." He walked behind his desk and dropped into his office chair. Andy dragged a chair back from the front of the desk, angling it so he could see the door and the desk, and sat down. Darryl opened a drawer, pulling out a bottle of Dalmore and two glasses.

Watching him splash the expensive whisky into the glasses, Andy arched an eyebrow, picking up one of the them and swirling the amber liquid before taking a drink. He waited patiently, knowing Darryl wanted to make a point, or at least had something he felt needed to be said. "Andy, is this because of what happened to Edith? You know there was nothing you could have done, right? She had made her own bed, with both eyes open." He opened his eyes wide, emphasizing his words.

Andy shook his head slowly back and forth. "I know I couldn't do anything, since I didn't know she was in danger. I don't lose sleep about her dying, D." He tossed back the rest of the whisky and carefully set the glass back on Darryl's desk.

"I lose sleep, because she died alone, man. She had no one, not a single person to give a fucking shit about her. No one had her back; no one told her she was making a mistake. She was fucking alone in the world, and that ain't right. A stranger like me shouldn't have to pay for her cremation, and then her ashes shouldn't be turned over to that same goddamn stranger."

Standing, he pushed the chair back a few inches, "I don't want to be Edith in ten years. I don't want to be alone, but I won't settle just anywhere. I haven't found my place yet, D, but I need to. It's like a pull in my blood, and I have to answer that call." Drawing in a deep breath, he ran one hand through his hair, and then smoothed it back down. "I'll know it when I'm there, when I find my place...but it ain't here."

Darryl stood and walked around the edge of the desk, holding out his hand in a traditional handshake. Andy grinned and grabbed his forearm in a warrior's shake, pulled him close for a one-armed hug, and thumped his back hard three times. Turning in place, he heard from behind, "I hope peace follows you, Andy," and he lifted one hand in a wave as he walked through the door.

Before rolling out, he stopped at a shop in Germantown, where over the past few days, he'd gotten a start on a tattoo. This would be his last two-hour session, drawing in the crisp details of feathers on the blackbird now inked on his right shoulder. Captured in flight, the large bird soared without fear, carelessly losing feathers with its tail spread in the wind. It looked the way he felt when he was riding his bike.

***

Andrew bypassed St. Louis in favor of going straight up towards Chicago. Looking at the map, Lake Michigan seemed impossibly huge, and he wanted to see this lake that was as large as some inland seas. Rolling up I-57, he pulled into the outskirts of town, watching the overhead signs closely and taking the exit towards 41, which ran right up along the edge of the lake for miles. He planned to drive the lake, and then find a motel for the night.

Since being inside the 294 loop, he'd seen several groups of bikers heading each way. He still felt a thrill when they acknowledged him, waving low in that gesture of brotherhood. Idling down the ramp for his exit, Andy heard the unmistakable sound of motorcycle pipes coming up behind him. Pulling to a stop at the light, he put his feet down and looked over his shoulder to see about sixty bikes bearing down on him.

Since he was already stopped, he couldn't easily move out of their way, so he sat at the light, looking cautiously left and right as the bikes stopped close to him—really close—way too close for comfort, as in right up alongside him. *Fuck.* He cut his eyes to the side again, and seeing one of the bikers on his right give him a chin lift, Andy returned it. He wasn't sure what the protocol was for being caught up in the middle of a club riding on what was clearly an official run, and all the men on bikes surrounding him made him nervous.

On his other side, the biker's head was shaved, and he had a helmet tattooed onto his skull. The guy had on a black leather vest with several patches sewn onto the front lapels, including a red diamond patch with '1%' embroidered on it, and one that said 'President', with 'Bones' right below it.

He had full tribal sleeves, and a small, black goatee. Lifting one fingerless-glove-covered hand for a fist pound, he grinned at Andy and yelled, "Sweet fucking Indian. Jesus, she's a beaut."

Nodding, Andy grinned in return, bumping his knuckles against the guy's fist. "Thanks, man. She's my baby."

The guy's face turned serious suddenly, and he looked down one of the side streets, and then turned back to Andy, saying harshly, "I need you to sit the fuck here and let my club ride around, man. Respect. Then you turn, and you go a different fucking way. Keep clear of any blowback. Any brothers get in your face, tell them Bones said don't fuck with you."

The light turned green, and the biker named Bones nodded at him, pulling away without another word. Andy sat there stupefied, not even able to nod or wave at the bikes as they moved. He waited, watching the bikes flow around him like water around a rock in a riverbed.

There was a top rocker patch that said 'Skeptics' on nearly every man's back, along with a large middle patch of a skull with one bony finger against its cheek, and a smaller MC patch beside it. Every rider had a bottom rocker that said 'Chicago Chapter'. None of the riders had women with them; there were a few doubled-up, but they were all men.

The light had turned back to red before they were all through, and the remaining fifteen bikes pulled up all around and on either side of him, just as the first ones had. On Andy's right was an older dude with a lean face, sporting a short, white Vandyke, sunglasses, and an army cap on his head. He had intricate and colorful tattooed sleeves covering nearly all the skin on both arms, and was wearing at least a dozen neon-colored Mardi Gras beads around his neck.

Looking at Andy's bike with delight, he pointed to his own Indian and offered his fist for a bump. "Goddamn, that's a pretty Chief. Yes, sir, that's a pretty ride." He laughed, looking across Andy at the man on the other side. "Six-Pack, you see this shit?"

Andy turned to look at the other man, who was a little tubby around the waist, thinking, *'Six-Pack' must mean his drinking preferences, not his physique.* The man pulled off his bandana to wipe the sweat from his face and neck, and then tugged it back down over his balding head. He had on a mechanic's shirt under his vest, and the name 'Walt' was sewn over the pocket. "Fucking fringe gets Shades hard every time," Six-Pack called with a laugh.

Sitting with his feet wide, balancing the bike, Andy watched as the light turned green again, and the rest of the bikers drove through the intersection. Some of these had 'Prospect' in place of the chapter rocker. They all raised a hand and waved at him, and as the last ones cleared the crossroad, he heard the distinct *pop, pop, pop* of gunfire in the direction they were headed.

Opening up their throttles, they roared into the dusk, disappearing into thin air as if they'd never existed. "Fucking surreal shit," Andy muttered, turning the bike to the right and motoring towards the lake. "Fuck me."

12 -   Neutral territory

Several days later, Andy surprised himself by waking up to yet another morning in Chicago. If he was going to stick here for a while, he needed to start looking for a job. Calling Watcher, he first checked on Carmela, finding out she was doing well in school and had stopped having nightmares. That was good to hear, because he knew that during the first months out of Mexico she had screamed the house down nearly every night, even with such a good disposition during the day.

Andy casually brought the conversation around to Chicago, asking about job opportunities and clubs that didn't mind someone who simply wanted to hang around. Watcher knew of a bar known to be neutral territory. They had ties with a garage where Andy might be able to look for a mechanic job. He told Andy to mention he'd been sent by Watcher.

He'd gotten a lot of practice at it in Las Cruces, and across the country afterwards, and since he'd been picking up tools one at a time, he had a good assortment of things needed to wrench on bikes. Jotting down the bar's name—Jackson's—Andy wound up the call talking about Memphis, telling Watcher what had gone down and why he'd left.

"No brothers for you to hang with in Memphis?" came the snarled question.

"Nah, the clubs and members I met there all seemed to be looking out for themselves. Hell, one of the clubs didn't even have a clubhouse, and they had church in the basement of the YMCA," Andy said and laughed, but then quieted, listening to the telling silence coming from the phone.

"Did they have MC patches, or RC?" Watcher finally asked.

"I'm honestly not sure. What's the difference, man?" Andy shook his head.

"Sounds like a wannabe club; they probably had a single large patch on the back of their cuts, right?" he asked, and then Watcher yelled away from the phone indistinctly.

Andy smiled at this audible reminder of Watcher's home life; even long distance, it sounded like it was never dull. "Yeah, they did have just the one patch," he replied.

Watcher's voice sounded confident as he said, "Riding club, then—RC. They gather wherever and hang out, pay dues. New members buy into their patches, so they'll have someone to ride with on the weekend—no business, no real loyalty or commitment, just riding—not brothers.

"You might see an MA; that's a motorcycle association, and it could be a ministry or some other squeaky-clean group. Some are badasses, though, so don't ever make a fucking assumption, Ice Man. MC, motorcycle club, is where you'll see the brotherhood like we have out here in my Southern Soldiers. Patches are earned in equal measures by dedication, effort, and respect...never bought. Club business is sacrosanct, and conducted in church behind closed and fucking locked doors that even the prospects don't breach.

"Even here in my Soldiers, we have specific requirements for most members. Ideally, we want everyone to be retired military, because that gives us the mindset we're looking for. The club might not be a fit for everyone, as you found out, but it works for us. We watch each other's backs; we take care of business, love our families, and try hard to manage all the crazy that kicks in the doors. My Soldiers are completely independent, but a lot of clubs negotiate support agreements with other nearby clubs, which effectively extends their territory.

"This bar that I told you about, it was the property of the Skeptics MC, but I heard it was recently sold to one of the Rebel Wayfarers members. It should still be a neutral location, because I heard Davis Mason bought it, and he's a pretty straight arrow." Watcher yawned.

"I met Bones, the president of the Skeptics," Andy said.

There was silence on the line again, followed by a gruff, "You *met* him?"

"Yeah, first day in town, a bunch of them pulled up beside me at a light, and he talked to me for a minute. Told me if any of his men bothered me, I was to tell them Bones said not to fuck with me."

"No shit, Andy?" Watcher laughed.

Shaking his head, Andy responded, "I shit you not, man."

"That's fucking interesting. You watch your six, brother. Call me if there's need, okay, man?"

He realized his forehead was a mass of wrinkles; Watcher had thrown a ton of info at him. "Um...thanks, brother. I will."

***

Pulling into the side lot of Jackson's, Andy backed his bike into a parking spot at the end of a long line of other bikes, looking at the shining paint and chrome with pleasure. He was glad he'd taken the time to polish up his girl a couple days ago; a few days on the road could put a layer of grime on things, and he liked it when she shone.

Taking his time putting gear away in his bags, he surveyed the rest of the lot. He noted that the bar seemed to have brisk business for an early mid-week afternoon.

Taking a breath, he realized he was nervous, which threw him a little. He'd been doing this kind of thing for a long time, and wasn't sure why he was suddenly anxious about walking alone into a bar. Pulling the door open, he stepped in and to the side, letting the door close as his eyes adjusted to the interior lighting. Shrugging out of his jacket, he saw an empty stool at the bar, laid his jacket over it and sat down.

The music was low, background noise, and there was a swelling murmur of sound from the booths as the conversations interrupted by his entrance began to resume. Tapping out a faint beat against the bar top, Andy used the mirror on the bar back to check out the other customers seated at the bar.

He saw many rough faces covered by scruff, and beards of various lengths. Most were wearing leather vests, and almost every one of them was using the mirror for the same thing he was, but they were all looking at him.

The bartender strolled out from the back room and saw him right away; he walked over to lean on the bar across from Andy. "You in the right place, man?" came the puzzling question.

"Yeah, I think so. Watcher from Las Cruces said I could find a cold beer here." Stopping his thumbs from tapping, Andy cocked his head. "Was he wrong?"

Barking out a laugh, the man pulled a frosted mug from the slide-top freezer behind him. "Nah, Watcher knows his fucking shit, that's for sure. He tell you to use his name?"

Andy nodded. "He did."

Drawing the beer into a mug, the man slid it across to Andy, saying, "Buck-fifty, no tabs." He stood wiping his hands with a bar towel while Andy pulled a bill from his wallet. The guy was tall and heavily muscled; he had a Harley stocking cap on his head, and his hair was barely long enough to curl out from under the back. With a couple days' worth of growth on his face, and a closed-off expression, he didn't let any emotion show through, even when he laughed.

Taking the cash, he turned to the register, and Andy saw he was wearing a cut. It had a central patch with a skull wearing a black paisley bandana, the head framed by handlebars with a three-pronged skeleton key clenched in its teeth. The top rocker said Rebel Wayfarers, and the bottom one indicated that Chicago was the mother chapter. He turned away from the register to face the bar again, and Andy saw the President patch above the man's heart. This must be Mason, the guy whom Watcher talked about.

He had nice-looking art on his hands and arms, with a striking tattoo of a brilliantly colored bird wreathed in flames climbing up his arm. Most of Andy's ink was covered by his shirt, but the man fixed his gaze on the words showing on his shoulder and pointed to it, asking, "Lose somebody?"

"It's for my little brother; he's back in Wyoming, but I watch out for him as best I can from a distance," Andy explained. "Have to watch out for our brothers, right?"

Nodding, the man moved away and efficiently mixed a few drinks for the lone waitress to distribute to the booths and tables. Then, he wiped down the bar top, and served the patrons at the bar as needed.

Andy was quietly sipping his beer, keeping track of movement in the mirrors. There were two greybeards coming over from across the room, and the bikers on either side of Andy suddenly abandoned their stools, standing and walking away. Andy sighed, locking eyes with one of the men in the mirror as they sat down.

He turned his head first one way and then the other, acknowledging them with a chin lift each, then he picked up his beer and took another sip. The man on his left had long white hair tied back with a bandana, and wore a thermal shirt under his cut. He sported a heavy chain that dipped in the front underneath his shirt collar, and his long mustache was dark, contrasting starkly with his hair.

The other man had a long, full, and bushy beard streaked gray and black. His lengthy, gray hair was braided into a single tail, wrapped with leather to midway down his back. He took off his sunglasses, parking them on top of the baseball cap he was wearing. His cut was worn over a long-sleeved, white, button-down shirt, and he had on a western string tie, with a huge piece of turquoise at the clasp.

They sat in silence for a few minutes until the bartender returned to their end of the bar, and a conversation started up as if it had never been interrupted.

"Don't know why you are dragging feet, Bingo. Fucking own that shit and start a chapter," said the man with the bandana.

"Mason don't want no more chapters, and you know that, Tug. I'll have to go nomad if I go home." The man with the string tie must be Bingo.

The bartender looked at Bingo with narrowed eyes, and said harshly, "I never told you that, motherfucker; don't fucking put words in my fucking mouth."

Bingo grew pale. "You told BamBam no more chapters in church last week, Mason. What the fuck am I supposed to think?"

"Goddamn well ask me, brother. Fort Wayne isn't that far, and I told BamBam no for Lauderdale. Different fucking thing—he'd be too far away to control without chapters scattered between. If you need to go home, fucking go home. If you have brothers who want to go with you, then you fucking better be willing to chapter up, asshole." He slapped the bar top hard, rattling the bottles and glassware.

Tug sat back, grinning. "Own that shit, Bingo."

"Church tomorrow, Mason, can we talk about it with the members?" Bingo fiddled with the brim of his hat for a minute. "I gotta be there for her, brother. I got to go home; she's the only sister I got."

Mason reached across and clasped Bingo's wrist in a tight grip. "Then go the fuck home and take care of family. I want you to figure out a revenue stream fast, though; I won't support more than twelve months of fucking around."

Andy had first tried to ignore the conversation that flowed over and around him, but gave that up when they clearly didn't care if he listened or not. This seemed like the type of shit Watcher deemed private—club business— and he felt awkward they discussed it so openly in front of him.

His eyes followed the back and forth chatter, and when they stopped, he realized they were all looking at him. He swallowed nervously, and looked in their faces for a moment, then picked up his beer to drain the mug. "Round's on me," he said, sounding bolder than he felt, and pointed to the men on either side.

All three men burst out into laughter, and Tug thumped Andy hard on the back, knocking him forward into the bar's edge as Mason went to pull four beers.

"Fuck me," Andy muttered as he pulled another bill out of his wallet. After he set the mugs down, Mason pointed to his own chest and introduced himself. Then, he confirmed Andy's understanding of the names for the other men. Taking a deep drink from his beer, Andy nodded and said his own name, acknowledging the introductions with a nod.

"What did Watcher send you here for, kid?" Mason asked. "You aren't wearing any colors, so you better not be affiliated. Jackson's is neutral, but we don't fucking tolerate anon shit."

"Nope," Andy said, popping the 'p', "Watch said you might be able to point me to someone needing a wrench for a bit. I've been traveling and need a place to sit a while to earn some cash. I can tend bar too, but I fucking love tuning and stroking chrome."

"What do you ride, man?" That question came from Tug, leaning his elbows on the edge of the bar.

"My baby is a '47 Indian Chief Roadmaster flathead. She's a fine, pretty little thing," Andy said fondly, grinning at him.

"Holy fucking shit, this I gotta see. '47 Chief? No shit? Holy fuck," Bingo shouted, standing from the barstool and grabbing hard at Andy's arm. Pulling back sharply to get his arm out of Bingo's grip, Andy quickly slid from his stool, turning it over in his haste as he took two large steps backward, adopting a defensive stance.

Mason reached out and smacked the side of Bingo's head. "You don't go grabbing strangers, Bingo. What a fucking moron. Sit back down, kid, or take him outside so he can stroke off to the Indian. It's a secret fantasy of his."

Some of the tension left Andy's body as he saw Bingo look first at Mason, and then him. "Oh man, sorry. Sorry, didn't mean to overstep. Respect, man." Bingo seemed genuinely apologetic, and righted Andy's stool; he picked up his jacket and draped it across the back.

"It's okay," Andy muttered, still somewhat uncomfortable with their lack of serious reaction to the near scuffle. "If you want to see her, that's fine. Let's go." He moved towards the bar and reached out to pick up his mug to drain it, and then leaving his change as a tip, he grabbed his jacket and turned towards the door.

There were mirrors mounted alongside the doorway, and he saw Mason give a signal up the bar as he stepped around the end to walk with Tug and Bingo. Andy pushed the door open, and then quickly stepped towards the side lot where he'd parked, moving past his bike. He turned back towards the men who walked his way, trying to keep everyone in view.

"Fucking *fringe*," Bingo moaned as he stood and looked at the bike with longing on his face, "there's fringe on the fucking seat. Oh God, look at those fairings. She's so fucking pretty."

"Goddammit, Bingo. I was kidding when I told the kid you'd get hard," Mason said and laughed.

Andy smiled tightly, still uncomfortable, and asked the men, "What do you ride?"

Mason pointed to a bike barely visible around the back corner of the bar. "That black and white panhead is mine, Tug has the solid black Road King down there," he shifted to point to a bike far down the row, "and Bingo has this Fat Boy with the low-rise handlebars," he gestured towards a gorgeous bike only two down from Andy's Indian.

Andy's mouth watered when he looked at Bingo's bike—flames on the tank and shiny chrome, and a tiny little tail seat on the back fairing. "All very nice, man. That Fat Boy is pretty."

A low roar came from the front of the building, and Mason spat a curse, taking running steps back the way they had come. Andy followed him, and he rounded the corner just as the door burst open, and a dozen fighting bikers wearing colors from several different clubs spilled onto the street. He quickly zeroed in on the only two participants who seemed focused on doing real damage with their fists. He maneuvered himself around the edge of the group towards the two men.

Mason was wading into the group; he yelled and smacked with an open hand as needed to get their attention. His voice was enough to drag most of the activity to a halt, but the two men Andy tracked were locked in their own bubble, and they didn't seem to hear Mason or anyone else.

Looking back at Andy, Mason said, "Come break these fuckers up, man."

Without questioning, Andy stepped forward and watched for a pause in the action. Seeing an opportunity, he grabbed the backs of their heads and cracked their foreheads together, dazing both men before he pushed them apart into hands willing to hold them back. Stepping back, he shot a look at Mason, "How's that, boss?"

Bending over and putting his hands on his knees, Mason laughed hard for a minute. "Pretty fucking priceless. That was classic, man. You are a hard-ass."

Andy shifted so there were no bikers at his back; he didn't want to get ambushed if he'd been jockeyed into some trouble. The movement wasn't missed by Mason. "No motherfucker here will put a hand on you for this," he said, raising his voice. "You fuckers hear me?"

There was a grumbling acknowledgement from the men on the sidewalk, and Tug broke the silence with a laughed out, "I need a beer," and pulled the door open to reenter the bar.

Andy lifted a hand in a casual goodbye, walking towards the side lot. He'd had enough excitement for the night, but damned if he wasn't sorry to leave the bar. It had felt pretty comfortable. "Where the fuck are you going, man?" came from behind him; Mason was calling from the doorway.

"Headed out, thanks," Andy tossed over his shoulder as he rounded the corner to see Bingo still standing in front of his bike.

Sharp laughter came from behind him, and he turned to see Mason had followed him. "Bingo, what the fuck are you doing, brother? Your girl is going to see you cheating on her, and she'll take her revenge…you know she will." He laughed again.

Bingo looked up at Andy. "She's beautiful, man. I'd give a fuckuva lot for one just like her; cherry red, virgin white, fringe on the seat, chrome so bright—that poetry nearly fucking writes itself."

Mason slung an arm around Andy's shoulders. "Come back inside and have a beer; I'd like to offer you a job." He turned them around and started walking back to the door of the bar. "Bingo will be out here for another hour, but he won't fuck with your ride. He'll simply lust from a distance."

Andy hadn't heard anything after the word 'job', and he was wondering what kind of position Mason had available. Pulling a stool behind the bar, Mason gestured that Andy should sit there, his back to the wall. Nodding, Andy slid onto the seat, propping his heels on the rungs and leaning back against the wall.

The waitress came up and stuck her hand out. "Hi, hon, I'm Merry, as in Christmas, not the mother of Jesus." She laughed at his expression. "And you are?"

He shook her hand gently, careful not to grip too tight. "I'm Andy, Andrew Jones. It's real good to meet you, ma'am."

She looked past him to Mason. "He's polite; I'll give him that. Cure him quick, or he'll be fodder to the masses." She turned and picked up beers and glasses, filling her tray as she went back out onto the floor. Andy sat patiently, waiting for Mason to tell him about the job.

Three hours later, he was still waiting, but at a look from Mason, he'd gotten up twice to settle altercations before they turned into full-fledged fights. Being behind the bar seemed to grant him some authority over these men, regardless of their club affiliations. Settling back onto his stool after standing and staring down another group, he was pleased; he hadn't even had to take a step to calm them down.

Mason walked up, wiping the bar. "We're open ten to two, six days a week. I'll need you here from three or four in the afternoon until we close, and then escort service for the waitresses to their cages." Seeing the horrified look on Andy's face, he chuckled and clarified, "Their cars, brother, fuck. Pay's a grand a week, and there's a room in the back with access to a shower if you need a place to crash for a while. Interested?"

"What's the job?" Andy quizzed him, not sure what was being offered.

"What you're doing, man—keeping everybody in line and stopping the place from getting trashed. I need an unaffiliated badass to keep the peace here. I haven't owned the bar long, and I'm trying to keep it neutral territory. I'm pretty sure if I had one of my Rebels pulling this job, it could cause problems." Mason shrugged. "I also called Watcher, and he vouched for you. That's fucking rare, man. I have to ask, though—are you looking for a club? He indicated he has hopes you'll go back to Las Cruces and join the Soldiers. He said you were rock solid during some business of his down in Old Mexico."

Shaking his head, Andy responded, "He's a good man, and I'm proud he calls me Brother without me wearing his patch. The Soldiers are a good bunch of guys, and they take care of their own. I'm also proud they would have been happy to have me join the family, but New Mexico isn't for me. I haven't found my place yet."

Scanning the room, he noticed that the clientele had changed in the after-work hours, and there were now what looked to be some business executives scattered at tables around the bar. "What's the deal with the suits? I've never seen a biker bar that drew in citizens like this. Is it because it's not a club bar?" Andy saw not all of the men were limiting their interactions with each other; some of them were gathering at the end of tables filled with leather and colors.

Mason grunted. "A few are RC members looking for a ride hookup; most are friends of ours. We own a few other businesses around town, and our garage is well known with the high-dollar weekend riders. They like the custom shit we turn out, and when they hang at the garage, they hear about Jackson's and show up. They feel like it gives them an in with us when they spend 10K on a bike we build."

He folded his bulky arms across his chest. "It's a good thing to have them see we aren't always doing business. There're lawyers and a couple of doctors in this group today; that guy talking to Bingo is a federal judge, and then we have Chicago's lead homicide detective sitting at the other end of the bar. It helps keep our options open in some situations."

Andy nodded, understanding. "They're not in your pocket, but know your face."

Mason swung his head to look searchingly at Andy. "Exactly."

"I'd love the job, man. Can I see the room in the back? Is there a place to park my bike at night so she's safe? I've been taking her into my motel room," he laughed, "but that doesn't leave a lot of room to maneuver. You should know that I've tended bar, in addition to working security, so I can cover a shift or fill in as needed."

"Yeah, there's room. Lemme show you; it's back here. Merry, watch the bar," Mason raised his voice as they walked into the back room. "It's good to know about the expanded skillset, man. I'll probably take you up on the bartending some days, when there's club business to deal with."

"Down the hallway to the left are the private rooms for parties; there're also doors from the main bar room into each of them. We get reservations a few times a week; they sometimes come with their own security, but we'll know ahead of time so you can coordinate." He paused for a minute to look at Andy's face to make sure he understood.

Satisfied, he continued, "On the right are the storerooms and our walk-in cooler. Shower and shitter at the far end, and the door on this side is where you can crash. There's an outside door from that room, and it's plenty wide to roll your bike through." He pointed up and down the hallways. To Andy, it seemed the building was a lot bigger than it looked from the outside.

"That gives us two doors from the back, and the one from the front to keep track of." Mason pointed towards the centrally located door. "Employees park in the back. They come in that way, and they leave that way, no exceptions, and make sure the night girls don't step outside without telling someone. It's a rule, man."

Sticking his head into the doorway of the room he would soon be calling home, he saw it looked like the rooms he'd stayed in when he crashed with the Soldiers at their clubhouse—functional and sparse, but provided everything needed, with a bed, and a dresser to store his clothes. It was big enough to bring his bike in, and that made him happy.

"Hey, Mason, do you mind if I run and grab my stuff from the motel and bring it back now? Then I can be here for the later hours, when shit is more likely to stir." He looked back at his new boss.

"No problem, take Tug and Bingo with you," Mason instructed, and Andy frowned at him. Mason shook his head. "Seriously, fucker? Are you questioning my wisdom? You just beat in the heads of the Sergeant at Arms for the Milwaukee Disciples and the vice-president of the Chicago Dominos; I think you might want someone on your hip." He laughed at Andy, who had blanched. "Consider it a courtesy to me and fucking say, 'okay'."

Andy nodded, walking back towards the bar. He grabbed his jacket and walked out to where the two greybeards were sitting, letting them know what Mason had volunteered them for. Without any argument or discussion, they stood, finishing their drinks. Aiming a chin lift at Mason, they turned to leave the bar with Andy. This was the kind of thing he had missed in Memphis, the feeling of brotherhood, and the security of knowing people around you would help as needed. This is what he'd been looking for.

He thought to himself, *I could get comfortable here*, as they kicked their bikes to life and motioned Andy to pull onto the street first.

13 - Becoming

He liked varying his sitting location night-by-night. It made it easier to spot the troublemakers, who looked for patterns in his position. He'd gotten good at clocking them when they walked through the door, and was seldom taken by surprise with eruptions of violence anymore. It had been weeks since any furniture was broken, and he thought his boss was happy about that, for sure.

After nearly three months of working for Mason, this bar had become his home, and the regular citizen customers and Rebel members were his family. Individually, he'd gotten to know them well enough to recognize when something wasn't tracking right, or when something was going on at home that had bled over into club business.

Not that he was in the club...yet. Mason always added that 'yet' when they discussed anything to do with the club and his application for membership. Andy believed he had found his home, that this was where his compass had been pulling him all his life. He wanted it, but was worried about the dangerous side of being a club member. After seeing how ugly and nasty things could get when he was hanging around the Southern Soldiers, he wasn't sure how to rationalize intentionally pulling that kind of shit into his life.

Mason was still on a campaign of clean up; he had taken over his old club by coup several years ago, and had formed the Rebels out of the remnants. Some of the older members still missed the easy money from more illegal aspects of the old club's businesses, though. Mason had outlawed certain activities, so the Rebels didn't run any girls, only did non-military, light guns, and wouldn't touch heroin. While that left a lot of money to be made with gun sales, blow, and pot, compared to what the club made in the past, to some members, it looked like they were leaving too much money on the table.

One thing going for the club was the number of legit ways for money to flow into it, all owned by Mason, but ran by Rebels. Eventually, Mason wanted to get entirely out of the drugs, but needed to ease some of the brothers into the business side of things.

Jackson's was his title business, in a way. In addition to this bar, there was a strip club, three garages with attached parts stores, half-dozen bars, two restaurants, and a motel up north. Andy had been sent on errands to all of them and introduced to the managers and workers. He knew where the backrooms were, and had used them to take care of a couple of problems for Mason along the way.

The Rebels didn't have any grief with other clubs in the area, as long as those clubs respected the territory lines. In some cities, those lines might be fluid, going back and forth as clubs rose and fell in power, but not in Chicago—

not with the Rebel Wayfarers. Their shit was solid, and their space was defined and defended.

Knowing what you want, and being brave enough to grab it by the balls are two different things, Andy mused to himself as he watched two Rebel members play pool. Tug pulled a stool up beside him, and he tipped the tall wooden chair back against the wall in a lean Andy could never manage.

"We got a run in the morning, Andy, and I'd like you there," he said as he folded his arms and watched the pool game.

Shaking his head, Andy responded, "That sounds like club business, Tug. Not sure your Prez would be pleased with taking a hangaround on a run."

"You did this kinda shit for Watcher and the Soldiers; I know you did. I've talked to him, and he said you exhibited proper loyalty and respect each time, that you were happy to help. Not for us though, I guess. Do you have less respect for the Rebels than you did that Las Cruces club?" Tug's voice was tight and angry. "You're going to have to make a decision soon, Andy. You can't ride this line forever, wanting the security and company of a club without shouldering the responsibilities that come with it. It's disrespectful to the club, the members...me...*Mason*...and that shit don't fly."

Not giving Andy a chance to respond, Tug let his stool fall back onto four legs with a bang; he stood and stalked away and snarled at a bar regular who spoke to him. That made Andy feel like a shit. The worst of it was he knew Tug was right. He was coasting, and it wasn't like him. He'd been a hardworking caretaker all his goddamn life, never one to shirk duty simply because it was fucking hard or distasteful.

This was no different. If he wanted this—if he wanted the brotherhood and knowledge there were people who he would happily die for, and would die for him...and he did want it...dammit, he did—then he needed to ante up, get in the game.

Looking across the bar, he saw Tug had sat down next to Mason in a booth with Tats, Red, and Wheels. He spoke, and Mason sent an annoyed look over towards Andy, then turned back to Tug and responded. These men were all officers in the Rebels, and they would be the first jury for him to convince he was worthy of becoming a prospect. Pitching his voice to carry, he called out across the bar, "Tug," and waited until the irritated old man looked up. Andy continued, "You're right, friend. I'm in."

Mason cocked one eyebrow up at him, questioning. Andy nodded at both him and Tug as he walked across the floor and stood nearer the table, asking, "What do I need to do to app as a prospect?"

Tug laughed, thumping Andy on the shoulder. "You just did, kid."

***

Andy missed Bingo, who'd left a couple weeks ago to move home to Indiana. There were a few members who were from there originally, and they'd gone with him to open a Fort Wayne chapter of the Rebels. He thought Bingo's absence was why Tug wanted him along on this run, and he was kinda glad he'd been cornered into a decision, finally, to become a prospect.

Tonight, he rode between Tug and Red, alongside a kid named Dirty Dan, who was three months into his prospect period. His road name was clearly a reflection of his personal hygiene; everything he wore looked like it had been dragged through the mud.

There was money trouble at the strip club. From what Andy knew, there was always trouble of some sort there, but it was normally a profitable business, and the cash always balanced all the hassle. Pulling up at the business, they looked at the full parking lot, and found the bike parking across the front was nearly full too. They carefully parked at the end of the row, with scarcely enough room for their four bikes.

Andy shrugged his shoulders, settling the black leather vest across his back. Mason'd had a cut ready for him. Andy had no idea how long it had been waiting in the drawer behind the bar, but it felt good to wear it, and to be part of this club he had come to love.

Walking into the building, the four men surveyed the area in front of the stage, where two girls were working the main pole in a synchronized dance. The customers were mostly facing the entertainment, but Andy saw with surprise that a number of them had chairs turned around, watching the entrance.

Andy realized Tug and Red had noticed it too, while Dan was still looking around. "Tug, this feels off; those aren't all Rebels," he said quietly, and saw a nod in response.

"Let's find Delilah; she'll have the ledgers that Tats needs," Red said, and they all started walking towards the office at the back of the room.

The music drew to a close, and there was a brief, desultory smattering of applause for the girls, who stooped and picked up their discarded clothing as they made their naked and nonchalant way back to the dressing rooms. The speakers boomed as a voice announced the next act as Little April, and some kiddy music came on. Andy saw a girl who looked like she couldn't be more than fourteen come onto the stage, stutter-walking towards the pole, squinting against the spotlights that glared down mercilessly on her.

Taking a position outside the office, Andy stood alongside Dirty Dan, and they turned to watch the room carefully, while Tug and Red went in to have a chat with the strip club manager, Delilah. They had made this unannounced visit, because for the last couple of months, there had been a significant amount of money missing from the accounts each week. It was unlikely to be anyone other than the manager, and they were here to get to the bottom of the problem quickly.

"Indian." Andy heard the name called from across the room. He looked up to see Bones, the president of the Skeptics, walking towards him.

He called into the office quickly, "Tug, Skeptics Prez is here; need an officer out here ASAP." He knew protocol dictated that as a prospect, he should not speak to another club's members, much less their president, without an officer of his own present.

"Indian," Bones said again when he had gotten close enough to speak comfortably, "you prospecting into Rebels, I see. Tough luck for me—you'd have been a fucking winner in the Skeptics. You got balls of steel, motherfucker."

Andy nodded at him, relieved when Tug stepped out of the office, and he was granted a reprieve from responding. "Bones, how you doin', man?" Tug asked, folding his arms across his chest.

"Tug, good to see you." He swept a mocking bow.

Damn, this felt tense to Andy; they were not using the word 'brother', and there was no handshaking or backslapping. "How's Mason doin' with his cleanup? That shit's hard to rub out once it gets hold in a club." Bones laughed. "I should know; I don't fucking try it's so ingrained in the Skeptics."

In a singsong voice, he continued, "Plus, we make a lot of fucking money on it." Here his voice lowered and became rigid, "So Mason's Rebels can kick that trade to the curb all fucking day, and I will sit and suck up that money."

Andy heard voices from inside the office; it sounded like Red was making a call. Tug pulled at one ear thoughtfully, asking, "That wasn't disrespect I heard, was it, Bones?" The corners of his mouth pulled his mustache down morosely. "Because disrespect for my club would make me unhappy."

"Nah, man, no disrespect intended," Bones said. "We had a sit down not two months back; it's all good."

Tug looked at Andy, and then back at Bones. "So, how do you know my boy here?"

Bones laughed, slapping his thigh in amusement. "This motherfucker has balls of steel—no...no...fucking titanium. He has balls of fucking titanium. He's sitting at this fucking red light, like a good little boy, waiting on the green. Him and his Indian are in the way of a Skeptics run. I got sixty brothers at my back, and he just fucking sits there, middle of the road, just...waiting on the green. He had all the time in the world, waitin' on the green."

He laughed again as he kept going. "We pulled up all around him, crowding him like he was fucking honey and we were the big, bad bears, and he never...even...blinked, just leaned over and gave me a pound when I complimented his ride. The motherfucker sat there through another light until my crew had all cleared. Balls of fucking titanium," he chortled again.

"Yeah," Tug agreed with a laugh, "he's a keeper." He took a deep breath. "I'm surprised to see you in here, Bones. This is a Rebel business; it's citizens and Rebels here."

"Oh, ho, not anymore, Tugboat. This place was declared neutral." He made a grimace of surprise, asking, "You didn't know?"

Tug shook his head. "First I've heard of it, man. Care to educate me as to who made that claim?" He was pissed; Andy could hear it in his voice.

"*Fuck*," Bones hissed, "goddammit, it was Monster. He called me up about a month ago and said there were new girls, new rules, and that it was newly neutral." Bones voice had turned serious. "You telling me that's not the case, Tug?"

"I am telling you that's not the case, Bones. This is Rebel; it stays Rebel. Jackson's and Tupelo's are both neutral, but those are the only two, on my patch, brother," Tug said.

"Fucking shit," hissed Bones in a low voice again. "There's a dozen different patches in here tonight, Tug, and half the fuckers are at war. This shit will get strange and fucking bad in a heartbeat. *Goddammit to shit!* You know I would not have trespassed, brother. Monster is an officer; he's fucking VP. Why would I question him?"

Tug pulled on his ear again. "You wouldn't—I know that. No reason to, when a patch officer says something like that. The expectation is that they are speaking for the club. I know that." He rubbed his face with his hand, scrubbing hard. "Pros—you both stick here. Bones, come in; let's give Prez a call and let you two work this out at your level." He and Bones stepped into the office, and the door shut firmly behind them.

Andy saw that the exchange had not gone unnoticed; it seemed half the customers had turned to face the office, while the other half were facing the door. Only the citizens—the non-bikers—were still watching Little April.

Dirty Dan was watching the stripper too, and Andy shook his head, keeping his eyes roving between the dressing room door, the one to the back alley, the front door, and the entire fucking biker population of the room.

Outside, there was the roar of bikes approaching, loud pipes announcing their impending arrival. That sounded like a fuckuva lot of bikes coming into the lot. The tension in the room ratcheted up another couple of notches, and Andy was tempted to pound on the office door, summoning Tug and Red. He held his hand out, but stayed still, waiting and watching to see what would walk into the room.

He scanned his close surroundings, looking to find anything that would give cover. There were tables he could overturn and crouch behind, but they wouldn't give any protection, they'd simply blind any attackers to his movements. There was a stack of kegs near the wall, but they were probably too closely stacked to let him get behind them.

"Fuck me," Andy murmured as the outside door opened and he got his first glimpse of the thirty newcomers and their patches. He did reach now, and pound the door three times, cursing softly, "Fuck me, fuck me, fuck me running."

He watched as a full dozen of the sitting bikers abruptly stood, taking an aggressive stance and facing the group that had come in. For some, hands positioned at their backs revealed the presence of a piece in their waistband, but for many, their gun was already in their hand, hanging loose and ready at their side.

"Dan, this is fixing to go sideways bad, man. Get ready to cover," he said quietly as the office door opened. Tug stepped into the doorway, looking at Andy. "Tug, we got fucking Machos. I count thirty green patches," Andy quietly alerted him, not taking his eyes off the men near the entrance.

Tug let out an inventive string of curses and stepped out of the office towards the group. "Not today, Machos," he called out, letting his arms relax at his sides. Andy stepped up behind him and to the side, seeing Red do the same at Tug's other shoulder.

Bones came out and stood off to the side, his voice calling his brothers like the crack of a whip. "Skeptics, to me." Over a dozen men stood quickly and moved to stand behind their president. Andy saw Shades and Six-Pack among them. Dirty Dan pulled the office door closed, shutting Delilah inside, and stepped to Red's side.

"What do you mean, 'not today'," asked the man in front.

"I mean not fucking today. You are not welcome—actually, not just today, but not ever," Tug responded, taking another step. He pulled all the men behind him forward a step with his movement as if he were magnetic and they couldn't let him advance without a corresponding stride.

Andy saw another group of bikers stand and move as a unit to the other side of the room, not wanting to be caught in middle. One of the girls came running from the back and scooped Little April up, rushing her offstage.

"That is too bad," the man drawled. "I was told this was a place where all were welcome."

"That rumor is not true," said Tug, "and the lie has been put to bed."

There was a loud murmur of discussion from the bikers in the place as they realized they'd been duped, and had unknowingly trespassed on the property of one of the most powerful MCs in Chicago.

Bones spoke up, his voice carrying through the room, "This is true; I spoke with Mason. One of his brothers made a mistake, but the Rebels will not seek reprisal for any club represented here today, unless there is blood." Whirling his finger above his head, he told his crew, "Skeptics, ride."

They walked carefully towards the front entrance, which was still filled with Machos. It would probably have worked, except one of the Skeptics was shoulder-checked by a Machos member, and they both landed on the floor in seconds with flying fists and feet.

The first shot rang out, coming from the front of the room, and Andy heard a deep grunt beside him. He turned to see Dan's body slowly falling to his knees as his legs unhinged and fell backwards. His body sagged in an arch across his boots, arms and hands sprawled carelessly to his sides, head tipped back against the floor. There was a small, tidy hole next to his left eye, slowly bleeding a single red tear down the side of his slack face.

"Fuck me." Andy drew his handgun and turned over several tables near him, crouching behind one with Tug as bullets began to fly in the room. He listened to the ebb and flow of the fight; there were cycles to everything, and gunfire was no different. After a second, he chanced a look around the edge of the table and saw men scattered around the room. "Tug, we firing?" he asked over his shoulder.

"Yeah, Pros, Machos only, if you can," came the response, and Andy saw Red nod in agreement.

Drawing a slow breath in, Andy propped his arms on top of the table. Taking careful aim, he began pulling the trigger slowly and methodically, moving from target to target. He watched as man after man fell. He was trying to keep the shots non-lethal, but sometimes that was not possible, and he took the shots he was given.

Running out of ammunition, he quickly sat down behind the table again. Pulling a spare magazine from his back pocket, he ejected the spent one and slapped the loaded one into place. Getting back into firing position, he saw there were only six green patches still standing in the room, and he took them down quickly. That left him six shots in the gun, and no spare magazines.

He realized there was no more gunfire, and cautiously climbed to his feet, seeing Tug move quickly across the room. Andy walked over to Dan and looked down into his already cloudy eyes. "*Fuck me,*" he breathed out.

Red was looking at him with wide eyes, and Andy shook his head at him while walking away. He needed to have Tug's back, and he'd already let him get too far. Stretching his long legs into fast strides, he pulled up beside and barely behind Tug as he stooped down to turn over one of the dead.

Andy spun and stood there with his back to Tug, watching the rest of the room, his gun held loosely in his hand by his side.

"Goddammit to hell," Tug muttered, then shouted without looking up, "Bones!"

"Yeah," came the call from across the room, "you had blood, Tug. You had blood first, brother."

"I know," yelled Tug. "Goddammit, this is fucked up. How are your guys, any hurt?"

"Nah, we're all good, barely a scrape from the fisticuffs. I got no blood, no death," Bones intoned solemnly.

"Thank fuck," Tug muttered, "Andy, get started pulling the wounded over to the wall beside the stage." He stood, turning slowly and surveying the room, calling, "Red, civilians to the back, brother."

Andy got to work, dragging the wounded men by their feet or collars, depending on where they had been shot. He positioned them carefully along the wall, pairing ones that were hurt more seriously next to someone who looked okay enough to help, if they were so inclined.

He grabbed the first aid kit from behind the bar, and tossed it to an uninjured Machos member, then pointed him towards the wall of injured. Fucker must have been on the floor; Andy hadn't seen him until now. Fuck, another uninjured came waltzing out from behind the bar, so Andy herded him over too.

Bones and his men helped Andy sort out the dead. They first went to Dirty Dan and straightened his limbs where he lay, folding his hands across his stomach and covering him with a tablecloth.

Bones then had his men start stacking the Machos' dead along a different wall. They handled each of them with respect, tidying their clothes and straightening their cuts as they laid them out. Red was handling the citizen non-combatants, and had moved them into one of the dressing rooms in the back, putting all the girls in a different one.

It seemed like bare minutes later when Mason stalked into the room with a handful of Rebels, fists balled on his hips as he shouted, "What the fuck happened here?"

Bones stepped up. "My men were leaving, and Franks," he pointed at his man with a bleeding nose, "was insulted by a Mexican cartel biker, Machos, a green patch. During their exchange, one of the Mexicans fired off a shot."

Tug took a deep breath, interrupting Bones, "Killed Dirty Dan, Mason. Fucking shot him in the face."

Bones spoke again, "Sixteen green patches dead, ten more injured, four yet live unbloodied."

Andy saw Mason's face morph as his teeth bared in a snarl of pure, feral rage, his jaw tightly clenched, and his hands balled into shaking fists. "Who the fuck killed sixteen Mexican bikers in my fucking strip club?" he roared. "Who the fuck turned this into a warzone?"

Andy blew out the breath he hadn't even realized he was holding, stepping into Mason's line of sight. "Six injured and thirteen dead are on me, Mason," he said, standing straight and upright, not daring to call Mason by his club title. After this, he expected them to rip his cut off at any moment, and he wouldn't have the right.

"Machos turned this into a war, Prez," Tug said. "Three dead are mine, three injured."

A low voice came from Red, "One injured is mine, Prez."

"This is a fucking goddamn pile of shit topped off with drug cartel dead, brothers." Mason was calming down a little. "First, the call about Monster, and then this shit? Is this officially Fuck Mason in the Ass Day or some shit? Fuck me with a whole bo—no...a *case* of fuck, not a box, a fucking case...a case of fuck. *Fuck me with a case of fuck.*" He continued his rant as he surveyed all the chaos that had gone down in his absence until Tug stepped over to Mason's side.

"No other club was involved, thank God. The call to return fire came from me; Andy asked permission, and I fucking gave it, because they were firing on us. Machos brought the war, Mason. There are no local club injuries other than our own, and Bones has stated in plain English, in full hearing of all present that first blood was drawn by Machos firing a weapon. There are four uninjured, two of which are officers. The ten injured will all live, and they all know this shit is on them. Prez, there should be no blowback from this. It's as clean as a fucked up piece of shit can be."

Red cleared his throat. "I, uh...I do have eight citizens locked in a room in the back, all unhurt." He rubbed his face with both hands. "Their, uh...their phones are in a box behind the bar, along with their car keys, and wallets. The girls are in lockdown in the panic room, all unhurt. Delilah is in the office, unhurt."

Mason snapped to Tug, "Call Tats; lockdown at the clubhouse until we're sure. Pull in families for now, and let's plan on a week."

Tug nodded, took his phone from his pocket, and initiated a call that would bring all Rebel members and their immediate families into the extended clubhouse. Andy'd heard it discussed over the past few weeks, and the facility located in southern Wisconsin sounded like more of a compound than any MC clubhouse he had seen before; it could house up to three hundred people.

"Bones, what we discussed on the phone still stands. No blowback, no issues, the change in status of this business was a miscommunication. I thank you for your help today." Mason walked over and offered his hand. "I owe you, brother."

Bones gripped his wrist firmly, shaking slowly up and down. "I will hold you to that, Mason. A Rebel marker is a significant thing; I appreciate your respect." He pointed at Andy with his other hand. "If you get tired of this one, I would like to know. Balls of titanium, he has. Easy as you please, just fired...*a plunk, a plunk, a plunk*...like he was at a carnival, shooting balloons. Never even broke a fucking sweat, simply took care of business." Releasing Mason's arm, Bones reached out to Andy. Shooting a look at Mason, who nodded, Andy accepted the grip on his wrist, returning it. Bones asked him, "Who the fuck *are* you, brother?"

"This is Slate," Mason responded proudly, "our newest and best prospect." Andy looked at him in confusion, and Mason continued with a hard laugh, "Just named the fucker; take a look at his face, Bones, knocked him senseless. Slate—it's a hard fucking rock, takes a fuckton of abuse without breaking. Joining an MC is also a chance to begin again, so you are officially a clean slate as of today. Write your own fucking story, Slate, hard and unbreakable. It's a good name, brother. Write your own story."

***

It had been a tough year-and-a-half for Slate, since he walked into Jackson's for the first time. Tough, but exciting, and if he would admit it, it had been fulfilling too. Moving through the ranks of the club from prospect, to member, and then now as a trusted confidante of the national president—every step forward just worked to validate his decision to keep moving for so long. He'd finally found what he'd been looking for...where he belonged.

Sitting in the waiting area of Ink Me, a tat shop a couple of blocks up the street from Tupelo's, Slate ran his hands through his hair distractedly. Tupelo's was a neutral bar owned by Rebels; he'd been working there for the past couple of months. Located on Cicero Avenue, it was in a part of town where it was necessary to keep a guard posted in the parking lot to ensure everything stayed where it was supposed to be.

He was there for the last session on his back piece, ready to ink the final bits of color into his commitment to the Rebels. In addition to completing the patch design that was being etched into his skin, complete with rockers, Slate had asked the artist to work up a sketch to go across his lower back, hip to hip. Framed with a faintly French-flavored fleur-de-lis design, he wanted the words, 'Bleed with me and you will forever be my brother'.

"Yo, Slate," came the high-pitched call from the back of the shop. He climbed to his feet, walking the hallways between the private stations until he arrived at the last one on the left.

"Silly, you ready for me, baby?" he teased.

"Always ready, big guy." She nodded her neon head; if her hair color was any indication, she must be feeling a little frantic today, because that particular shade of green looked like it should be buzzing. It looked striking against her dark, Hispanic coloring. She held out her hands, flicking them under his nose. "Lookie, Slate, aren't they pretty?"

He pulled back his head, focusing with difficulty on the dermal piercings she had on the backs of her moving hands and fingers. "Roses, Silly?" he asked, not quite sure he had made out what the design was.

Her response was a shrill, "Yeaaahhh, *look*—orange and lavender roses. Orange means desire and enthusiasm, and lavender means enchantment. I'm enchantingly enthusiastic and desirable." She admired the backs of her hands, squealing, "Aren't they pretty? You know, I thought about a day of the dead skull, but the roses were so *pretty*!"

"Sylvia, they are definitely beautiful, just like you," Slate said solemnly. Taking off his cut and shirt, he hung them up carefully and unfastened his pants, pushing them down barely off his hips, giving Sylvia plenty of room to work on the back piece. Straddling the chair, he leaned forward and cushioned his head on his folded arms, waiting.

She slapped his ass hard, laughing when he jumped. He was looking at her, watching carefully, and laughed silently to himself when he saw the transformation from silly-Silly, to work-focused-Sylvia. She pulled out her portfolio book, refreshing herself on the requirements before beginning. Her hands stretched out for the machine and ink, her foot automatically pushing the pedal into position as she readied the colors needed for his tattoo.

He saw her retrieve a piece of paper from the table, and took it when she wordlessly offered. It was a sketch of the tattoo for his lower back. "That's perfect, Sylvia. Can we do that today after you finish up on my colors?" He was pleased with her work so far, and already had a half-dozen more ideas floating around in his head. He knew she'd do each vision justice.

Her voice had dropped two octaves, sounding raspy and whisky-filled; this was definitely her alter ego, Sylvia. "I'm ready, Slate. Get still and hold the fuck on, man. We're gonna ride, so let's get this party started." He heard the buzz of the machine and relaxed into the sting on his skin as his eyes drifted closed.

Later that evening, he was standing near the back wall in Tupelo's, his back burning pleasantly, reminding him he shouldn't lean against anything. As a neutral territory bar, they had their share of regulars who came in to meet with friends patched into other clubs. Tonight, however, he'd seen quite a few men come in he didn't know, and even more unusual—he didn't recognize their patches, and they didn't introduce themselves. That meant they were either gypsies from off, roaming and looking for places to start a chapter, or new clubs in the area, who were unaware of protocol when coming into the bar for the first time.

Slate moved his position to halfway between the door and the bar, barely getting there when the door opened. Looking up, he grinned. "Bingo, son of a bitch, it is *good* to see you." They clasped wrists, pulling into a one-armed hug, and Slate winced as his raw back was pounded by Bingo's fist.

"Oh fuck, man, you had your colors done today, didn't you?" Bingo apologized as he beat Slate's back again in painful affection. "Sorry, man, I forgot. How'd I forget? That's the reason I'm back this weekend. I'm a forgetful fucker sometimes, I swear." He struck Slate's back one last time, releasing him to stand back and give him a wicked grin.

Slate laughed, wincing still. "No worries, brother. How's your family in the Fort?" He'd visited once, checking the set-up of the clubhouse in Bingo's hometown. He knew the sister had died; her kids moved in with Bingo, and he was raising his nieces and nephews as if they were his own.

"Kids are great, man. Fucking kids can bounce back from anything. Hell, Tyler broke his arm playing football a month ago, and I caught him trying to cut his cast off yesterday with a hacksaw," he said proudly.

Slate laughed again. "Tough fucker, man."

Bingo moved to stand next to Slate, and together, they surveyed the crowd in the bar. "How many different patches you got here tonight, you think?" he asked softly.

Slate paused for a second, thinking before he answered. "I'm tracking fifteen right now, but I am missing one guy, who was at the bar...maybe he had to piss. Yeah, he's coming back out now, so...fifteen patches. It's a mix of RC and MC. We don't get many MAs in here; it's too coarse for them usually." He narrowed his eyes towards the pool tables; there were voices raised in an argument for a moment until they saw his focus on them. Without even moving a step, he calmed that shit right the fuck down, and turned to see Bingo grinning up at him. "What?" he asked innocently, and then laughed.

His and Bingo's phones buzzed, as did a few others in the room, and each looked up at the others with alarm on their face; incoming texts to multiple members were seldom good news. Pulling his phone out, Slate saw, **Machos on cicero abt 50 - help inc**, and heard a far-off roar of bikes as he finished reading the text.

"Fuck me," Slate whispered to himself before yelling to the crowd, *"Machos! It's war! Fucking war."* He watched the bikers and customers scramble and scatter as they heard the first gunshots down the street. Running behind the bar, he grabbed a spare 9mm and a half-dozen loaded magazines from the locker on the floor. Turning, he shouted at a waitress, "Tara, lockdown," and saw her nod as she began gathering the employees, using words and motions to sweep them towards the panic room in the back. "Rebels, arm your-fucking-selves," he yelled, pointing to the now-open armory Bingo was coming out of, his hands filled with weapons.

Shades trotted up. "Skeptics stand with Rebels. You got guns for us?"

Slate nodded, jerking his head towards Bingo. Positioning himself behind a stout pillar about thirty feet from the front door, he listened as the roaring of bikes peaked close by, and then died off, leaving no echoes.

He looked behind him, and saw a green patch trying to sneak into the bar from the back; the door must have failed. He pointed at Bingo and then the door, and heard the thwack of the knife without ever seeing it pulled and thrown. The Machos member went down soundlessly, the hilt of the knife having hit him hard in the middle of his forehead.

Shades saw the action, and he cautiously went into the back to secure the door; he returned in a minute with a second man, also unconscious. He piled his guy next to the one already on the floor, and placed himself behind the bar, waiting.

The quiet didn't last long, and Slate gritted his teeth, hearing screams he assumed came from his Rebels who had been positioned outside, and then the silence that meant they were at least beyond pain. This was the first attack the Mexican club had made in retaliation for the deaths at the strip club. The Rebels had been waiting for this shoe to drop, because the Machos' brutality was well known. "Shades," he called quietly, "can you see if the back is open? I want to flank them if we can."

"No way, man. They've got two guys on that door, Slate. I've got it locked and blocked, but it's not a way out right now," Shades delivered that unwelcome news.

"Fuck me," Slate breathed. "What are they waiting on?" His phone buzzed, and he pulled it out; the number was unknown, but given the situation, he answered it readily, saying gruffly, "Yeah?"

"Nearly there, brother," came Mason's voice, and Slate all but sighed out loud in relief.

He started giving Mason the rundown. "It's quiet outside now, but pretty sure they've killed Buzz and L.J.; I have six brothers in here, and another five Skeptics who stand with us. Girls are in the panic room, and we are staged in the main room with the backdoor locked. We have two unconscious Machos in here. Tell me what you need, Mason. Tell me what to do." He heard, "Just hold, brother," and the connection was cut. "We hold," he called out to the room, looking at his men and nodding confidently. "We got this. We hold."

There was a scuffling noise from the front of the building, and they heard bikes being started. Slate remembered he'd installed closed circuit security cameras after a customer's bike was trashed, and he ran behind the bar, ripping the sliding door off the cabinet.

He punched the monitors on and stared at the four screens that showed up. There were about forty men spread across the parking lot in front of the building, and then he could see another ten in the back alley. There were two men he focused on, standing between their bikes and the bar door, confident in the protection their club status afforded them. He knew that one of the men would be Estavez, Carmela's uncle. He had brought war across the border in a big way.

He saw several bodies lying a few feet from the outside door. It was hard to tell on the black and white screen, but one of them looked a lot smaller, maybe female. The killing must have pulled in civilians, which would make this a much more difficult thing to contain.

They felt the low rumble before they heard it; there had to be at least a hundred bikes coming from multiple directions, because the noise and vibration was everywhere. Outside, the men in Machos' colors scattered to their bikes, looking as if they were ready to evacuate.

On the monitor, Mason was clearly visible on his motorcycle as he led a double column of bikes into the camera's view, and Slate broke for the front door. He pointed at Bingo and called, "Stay with the greenies in here," as he pulled the door open, striding into the open with his gun held low by his side.

Mason pulled within inches of Estavez, idling to a stop as the two men stared each other down. Slate couldn't hear what was said, but Mason's face swung his way for a moment, then back to the Mexican. The male bodies piled in the parking lot all had on club cuts. They were laid out in such a way that he couldn't see the patches, but none of the men looked familiar. Scanning the lot, he saw Buzz and L.J. leaning up against the outside wall of Tupelo's, their wrists and ankles secured by zip ties, and he whispered, "Thank fuck."

Stalking over to the stack of bodies, his steps slowed and stopped as he recognized the hair on the lone female figure. His chest hurt, and it became difficult to pull in enough breath. He looked over and saw Mason shaking hands with Estavez, and his brain froze for a second at that sight. Mason climbed off his bike and motioned for Slate to come over to him.

He looked back and forth between that bright green hair and his chosen brother, between his friends. This was insane. How could Mason be standing so casually with the man who killed Silly? Slate walked halfway and then stopped. Pointing backwards to the still forms, he asked, "Sylvia? *Silly*? Fuck, Mason, what is going on?" Mason motioned him over again, irritated, and Slate took another few steps to stand equidistance between Mason and Estavez, forming a triangle.

"Listen for two minutes, brother, and then you tell me what we need to do." Mason stepped back a pace, leaving Slate to face Estavez alone. Running his hands through his hair, Slate waited for the man to begin talking, and caught the calculating gaze that swept him up and down.

"Andrew Jones, I have wanted to meet you for two years," Estavez stated with a pronounced accent, but his English was spoken plainly enough to be easily understood. "In Juarez, you aided me with a serious problem, without any knowledge of the assistance provided. You did my family a great service, and for that, I am trying to repay your family here in Chicago."

Slate cocked his head, and made a hand motion urging Estavez to continue, then was staggered by what he said. "You saved my daughter, my heart, my life—Maria Luisa Carmela Estavez—my child, stolen by my brother and hidden from me for more than two years. I could not find her, but you saved her and brought her back into the light."

"Carmela is your daughter? She called you uncle and said you had sold her into slavery. You told us to bury her with the fat bastard who had been given a girl as a sex slave. How the hell is she your daughter, your *heart*?" Slate was angry, as furious now as he had been while sitting on his bike in Juarez, watching Devil seat the girl in front of him, taking her across the river with them into America.

"May we sit, Andrew? Mason?" Estavez asked. Mason looked at Slate's face, and nodded without shifting his gaze. Slate looked around, aware for the first time of the men standing near the three of them. There was a mixed ring of Machos and Rebels about ten feet from them, and then beyond that, there had to be more than one hundred members of the Rebels and their local support clubs circling the entire group. Slate stepped back, watching as an aisle appeared towards the door of the bar.

"Mason, we can't fit everyone," Slate said low and quiet. "We can put a couple of kegs inside the door and pass out cups."

"Do it, brother," Mason agreed. Slate led the two club presidents into the bar, quickly making the arrangements for the beer to be set up as he had suggested. He walked over and used the intercom to reassure Tara, releasing her from the panic room. He saw Bingo was still watching the two Machos they'd disabled inside the bar, and relieved him of that duty by asking L.J. to escort the two men outside.

Bringing three beers with him to the table, he sat down beside Mason carefully. "Estavez, I don't understand," he started, and the man nodded.

"I can explain, Andrew, and it's important for you to comprehend." Estavez took a shaky, deep breath, and then a long, slow drink of his beer. "My brother and I had no love lost between us. I had the esteem of the family; he had the approval of the cartel. I was a businessman in Mexico City; he was a gang member in Juarez. My child, my daughter—my *only* daughter—was a favorite of us both, one of the few things we had in common. We had a falling out when our parents died, and things that had been difficult or strained went to antagonistic and hostile. I wanted him gone, and I talked to an official in Mexico City about his activities in Juarez. That was my mistake, and my family paid for my error, because that official worked for him.

"My brother, he came to Mexico City and stole my daughter from my home. He took Maria...my Maria. You have to understand the police were of no help. There are so many abductions in Mexico, so many kidnappings, that they do nothing unless there is a benefit for them in the recovery. I didn't understand how they could be so mercenary, but I had to find her. So, I took things in hand looking for her, stalking my brother. It wasn't until Maria—Carmela, as you know her—was at Watcher's home that she was able to contact me."

He smiled briefly, but it didn't reach his eyes and the expression faded quickly. "Her uncle asked for her death. Her uncle threw her away for a favor with the cartel, and into hell. For more than two years, she was trapped with the man you killed that day. My Maria called me from America, from safety, and Watcher listened to my tears as I heard my dead daughter's voice once again," he spoke quietly.

"I decided I needed to deal with my honor in a lasting way, so I began to systematically take out my brother's allies." He sneered. "I am a businessman at heart. I can patiently strategize, and then execute on those strategies. Within eighteen months of your rescue of Maria, I gained control of his club, the Machos. My brother lies dead at my hand, as well as all of his main allies. It is now my club; these are *my* Machos."

He took another long drink of beer, his throat working hard. "But a debt remained. Maria told me of your part in the events in Juarez, and your kindness and comfort to her. Your assurance of her safety allowed her to trust and be saved. She holds you in high regard, Andrew Jones. I cannot ever repay what you mean to her by becoming her shelter of security in a storm of terror, but I acknowledge a debt to you. I have tracked you from Las Cruces to Lamesa, from Longview to Memphis, and now to Chicago. Along the way, I have continued to clean up my brother's messes, as I did today.

Motioning towards the door, he explained, "The ones killed today were loyal to my brother, and had planned on creating more difficulties for you here. The woman lying dead in the parking lot is not your Sylvia. It is Silverio, my sister-in-law. She came to Chicago months ago with the intention of replacing your Sylvia, knowing she could use that relationship to get close to the Rebel club members, and be able to hurt them.

"Silverio was also behind the attack you experienced a few weeks ago. She and her cadre of accomplices have been dealt with most persuasively, as you saw." He pushed back from the table, standing and holding out his hand to Slate. "My word to you, Andrew, Machos will not bother you or your family again, but you must tell me how I can repay you in my daughter's name. I will not rest well with an unresolved debt such as this."

"I have to think on that, man, seriously, but as long as Carmela is safe and happy, I'm good. Yeah, I'm good." Slate stood, accepting both the handshake and the commitment somberly.

Estavez shook hands with Mason too, and then stepped back. "I would like permission to remain in Chicago for a few days, to be certain I have cleaned up this rubbish in its entirety, if that is acceptable."

Mason nodded. "Sure, brother. We can house you if needed." Estavez accepted the offer, and Mason asked Tug and Bingo to begin the process of getting Machos to a secondary clubhouse in Chicago. After seeing the groups off, Mason and Slate headed back into the bar.

Drinking and talking to Mason late into the night, Slate told him the full story of the events in Mexico. He had a feeling Mason already knew about it, but felt the need to explain all that had happened, and what it meant to him. He talked for hours about the girl they had saved, and how Carmela had changed his life, showing Mason the tattoo he'd gotten in her honor.

"I need to know I make a difference, Mason. I think that's what it boils down to; I need to make a difference," he slurred his words, but the sentiment was honest. "My brother, my little brother Benny might need someone one day, and I wanna know I've racked up enough good things to give him a chance." Slumping in his chair, he ran a rough hand through his hair. "My brother Benny, my brother Mason—I love you both, man. Karma, my brother." He sighed. "Fuck me, I'm tired, and I think a little drunk. Can I crash here?"

Nodding solemnly, Mason helped him up and got him into the back room where the bunks were. "You need to sleep," he said as he threw a blanket at Slate. "We'll talk about the marker tomorrow, man. It's all good." The last thing Slate thought about as he fell asleep was the carefree look on Carmela's face the last time he'd seen her at Watcher's house.

***

Six years ago

They were arguing back and forth, debating the worth of a recent prospect who had app'ed to the Rebels, Reuben Nelms. Slate had met him a few years back in Texas, but didn't really know him. Reuben had shown up in Jackson's a few months ago, and like a lot of them, it seemed like he was looking for a home, a place he could set his demons to rest. Mason liked the guy a lot, but he wanted to evaluate Slate's recommendation. He was trying to make Slate his lieutenant, and planned to have him do these kinds of things going forward.

"Tell me about the girl, Mason." Slate thought this sounded like a long-term issue, and wanted to figure out the potential blowback for the club if anything Nelms did went sideways.

Mason leaned back in his chair; they were sitting in the meeting room in the Chicago clubhouse, with a couple dozen Rebels in attendance. The other members were scattered around the room, sitting at the bar or high-top tables, or playing pool. Two prospects were tending bar tonight, and Slate held up a hand to catch an eye for a refill.

Bear brought them two more beers, wiping the table before setting down the new bottles. Bear'd been in the process for about a year now, and was a solid, settled brother. His past was tragic, but Mason had found a way to connect with the man. They were going to vote on patching him in the next time they met for church, which would be when they decided whether to welcome Nelms or not.

Gypsy was the other prospect here tonight, and he 'd only been wearing his colors for a couple months; they'd have to take him on a run soon, see how he shook out. He was good at keeping order here in the clubhouse; he'd been a cop in Fort Wayne before he came to them, and the brothers all respected him.

Mason waited patiently for Slate to return his attention to him, picking up his bottle and turning it in his hands. "She's a student at UI in Springfield, and he checks up on her every couple of days. He's got a shit-for-brains brother who hurt her. When you met him in Texas, he'd ran from what was happening, and now he feels responsible. When I say the brother hurt the girl, it sounds like it had got real physical before she was able to get away. He's loyal, he's fearless, and he's got a heart the size of fucking Texas. I think he is a good fit for us, but I want to know your thoughts, brother."

"Does the girl know Nelms is watching over her?" Slate mused, "It seems weird, man. I know you helped him get his scoot, but have you been down with him to see her? Do you trust him? Does she meet with him and have fucking coffee? Fuck me, but this feels off."

"Nah, I haven't run down with him, but he talks about being careful that she doesn't see him. I think she'd bolt. Sounds like he just ducks around corners and shit. He's not perving on her, simply making sure his brother isn't catching a sniff of her." Mason grinned. "Maybe she's hot. Reminds me, we need to get you an old lady soon, or you're going to be too ancient to fuck."

Slate flicked a coaster at Mason, grinning. "Fuck you. You're the old man at the table. Where's your old lady, hmmm? Haven't seen anyone riding tail with you in months. You give up fucking for Lent and forget to start back up?"

"No man, I gave up talking to assholes; that's why it's been so long since you heard from me," Mason shot back. The two men grinned at each other; they'd become close friends over the years, seldom apart.

"I'll ride down with him tomorrow, get a read on this shit. I can take Gypsy with us, maybe Bear? That would leave you two prospects as gofers if needed, Hoss and Tequila. We still thinking about voting Bear in on Saturday?" Slate stretched in his chair, sliding his ass down in the seat and crossing his legs at the ankle.

Mason nodded. "Yeah, at Saturday's church we need to vote on Bear and Tequila as full-patch brothers, and about Nelms and Steward as prospects." He dropped his voice. "We also need to vote on Monster, figure this shit out for the last time. Motherfucker has dogged me too often in the past few years, and I've found proof he's skimming on runs. I don't want to take him down without a consensus, but the bastard is going to be sorry he fucked me. I am the Rebels, and he's fucking with them, so he's fucking with me."

Slate looked at him levelly. "Mason, full fucking backing here, and you know it. I've been hungry for his ass since his lies cost a brother's life. I can take care of that fucking business before sunset today; you just gotta give me the word."

Waving a hand casually, Mason brushed off his offer. "Nah, man. Church, consensus, closure—it will do us all good."

14 - Mica

Four years ago

"Are you fucking kidding me, brother? She bought the house next to Mason? Does he know yet?" Slate listened on the phone he was holding against his ear, lying in his bed at the clubhouse with eyes closed. The call had pulled him from sleep, but he wasn't ready to fully commit to waking up yet. He jerked as a hand pressed against his bare chest, sliding down towards his belly. Reaching down with his free hand, he stopped the progression of the feminine fingers, trapping them against his chest with a hard fist.

"Mason needs to know, but this is a good thing, Duck. Makes it almost a joke to keep an eye on her. No fucking way will your dickhead brother get a finger on her now." He paused, listening again. "Yeah, I know. I'm here; I'll see him in a few, and I'll get a read on this shit. Later, brother," he said as he pressed a fingertip against the screen, cutting the call.

Turning his head, he stared at the woman in his bed. "Tawny, I told you to get the fuck out last night. Don't fucking do this shit again. I'm not sleeping with you. I'm not fucking you. You're not giving me head. I got nothing to do with you." He sat up in bed, flipping the covers off her. "Now get the fuck out." He watched her slide from the bed, glad to see she had on a t-shirt and panties at least. Without a word, but with more than one dirty look his way, she pulled on a short skirt and slunk from the room.

"Goddamn shit," he muttered to himself. "Fuck me." Dragging his body to the bathroom, he took a hot shower. Half an hour later, he strolled into the meeting room, seeing Digger on bartender duty. He was a good prospect, but damn shy. "Where's Mason, Dig?" he asked as he rolled his shoulders.

"In the office, Slate. He said to let you know he wanted to talk to you when you got up." Digger slid a glance over Slate's shoulder, and then back to his face.

Slate turned to see who was in the room, and was surprised to see Tug, a favorite brother and long-time friend. Grabbing him in a tight hug, Slate pounded him on the back. "Good to see you, greybeard motherfucker. When did you get back from Fort Wayne?"

Tug laughed. "Good to see you too, Slate. I got back last night. It's not a far run; dunno why you seem allergic to the town. Bingo said he'd like to see your face once in a while."

Nodding, Slate responded, "I'll head that way in a couple of weeks. I need to take the prospects down to meet the club, get the lay of the land. Will do everyone good to get me the fuck out of here for a few days.

Brother, sorry for this, but I gotta talk to Mason now, but I'll be back out in a few. You sticking around for a bit?"

Tug nodded, stroking his mustache. "I'll be here. Take care of business."

Knocking twice and pushing open the door to the office, Slate stuck his head in. "Hey, is now a good time, Prez?" he asked, and waited on the affirmative response before he fully entered the room.

"I got something to tell you," Mason started with a big grin on his face. "You are not going to believe what happened yesterday. Pretty little gal moved into the house next to mine. Man, she is fucking hot, feisty as all hell too. Movers were giving her shit about fixing her yard after they drove all through it, and she was up in their faces about it." Mason was smiling as he talked. "Her name's Michaela Scott, and I need a favor, man. I want to know about her. I was at Jackson's last night, and no one seemed to know shit about her. I want everything you can get, okay?"

Blowing out a sigh, Slate wrinkled his forehead, frowning at Mason. "Brother, I already have some news on this one. Want a beer?"

Mason frowned back at him, his expression sobering. "Sounds ominous if you think I need a beer this time of the morning, so spit it out. Tell me what I've missed."

Slate nodded. "You remember Duck's girl, the one we've been helping him protect and watch? Mica Scott, from Texas, by way of Springfield, Illinois...Michaela— that's who bought the house. I think everyone in the club except you went down to Springfield, and they've been hanging around the business she started after college. We still check on her every couple of days. A few months ago, she started renting office space in a Rebel building; it helps make it easy to watch over her."

He laughed, gauging Mason's response, "But, dude, buying the house next to you? Not organized by us, but I can't help but feel it's a happy circumstance. It will make it a damn sight easier to keep an eye on her, for sure. It's been so many years since she ran from Duck's brother that we keep hoping Nelms has given it up, but we watch anyway."

Looking down for a second, Mason said, "Slate, goddammit, I get it now. I see why Duck wanted...no...*needed* to keep her safe." He looked up at Slate. "I get it. That's why the brothers never get tired of babysitting. She's something, man, and you can tell she's been tore up, totally fucked over and back again, but she's pulled herself together better than before, strong as shit. She turned her back on me to tear into the driver, with me offering to help her sort it out. Turned her back on *me*— didn't give it a second thought. Fearless, or at least courageous, she's..." he shook his head, "...she's a fucking treasure, man." Taking a deep breath, he urged, "Tell me what else you know."

Pressing his lips into a straight line, Slate organized his thoughts. "She's a Web and software programmer, and her business is doing all right for being new. She's got one employee; you've met Jess in Jackson's, and she dates the gal who owns that bakery we all like. Mica's got a fuckwad of a brother back in Texas, and beyond that, there's some deep shit with her family back home. She never goes back, and barely sees a select few family members at scattered destination cities. Her sister lives with family, but not the father and brother."

He cut his eyes up at Mason. "Prez, she has a terrible enemy in Duck's brother. He's never stopped talking or threatening about getting back at her for leaving his ass all those years ago. He's got a fucking screw loose, and we make goddamn sure he's never close enough to get even a fucking sniff of Mica. For the gal herself, she's isolated. She's got damn few people in her life here. Jess is her friend, as well as an employee, but in all the years we've watched her, there's been no boyfriend, no steady man...she's never been married...never even spent the night with anyone that we can tell. She doesn't trust people...at all."

Blowing out a deep breath, Mason looked like he made a decision. "There's something about her, Slate. I want it known that she's under our protection, that she's Rebel. We make her Rebel property. You make it as blatant and plain as needed, and have it be known this shit comes from me, not Duck. I'll talk to him and take care of letting him know, but starting right now, we put anything we need on the street in order to keep this woman safe."

Mason nodded, excitedly planning on the fly. "We can do more for her than that, though. More than just protection, let's get her comfortable. I don't want her leaving. We can steer a few clients her way, and get some extra security online in her offices—tell her it's a landlord's upgrade or something, and hell...just fucking be there for her as needed. Let's get her into Jackson's. That gal Jess should be able to help out there; she knows some of us. I want Mica...it was Mica, right?" he paused, questioning.

Slate nodded slowly. "Yeah, she doesn't go by Michaela, just Mica."

"Okay, I fucking want Mica comfortable with us as fast as we can get it done. Slate, she's a fucking treasure, and...well...let's get shit moving, okay?" Mason tilted his head back, looking up at the ceiling. "One more thing, let's make sure the other clubs are crystal that she's our Princess." He nodded at Slate. "Use the title, man; that's a sure way to make it clear."

Slate opened his eyes wide in surprise. It was not a title he'd ever heard used around the Rebels, but he knew from years of conversations that a club offering that level of protection was also establishing ownership. This would identify Mica clearly as Rebel property, and untouchable.

Licking his lips nervously, Slate nodded. "I'm on it, boss. I got this."

* * *

One year ago

Goddamn, Slate was tired of babysitting this woman. He had years put into this bullshit. Nowadays, about four nights out of the week, he slept on the couch at her house, because Mason was certain the shit was about to hit the fan.

Following a nasty beating and near kidnapping, which took her weeks to recover from, Mica received some pretty frightening threats. They didn't have any proof it was Nelms, but everything pointed that way, so they'd ratcheted the security up to a crazy level. Before he moved to Chicago and in with Mica, her brother had met up with her ex-boyfriend. Then, on the very day she kicked her brother's sorry, lazy ass out, she'd gotten the shit beat out of her.

Mason had been right there when it happened, and had helped save her. Slate helped him clean up the mess once they got their hands on the men, but unfortunately, they hadn't learned any useful information from them. Now, they were months down the road from the event, but the threats still felt real.

Sitting in her kitchen with Tug and Tucker, a prospect, they had barely finished eating when Slate thought he saw something outside. He watched the window out of the corner of his eye, catching another hint of movement against the horizon.

He poked Tug in the arm. "Watch the window, man," he mumbled, and stood to walk across the living room. Mica was sitting on the window seat, like she did most evenings, with her head lying on her folded-up knees, simply staring outside. Slate stopped behind her, looking at her face in the reflection of the window, and saw her eyes were closed. Tilting his head down, but keeping his eyes up and looking outside, he reached down to touch the top of her head, and then ran a lock of her hair through his fingers.

He bent over and inhaled near her hair, surprising himself by thinking, *God, she smells good*. With a sizzle-like electricity, he saw her eyes jerk open, and her hand swept up to knock his away. Strolling back to the kitchen, he sat back down in his chair.

Tug leaned up. "There was movement out along the road, brother. What are you thinking?" Slate shook his head and waved his comment away. He knew it was probably nothing; they were all jumpy as hell about everything going on. Mica stood up and told them she was headed to bed. Slate sat watching her as she walked up the hallway to her bedroom, waiting. He'd seen this routine often enough to be surprised when something varied. Her bedroom light didn't turn on.

"Be right back, man." He stood abruptly, walking towards her room.

Tug sat up straight. "You sure that's a good idea, Slate?"

Tucker simply looked from one to the other, unsure of what was going on. Slate thought he might not make it past prospect status; there was something missing in this kid. "I got to see after her, Tug," Slate muttered.

Tug caught up to him with quick strides, putting a hand on his arm. "Not a good idea, Slate."

"Tug, if you want to keep that fucking hand, you'll take it off me, *Brother*," Slate put emphasis on the word, wanting him to back off so he could fucking focus. Something wasn't right; he could feel it.

Pulling away, he watched Tug shake his head and move back towards the kitchen as Slate strolled on towards her bedroom, where he thought he heard muttering. He stayed back a little, not wanting to scare Mica if it was nothing, while staying out of sight if there was. There was barely enough light from the hallway to see something on the floor. It jerked and rolled, and as he saw a booted foot flash into and out of the light, he realized the figure on the floor was Mica.

Hands came into view, pulling her pants and underwear roughly down and off her legs, and then the booted foot flashed again, kicking her hard. Slate yelled and jumped into the room, catching himself before he stepped on Mica. He put up a defensive hand just as a hard kick to his face took him off his feet, smashing him into the wall. *"Fuck,"* he grunted out, sliding down the wall, unable to think or breathe.

A short, dark-haired man ran up the hallway, and Slate heard the front door open and knew the man was gone. He looked around, but couldn't find Mica anywhere. *What the hell?* How had the woman gotten out of the room without him seeing her? The man hadn't taken her; he'd seen him clearly as he ran towards the light and fucking knew it was Nelms, Duck's brother, and he'd been alone as he made his escape. Tug and Tucker burst into the room, taking everything in. Tug reached down and grabbed Slate's cut, slamming him hard against the wall, yelling, "Slate, where's Mica?"

Fuck, that hurt. He had something wrong with his ribs, and his face was on fire. Shaking his head, he pointed towards the bathroom, reaching up to put a hand on the side of his face. Tucker stepped back, and turned on the light in that little room, which illuminated the blood-spattered walls and floor in Mica's bedroom. The prospect stopped and stooped low at the end of the bed, reaching underneath, causing a commotion of noise and screams. "She's naked under the fucking bed," he said incredulously.

Tug dropped to his knees, looking underneath the bed while Slate could only stay slumped against the wall. Tug reached under the bed slowly as, over his shoulder, he softly told Tucker to call Mason. Waiting patiently, he finally began to pull something slowly towards him. Slate saw Mica's hand was folded tightly in Tug's as he dragged her out from underneath the bed. Her face was bruised along her jaw, but the worst was the deep color marring the column of her neck. Purple finger marks clearly spanned the flesh of her throat, and through the rips in her shirt, he could see bruising already forming along her sides and hips.

Tucker handed Tug the phone, and he relayed to Mason what had happened, telling him to come quickly before he hung up and tossed the phone towards Slate. Too slow, he fumbled the catch, and the sound brought Mica's eyes towards him. She could barely speak through her swollen throat, but she said something to Tucker that Slate couldn't make out, because her voice was so ragged. She crawled across the floor towards him, shrugging out of her torn shirt, and pressed the fabric to the side of his head.

"He kicked you, didn't he?" she asked in an aching whisper. God, that had to hurt her as badly as his face and ribs did. It sounded so raw and painful he didn't want her to speak again. She moved and he realized she was naked except for her bra; he watched her long legs accordion as she knelt back on her heels, letting the shadow of dark curls nestled between her thighs flirt with the light. She was classy and beautiful, even broken and bruised like now; he could see what made Mason want and love her.

She had asked a question while he was woolgathering, and Tucker threw something at the wall. As it flew into view, she screamed through her agonized throat and crab-walked backwards, her moving legs exposing brief glimpses of her pussy. A black cowboy hat slid to the floor beside Slate, and he realized her eyes were locked on it, with a look of pure terror on her face. "Tug, get her to the kitchen. Get her out of here," he said softly. Rising painfully to his feet, Slate put his hands flat on the wall behind him, wincing as his face and ribs throbbed.

He followed them to the kitchen, sitting back down in his chair. He didn't dare offer any resistance when Mica forced him to sit still for her inept treatment of the long split on his face. She ignored their repeated requests to put her sweatpants back on; it was like she couldn't make sense of the words.

The door burst open, and Mason suddenly filled the room with his rage. Slate was uncomfortably and totally aware that a nearly naked Mica was draped over him, finishing up with his face. Mason swept her into his arms, wrapping her up gently as he buried his face into her shoulder and neck for a second. The relief on his face was in stark contrast to the furious tone in his voice as he said, "Living room," as he picked Mica up and carried her out of the kitchen.

Slate climbed slowly to his feet again, following them into the other room. He took a beer from Tucker, and told Mason, "He was in the house, Mason. We cleared it, but then he was in the house. He unscrewed the lights in the bedroom, and ambushed her on her way to bed."

Tug added his insights, but Slate was thinking; he'd been trying to figure out how that fucker had gotten into the house after they did a sweep. He was certain the house had been clear, but then Nelms had gotten inside...unless..."Go check the windows in the guest bedroom," he told Tucker.

It was the only explanation; it was the only room near Mica's bedroom that was vulnerable, and Slate wasn't surprised when Tucker came back with the message that the windows were unlocked. Jerking his head back towards her bedroom, he told Tucker to bring the hat out. Turning to Mason, he said, "At least we know how he got in after we cleared it. I'll get our guy out tomorrow to work on all the entrances. We need alarms on shit."

He watched as Mason checked Mica out, cataloging all the bruises and marks where that bastard had put his hands and feet on the woman they were supposed to have been keeping safe. *Fuck*, he thought, *we didn't do a fucking thing right tonight*. Carefully covering her back up, Mason cut his eyes over to him and Tug. Mason asked Tucker to bring in her clothes, and Slate had a sudden thought. "Thinkin' trophy, Prez? Her shirt was torn to shit, but she still had it on. She took it off to use it on my face."

Tucker came back in, and it was clear her underwear was missing. Mason nodded. "Trophy."

Tug and Slate glanced at each other, recognizing the guilt each felt. Mason caught it. "I'll kick your asses later. Right now, focus on the reason, brothers." They nodded, tapping fists against hard chests, mouthing the now-familiar *fucking treasure,* which was what the Rebels all said about Mica, echoing their president's sentiments.

***

Months later, Slate was still tasked with organizing and scheduling the protection detail assigned to Mica. In the past few months, she'd hooked up with a hockey player, Daniel Rupert, and had all but moved in with him following the attack in her home. It had looked pretty serious, but then she'd bailed on the dude one day, abruptly moving back home. All along the way, Mason had focused on Mica, on keeping her safe, healthy, and happy, but never making a move on her. Slate had been confused by how fast Mason gave up on a relationship with her. It was like he had checked out of the race, but more than that, it was as if he had intentionally pulled over and let this Rupert guy sweep in and take what was his.

One night at the clubhouse, Slate had been drunk enough to ask about it. "Mason, where do you see this thing with Mica going, man? Do you see her in your bed, in your home?" Here, he looked around the room, taking in a nearly naked blonde's head bobbing up and down in a brother's lap. "You see her in this clubhouse? I know you've had a thing for her for years now, but is it a realistic thing? I don't want you hurt, brother, and she seems to have the power to really do you some harm."

Mason had laughed, then responded, "Slate, I haven't been able to see anything except her since she moved in next door to me. I see her." He took a drink from his beer. "I see her with me, every part of me. I see myself in her bed, and her in my home. She rides on the back of my bike, wraps those sweet legs around me, and that's all I can think of for hours, or shit, man, *days*. I hear her laugh, and I want to bottle that shit up and keep it around forever. I see her smile, and it breaks my chest wide open, it fills my heart with too much."

He took a breath. "But I know...fucking *know* she needs something I can't give her. I can love her, I can hold her, but I can't be her everything. I can't give her stability. I can't offer her anything but what you see, and she doesn't need this shit.

His face grew somber. "Daniel loves her more than life itself. He sees nothing but good in that woman, and she's growing to love him. He'll be there for her no matter what. He won't wind up in jail, or dead from a fucking war he didn't start. It's not about money, or stature; it's about more, fucking longevity and reasonable expectations. You and I know this life, the MC life. This is what we need, the life we want. The club and brotherhood fulfill something in us that citizens don't understand; Mica can't understand. Our needs are honest and real.

"Slate, her needs are just as honest and real, and just as inexplicable to me. For Mica, I could almost see myself trying to be what she needs...but almost isn't enough," he barked out a harsh laugh, "because, *fuck me,* if she doesn't also need *me,* just me—raw and motherfucking mean as I am—sometimes. That means I have to preserve what I am and what I can do for her. So I push her towards her need that isn't me, and I keep myself in reserve for the hard shit that seems to follow her around."

Slate stared at him. That had to be the most heartbreaking thing he'd heard in a long time, maybe ever. Loving someone like that, and recognizing that not only weren't you what they needed, but wanting to make it right, help them make the right choices, even if that meant they'd travel a different path...that was *real* love. He reached out and softly punched Mason's shoulder. "That's heavy shit, brother. She might be able to settle with the club business. Have you thought about giving it a chance, letting her in, allowing her to find out what you've been protecting her from?"

Mason took off his toque, rubbing a hand over his head. "Are you seriously asking that question? I've only thought about it every single, fucking, squandered day, brother, but it's not the answer, and you know that right alongside me. She would hate knowing what we've done, the lengths we have gone to in order to keep her safe. Mica would be furious if she thought we knew her secrets, and more furious if she saw the skeletons in our fucking closets."

Holding his empty bottle up to a passing prospect, Mason continued, "Slate, I had one night with her, and it flat ruined me for anyone else. I held perfection in my hands, in my arms. I rocked her to sleep, and held her when she cried out in fear of her dreams. Every single day, I think about how I can save that, how I can keep that. She's a fucking treasure, and she's *mine,* but she's also ours; she's Rebel. Now, she's Daniel's, and that's a fit for both of them. She's mine, but never going to be mine. People don't always end up with what they want." Both men were quiet for a long time after that.

***

"Fuck me," Slate muttered, yanking at the collar of his shirt. He was on office duty today, and Mica had an important customer presentation. So, he'd had to dress up like a fucking monkey, jacket and everything. Now, he had to suffer Mica's wrath, because she didn't want him to go with her, but he was under orders. Beyond orders, he'd failed her once, and she'd paid for his mistakes with her flesh and blood. He wouldn't fail her again. Looking into her face as she tried again to talk him into letting her go alone, he calmly told her, "You go, I go."

She argued again, but he knew he was wearing her down, because she was less vehement about it now. He shrugged. "Mason's decree, princess, so I can't let you go without me, especially not now. You go, I go—simple as that."

She rejoined, "I hate this sometimes, Slate. Don't ya get tired of babysitting me?" She stalked to the elevator in front of him, her fury evident in every line of her body.

He imitated her accent, drawling out his response, because he knew it made her crazy, and he'd decided today was Pick on Mica Day. "More than ya fuckin' know, princess, more than y'all will ever fuckin' know." He pulled on his collar again, thinking, *Fuck a damn tie.*

At her client's office, he sat near the elevator, making sure he could keep her in sight while she was in the conference room. He leaned back against the wall, knowing his presence in that room would have only made things difficult; by leaving him out here, she wouldn't have to explain him to anyone. Keeping to himself, he sat quietly waiting. It was more than an hour later when a teeny little brunette swayed her way out of the elevator, walking to the receptionist on stilted heels in a too-tight-for-imagination skirt.

"Is Thomas available?" she curtly asked the receptionist.

"Mrs. Rupert, he's in a meeting, but it should be finished soon; it has already gone over schedule."

Tapping her crimson nails on the desktop, the brunette glared around the waiting room, and her eyes stopped on Slate as he sat quietly on a couch. "Oh my, well aren't you pretty," he heard her say as she sauntered over towards him and settled down on the cushion next to him. She tucked one shapely leg underneath herself, letting the hem of her skirt ride high up her thighs. "Hello there, I'm Amy," she purred at him. "And you are?"

He lifted his chin at her. "Slate."

"Just 'Slate'? No given name?" She scooted a little closer on the cushion.

He nodded. "Just Slate." He realized this was Daniel's ex-wife—Mica's Daniel, even if they weren't exactly together right now, and that was only because Nelms had threatened Daniel's family. Mica was trying to balance keeping everyone safe, while not telling anyone a damn thing—the club had only found out about the threats when Tug made an unannounced visit to her workplace and heard Mica and Jess discussing it. That's when work duty had become a real part of the security schedule.

Amy saw some of his ink that stretched down his arm past his cuffs, and she squealed, "Oh my God, look at those tattoos. How pretty. Do you have more surprises hidden under all that fabric, Mister Just Slate?" She reached out to trace the ink and he pulled back. He didn't want her hands on him; she felt slimy, and there was probably a good reason why Daniel had tossed her ass to the curb. He wasn't certain he wanted to know what it was, but he was going to try to avoid her without being his usual jackass self.

Pressing her thigh against his, she leaned in, whispering, "You are hot, Mister Just Slate. I'm not impressed by much, but you are something else. I want to lick those tattoos, and I'd love to see what else you have underneath your clothes. I'll be at the Drake at seven; meet me in the bar." She reached out one finger, touching the back of his hand and skimming the black lines with her fingernail. The inner door opened just in time, because that unwelcome touch made his skin crawl. Mica came out, shaking hands with the guy she'd come here to meet.

She saw the brunette sitting close to him, and must have read in his face how unhappy he was with the woman being in his space. Mica was scarcely bothering to hide her amusement as she looked at him and inclined her head towards the elevator. He got up and walked over, listening to the two women chat, and he heard Amy call him 'Mr. Slate', which he found amusing.

Taking Mica's computer bag, he turned to see her client pull Amy back into him tightly, grinding his crotch into her ass. That was more than he wanted to see, and he thought it was a good cue to go; this guy was a sleaze too. The client and Amy were still talking, and Slate heard the name of Daniel's hockey team...and that Amy was his ex-wife. If he could hear it, then he was certain Mica could.

He knew this was not going to go well, and sure enough, as they were entering the elevator, Mica finally put two and two together. She stiffened and stopped in her tracks, suddenly realizing from what they overheard that Amy Rupert was Daniel Rupert's ex-wife. Slate leveraged his mass to push her gently into the elevator so the doors could close behind them. It didn't seem like she'd known about Daniel having an ex, and he had a suspicion she'd have a hard time dealing with this shit.

***

Back at Mica's house, Slate was frustrated, because she just kept talking about that fucking brunette. Daniel loved Mica, and to Slate, it kinda looked like she'd fucked him over. She'd left him without a real explanation, and then stood back while he nearly drank himself and his hockey team out of playoff contention. Instead of obsessing about Daniel's past relationships, he would much rather she focus on her own fucking problems.

Today, all she could do was pick the encounter apart, trying to find justification for her anger, and she was quickly settling in to stoke and feed that emotion. He'd pulled up a stool in the kitchen, waiting for her to finish yelling from her bedroom while she changed clothes, so they could decide what to eat for dinner. He was on babysitting duty tonight, along with two other patches, and it looked like it was gonna be a long night.

He'd offered his insight about Daniel and Amy, but she brushed it away, discounting it as dude-talk, pissing him off even more. He was so tired of minding this woman, but because of what had happened in this house, at the same time, he felt accountable for any injury she might receive, whether it was on his watch or not. She came out of her bedroom, admitting that she'd looked Daniel up online, and learned all about his ex-wife in the process.

"Princess, maybe he didn't want to talk about his old lady with his new lady?" He rolled his eyes at her, taking a deep, frustrated breath. "Sometimes, it's the simplest shit that tears us up inside. Did your Googling tell you why they split?" She recounted the rumors of affairs she had found online, and they chatted for another minute about Daniel and Amy, not making any headway against her anger and sense of betrayal. Slate began shucking out of the dress clothes, and once he removed the tie, he started feeling better.

Looking over at Mica, she was chewing on the side of her thumb. He thought it was a terrible nervous habit, and she'd probably pull back a stub one day if she didn't quit it. She was so clearly upset he decided to lighten the tone. "Wish you could have been there when just 'Slate' wasn't enough for her; she had to turn me into *Mister* Slate, like I'm some big shit or something." He saw her smile, and knowing her sense of humor and jokes, he thought he should nip this in the bud right now. "You fucking tell the brothers about that shit, and I'll send Tucker over in my place."

She startled him by reacting physically to that in a negative way, recoiling backwards and flinching. *Whoa,* there was some history clearly, and while he knew Tuck wasn't her favorite person, he didn't know why. Slate decided now was probably the best time to ask her about what had happened between them. He needed her to sort this shit out, because it made it difficult to schedule her sitters, since she didn't want Tuck to be the most senior guy on duty, and thus in charge.

She blew him off, or tried, and he pushed her fiercely, not backing down this time when she got upset at his questions. She was reacting emotionally, as well as physically, shaking her head and frowning hard at Slate. "Princess, there's gotta be a real reason behind that face you are making." He stalked across the kitchen towards her, starting to get into her space. "Give it up; tell Uncle Slate all about it. I can straighten shit out if needed."

She turned her back, shaking her head again, hair flying out in a halo. She was stalling and filling time by fucking with the teapot in the sink. "I simply do not like him...here," she said. "He was here the night Ray was, Slate."

What the fuck? He thought he might get it now, oh...but this had larger consequences if she blamed them all. "Do you blame him for what happened, Mica?"

"No, never," she yelled at him, eyes beginning to well with tears, "he did...you *all* did everything asked of you, and more."

"Then what exactly," he moved quickly towards her, pushing within inches of her back and trapping her into the corner by the sink, an arm on either side of her torso, "is the fucking deal?" He was trying hard to get her off-balance so she could simply react and answer without thinking.

She spun back to face him, shoving her face up into his. She was close enough that he could feel every gasped breath on his lips. "He saw me naked, okay? He saw me naked, and I don't like it." She whipped back towards the sink, hiding her face in the curtains of her hair.

Slate took a slow step backwards, releasing her from the frame of his arms. "Mica, Tug and I were here that night too. Mason was here. Tucker wasn't the only one. We all saw you. Hell, you were practically rubbing your titties all over me when you were putting Band-Aids on half my face. You can't be upset at just Tucker for that." He looked at her, cocking his head to one side quizzically. "You didn't even realize you didn't have panties on until the next day. What the fuck? We were not focused on your pussy, or your titties, or your ass. We were *all* focused on minimizing the damage and keeping you safe."

She started crying; he could see her shoulders moving jerkily, and he reached out to lay a calming hand on her back, anchoring her to him physically. He knew what he needed to say next, but he hated doing this, reminding her he was one of the guys she didn't like.

He'd known for a couple of years he was just about her least favorite Rebel, but his position in the club meant he had to take over for Mason when needed. He had a real fear she'd close off and turn away from him, but he needed to know what was in her head, and Slate was closer to cracking this than any of them had been in weeks. Taking a leap, he started, "Fuck, if you wanted someone gone for seeing you all naked, why not me? I'm a fucking asshole more often than not, and I know it. Shit, Tucker is a boy, hardly fearsome."

She was seriously pissed off when she turned back to him, tear tracks visible on her cheeks. He'd been right; she was crying. She shouted at him, "Because he touches me, okay? He keeps touching me every time he's here—on the arm, pulling my hair off my neck, on my back." She spat the words at him, tears welling out of her eyes and streaming down her cheeks as she struggled to keep talking. "Every time he is around me, he finds a way to touch me, and I hate it. It's like, because he saw me naked, he thinks he has a right, and I hate it. It's nothing blatantly sexual, not really harassing…but he puts his hands on me every time, and *I hate it*."

Oh, good goddamn, this was fourteen kinds of fucked up. Slate snagged her arm and jerked her into a tight hug; he wrapped her up tightly in his arms, and held her carefully against the hard planes of his chest to comfort her as he'd seen Mason do so many times. Slate hoped he hadn't read her reaction wrong, and that she'd come to trust him, if not like him, because he wanted to be supportive and helpful, instead of a threatening asshole. He shushed her, stroking her long hair slowly. "He won't be back here ever, Mica. I got this; I promise you. Shhhh, princess, it won't happen. I got you. You are a fucking treasure, and I won't let it happen. I got this for you."

He was physically still, but his brain was working a hundred miles an hour thinking of all the things they needed to do to keep Tucker away. *Oh fuck*, Slate realized Digger would be coming over soon. He calmly and softly asked Mica if she was okay with Dig or wanted him called off, and Slate reassured her whichever she wanted was fine.

Dig seemed to be safe, because she quieted down, shaking her head. He told her, "That's okay; he's a good guy. Do you want to go wash your face, princess? I'll order pizza and call Dig real quick to pick up some more beer. We'll watch some fucking reality show and laugh our asses off, yeah?"

It wasn't even a minute later before he regretted offering up that reality show, because she reminded him there was a dancing show she liked on TV that night. She also told him—with no visible joking—that he was a good guy, and thanked him for holding her while she cried. Slate grumbled, "Fuck me...dancing?" then pulled out his phone and dialed Digger, telling him to bring the beer. He stopped for a minute, and decided to keep things cool for now, just leaving a message for Tucker that he wasn't needed tonight.

Now came the call he was dreading, because Mason had to know what was going on with Mica and Tucker. This shit simply wouldn't fly; no fucking way would that little piss-ant get to put his hands on their princess. Tapping his chest with his closed fist and mouthing *fucking treasure*, Slate hit Mason's number on his phone. "Prez, we needa call a meeting. We got a fucking serious problem in the club, man. Gonna cut a rocker I 'spect."

Mason snarled in his ear, "What the fuck do you mean, Slate? Because I gotta tell ya, I don't fucking have time for this right now. I just heard that Bones is ready for a sit down. While Bones is a no-brainer, and we're just solidifying some of the shit you've been setting up for us, it still requires fucking focus. Then after I get done with Bones, I'm headed over to Fort Wayne. I need to talk to Bingo tonight, because he's got trouble with the gangs crowding him. I'll be back in town tomorrow, and we can meet at the clubhouse or Jackson's." Mason sounded exhausted.

Slate scrunched up his face. He'd wanted to be at that sit down, but he knew he couldn't be in two places. Making a decision, he decided he needed to be here with Mica for now. "Yeah, okay, tomorrow is soon enough. I'll take care of what I need to tonight, and you can let me know the time and place. I got this, Mason." His final call was for a replacement for Tucker, and he called Roach, knowing Mica was fond of him.

15 -   Essa

Beer and pizza helped make the bad dancing show bearable, and so did seeing Mica relax. Her improved mood had a lot to do with Digger and Roach; she was comfortable with them both, friendly and interested in what they had to say, all hugging and tickling, and generally having a good time. Slate was sitting on the floor in the living room in front of the TV, leaning back against the couch. Mica was sitting directly behind him, and every time she moved, she jostled him and his precariously balanced plate of pizza.

Snarling, he brought his head up to complain again and saw something...someone...walking past the big window. It looked like they were going towards the backdoor that opened into the kitchen. He reacted quickly, shifting to his feet smoothly, and issuing orders to Roach to secure Mica as he turned off all the lights.

Slate made it to the kitchen in a few long strides, and sidled towards the kitchen door, keeping his back to the wall without windows, waiting for movement or noise from outside. There was a sudden, hard pounding at the door, and he jerked it wide open. This had the advantage of getting the person outside off-balance, and he leveraged that by grabbing an arm and yanking them hard into the house, slamming the door closed behind them.

He manhandled them into the wall face-first, slamming them against hard surface and using his body to immobilize them. *Fuck*, this guy felt tiny, like it was a little kid, but he wouldn't take any chances with Mica right now, so he stayed mashed up against him. *Goddamn*, there were some deliciously soft curves back here, so it was probably not a him. He was pressed up against them, and *holy fuck* it all felt good. He snarled at Digger to turn on the lights, and was not surprised at all when the body was revealed to be a young woman. *Fuck*.

He released her, stepping back quickly, and was nearly taken by surprise when she attacked him without pause. She tried to sweep his feet, and was smacking at him hard, so he captured her hands again. "What the hell?"

He stared down into dark brown eyes, with a golden ring circling the iris. Those eyes were centered in a beautiful face, tanned and full of angles he would love to trail his fingers along, and it was framed with dark hair he could surely sink his hands into.

Fuck me, he thought as the gal yelled for Mica, using her full name. He released her again, but he stepped carefully between the two women as Mica ran towards the room. Digger did his part, stopping Mica from entering just as Roach ran in behind her.

Mica apparently knew the girl, talking a mile a minute, even as Rebel hands kept them apart. She didn't have any fear of the girl, and Slate motioned to his men to let things go, allowing the two women to meet in a fierce hug in the middle of the room. The gal's name was evidently Essa, and while she was a little taller than Mica, she was a lot younger. In the full light of the kitchen, she looked about seventeen, but was lean and athletic, so he thought that might be somewhat misleading. God, she was pretty, dressed all casual in jeans and boots.

"Mica?" he asked carefully, wanting clarity for what was going on. He wasn't sure yet that everything outside was okay, so he sent the men out with a gesture, watching as they split up outside to check the yard and house. Mica moved slightly, but kept her hands on the girl, introducing her, "Slate, this is my little cousin, Essa." She pointed at Slate, grinning. "Essa, this is Slate, but don't worry—he's not as tough as he tries to look."

The woman—*Essa*, he tested out in his head—looked up at Slate with a pleasant, but cautious stare, and then totally ruined the moment. "Mr. Slate, pleased to meet you." Fuck him, that was twice in one day he'd been called 'mister', and he knew Mica would capitalize on it. Sure enough, confirming she'd picked up on it, Mica grinned hard at him while clarifying for her cousin, "Just Slate, Essa, he's...just Slate. What are you doing here? Have you had supper?"

Slate watched Roach and Digger come back in from outside, Roach indicating everything was in order. "Just a truck and horse trailer, no one in either, unless you count the pissed off nag."

Slate saw Essa stiffen at that; the horse must be hers, but she didn't say anything back. Slate thought a little arrogantly that maybe she was intimidated by all the bare skin that surrounded her; he and Digger had a lot of ink, and they were shirtless. Plus, Digger worked out at the gym every day, and Slate had his own version of strong and lean going on.

Mica organized a quick plate of food for Essa, pulling her into the living room for a chat while the guys got things ready in the kitchen. Slate followed them, and listened as Mica asked a few quick questions of Essa. He noted in one of the answers that the gal said the horse had been in the trailer for too long already, so he thought he should probably unload it and make sure everything was okay. Essa was obviously attached to the horse, and for some unknown reason, he would hate for anything to happen that would upset her.

His head snapped up as Essa burst into tears, surprising him. She was crying so hard that he couldn't understand anything she was saying, and he hadn't been paying attention to what Mica had asked. She wrapped the girl up in her arms, and asked him to take care of parking the rig and get the horse out, explaining things carefully, but like he was an idiot. He nodded, disarmed, because he thought it was funny she'd asked him to do something that was so familiar to him, but she was worried he would fuck it up.

He nodded, turning to walk outside, telling Mica over his shoulder, "I'll move the rig and unload the horse, and I'll make sure he has water, a little feed, and see if there's a blanket for him." *Fuck*, this little girl had him on edge. He couldn't think straight when he was unsettled like this, and that was probably more of his history in one sentence than Mica ever knew about him before. He could feel Mica's eyes boring into his back questioningly as he grabbed his leather jacket to go outside. He laughed. *I'm a fucking enigma.*

Walking out, he saw the crew cab truck and a two-horse trailer sitting nearly in the road. Opening the door, he found the keys thrown carelessly on the floorboard, and snagged them. Pulling the truck safely off the road, he set the brake and shut down the rig. Climbing out, he opened the small pass-through in the front of the trailer to look at the horse tied inside.

The dappled gray horse looked aggravated, and rolled its eyes at him. He stepped back, opening the gear and living quarters in the nose of the trailer, quickly finding what he was looking for in the form of feed, water, buckets, and a blanket. Setting things out where he could reach them easily, he opened the gate and unloaded the horse, letting the gelding step slowly and cautiously backwards down the little ramp.

Calmly patting and stroking the horse's neck, Slate pulled out the bucket of water, securing it to the side of the trailer. He tied the horse off, giving him only a little slack to sidle sideways a couple of steps. Grabbing the horse blanket, he fitted it onto the horse, clipping the belly and neckbands comfortably. He closed up the back of the trailer, securing the ramp.

Sitting on the fender for a minute, he patted the gelding's nose and watched him settle down. Slate could see there was some puffiness in his legs; he needed to walk it off, get the blood flowing again. Fuck, she'd kept this horse standing immobile in the trailer for several hours too long in her efforts to get to Chicago and Mica.

Untying the gelding, he slowly walked him down the block and back, pausing a couple of times to run a hand down the horse's legs. He was still a little hot when they got back to the trailer, so Slate tied him again and found some alcohol, then rubbed him down for a few minutes. That was rewarding, because the gelding's head dipped slowly as he relaxed into the indulgence.

He dipped out a small ration of oats for the gelding, wanting to give him enough to ease any hunger he might have. Headed back into the house, he found that the women were in the guest bedroom behind a closed door. He snagged a beer, and laughed out loud when he saw the guys were still watching the dancing show, even without Mica to goad them.

Roach looked over at him, raising an eyebrow. "Cousin from Texas?"

Slate blew out a breath and nodded. "Seems that way."

Digger looked up, a gleam in his eye and humor written on his face. "That little girl nearly popped you one, Slate," he teased, grinning widely. "That woulda been something to see."

Fucker. If she had been successful in clipping him, he wasn't one hundred percent sure what his reaction would have been, but given the rock-hard erection he had been sporting from pressing her against the wall, it could have gone either way.

A couple of hours later, Mica finally came out of the guest bedroom without Essa, and Slate gathered she was asleep since Mica was careful with noise. Roach and Digger had gone to sleep too, and since Slate had turned the TV off a while ago, he pointed silently towards the kitchen. Once they were both sitting at the breakfast bar, he asked Mica, "She okay?" Mica shook her head without saying anything, her face concerned.

He wanted to distract her from whatever was keeping her mute, and thought about the dappled gray horse and rig. He knew that Mica was a rodeo gal before college and Chicago, and he figured she would want to know all about the horse. "She has a nice gelding; come outside and see." He handed Mica her jacket and opened the door, grabbing a flashlight to bring with them. Once they got outside, he found he was inordinately proud she seemed impressed with the job he'd done parking the rig and settling the horse.

The gelding was dozing, still tied securely to the off-side of the trailer. Just after the guys had gone to sleep, he had come out and tidied up the empty buckets; he knew from experience that a horse left with loose equipment would quickly find a way to get into trouble. The horse was nice and warm in the blanket, and was relaxed and resting. Slate ran a hand down his legs, relieved there was no heat anywhere. Mica had him shine the light on the horse's halter on the side of his head, revealing a nameplate bradded into the nylon halter. She spoke the name aloud, "Summer Breeze."

Slate wondered about everything; this gal had shown up out of the blue, when none of Mica's family was supposed to know where she was, except her shithead brother...who had gone home. Michael Scott was probably the reason behind this visit. He asked Mica brusquely, "What's she doing here?" He had a sudden thrill of fear that it wasn't because of Scott at all.

Mica physically avoided the question, rolling her shoulders in a huge shrug, so he pushed the topic. "Princess, does this have anything to do with Nelms?" She nodded, looking at him silently, and his anxiety level shot through the roof. *Fucking shit*, she was out here in the goddamn open. He wasn't even glancing around, or trying to clock anyone, or anything; he was playing with a fucking horse.

He quickly and roughly manhandled her towards the house as fast as he could, short of picking her up and carrying her in, his eyes scanning the surroundings for any danger or threats. "The fuck was I thinking, taking you outside with only me out here?" *Goddammit,* he was pissed at himself. He forced her into the house, and then just as quickly, he moved her away from the door and windows. Protecting her with his own bulk, he kept himself between her and any openings to the outside. He scowled and snarled at her, "Talk, Mica. I need to know. Everything."

She moved her head, and he heard her neck crack, and realized how tense and afraid she had to be. Something Essa told her had to have been bad, probably whatever made the little gal cry like she was earlier in the evening. Slate chopped out a quick, "Sit," and then just as quickly reversed himself with a, "Wait," as he moved to grab pillows and blankets from the living room to make a pallet. He threw the bedding on the kitchen floor between the sink and the kitchen island, pointed, and said again, "Sit." He sat down next to her, leaning his head back against the sink cabinet. "Start with Essa—who is she to you?"

Mica was still strangely calm and was clearly fond of her cousin. "Essa, or Esmeralda, is my cousin. She's the daughter of my mother's sister, and two years younger than my baby sister, Molly. They've grown up together, more like sisters than cousins."

Slate knew her sister was placed with her family after her daddy was convicted of raping Mica's best friend when she was barely seventeen. During his trial, Mica had come forward with testimony about years of abuse at her daddy's hands, and she had been important in his final conviction. Being apart from her little sister was hard for Mica, and her statement just now had been made with a tone of both sadness and ruefulness. It sounded like she'd missed so much of her sister's childhood. Mica continued, "Aunt Janet and Uncle Rob don't know she's here. They know she's on the circuit, and she was supposed to be headed to a rodeo in Urbana. She kinda detoured to here."

Slate interrupted, because for him, this was the most critical question of the night, "How did she know where 'here' was?"

Mica rolled her neck again, pulling and stretching her muscles. "According to Essa, she got a letter a few weeks ago. All it had in it was a picture of this house, a picture of me, and an address. Molly got one too, but her age division had more events out west, so the girls decided Essa should investigate while up this way."

Leaning over, Mica laid her head on a pillow. "The pictures are some of the ones Ray had, so I think he must have sent them to the girls. I don't know why yet...can't figure it...but I am sure there's something going on. It's like something is just outside the range of hearing, you know? I can almost grasp it, but it slithers away. She's also got something else going on I need to figure out. She wouldn't talk about it, but it's there." Mason and the Rebels had found out about the pictures Nelms had taken weeks ago; it was one of the things that had caused the huge uptick in security.

She yawned, snuggling into the pillow. "I'll go down to Urbana with her in the morning, make sure she's solid, and then watch her compete. That will be fun, to be behind the scenes again. I miss it sometimes." Pulling one hand out from under the pillow, she started chewing on the side of her thumb again, a sure sign she was nervous. Her voice was uneven as she added, "Ray's taken so much from me, and I hate him, Slate. *I hate him*."

He hated seeing her like this, not just stressed out, but so clearly and evidently fearful. It had been a long time since he'd seen her face without that dark shadow of fear on it. Maybe if she saw him as a person, not merely one of Mason's Rebels, but as a man...a friend...then, maybe she'd have confidence that he could keep her safe this time. He knew he had failed her, badly, but he was much more committed now. He wanted to build on a friendship he felt was budding, so reaching out a hand to smooth her hair down her back, he gave her his name—not his road name, but his real one. "Andrew Jones."

She was confused, looking up into his face. "Huh? Who is Andrew Jones?"

"Me." Slate smiled at her, seeing the recognition in her face of what he had offered her. It was a window into him as a man, into who he had been before. She seemed to accept this as a precious gift, and he felt a little less exposed. "Sleep, princess, and tomorrow," he waited for a beat, watching for a nod from her before he continued, and reminded her, "you go, I go, remember?"

They stayed on the floor for a time, Slate watching over her as she slowly relaxed into the pallet on the floor. He curled around her, feeling her loosen and ease into sleep. Waiting patiently beside her as she delved deeper into a healing rest, once he thought she was far enough under, he picked her up and carried her to bed. After straightening the house and putting up the bedding, he settled into a chair in the living room, keeping watch for the rest of the night.

Once the sun came up, he shrugged on his jacket and strolled outside to check on the gelding. Standing near the horse, he saw Mason coming down the street, and watched his bike slow as he took in the strange vehicle set-up and the sight of Slate comfortably handling the horse.

Slate waited on Mason to walk over after he parked. Meeting him with a chin lift, Slate gave a succinct summary of the evening. "Rig belongs to Mica's cousin, Essa; she's eighteen. She and Mica's sister, Molly, got letters with pictures and this address, so she came to see. We're taking Essa to Urbana this morning, where she's competing in a rodeo. Mica and I both think the letter and pics probably came from Nelms."

Mason nodded at him; their version of shorthand worked both ways, and he'd gotten all the key details from what Slate had said. He looked at Slate, narrowing his eyes. "Okay, got it. Sounds under control. Now tell me about trouble in the club."

Fuck, he'd nearly forgotten about Tucker with everything that happened last night. Slate blew out a long breath, looking into Mason's face as he told him what Mica had said about Tucker. Mason was visibly upset, his dark grey eyes turning steely and hard. Slate watched as the muscles in Mason's jaw tightened and jutted out; he was grinding his teeth together. His question was a snarled, "Tucker put hands on her? Before or after we patched the fucker in?"

Slate frowned; he knew it was an important question, and one that would determine the future of the biker, and perhaps their club. "Both, I believe, Prez."

"Think anyone saw?" Mason asked. "Because if they did, and didn't tell, we'll rip more than one rocker off a fucking patch's cut."

"Nah, Prez, this will be a he said/she said if I've ever seen one." Slate didn't think any of their brothers would have covered up for a freshly patched new member, not when everyone knew how important Mica was to all of them. Slate was a little worried about their ability to defend the accusation, but he knew in his gut she'd told the truth. He shared that confidence with Mason. "I believe Mica though; I pushed her until I got a real reaction, and I know what I saw was truth."

Folding his arms across his broad chest, Mason shrugged. "Then there's only one question: Do we stop with the rocker?" He turned and walked towards Mica's house.

***

Headed into the house behind Mason, Slate grabbed a hot cup of coffee and lounged for a bit, cocking one hip against the kitchen cabinet. He watched the girl stumble into the room, her eyes still half-lidded with sleep. He reached out to set a mug on the cabinet near the coffeemaker, and watched as she filled it and carried it over to the breakfast bar. She wriggled that rounded ass onto one of the stools, leaning far over onto her elbows and keeping her hands wrapped tightly around the mug.

After a few sips of coffee, she seemed more aware of her surroundings, and he caught her looking between him and Digger more than once. He knew that Dig was probably a lot closer to her age, but he was intrigued by this girl, and found himself frowning whenever he caught her eyes on Dig. Mason grabbed her mug and refilled without saying anything to her, and Slate saw her shiver when she looked up at him. She blurted out an "I'm sorry," to Mason, making Slate want to tell her she'd done nothing wrong. Mason beat him to it, asking her "What the fuck for?" Essa's response was nonsensical, and Roach laughed loudly at her, bringing quick tears to her eyes that she tried to hide.

Mica checked the time and began hurrying everyone along, so Slate headed outside, saying, "I'll go load the gelding and get the rig ready to go." As he swung through the door onto the little back porch, he heard Essa yell, "Breezy, his name is Breezy" and he laughed at her constant defense of that pretty, gray gelding. He loaded the horse, stripping the blanket and putting that and the water bucket back into storage in the living quarters. He closed and locked the gate, shaking it back and forth to ensure it was latched securely.

He headed back into the house, hoping to get another half-cup of coffee, but saw Essa walking through the kitchen with a black cowboy hat in her hand. He grabbed it from her, thinking it was Nelms' hat, but then he realized it was much too small. By this time, though, he was committed; hell, he had the hat in his hand already. So, to cover, he asked Essa, "Where are you going with that?" wondering what she'd say in response.

She looked confused, responding, "It's my hat; I'm taking it to my truck."

He wanted to keep talking to her, but he couldn't think of anything else to say about the hat. He spit out the first thing that came into his mind, "It's black." *Fuck, that was random.* She was going to think he was crazy at this rate. He needed to shut up now, before it got worse.

She responded very slowly, "Yes. It is black. Black goes with my outfits."

Slate closed his eyes and shook his head, handing her the hat back without speaking. They headed out, and Essa checked in the trailer and then leaned in to start the truck, grabbing a tire gauge from the glove box. He watched her shirt and jeans stretch and tighten across her body as she moved. God, she smelled good as she brushed past him towards the trailer. She was wearing the same clothes as last night, and he had caught a quick hint of a musky, sweet scent. It smelled of arousal and sexual frustration. As she moved away, he climbed into the truck, sitting in the driver's seat. Essa made the rounds with the rig, checking first on the horse, then on every tire and light. She made sure the gate was closed and latched, returning to the driver's door, and gaped when she saw Slate sitting there. "Umm, you're in my spot," she said, opening the door.

Slate was focused on her, and saw the firm lines of her mouth, thinking to himself, *This has to be her annoyed face.* He couldn't keep looking at her, or she'd soon see the evidence of his arousal from being around her. "Nope, I'm driving today; I am your chauffeur and bodyguard, Ms. Essa." Slate stared straight out the windshield in front of him, not daring to look her in the face.

"Look, dude," she started and he glanced over at her, laughing.

"Did you just 'dude' me, little girl?"

Unfazed, she argued with him, "Slate, it's my rig, my horse, my responsibility...so you need to get out of *my* seat, now." Slate turned to look at her, and she was so beautiful he couldn't breathe. He felt his eyebrows arching up towards his hairline. He was trying to take her in, drink in the spirit of Essa. She stumbled verbally, stuttering as she said only his name, "S-slate," before Mica squashed her defense, supporting his decision to drive. Essa had a petulant look on her face as she slammed the door beside him, muttering, "Fine, but it's my rig," which made him smile.

Arriving at the fairgrounds in Urbana, they unloaded and setup, and Essa walked with Mica to pick up the paperwork for her event entries. Essa and Slate stalked cautiously around each other, each seeming to recognize there was a connection between them, but unsure whether to acknowledge it.

Essa worked the horse, and Slate was impressed with the skill and patience she exhibited during the session. She was also very attuned to the horse, and noticed quickly when a shoe became loose. He watched as she gathered her farrier bucket and secured the horse, removing the loose nail and quickly replacing it with a new one. Crimping and trimming the nail, she tightened the shoe down and he saw how her tight jeans caressed her legs and ass, forming into a deep "V" at the apex of her thighs, where he imagined being buried deep inside her.

As she worked, Essa asked Mica if she and Slate were dating, which he found hilarious. Then she asked about Mason, and he was surprised to hear Mica easily dismiss any thought of her and Prez being together. He frowned, wondering if she knew just how deep into Mason's life she had drilled, how much she mattered to him—*shit*—to all of them.

He focused back on what Essa was saying, just in time to hear her say, "Mica, there were four really *HOT* men in your house this morning, example: this guy," and watched as she pointed at him, and he shouted with laughter again. "Four *REALLY* hot men, with muscles like Greek gods...and you are telling me that not a single one of them is your boyfriend?" She shook her head at Mica's response of, "Not any one of them." Laughing, Essa asked her, "Cuz', I'm sorry. How did *you* get friend-zoned like that?" Slate didn't even try to hold back his laughter this time, and he roared even harder when he saw Mica's face, her mouth opening and closing like a goldfish, because she was speechless. She stalked off, and Slate followed her, leaving Essa standing next to the trailer.

***

Returning to the trailer, Slate saw the door to the living quarters standing open, and the horse was tied to the side, saddled and ready to go. He stepped over to the door and peered in to see Essa standing there dressed only in her underwear. Facing away from him, she was bent over to pick up something from the back of the closet, giving him a clear view of the dark shadow between her legs and the high-arching cheeks of her ass. "Essa, fuck," he choked out, startling her.

She turned quickly and grabbed something to cover herself, yelling at him, "Pervert, what are you doing, peeping? Get out! Shut the door!" He grabbed the door and slammed it shut, and then heard her yell in a panic, "Open the door! Open the door!" So, he opened the door in fear, and then saw her still standing there in her panties and bra, and he slammed it quickly again.

Oh God, she was so much more than beautiful; her body was glorious. His cock was hard as bone, and he was breathing like he'd run a marathon. He couldn't imagine touching her without having her, and Slate was struggling against opening that door again. The mounds of her breasts had been plumped up by the low-cut sports bra, and those thin little panties didn't cover anything. *God,* he wanted her. He walked over to the horse and leaned his head against the gelding's hip, trying to get himself back under control.

He heard movement from within the trailer, and a couple minutes later, the door slammed open, and Essa stood in the doorway. She yelled, "What were you doing looking into my trailer?"

He shook his head, leaving his forehead against the horse. Closing his eyes, he asked, "Why was the door open, Essa?"

She sighed. "Because it's hot in there, and there's no one else over here. It was not intended as an open invitation."

Lifting his head, but keeping his feet planted, because he still didn't trust himself, he slowly looked her up and down. She was even more beautiful with her eyes blazing and color in her cheeks. Her black shirt didn't have buttons; it had pearl snaps, and he could see himself ripping it off her. "God," he muttered, "it's black."

She looked puzzled, but responded, "Yes, my outfit is black, and so is my hat." She moved to untie the gelding, and Slate stepped back, watching her. When she lined herself up to get on the horse, he slid in behind her and gripped her leg firmly. His hand slid up her calf, to the bend of her knee as he lifted, boosting her into the saddle. She thanked him quietly, and then asked him "Where's Mica?"

He looked around...*no Mica.* "Fuck me, goddammit," he growled. "Mason's gonna kill me."

He stepped around the trailer, and saw Mica walking towards him eating cotton candy that was the color of Smurfs. "Mica, you know better, damn it. You go, I go...you get me?" he scolded. She held out the neon blue spun sugar, offering him a bite. He shook his head. "Goddammit, Mica, I don't need this shit. I'm the only one here right now, and what if fucking Nelms walked around the corner? I need you to fucking pay attention, and I want to hear you say you get me. So give me the fucking words, princess. Say, 'I. Get. You. Slate.' *Goddammit.*"

She looked over his shoulder at Essa working the gelding on the grass. "I get you, Slate. I'll stick close; I'm sorry."

After the first runs for her events, Essa came back to the trailer and dismounted. Slate grinned at the wide smile on her face, and he grabbed a bag to rub the horse down. He knew that would give her a few minutes to relax. While he worked on the horse, he watched her sit beside the trailer as she grabbed a book and pencil. She looked cute as she concentrated, making her notes in a stop and start fashion as she jotted things down. Sitting like this, she looked very young, but he only had to close his eyes to see her nearly naked form in his mind again, remembering she was all woman, and found himself getting hard.

He watched her hat tip backwards; she let it hang by strings around her neck. *God*, he imagined his hands sliding up the column of her throat, caressing the edges of her jaw. He leaned his arms against the horse and locked his eyes on her, watching the movement of her mouth and lips as she chewed on her pencil.

Essa looked up, catching his eye, and she watched him as he stared at her. He saw color rising in her cheeks again, and wanted to see her eyes flash like they had earlier, but instead of from across the room, he wanted to see them looking up at him from a bed. *Fuck*, he needed to get this under control, had to sort his shit. He shook himself and went back to working on the horse, thinking this might be the hardest order Mason had ever given him, and he couldn't fucking wait to go home.

He was startled when he glanced at her and she stuck her tongue out at him, and a frown slipped onto his face. What the fuck was he thinking? He was nearly twice her age; nothing could happen here. This was Mica's family; Essa was off limits, and he knew that was an important thing to remember.

He continued working on Breezy, and asked Essa when she was supposed to compete again. He assumed it was soon, since she hadn't untacked the horse. She checked the time, and responded, "In about forty-five minutes...they'll get team roping done first. Poles aren't until tomorrow, so I only have the two barrel events today."

He shot a look at her. "Tomorrow?"

She leaned back, nodding. "I've got four events tomorrow; it will be a faster-paced day."

Fuck, fuck, *fuck*. Slate looked over at Mica, and asked hopefully, "Home tonight?"

Shit. She shook her head no. "Mason will be here soon; he is coming to pick me up, but we need someone to stay here with Essa," she informed him. *Oh no, Mason had better be bringing someone...but not Digger.* He didn't want Dig around her...and not Tucker either; that fucker didn't need to be around any women. Slate mentally rejected every Rebel he could think of, and felt his face pale as he realized what that probably meant.

Essa yelled at Mica, "I do not need a babysitter, Cuz'. I've been doing this on my own for nearly three years now; I do not need someone to stay with me...especially him!"

Still hoping it was a terrible joke, Slate asked, "Mica, you shitting me?" as he looked over towards her, frowning. She tossed him her phone, and he read a long text from Mason that told her to let Slate know he was on babysitting duty for the night, and that Mason would be down soon to pick Mica up to take her home. He closed his eyes and turned away. "Fuck me. Looks like you are stuck with me, little girl."

When he arrived, Mason had brought dinner for them; he started handing out food containers to Essa, who slammed them down on his hood. She began her tirade with, "Okay, Really Angry Guy, let's be clear here—you are not my daddy or one of my brothers; you are not even any real kind of family. You are not dating my cousin. You are not the boss of me. I do not want *him* to stay with me, because I do not, let me repeat...I do *not*, need a babysitter. Plus, he doesn't even want to. So, you can take them both with you and leave me alone." She stood there with her hands at her waist, one hip cocked out and her chin tucked down angrily.

Stopping a moment, Mason looked at her puzzled, and then grinned. "What did you call me?"

Mica made a rude noise in response as Essa repeated, "Really Angry Guy, but that's not the point."

Mason asked Mica on a laugh, "Were you this bad when you were eighteen?"

She responded, sighing and nodding her head, "Worse, probably."

Mason laughed again briefly, but then Essa seemed to catch his mood change as his eyes turned steely. He stopped laughing and leaned forward. "You *will* have a fucking bodyguard tonight, Essa. You are Mica's cousin, which puts you under my protection, like it or not. We are family, whether you recognize it or not. Now, Slate can stay, or I can, but one of us will...so choose, now."

Essa looked stunned, and then jumped in again with, "Hello? No one is staying with me. Why is that concept so difficult to understand? Are you simian? Seriously, dude, *go away*. I'm fine."

Before Mason could respond, Slate distracted Essa by reminding her, "Little girl, don't you need to warm up? It's nearly time for your run." He thought he had effectively derailed her argument until she told Mason, "This is *so* not over."

Slate gave her a boost up onto the horse again, patted her leg encouragingly, and then handed her hat up. He, Mason, and Mica all watched her warm up, and then Slate asked, "Nelms has dropped off the radar, hasn't he?" Mason responded by nodding silently. Rubbing his hands distractedly through his hair, Slate frowned, and then cut his eyes over at Mason. "I got this, Prez. He's gonna show up. After all, he sent her here, right? We'll get him, Mason. I got this."

They followed Essa to the arena, preparing to watch her compete in her event. Sitting in the stands, his elbows to his knees and chin in his hands, Slate leaned forward and watched as tiny Essa raced her horse at full speed out of the darkness of the alleyway and into the brilliant sunlight shining down on the arena. She deftly moved him in a cloverleaf pattern around the barrels, using her heels and hands to guide him into each turn and pivot point with precise movements. Riding fast, but skillfully, she cleared the final barrel. Leaning far forward and over his neck, she rode like hell out of the arena whooping, laughing, and fanning him with the reins.

Stunned by the sheer brilliance of her athletic grace and confidence, Slate sat still for a moment, listening as the announcer called her name for best time. They met her back at the trailer, and before she slipped off the horse, she looked down, locked eyes with Mason, and said, "Okay, you win. I choose him…Slate." Dismounting, she unsaddled the gelding quickly, starting to work on grooming him.

Mason looked between Slate and Essa, asking casually, "Mind telling me why?"

Essa kept working on the gelding, responding to Mason with, "He's already seen me in my underwear."

Slate's head fell back and he groaned at her words, knowing it would bring Mason down on his ass. Sure enough, Mason's hands formed fists as he looked at him and asked, "What the fuck, Slate?"

Fuck me, Slate thought, and he quickly responded to Mason, "It's not like that, Prez. She was in the trailer with the door wide open, and I stuck my head in to see if there was anything I could do. She was changing. All I did was close the door."

Tossing a coin in his head, he fed Mica into the Mason-maw by letting him know she had been unguarded for a time. "It was about then that Mica gave me the slip, risking her life for fucking cotton candy."

Mica glared daggers at him, and Mason looked between them, laughing. "Seems like everyone had an interesting day. What do you say, Mica? Let's go home."

Much later, Essa and Slate were winding down after eating and finishing chores. They'd walked the fairgrounds, and she'd introduced him to a few of the entrants she knew well, explaining to him they'd all practically grown up on the circuit over the years.

He spent a few dollars winning her a cheap stuffed animal at the baseball throw, and then laughed with her when the carny admitted to giving him the easy balls and target. They shared cotton candy and a turkey leg, and then Essa stole a sip from his mug in the beer tent. It was comfortable, feeling safe and familiar, and Slate knew it was dangerous.

Back at the trailer, he waited outside as she changed, entering once she called out she was settled in the bunk. He pulled out a couple of blankets to pad the floor, arranged a bag of feed as a pillow, and took off his shirt before lying on the floor.

Calling a quiet good night, he listened for her response, smiling to himself when she sounded annoyed. She was tossing and turning on the bunk, the narrow mattress doing little to hide the noise as she rolled restlessly. Even though they'd had fun tonight, Essa still wasn't happy he was there, not just because she felt a babysitter undermined her efforts to be self-sufficient, but also because he was in her space, and the living quarters weren't that big.

Listening to her move, Slate clenched his teeth; the restless sound alone was enough to have his cock hard and straining against the button fly of his jeans.

He rolled the events of the day around in his head, thinking about her stunning ass covered only with thin panties, her breasts round and full, her calling him hot, and watching him out of the corner of her eyes...*God.* He had to think about something else. She's a kid, barely eighteen. *Fuck me,* he thought, *I'm old enough to be her father.* She was fucking off limits, and Mason had made that crystal today.

The noises continued from the bunk, and he took a breath in, catching a hint of musk. Taking in another breath, he broke the silence, his voice husky and rough. "Tell me about Breezy. Is he yours?" There was a little light that leaked around the door, hardly enough to allow outlines of dark against black, but he saw the silhouette of her head pop over the edge of the bed. He wasn't sure she could see him; it was dark where he was on the floor, but she hung over the edge like that for a few seconds, holding still and looking down where he laid.

She began speaking confidently, "Yeah, he's mine—well, my daddy's, but I bred him. He's out of my favorite mare and a good stud from Missouri." She eased out of sight, lying back down. "He's been mine since he first dropped to the straw in the stall, and I've trained him too. I'm proud of how well he's doing; he's gonna make a great college event horse. I plan to bring his full brother out on the circuit next year. Summer Storm, he's a year younger than Breezy, but he's not cut, so I am not sure if I'll trailer the both of them, or just the one. Studs are trouble sometimes."

God, her voice was so sexy, sounding low, intelligent, and strong. She paused and moved again, and he was drawn back into his memory of her standing in the trailer earlier today—facing away from the door and bent over, that ass right there in front of him. Fuck, he was hard, his erection begging for release. In this low light, he was confident she couldn't see him, even if she tried. He slid a hand down his front, adjusting himself; then he grasped his cock through the fabric of his jeans, and pressed down firmly with the heel of his hand. His cock was throbbing, and it twitched at the attention.

Stifling a groan, he swallowed hard, running his hand down the length of his cock again, cupping his hand over the head and stroking slowly through the thick fabric. He wanted to hear her voice again, and asked, "Have you been riding barrels and poles long? Is there anything specific that you enjoy about the competition? What do you like about it?"

There was a smile in her voice, "I've been riding since before I could walk; horses have always been part of my life, and I love it all. With the competition, what's not to like? You work in collaboration with an elite, equine athlete, testing both your skills against the pattern and the clock, again and again."

As she spoke, he remembered pulling her into Mica's kitchen, besting her physical reaction and pressing her up against the wall. He'd been hard, pressed against her ass; remembering it now, he shifted the hard length of cock to a more comfortable position, sliding it sideways across his hip.

She continued to move, and he heard her turn over, tossing her blanket off her body and against the back wall of the bunk. "It's not a competition against the other riders, other than how they can get under your skin and into your head. It comes down to training, emotional resiliency of horse and rider, skilled event riding, composition of venue, and the luck of the draw."

God, she was amazing, there was an incredible intelligence and analysis revealed in her outline of what she did. He smiled, thinking that he wanted her to keep talking, so he urged, "You make it sound technical and scientific, and then say something like 'luck of the draw'?"

It's dark in here, he reminded himself, brushing across his cock with the heel of his hand again. *She won't know, she can't see.* He unbuttoned his jeans soundlessly and took his cock in hand. He stroked slowly, holding it loosely in his fingers, rubbing his thumb over the head and across the tip.

"Yeah," she breathed softly, startling him by speaking from right over his head. "For some horses, running too early in the day is tough, and others don't do well waiting around. So when you draw for your positions and run times, it really can be the luck of the draw."

She continued, shifting away from the edge of the bunk again, "Some riders don't do the head game very well, and they amp their horses up unnecessarily, either by tacking up too soon, or not following a good, predictable routine."

He was stroking himself slowly, changing his grip and tightening it as he slid his hand from root to tip, again and again. Concentrating on keeping his breathing under control, he listened as she continued talking, "Or they don't pay attention to fatigue levels, and work their horses when they are too tired. It's hard on the horses to be trailered for long distances, so you have to give them time to recover before working them hard. Um. Are you jacking off, Slate?"

At her question he froze in place, *how did she know?* Taking in a short, light breath, he asked softly, "Why?"

Her voice came from the bunk, directed towards the ceiling, but very soft and low. "Because the sound of your hand moving up and down the length of it is pretty sexy sounding, and your breathing has gotten shallow and fast, and that's sexy as hell, too."

Slate debated lying to her, but then opened his mouth and groaned, "Yes," while he kept stroking his cock slowly, root to tip.

He heard a smile in her voice as she whispered, "I thought so," and the sound of that smile nearly pushed him over the edge.

He could imagine it on her face as she looked over her shoulder at him, while he drove into her from behind. He tipped his hips forward and upward, fucking hard through his fist for a few long strokes. He was listening to the noises he made with his movements, knowing she was listening too. "Talk to me, Essa," he urged her quietly, wanting her voice again.

She was at the edge of the bunk again, right over his head, and when she spoke, her voice came from bare inches away, her breath stirring the air around him. "Does it matter what I say, Slate?"

Fuck me, he thought, *she has no idea how sexy she can be.* "Yes, it has to matter to you. I fucking love the passion in your voice when you talk about all this." He reached down with his other hand, pushing his jeans open further as he arched his back, gritting his teeth.

He thought he'd ruined it for a few seconds, because she was silent and moved away from the edge of the bunk, gaining distance between them, even in the small space. *Please*, he begged silently, *talk to me.* He was listening so closely for her voice it took a second for him to recognize the sounds she was making. There was a brief, wet, sliding noise, and her breath caught in her throat. *God, she's...* There was the noise he had heard again. He almost couldn't believe it, but he had to know, so he whispered on a breath, "Essa, are you touching yourself?"

She answered soft and low, "Yes."

Slate groaned quietly, stroking himself harder and faster, and felt himself come closer to the edge. He realized he couldn't care less about the noises he made. He had to know about Essa though, had to know how aroused she was, asking her, "Are you wet?"

There was a soft rustle of clothing, and she answered with a hitch in her voice, "Yes."

Oh, fuck me, the vision of her body from today was burned in his brain. He could still see the dark shadows between her thighs that had been barely covered by her panties, and he *had* to know if she tasted as good as she looked. He released himself, sitting up and reaching for the edge of the bunk as he groaned, "God, Essa, I want to taste you. Let me...let me touch you, have a taste of you. I need to know if you are as sweet on my tongue as your scent is in the air."

Reaching out, he wrapped his hands around her thighs and hips, pulling her body to the edge of the bunk and inwards towards him. Positioning himself between her legs, his shoulders held her legs apart as he rested back on his heels, feeling his cock bump against his bare belly.

He never took his hands off her, wrapping his fingers around her legs, smoothing slowly down and then back up the inside of her thighs. "If you don't want this, you need to tell me, little girl. It's your decision, baby, but you have to tell me yes or no." Bending his head, he trailed soft kisses against the inside of her knee, working her flesh with his lips and hearing her groan in response to his touch.

He slid his hands up, following them closely with his tongue; she was so femininely muscular, so strong. Her thighs were corded and taut, and he ran his hands over every inch of them on his way to his goal. He paid close attention to every reaction to his touch; he wanted to learn what pleasured her, and he loved her vocal responses of moans and gasps. Slowing, and then stilling, he waited for her answer. "Please, Slate, don't stop," came from the shadows.

He sighed in relief, and then kissed and nibbled up the inside of one soft thigh, taking in the scent and flavor of her skin; her hips were moving impatiently on the bed as he moved to pay the same attention to the other. He framed the apex of her thighs with his hands, using his thumbs to stroke the crease where they met her lower lips, but deliberately not touching her most sensitive places. He smiled gently as he heard the quiet sound of disappointment she made, holding her hips to the bed as she attempted to arch up against his touch.

Running his hands across her belly, he spanned her smooth skin from hip-to-hip, stroking and kissing along that line, and then back downward, finding no fabric barrier in his way. "You took off your panties," he groaned harshly against her, rubbing and dragging his nose across her belly hip-to-hip again, then kissing and licking along the crease between her hip and her thigh.

Her fingers were uncertain when she first reached down, tentatively touching his head, then she pulled her fingers gently through his hair. She tugged at his hair lightly, cautiously urging him. He let her guide him, angling his tongue towards her clit, but just avoiding the engorged bud peeking out of its hood.

He kissed and licked again, drawing his nose through those beautiful curls, dragging in a deep breath of her scent, musky and rich. She was so soft and needy, and he loved how she moved, pressing her hips up against him.

She sighed loudly, then called his name softly as he brought his hands down, never losing touch with her skin. He slid his roughened, callused thumbs gently along either side of her clit, separating her folds and following them with his tongue, getting closer and closer to what he wanted so badly. He ran his thumbs down, circling her opening and dipping one tip inside just as his tongue found her clit.

His cock twitched as he listened to the sounds she made deep in her throat while he tasted her. He nibbled and licked the nubbin of flesh and nerves, circling it with the tip of his tongue and flicking it hard, then dragging his teeth across it and gentling the sting with a soft laving of his tongue. Keeping his mouth on her, he let her feel his lips move against her as he asked, "Do you like this, Essa? God, you taste so sweet. Does this feel good?"

He kept kissing and working at her, dipping his thumb in and out of her entrance while waiting on her response...because he simply couldn't get enough. He could not get enough of her. He'd never enjoyed going down on a woman like this; it had always been a way to learn their responses, but this...this was different. Fuck, he loved how she tasted, and he felt like he could do this all fucking night if she would simply keep making those noises.

"Yeesss," she groaned, drawing in a deep breath and hitching her hips up as he slid his thick middle finger deep inside her. He was thrusting deep and fast with that one finger, while his mouth continued to work her sensitive folds and nub.

Pulling back for a second, he asked, moving his mouth against her again, "Is this what you want, little girl?" He flicked hard with his tongue, then brought it down to her opening and wound it around his finger as it slid in and out of her, licking the wetness greedily. "Do you want my mouth on you? My hands on you?"

Pausing in his assault for a second, he blew a cool stream of air against her drenched heat and she groaned loudly, her hips pumping up against his face, grinding and circling. She called out to him, tightening her fingers in his hair, "Oh God, yes, please, Slate." Her inner muscles were tightening and gripping his finger, and his cock jerked against his belly again, twitching hard as he talked to her.

"Baby, you are greedy, aren't you? Want my fingers deep inside you?" He pulled his finger out, and slipped back in with the addition of a second finger. He pushed hard and deep, using them to spread her apart inside, feeling the tightness and grip of that so-soft flesh. Pressing his thumb hard on her clit, he teased it out from under the tiny hood as he licked the folds beside it, lapping up her taste and wetness. She was tensing under his touch, her thighs tightening on either side of his head, so he called softly, "Are you going to come now, Essa? Go ahead. Come, baby, for me."

He waited for her release, unable to see, but feeling it through every fiber of his being. Her orgasm swept over her, hips jerking and rising against his mouth and fingers. His hair was pulled painfully as her fingers tightened and released in his hair, holding his mouth hard against her as she rounded her shoulders up off the mattress.

The sounds she made were so beautiful; she was unrestrained in her passion, and he loved everything he felt and heard. He whispered, mouth still against her pussy, "Oh, baby, yes...God, yes." He kept the rhythm of his mouth and fingers in and against her, slowing and caressing her until she crumpled bonelessly back down to the bed. Sagging against the bulkhead wall, her fingers were smoothing his hair back from his forehead now, instead of convulsively using it to tug him tighter and closer against her.

How could he walk away from this? How could he set her aside? *Fuck me*, he thought, *I can't do this to her. I have to stop. Please, God, give me strength.*

He gave her a final soft kiss against her sex, and slowly slid his fingers from inside her, licking them clean as he caressed the inside of her thigh with his other hand. His breath was slowing along with hers as he sat back away from the edge of the bunk, gaining room enough to stand. He carelessly shoved his cock back into his jeans, buttoning them tightly against his painful erection.

Stepping back towards the bunk, he pushed her legs together, shifting her sideways on the mattress. Slate climbed in behind her, snugging an arm tightly around her waist. He pulled her back against him, tucking her into him and tangling their legs together. She put her hands on top of his arm, rubbing slowly up and down. She sighed deeply and wriggled her ass, causing him to groan when she pressed against the front of his jeans and his still-enthusiastic cock.

"Slate? Are you okay?" she asked sleepily.

"Shhhh, little girl, go to sleep. Everything is good; everything's fine. " Kissing her hair, he reached and pulled the blanket over to cover them, and then he quietly laid his head down on the pillow beside hers. He kissed her hair again, snuggling her and hitching one leg up with his. "Shhhhh."

***

He couldn't ever remember being this angry at anything before...not his dad dying too early, or his mom's slow degeneration into the hell she created for herself. Nothing compared to this. Slate was standing outside the trailer the next morning and he was pissed—really fucking pissed—at himself. After caring for the gelding, he settled himself to wait and think.

He'd betrayed both Mason and Mica's trust in him last night. Essa was just fucking eighteen, a little girl, just like he kept trying to remind himself. Beyond that, she was family, Mica's family.

He had to tell Mason, and that would break him. If he lost his family, he didn't know what he'd do, and this was an offence that could...should, yeah...*should* get his rocker cut the fuck off. He'd been in such a rush to taste her last night he hadn't considered things, like what the club would say. At least he hadn't fucked her; he'd stopped short of that.

Feeling the trailer move, he assumed she was up finally. He still had no idea what to say to her. He couldn't let her believe this would lead to anything, but he didn't want to make her embarrassed at what had happened. It had been beautiful, but he had to be clear this was a one-time thing, not something that could repeat. Turning to face the living quarters door as it pushed open, he tried to keep his face impassive.

She stepped out of the trailer and smiled politely at him, reaching over to pet the horse. "Did you eat yet?" she asked. He felt his mouth drop open, but couldn't form words. She blushed deeply, the color moving swiftly up her neck and into her cheeks when she realized what she'd said and clarified, "Breakfast, I meant. Did you eat breakfast yet?" She tucked her chin down and turned, walking quickly away from the trailer, calling over her shoulder, "Gonna see what the stands have ready; I'm hungry."

Shaking himself, Slate called, "Essa, you okay?"

She turned around, considering him for a second, and then she stalked back towards him, "Yes, I'm okay, thanks for asking. So...let's get this out of the way now, okay?" She came to a stop in front of him, and put her hands on her hips. "Slate, that was real sweet last night, but I have to focus on my competition this season, so it's not gonna happen again." She lightly shrugged in an attempt to be casual. "In fact, if we could agree to not say anything to Mica about what happened, I'd appreciate it. I don't want her to worry about me getting into trouble with the first hot guy I see. Now, I'm hungry. I'm going to get food. Do you want anything?"

She turned on her heel and walked away from him, heading to the fairgrounds. Slate walked fast, catching up to her with his long strides. He waited until he was beside her to answer, "I could eat," he said, pausing for a beat and watching her stumble a little, "breakfast."

His phone rang near lunchtime, and he felt the blood leave his face when he saw the caller ID come through—Mason was calling. Slate and Essa were sitting in the shade beside the trailer, having a comfortable conversation as they watched the other contestants working their horses.

He answered the phone with, "Yeah," and heard Mason ask, "Slate, got a report for me, brother? Was it quiet last night after I left with Mica?"

Slate responded, "It was good—quiet, but good." Fuck him, he had just lied to his Prez, his brother, his family...the only family he'd ever really had. He closed his eyes, feeling sick to his stomach. Mason was talking, but Slate couldn't hear him through the roaring in his own ears, and he asked, "What was that, Prez? I didn't catch it."

Mason laughed low, and repeated himself, "Slate, I think you should stick with her, travel for a couple of weeks with her. We still don't know where Nelms is. Steve's looking, but he hasn't found anything yet." *God no, no, no*...he thought, shaking his head. He listened to Mason continue, "I've reached out to MCs along the route, and they are watching and will be a resource if needed." Fuck, he couldn't do this.

Keeping his eyes closed, Slate warned Mason, "Not sure I'm the right one for this, Prez. I got something to tell you." He felt Essa land a hard kick to the side of his leg, and opened his eyes to see her shaking her head frantically at him, her wide eyes in her white face silently willing him to not say anything else.

Mason barked out a clipped, "What?" and Slate closed his eyes again before continuing.

"Last night, I messed up, Prez, with Essa."

He heard a heavy, disappointed sigh on the line, then just one word, "Bad?"

"Enough," Slate responded in kind, knowing Mason would get what he was saying.

There was a ringing silence on the line for the longest time, then Mason asked, "Not telling Mica then?"

Slate gritted his teeth and took in a sharp breath; Mason wasn't asking for his colors, and that was fucking amazing given his transgression. "Not if I can help it."

Mason spoke again, using the familiar club address intentionally, making sure that Slate knew the full extent of his responsibilities, "*Brother*, if you don't go, if we send someone else, she'll know something is up. You better get it the fuck under control and fucking keep it that way."

Slate opened his eyes and saw Essa looking at him with tears welling in her beautiful eyes, slowly shaking her head back and forth as her mouth and face tightened in sadness. "I got this, Prez. I won't fuck up again," Slate was reassuring all three of them with that statement. "It won't happen again."

As fast as he hung up the phone, Essa's sense of betrayal and sadness turned into anger, and she yelled loudly at him, "I cannot believe you did that. You are such an asshole."

He expected more from her, and so he waited for a second before he responded. He needed to explain, and wanted to be sure she was listening, "Are you finished? It was Mason, and he doesn't want to say anything; he won't say anything, but he's my *Brother*, the president of my club, and I have to respect that. He has to know when I fuck up, when he can't depend on me, but no one will tell Mica unless you do. I promise. Sorry, little girl, it seems you are stuck with me for a while. I'll be traveling with you for a couple of weeks." He shook his head, stood, and took a long step away from the trailer, thinking this would be a long ass trip.

***

Fourteen long days later, Slate smiled grimly as he remembered that prophetic thought. It had indeed been a long couple of weeks, long and hard in a myriad of ways. Essa quickly got over her anger about him still traveling with her, and she determined that in order to run him off, torture was her best weapon.

Every single night they spent in the trailer, he took the floor, lying on top of the blankets as he had that first night. But unlike that night, he didn't tease conversation out of her, because she was otherwise occupied. He would hear the shifting of her clothing against the sheets, and then that soft gasp when her fingers first found her clit.

Every night, he had to listen to her touch herself while she was only a few inches away from him. He would hear her breathing change and quicken as she moved towards her climax, feeling the trailer shift slightly as her legs stirred restlessly against the mattress. Her soft panting as she rode the wave back down, and then he would hear Essa's husky voice taunt, "Sweet dreams, Slate," making sure he knew exactly what she was doing.

Several nights, they stopped at a hotel and he paid for a room. He would escort her to the room, and then return to the trailer, claiming the bunk for the night. That first night, he hadn't counted on how the pillows and mattress would smell of her, the soft, sweet scent from her shampoo, and the musky scent of her sex on the sheets. He had not slept well that night...not at all.

She found every opportunity to torture him, even in simple things, like when he used the hotel bathroom for a shower. There were a number of times he'd exited the bathroom to see her in the middle of the bed, sitting cross-legged in a tight, little tank top and sheer panties. She would simply sit and grin at him, knowing it aroused him to see her so nearly unclothed, her shoulders and arms bare, her legs and hips spread open for inspection, barely covered.

He'd finally gotten wise and now confiscated both room keycards before showering. That lack of access kept her somewhat at bay, and gave him a few minutes of peaceful solitude. He shook his head, at least until she figured out a new way to play with him. He spent half of every day painfully hard, and the other half, he was angry with frustration. Mason called regularly to get updates, but had shown continued trust in Slate by not questioning his behavior again. When Essa brushed past him in the trailer, or pushed between him and the gelding, he held onto that trust in his mind, trying to do the honorable thing. She was often amused by his restraint, and would grin at him in a way that told him she knew how close to the edge she could bring him.

Carrying a bucket of water back to the trailer, he thought about last night and something that'd happened. He'd woken in the middle of the night to a light playing slowly over the ceiling, shining up from the mattress. He heard Essa's soft voice whispering under her breath, and when he listened closely, it sounded like names and numbers.

The light paused and held on a picture of a beautiful young girl with long, dark hair caught in a side braid. It showed her mounted on top of a gigantic sorrel; the horse was so big that the saddle on his back almost looked like a toy. Slate thought the girl pictured riding it seemed much too small to control such an animal.

The camera had caught them as they rounded a barrel, frozen in time as the horse turned back hard on his hocks. Both sets of eyes were already looking ahead, completely focused on the next obstacle. Essa whispered, "Michaela Trenton Scott, The Governor, 1997, winning junior nationals in Vegas," and Slate realized she was naming the people and horses in the pictures.

Now, in the light of day, he stepped into the living quarters, and looked up and around until he found the picture of Mica. He smiled at how young and determined she looked in that picture, but he could see hints of the woman she would become too. This picture was taken before Nelms had tainted her life, before he took so much from her.

Slate's smile faded away, thinking about his conversation with Mason earlier. Mason had growled, "Steve got a lock, Slate; we got a fucking lock on the bastard. His stock company is contracted for the Texarkana Rodeo, just like we hoped. There's no chatter about him on the grid, and strangely, no chatter about you on the circuit. Nothing to warn him off, so we think he's going to show, brother."

"Fuck me," he'd said softly, "you really think he's coming here, Prez? It's a small rodeo, smaller than the last three have been for sure. He can't hide here, man; it's pretty wide open, and all the contestants know Essa. I hope the fuck he does; I'm ready to hit my own bed, man. This fucking babysitting is tiresome. I'll be ready. I *am* ready."

This was the last event before Essa headed back home for a couple weeks, just outside Longview, Texas. They'd pull out in the morning, he'd see her safely back to her parents' place, and then hop a plane home. Home, sweet fucking home.

Sighing heavily, Slate looked back up at the picture of Mica one more time, and had turned to step out of the trailer when he heard Essa's voice on the other side of the wall. "Molly, I'm telling you—you can do this, sis." Her voice slid a half-octave up. "No, you can't tell Mom and Dad, not yet." Molly was Mica's little sister; he wondered what the fuck was going on with her.

He heard Essa sigh, and then heard her slide along the metal as she leaned her back against the trailer. "It's only been five weeks; how can you even know for sure? Molly, hold tight. You can do this; I know you can. You are one of the strongest women I know, and once I tell Mica, she can help us." There was a pause, but he couldn't make out any words from the other end. "No, I didn't get a chance; she has like an army of bikers that hover around her all the time. I'm going to call her tonight, and I'll be home tomorrow."

She must've shifted and pushed herself upright, because he felt the trailer rock a little. "Nelms hasn't been at any of the events yet, but I'm looking for him to show here. Molly, I swear to God—I'll kill him if I see him." Her voice had dropped, the tone terse and heavily accented in her vehemence as she talked over Molly's voice, which had risen to a shriek Slate could nearly make out through the phone. "I will too goddamn well kill him. He can't get away with this." Essa was silent, and he heard her footsteps move alongside the trailer, so he stepped out just as she rounded the vehicle.

Startled, she looked up at him. "Hey, I'm gonna warm up for practice." Slate was still mulling over what he had overheard, and tried to figure out where Essa fit into everything. Clearly, something had happened to Molly, and the Rebels had inadvertently gotten in the way of what Essa had intended to tell Mica. Just as clearly, it was Nelms at the root of the problem, as he'd been for so long.

He looked at Essa, reading her lying intent in her face, and he thought it was time to pull back the veil a little. "Little girl," he held on those words for a bare second, waiting for her to focus fully on him, "if I find Nelms first, you won't have to do a fucking thing." She paled, and must have realized he overheard her conversation. Slate watched the war written on her face as she decided how to proceed with him, with trust or lies. He knew which he preferred, but wanted it to be her decision, so he waited silently and patiently.

"He's going to be here," she clipped. "I feel it."

Slate nodded proudly at her, knowing she'd made a conscious decision to trust him. "Good girl. Yes, he's contracted to bring the bulls in tonight. I have reinforcements on the way, because I believe he's going to show too, but before I let you get on Breezy," he padded slowly towards her, "I want you to tell me what he did to Mica's sister. No, not want, I *need* you to tell me." He reached out, wrapping his hand gently around her arm above her elbow, urging her towards the living quarters of the trailer. This was the first time he'd touched her in days, and the heat of their contact seared him. He ground out through his gritted teeth, "You're going to sit on your ass until I'm convinced I know everything you do."

She struggled and squirmed for a minute in an effort to break his hold, and then, when she couldn't, she walked alongside him with a peevish attitude, asking, "Do you always get what you want, Slate?"

He barked out loud laughter, surprising her. "Oh hell no, little girl, not by a long shot. Now start talkin'."

It was hours later when the bull trucks finally pulled in, but without Ray Nelms. He didn't show, and his drivers said they were surprised, because he had intended to come to Texarkana. An Arkansas chapter of the Rebels had come out in force in response to Mason's request for assistance, and Slate spent a bit of time talking to the president and members who'd come down from Little Rock.

He arranged for food while he and the bikers discussed Nelms, making sure they were all on the same page with the intended outcome. Once they were all comfortable, he asked them to scout the drivers and locals who might know Nelms, in order to come up with a list of locations where he might be staying. He thanked the Little Rock members, gripping and shaking forearms with the group, feeling good about this chapter having their backs. He'd been surprised but pleased to see Bear riding with them. Between him and Bear, they'd have a positive report for Mason, and the local president knew it; he was proud of how his members had acquitted themselves.

Slate pulled Essa into his side as they stood and watched the bikers pull out as quietly as their rumbling pipes would allow. He looked down at her, and lifted her chin with one finger. "You gotsta make a call, little girl. It's time to talk to Mica." She drew in a broken breath, and she buried her face into his chest with a sob. He lowered his cheek to the top of her head, wrapped his arms around her, and held her gently against himself.

Speaking gently to her, he deliberately roused her protective feelings towards her cousins. "I know it's hard, baby, but Molly needs her sister, and Mica has to know what happened, but she has to have some space to deal with her own shit before she dumps that on Molly by mistake. You are the only one who can help guide them through this.

"Essa, I shit you not, talking to Mica like this—now, and telling her over the phone—it might seem cold, but it's not. You don't know the shit Nelms did to Mica, and that's her tale to tell, not mine, but I guarantee she's going to feel guilty for bringing this shit home. Her shit seeped out all over Molly, and that's going to fucking eat at her. I know her, and I know her heart. Give her a day, and she'll sort her own crap out, especially with Mason there to help her, and then she can help Molly with everything else."

Standing there holding her, he called Mason, saying simply, "No Nelms, got the brothers looking in his hidey holes. If he's here, we'll find him, Prez." Mason grumbled back at him, cursing Nelms and his ability to avoid them when they could've taken care of fucking business.

He interrupted Mason, and heard his attention snap fully onto Slate as he grasped the importance, "Mason, I need you to go to Mica's and be with her. She's gonna get a fucked up call from Essa, and it's bad news about Mica's sis, Molly. Nelms is involved, and she's gonna need you, Prez. She's gonna need us all."

Mason growled underneath his breath, "On my fucking way, give me two minutes," and the connection closed, leaving dead air in Slate's ear.

He pulled Essa gently into the sleeping quarters, settling her on the bed and sitting quietly behind her. He kept one hand on her neck, merely anchoring her with the touch and warmth of his hand. He pulled out his phone, dialing Mica and first making sure Mason had made it over to her house.

Once he was reassured, he handed the phone to Essa, and listened as she launched into the bare bones of what had happened. She got the worst of it out into the open, so Mica could begin to understand, and Essa bravely stayed on the phone with her as the rollercoaster of emotions swept through her cousin. Nelms had drugged and raped Molly, and she was nearly six weeks pregnant with the result of that rape.

Then, it was time to bring Molly onto the line, and Slate remained sitting on the bunk behind Essa. He was slowly caressing and rubbing the back of her neck as she sobbed on a three-way call with the two of them. She helped fill in the background she'd been able to dig up on Nelms, which wasn't anything more than Slate had already known.

Mica sounded devastated, and Slate was glad Mason was there with her. When Essa handed him back the phone, he put his arm around her tightly and scooped her across and into his lap. He settled her there, her legs draping across his thighs with his chin on top of her head as he felt her crying hard against his chest. She was wound tight and had wrapped her fingers around handfuls of his shirt, holding on with desperate strength. Lifting the phone to his ear, he grunted out, "Yeah?"

Mason responded to him in a low, pained voice, "Did you hear? Did you get that, Slate?"

"Yeah, Prez, I got it all," he breathed out across the top of her head, softly stroking her hair as she sobbed.

Mason told him, "Dig is booking tickets now. I'm bringing Mica. We'll meet you in Longview when we get in; I'll text you where." He sighed. "How's the girl?"

Slate looked down at Essa, noting how she was still clutching his shirt to her face as she sobbed and hiccupped against him. "Better, now that she's not alone in this." He heard an approving noise from Mason, and hung up the phone.

"Shhhh, baby girl. The hard part is done, and you were there for your family. You done good, babe," he said, trying to calm her. "No one could have done better. I'm proud of you, Essa." He softly kissed the top of her head, wrapping both arms around her as he scooted back across the bunk, leaning against the bulkhead. "Shhhh," he soothed, holding her like that as she cried herself to sleep, her face nestled against his neck in the darkness.

The next morning, Slate woke up with a start, jerking his eyes wide open as he realized she was still sitting in his lap. He shifted her slowly, easing her down onto the mattress and arranging her limbs before he covered her in a blanket. Stepping outside, he walked over to the gelding, checked on him, and then went in search of coffee on the fairgrounds. He passed and waved at other competitors, and grabbed a couple of breakfast burritos, along with the coffee he needed so badly. Back at the trailer, he knocked until he heard her answer, and then opened the door to pass in the food and drink.

She had only one event today, and he began packing things up to be ready to leave as soon as she was done with the competition. Before long, they were driving west and south towards Tyler, where they'd meet Tug outside the airport. He'd caught an early morning flight down, with Mason and Mica coming in on the first afternoon flight. Mason wanted the four of them to talk as they were heading to Essa's folks' place, and the plan was for Tug to take the rig and gelding home.

Sitting in the back seat of the truck Mason had rented, Essa reached over and took Slate's hand, sliding her fingers in-between his and holding on tightly. Mica didn't want to talk about Nelms or Molly, so the conversation flowed back and forth between the seats casually for most of the drive. Mason and Mica wound each other up into a fierce argument, which left them all sitting on the side of the road listening to a much needed air-clearing confession. What Mason and Mica disclosed floored Slate because it sounded very much like they'd slept together, and he thought it sounded as if they both harbored some guilt over the encounter.

Their palpable pain filled the words they threw at each other, but looking from one to the other he could see their love and affection clearly. In direct contrast with what he saw and knew, he heard them recite all the valid reasons they could never be together...and those reasons resonated with him, making him think again about Essa, sitting beside him, still holding his hand. He held his breath, listening to their words, and the silence that followed, hearing their harsh breathing that sounded in the truck cab before Mason reached out, enfolding Mica in his arms. He laughed silently at Essa, she'd broken the tension with a funny comment, helping bridge the moment and allowing the group of them to move past the revelations.

Pulling into the lane that lead to the ranch, they were met with a large group of people, mostly family. Mica's father was there, which was an unpleasant surprise, since he wasn't welcome on the ranch. Mica confronted him, with both Mason and Slate backing her up. He left, along with her brother, and Slate watched as Mason fairly vibrated with rage towards those men.

Mica took her aunt and uncle inside to talk about what had happened to Molly. He stayed with Essa, and they worked alongside each other to unload the trailer, settling all her gear into the barn and tack room. He smiled a little when he realized they were working in quiet tandem, not needing words for most tasks, knowing and anticipating what the other would do next.

He bunked with the ranch hands that night, soliciting stories of Essa growing up from them, and laughing to himself about some of the scrapes she'd gotten herself into, like the time she decided to take the tractor to school, but wanted to take a shortcut across a field and got stuck in a creek. The lead hand had been proud of her, because she'd gotten herself unstuck using a chain and winch, but she'd missed nearly an entire day of school and was grounded for a month.

There were lots of grins from around the room as they trotted out escapade after escapade that she'd gotten up to—moonlight rides, sneaking out of the house to meet her friends, trading a cow for a car three years before she could legally drive, skinny dipping in the stock pond, stink bombing the teachers' lounge at school, a few moonshine stories, and how she'd talked her younger brother into jumping off the barn roof one summer, which resulted in a broken arm. Those were all from when she was younger, and then as she gained focus in her life, the stories changed.

The hands all talked about how good she was with the horses, and listed champions she'd ridden and trained. They thought she'd probably get enough points on the circuit this year to get to junior nationals in Vegas. She'd nearly made it last year, but had broken her hand the last few weeks of competition.

Even though she was riding again the same day, the cast on her hand had her off-balance, and it had showed in her performance. It was a close competition, and even though she'd learned to compensate within a couple of days, by then, she'd lost too many points and couldn't make up the ground. One of her brothers laughed and complained about how she'd come home cussing a blue streak about the cast, but gotten grounded for only a week that time.

Slate wanted to know more; he couldn't get enough of the stories about her. He kept steering the conversation back to Essa every time it started to drift, and thought he was doing a good job of covering up his interest until he saw Tug looking at him with a considering gaze. Time to drop it, probably, but he'd gotten some interesting information. She'd only had one serious boyfriend the hands knew about, but when she'd caught him with another girl on the circuit, she dumped the boy and his horse on the side of the road in Oklahoma. A competitor who put her career above everything else, she had skipped out on proms, parties, and even graduation in order to compete.

As he lay back on the bunk, listening to the rustle of the men in the beds around him, Slate thought back over the stories, and saw a clear thread running through them all. Essa was a self-sufficient, confident young woman who didn't like asking for anything. She wanted to make her own way, and knew what she wanted from life. She was driven, passionate, caring, and he thought he could love her.

***

The next event on the girls' calendar was a couple days away in Houston, and the whole group stayed in Texas and went along. Mason was sticking close to Mica most of the time, as he normally did, and Slate and Tug were tasked with keeping track of the girls. None of them really expected Nelms to show now, but they were vigilant anyway.

"Slate," he heard, and turned to see Mason looking at him. He gave a head jerk, and Slate followed him away from the trailer and people. "Daniel's coming into town, man. His hockey team is doing an exhibition game, and he was already planning on being here. I called and talked to him about Mica, and he is willing to see her." Mason closed his eyes briefly, and scrubbed at the back of his neck with one large hand.

"She doesn't know he's coming, and I don't want to tell her yet, but I gotta head to the hotel and pick him up. Stay here with the girls; Tug will be with Mica. I'll call you when I get back to the fairgrounds to find out where she is, okay?" Looking more unsure than Slate had ever seen him, Mason lifted his eyes to Slate's face. "Is this the right thing to do, man? It hurts so fucking much it has to be right, right?" he asked in an anguished voice.

Slate shook his head as he answered, "Prez, I can't tell you that. I know you love her, but she's not club material, and we both know it. You called that a long time ago. She's only now putting herself back together; the life in the club would tear that all back down again, but you have to live in your head, brother. If you can see your way clear to keeping her, then push Daniel out of the fucking picture. If you can't see that—if you can't keep her—then you should let her go. She's a fucking treasure, and that shit is the truth."

Slate stared as Mason turned to look at Mica. She tipped her head back, laughing at something Tug said, and Mason's eyes darkened as he took her in, moving from tips of her cowboy boots, to the dark hair on the top of her head. His face tightened, he rolled his neck and shoulders, and then turned without a word and stalked away. Slate watched him until he went out of sight between the trucks and trailers, and then turned to walk back to the rig.

Tug and Mica went for a walk through the fairgrounds, while Slate, Molly, and Essa headed over to the local firemen's fundraising booth, looking for dinner. They sat and ate, laughing at the stories each girl took turns telling about the people they saw walking through the fairgrounds. This was a tradition they had with Mica, it seemed, and they made up more and more outrageous stories about the strangers they saw. Slate's phone buzzed, and he picked it up to see a text from Mason: *Pulling in now—where is she?*

He quickly typed back, *Looking*, and told the girls they needed to head back.

Walking up to the rig, he saw Tug sitting on the ground next to the trailer. There was one horse tied to the outside of it, and the back gate was down. Tug's hair was dark in the evening light, and with shock Slate realized he was covered in blood. He pushed Essa and Molly behind him, crouching down beside Tug. Essa gasped and reached out a hand, then pushed into the living quarters and grabbed up something from the floor, pressing it against the back of his head.

Slate and Molly heard the scream at the same time, their eyes meeting for a second before they scrambled to their feet. He yelled at Essa to stay with Tug, and was a half-dozen strides behind Molly when he thought he saw her stumble, going halfway to the ground and coming up with an odd twisting motion.

There was a yell from in front of them, and he saw a woman on the ground in front of a man. The man was holding a hand to the side of his head, and Slate saw Molly stoop and scoop something off the ground again, coming up with that same odd, twisting motion. There was another yell as the man clapped a hand to his forehead, and then Slate saw Mason running past as Molly yelled and hit the man with another rock.

Mason tackled the man, and Slate recognized Nelms' face as they went down together. Daniel was right behind Mason, and he stopped next to Mica, who was still sprawled on the ground, clawing and scrambling away from the fight behind her.

Slate's breath stopped, "Essa," he breathed, and rounded on his heel, running back to her where she was crouched by Tug. "Baby, are you okay?" he asked, and she nodded, handing Tug a bottle of water. He was sitting on his own now, holding a bandana to his head to staunch the blood flow.

"Mica, where is Mica, Slate?" Essa asked, "Is she okay? Please tell me she's okay. Oh, please."

He reached out a hand and stroked slowly up and down her arm. "She's okay; Mason and Daniel are there. Molly saved her. She's okay." They helped Tug move from the ground to the entry of the living quarters, which had been trashed. Slate looked up and saw Mica, Molly, and Daniel walking towards them, all huddled together in the middle of the road.

He stood, headed towards them, asking Mica, "You okay, princess? You look like shit on toast. Gonna go help Mason take out the trash, but I'll be right back." He waited for her nod, and then turned to Daniel. "Ice, ibuprofen, clean her up—you take care of her, Daniel, or you answer to me." He moved around them to walk quickly towards Mason and the unmoving Ray Nelms, stretched out face-first in the dirt. "Prez, you okay?" he asked low and quiet, looking around, but not seeing much of an audience.

Mason looked up at him from where he straddled the unconscious man. "Gonna end this, Slate. Gonna end it here. Walk away if you want, or if you don't agree, but this piece of shit isn't going to get another chance."

Slate shook his head. "No, I got your back, brother. He's fucking evil on earth and needs to go away. How do you want to play this? Because I'm in. I'm so in. If you don't want this on your hands, then stand the fuck up and let me over there."

Shaking his head, Mason thought for a second. "You have connections. Make a call. We're going to need a pickup and drop. See how fast they can get someone here; make sure they bring a cage, not just bikes." He looked down at Nelms lying there with blood crusting the dirt on his face into whirls and lines. "We need something to secure him. Go see what you can find, brother."

Heading back towards the rig, he saw Mica and Daniel beside it, standing close to each other with his hand at her waist. Slate paused for a second next to Mica, telling her quietly, "Get the horses out of the trailer, leave the ramp down," and then he was past them, looking into the living quarters and spying the roll of duct tape he needed. Grabbing it up, he turned and headed back out to where Mason was now crouched next to Nelms.

They used the tape to bind his hands and wrists together, and then taped his legs together, making it easier to pick him up and move him. Slate checked over his shoulder; it looked like Mica had things moving, and they'd be able to get Nelms out of sight soon.

He slid his phone from his jeans pocket, and pressed a couple of buttons to bring up his contacts. Hitting a number he hadn't called in a while, he wondered if it was even still good, until he heard a laughing feminine voice answer, "Ray's Crab Shack, need some crabs?"

His heart eased a little at the joy in that voice—this had been one decision he made that was good and right. "Lottie, it's Andy. How the hell ya doing?"

He jerked the phone away from his head as she squealed loudly, saying, "Holy cow, Andy! It's been forever. Randi, put that down; it belongs to your brother."

Slate heard a child's chattering voice from the background, and the beginning of a heartbroken wail. "Hey, Lottie, is Blackie around?"

Her voice got quiet, asking, "Club business?"

Slate nodded, saying, "Yeah," into the phone.

"Blackie, baby, Andy's on the phone, needs to talk business," she called, her voice moving away from the phone, then returning to the handset with, "He'll be right here. Good to hear from you, Andy. Give Blackie an address, and I'll send pictures of the kiddos. Randi hits middle school next year, and she's grown so much. Tater and Possum are both in third grade; they look just like their daddy. Punkin is nearly two, and," he heard satisfaction in her voice, "we're expecting again."

He grinned; she sounded so happy and complete. "I'll do that, Lottie; I'll make sure he has my address. You guys make cute kids. It's good to hear your voice too." He paused in the silence on the phone. "This is Blackie, isn't it?"

A deep laughter came through the phone. "Fucker, you gotta start calling her Peaches, or you gonna be Rabbit all your fucking life."

Slate said tightly, "Got some business, Blackie. Need some assistance in Houston—you got anyone down this way? You'll own a Rebel marker if so, on my word as Slate, Lieutenant of the Rebel Wayfarers, mother chapter from Chicago."

More laughter came from the phone. "Don't need no fucking marker, Slate from Chicago. I still owe you my life for bringing Peaches back to me, so no fucking talk of markers. Yeah, I got boys down there. Where abouts you need that help?"

"We're at the fairgrounds down here; we caught that motherfucker we've been hunting for years. Need a cage pickup, and then a *final* dropoff, man. Tell me now if that's too big a thing to ask, and I'll go away...figure it out on my end." Slate held his breath for a second, waiting on Blackie to back out.

"This your number, brother?"

That short sentence told him everything he needed to know. "Yeah, call me back with info, I can give you the row and space we'll be waiting in the competitors' parking," he said on a rushing breath out. "Thanks, brother," he finished, and the call was disconnected.

"Got assistance on the way, Prez. It's a personal favor, no club marker. This is me for her; you got what I mean?" he looked over at Mason, who nodded once. "Blackie is a good man." Slate ran his hands roughly through his hair. "His woman was nearly mine, Mason. She could have been my Mica, but she needed him, and he loves her. This is from me for Mica. He'll call me back in a few. Let's get things taken care of, yeah?" Slate stood, reaching down to pull Mason to his feet, and together, they stooped and grabbed Nelms' arms, lifting him.

"Fuck me," Slate muttered as he and Mason stood with Nelms between them. He saw Essa was facing Mica, and her wide eyes were frozen on him over Mica's shoulder. She moved her eyes between Mica and him, and then turned and walked away with Molly. Slate called out to Mica softly, "Don't turn around, princess. Just give me a minute here."

They manhandled Nelms' limp body into the trailer, which rocked and creaked as they moved inside to lay their burden down. Stepping out, Slate closed the gate and locked the ramp into place. Mica asked, "Okay now?" and Slate responded with, "Yeah."

The men all stood near Mica, except for Tug, who watched quietly from his place near the trailer. Mica looked at them a little frantically, finally whispering, "What do y'all want from me? You are all looking at me, and I don't know what you want me to do."

Slate laughed without humor. "I think we're checking to see if you are gonna freak, princess." She shook her head at that, muttering, "No freakage, Slate. It feels...I dunno...final—like it's over, after so many years of looking over my shoulder and not sleeping. It's over, finally. My face hurts, though."

He looked at Daniel, thinking that one of his tattoos was pretty appropriate right now, 'Three can keep a secret if two are dead', because Daniel looked like the weak fucking link here. He wasn't aware of the lengths to which the club had gone over the years to keep Mica safe. This was simply an extension of what they'd already done, but one word from the hockey player to the wrong ears and everything could go to shit. "Are you with us, man?" he asked, and watched as Daniel had a physical reaction to the question, shivering and folding his arms tightly across his chest as he nodded.

Mason stepped away, calling Blackie to extend his thanks, and Slate edged over towards the trailer, wanting to make sure no one saw anything. He remembered the mess in the living quarters, and moved up to start sorting through the girls' clothes, putting the few clean things on a bunk, and separating the rest into a wash pile.

Slate's phone rang, and he answered it, seeing Blackie's name on the screen, "Row fifteen, space three-oh-one," and waited on confirmation before hanging up. About a half-hour later, a dark van drove up, with three members of Blackie's club inside. Slate stood, walking over to greet them. "You Slate?" came the question from the leader of the group.

"Yeah, Slate, Chicago Rebel Wayfarers. This is my president, Mason, and our Sergeant at Arms, Tug."

The leader introduced himself, "JD," and then gestured with a thumb at the two men at his back, "Mouse and Devil. Y'all are a long way from Chicago, man. Welcome to fucking Texas."

Getting straight to business, Mouse spoke up from where he stood behind JD, "Blackie said you had some baggage we'd be happy to take care of for you. He didn't specify the condition, though. Got any preferences?"

"Yeah, end of the line would be good, man." Mason stepped up beside Slate and continued, "Not particular on the method of arrival, long as the destination is the same." The three men nodded, glancing at each other.

"You got it," said JD. "Devil, situate the van, please, sir. Let's get our baggage and get gone."

Slate moved one of the horses to block the view from across the way, while Nelms was retrieved from inside the trailer and bundled into the van. Mouse raised a finger to his brow, nodded at Mason, and then Devil drove the van away into the night.

16 - Out of mind

Days later, Slate was back in Chicago, trying to settle into some kind of routine. He'd been crashing in his room at the clubhouse, not wanting to face the quiet in his house. One of the club mammas had gone over and straightened up, chucking food from the fridge, tidying and getting a layer of dust off everything, so it was clean. But, he found that the house was too damn big after weeks of living squeezed into the tiny quarters at the front of Essa's trailer.

She was constantly on his mind, and it didn't help she sent him texts and pictures all the time. She sent pictures of Mason and Mica, her and Mica, her and Molly, and finally, one of only her he saved onto his phone. Someone else had taken the picture, and her hair was a little wild, curling out from underneath her hat, which was shoved tightly down on her head. Her brown eyes were sparkling, and she had the widest smile on her face. Slate reached out a finger, trailing it down the screen as he closed his eyes.

He wouldn't do this, shouldn't want her...couldn't need her like this. He was not the right kind of guy for her, and he wouldn't be the reason for her getting hurt, but he kept the picture on his phone, and he sent her one of him clowning for the camera.

Sitting behind the bar in Jackson's, he looked up as the outside door opened, letting in a blustery wind. It was early spring in Chicago, and the Windy City was living up to its name. Slate grinned as he recognized the men walking in, Jason Spencer and Gary Millson; they were from Daniel's hockey team, and were just rowdy enough to be fun without needing too much intervention.

"Hey, man," he called to Jason, watching as they altered their direction to come to where he was sitting. Slate held out a hand, stood, and shook with them as they all settled onto barstools.

"What y'all doin' in Jackson's on a weekday?" he asked. "Isn't today normally practice?"

"Motherfucker, we made the playoffs; we don't have practice for four days, and so life...is...gooood," Jason drawled, laughing.

"Fucking playoffs, that's great, man," Slate said, nodding. "How's Daniel doin' these days?"

There was silence from the two men, then, "Not good, Slate, not good at all. He's still crawling out of a bottle every morning, and his skating has gone to complete shit. He's gonna get himself killed if he keeps it up. Do you know when Mica is coming back?"

He shook his head. "She might not come back, from what I hear. Mason said she's pretty entrenched back home now. She's making up for lost time with her family, spending lots of time with her sister and cousin." He stood and stretched, stepping behind the bar, asking, "Draft?" and saw the men nod.

Grabbing three chilled mugs, he pulled the beer expertly, leaving barely an inch of head on each. He continued, "I get the feeling Mason will be coming back soon; maybe if she's down there alone, she can get her head together. I don't think she ever got a chance to tell Daniel what happened, you know—what really happened and why she left him the way she did? I thought they were getting back together for about a minute in Houston, but then he turned and walked away from her."

Jason looked at him, canting his head a little sideways. "What the fuck happened in Texas, man? Daniel didn't only walk away from Mica, he didn't even stay for the exhibition game, and he's been rocky since. For that matter, what happened with Mica? Why the hell did she leave him like that? We're his friends, and we...I'm worried about him."

Slate blew out a heavy breath. "Man, Mica had some shitty stuff in her life before she came to Chicago. A motherfucker of a father, a brother whose contact info is in her phone as 'BastardSon', and an ex-boyfriend who fucking defined the word evil. That ex made credible threats against Daniel's family, unless she agreed to leave him. So, because she liked him—liked his mom and brothers—she left him." Slate shrugged. "There's more to it, of course, but that's the general notion. She kept it to herself for weeks, and tried to keep us Rebels at arm's length too, but we were all used to fighting that fucking shit with her, so it just didn't work as well on us.

"Daniel, on the other hand, fucking let her walk away," he shrugged again. "He should have picked her up and carried her back, but he gave her space. That shit made it look like she didn't matter, or as if she wasn't worth fighting for. So now, we have a clusterfuck, and it's his loss...and it's her loss. Mason's loss too, because he's caught in the fucking middle of it. Fuck, *my* loss, because I have to keep shit going here without Mason's help. Fucking everyone's loss, I guess."

A few regulars drifted in, and soon, Jason and Gary were deep in conversation with some of the Rebel members they'd come to know from frequenting the bar. Jackson's had become the unofficial bar for the Mallets hockey team, and the big athletes and hardass bikers mixed surprisingly well together.

Jason was interested in getting a bike, and Digger was trying to broker him a deal for a Fat Boy. Slate's ears perked up; he'd had to retire the Indian several years ago, now a Fat Boy was his current ride, and he liked it. "Jason, a Fat Boy is a good bike, man. Go around back and check out mine." He tossed his keys over, ignoring the silence that fell over the bar. "Don't dump it, motherfucker, or I'll kill you."

Jason caught the keys and looked from his hand holding them, up to Slate's face, and then back down. Slate was aware everyone knew him to be very particular who he allowed to touch his scoot, and he'd never let anyone else ride it. "Fucking first time for everything," Slate muttered under his breath.

His phone buzzed, and he pulled it out of his pocket to see Essa's name on the caller ID. He stepped into the storeroom behind the bar, and answered, "Hey, you, what's up?"

There was some static on the line, and then he heard her voice, low and husky. "Slate, how's Chicago?"

He caught an edge in her voice, and knew this wasn't a social, chatty kind of call. "What's up, little girl? Something got you wired?"

She gave a half-sob, laughing wildly. "Mason is leaving, Slate. He's leaving, and she's staying. She doesn't even seem to care, but I know that she should care. She should give a crap about what's happening, but she doesn't." Essa took in a whooshing breath. "She's even shutting Molly out, and I know from talking to Mason that she's ignoring her business, too. Is she going to be okay? Tell me she's going to be okay, Slate. I couldn't stand it if me coming to Chicago was the cause of all this. It feels like it's all falling apart and it's my fault."

"Shhhhh, baby girl," he murmured into the phone, "shhhh now, none of this is your fault. You did nothing wrong; in fact, you are the main reason that things can now begin moving forward again. Mica is simply...stuck, I think. She'd been held tight in the same place for so long, because she had to protect everyone she loved, and now that pressure is gone. So now, there's nothing holding her back, except her own fear. You have to remember—she's lived with the fear for a long, long time, and even though we all know how strong and gutsy she is, in the mirror, she only sees the girl she was after Ray got his hands on her."

He heard Essa sniffling, and then she asked, "Will she ever be okay again, Slate?"

He smiled, knowing she'd hear it in his voice. "Yeah, she will be. Once she gets past this little hump, she'll be good to go again."

Essa sniffled again, and then her voice changed, and got tense instead of emotional. "Did you know Uncle Trent is missing?"

Trent Scott was Mica's father; Slate knew the fucker's name. "No, I didn't know that. What happened?" He held his breath, because he had a good idea of what was going on. It was one of two reasons he thought Mason had stayed in Texas so long, and the other was simply being there to support Mica.

"No one knows; he was just gone from the ranch one day. Michael is there, and is keeping things going, but he won't be able to for long; he's never clicked with the life," she said casually.

"How's Mica seem about her dad being missing?" he queried, wondering if Mica had any inkling.

"Oh, she's fine about that. She's *fine* about everything, but she's not *okay*. That doesn't make sense, but it's the best way I can explain."

He heard frustration in her words, and soothed her again, "Shhhh, little girl." Taking a breath, he asked softly, "Do you think you'd ever visit Mica again, if she comes back up here?" He waited on her answer, not sure which one he wanted. He wanted her, but couldn't see her fitting into the club, and he didn't want to get into the same kind of situation Mason had with Mica. He needed to cut ties, let this gal go find herself someone who fit her life, someone her own age, who wanted the same things she did.

"Yeah, I'd come visit," she said softly on a breath, nearly inaudible. In the same breathy tone, she said,

"Slate, I gotta go. Thanks for talking to me. I think you're right; she'll sort herself out eventually."

"Okay, little girl...be safe," he told her, and he waited for her to hang up, putting his phone into his pocket slowly once they'd been disconnected. She'd wound her way around his heart, and he feared the emotional toll, since he knew he had to let go of the idea of her. He wasn't the kind of man she needed; there was nothing soft about him anymore.

***

Several weeks later, Slate was sitting and listening to Mason talk about his plans, which had arisen from a recent confrontation he had with Daniel. Mason said, "I told him how much she'd taken on herself, made sure he knew the entire fucking history and why she felt she had to leave. Asshat couldn't see past his own hurt, even when I told him plainly enough that if I go down alone, I'm not gonna be looking out for his best interests anymore." Mason took a breath, looking over at Slate, "I love her, man. I want her back up here...in my life." Slate sighed and told him, "Yeah, but she loves Daniel."

"She doesn't think there's anything here for her anymore, not with him at least. He pretty much broke that shit in Houston, so I'm gonna do my damnedest to convince her that there's enough here to make her come back, that what we have is enough. Tug said she wants to learn to ride, I'll buy her a fucking bike and teach her myself. Denzie has a Road King that I want, and he's got a Sportster he'll throw in for a couple hundred since it's for Mica. I'll argue her back, bribe her back...any way I can get her, Slate," Mason groaned and looked away.

Rocking his head back against the wall of the clubhouse meeting room, Slate asked seriously, "You think she's into riding on her own now, man? Road trips can be brutal, are you sure you want her first introduction to be not only a thousand-mile trip, but one where she's learning how to ride? I like the idea of getting her a scoot—she'd look hot on a Sportster—but damn, Mason. You are hoping for a fuckuva lot from her."

He paused for a minute, letting that sink in to his brother's head, then switched gears, saying, "I get you wanting that Road King, man. Denzie has a sweet ride. I didn't know he was up for selling it, but glad it's coming up here. We're still looking for a Fat Boy for Jason; he's wanting a pretty bike to impress DeeDee." Slate yawned; *fuck,* he was tired.

Mason's head came up. "He sniffing around Winger's old lady? She okay with that? It's been a while since Winger passed, man, and about time she moved on, but a hockey guy? I'd hoped she'd find someone and stay in the club; she was a solid old lady."

Slate nodded. "She seems to be encouraging him, at least what I've seen. Jackson's is the only place I've ever seen them interact, and she's only here for a couple of weeks anyway."

"Fucking DeeDee, man. I should get Mica introduced to her, especially if she's moving out of the club. Would give them both something to have—kinda halfway, you know? Plus, if I can get Mica riding, she and DeeDee could run around together." Mason paused. "Fuck that; forget I said anything about them riding around. Mica learns how to ride, we'll need to have escorts lined up."

"Fuck me," Slate snarled, "security detail *still*, Mason? Isn't that taking this too far? The threat has been handled, man...Nelms is neutralized. Why should there still be a security detail?"

Mason thumped his hand on the tabletop, silencing Slate's argument. "Because she's our fucking princess, and while that gives her a lot of protection, it also puts a target on her ass. So until we are goddamn certain there's no blowback from anything associated with Mica, she gets a fucking security detail. You get me, brother?"

Slate rubbed his hands over his face, pushing them through his hair, leaving it standing at all angles from his head. "I get you, Prez. I'm on it."

* * *

Standing on Mica's little back porch, Slate stood with his hands on his hips, watching as the growing crowd helped put the final touches on the party to welcome Mica and Mason home. He felt pretty proud of himself; this was the first party he'd been in charge of, and he knew he'd enlisted the right help. Digger and Daniel's guy, Carter, had been in charge of the beer. There were several kegs set up and ready go to. Road Runner was handling the food, and that man lived for cooking.

Jess had proven valuable too. She'd opened the phonebook and called a dozen important Chicago businesspeople, who then told another dozen, and so on. It was like a crazy game of telephone, but the result was more than a hundred people milling around the connected backyards of Mason and Mica's houses. Nearly the whole Mallets hockey team had come, and Slate had seen two of the Rupert siblings earlier, but no Daniel yet.

Most of the Rebel brothers from the three nearest chapters were in attendance, but there was also a welcome, tension-less exchange with outside clubs' members who'd come. He'd seen Bones, Shades, Joker, VD, Six-Pack, and Ratman wandering around, all from the Skeptics MC. They'd offered nothing but respect to him and his brothers, and were waiting patiently for Mason to show.

Relations were good with the Dominos MC too, and their president Hawk had shown up with his old lady, Houlihan. She was a curvy brunette with a smart mouth. Hot Lips also happened to hold a Master's Degree in Special Education, and was in high demand at the local schools. Riding behind them were four full-patch members; it was the first time Slate had met any of them, but he shook and exchanged greetings before passing them off to Tug to wrangle.

He muttered to himself, "Fuck me," looking at the number of bikes parked along the street and alleyway. Tilting his head, he closed his eyes, biting his bottom lip. Straining to see if what he thought he'd heard was real, he became convinced that over the low roar of the crowd, he could hear the welcome, sweet sound of bikes coming from a couple of blocks away.

Jumping up on the railing surrounding the porch, he bellowed at the crowd, "Here they come. Pipe the fuck down, people." Making sure his message was heard and being passed along, he jumped down and yelled at Tats and Hoss to make a lane in the alley for when the bikes arrived. They moved to the street, shifting people out of the way as Mica came into view. She was riding along in front of Mason—he'd granted her pride of place—and she had the biggest shit-eating grin on her face.

Whispering quietly to himself, he muttered, "Put your feet down, put your feet down, put down your fucking feet..." until he saw her idle in and brake to a stop, putting down her feet to balance her bike. "Thank fuck," he breathed, seeing Mason pull in beside her and motion her to park up here by the house.

Nodding his head, he watched her roll the bike up to the pad, then back into what was now officially her parking place for the Sportster. She put down the kickstand and killed the bike, slowly taking off her helmet and looking around in what looked like surprise and awe at the people crowding around.

He knew her legs would be weak for a couple minutes after a long ride like today, so he jumped off the porch, coming up beside her and lifting her off the bike with ease. She twisted in his arms, hugging him, and then pulled his face close with both hands, kissing him softly on the lips. Smiling, she pulled back and whispered, "That's from Essa." A shock shot straight through to his cock, and he almost moaned at the thought of his girl asking Mica to pass that along.

Slate stepped back as others crowded around her, everyone wanting to touch her and make sure she knew how much she was loved and had been missed.

Watching Prez pad across the yard towards her, he recognized from Mason's body language that their relationship had shifted in the days since he'd last seen them together in Texas. *Fuck me*, he mouthed, seeing the long-standing, familiar, sexual tension had changed to what looked like a lover's knowledge of each other's bodies. Fuck...maybe it was a good thing Daniel wasn't here yet.

He had given a three-fingered salute to Mason before he turned to walk through the party, listening as the music went from *Blessed* by Black Water Rising to the favorite *Arms Wide Open* by Creed; the fucking music rocked. He wanted to make sure no one got too rowdy, and that the mix of brothers and citizens remained as friendly as they were right now. Running into Hoss, he thanked him for helping get Mica up to her house safely, clapping him on the back.

Hoss pulled him into a conversation about the benefits of an enforced perimeter around a clubhouse. He'd moved to the new Fort Wayne chapter a few months ago; he had some family down that way. Slate knew Fort Wayne had been having problems with gang activity near them, but this was the first he'd heard that they weren't enforcing a goddamn neutral zone. Tequila was also a Fort Wayne brother; he was up here with Bingo for a few days, and Slate pulled him into the conversation.

This sounded like sloppy leadership to him, which wasn't like Bingo. The club needed a secure area around their house, where they could be confident of safety for both members and family, if needed. If the gangs were pushing that badly, Mason needed to be told, so he could manage the situation and expectations.

Slate casually kept pushing on other topics, listening as much to what wasn't said, as what was. The strip club business was doing well, but they'd saved money by not testing the girls for drugs or disease.

Shooting range business was taking a hit; the lack of ammunition was impacting casual sportsmen's ability to play with their cock-replacements. On the other hand, local law enforcement officers, otherwise known as LEOs, had arranged private times for the facility, which nearly made up the missing income. Something smelled of kickbacks there, but it was hard to tell without being onsite.

The two bars sounded like business as usual, however he heard undertones of tension with the Highwaymen out of Detroit, which could be problematic. He was coming to the unwelcome conclusion that he needed to make a trip to Indiana soon. He'd have to track the shit there and figure it out.

He was leaning against a tree, chatting with Tequila, when he caught sight of Tucker weaving through the edges of the crowd. Rebels held church about his shit months ago, but the fucker had done a runner, and they hadn't been able to take things to the final conclusion. Anger boiled in his system and he found his jaw clenched, grinding his teeth together tightly. Stepping away from the tree, he caught Bones' eye, and the Skeptics' president strolled over. "Slate, my titanium-balled friend, you look positively enraged. Furious is also a good word." He eyed Slate's face closely. "Can I be of assistance, brother?" he offered quietly.

Slate tucked his chin down, and then lifted his face. "Naw, man, club business." He indicated Tucker with a nod. "We have some old news that just showed up; needa take care of it, is all. Your guys are probably gonna wanna watch, but I'd ask for some privacy, unless you hear otherwise from Mason."

"You got it, Slate," Bones agreed readily. Clucking his tongue, he called his members to him, pointing to Tucker. "See that piece of Rebel business? We will assist Rebels as needed, catch and...not release, I think. Just catch, yeah."

He nodded at Slate. "Go get Mason, Brother. This shit's contained."

Slate whistled low and then high, calling his own members to him. "Tequila, Wheels, Bingo, Duck—Tucker is here. Snatch him up, take him over to Mason's backyard, and wait." He looked around the ring of faces, seeing his own anger reflected there. He tapped his fist to chest, saying softly, "She's a fucking treasure," and heard the echo go around the circle of men. "Do not fucking fail her. We take care of this shit tonight," he snarled, watching for agreement on every face.

Bones walked with him for a few steps, his words pulling Slate to a slow stop. "It's for *her* then?" he asked. "The Rebels' Princess?"

Slate nodded, staying quiet. "I've often wondered what it was about her," Bones mused, "and then I saw her riding in today. I believe you Rebels have the right of it, and trust me when I say I mean no disrespect to her or the club as I say along with you that she is," he tapped his chest with a closed fist, "*a fucking treasure*. Mason is a goddamn lucky man." Slate silently nodded again, stalking off to where Mica stood between Mason and Daniel, symbolic of their months-long relationship struggles.

He heard a short struggle behind him, and knew Tucker had been located and detained. He stopped a little ways from where Mason stood, and got his attention with a yell of his name followed by a single word, "Tucker."

Mason disengaged from Mica and walked towards Slate. "Took him to your yard, Prez," Slate told him. They angled their steps that way, quietly acknowledging as Rebel members fell into step behind them. Mason nodded at the Skeptics guard standing outside the yard, bumping fists with Bones.

Entering the backyard through the gate, they saw three Rebels standing in the darkness at the back of the open area. Mason nodded at two of the men, and stared at the third for a long moment. He turned back to the larger group, waiting patiently as they gathered and settled into place.

"Rebel Wayfarers forever," he began, and the crowd took up the saying, finishing with, "forever Rebels." Mason nodded at them, trailing his gaze across every member present. "Weeks ago, we made a decision in church to remove a member. Has anyone forgotten the charges? Does anyone need a refresher on what the member did?" Mason had already begun the process of stripping Tucker of his place by reducing him to a member, instead of a name.

No one spoke up, and a few heads shook in negation. "Does anyone question the charges?" he asked the group, receiving only head shakes in response. "Do we all stand by our original decision?" he asked, finally receiving head nods this time in agreement. His eyes ripped across the group again. "God forgives; Rebels don't. Fucking right," he said, and pulled out his knife.

Opening the lock blade, he approached the group of three. Taking a step behind them and to the side, he waved his arm at Tucker, who was held facing forward by his arms between Wheels and Duck. "No longer Rebel," he reached out with one hand to steady the leather fabric of the man's cut; he ran his blade along the edge of one patch, severing the threads holding it in place, "no longer one of us," he took his time around the larger center patch, treating the club colors with respect and care, "not club," he said finally, releasing his hold on the leather, stepping back with the three patches held loosely in his hands.

Wheels and Duck turned Tucker loose, stepping away. He rounded on Mason, speaking for the first time. "This is fucking bullshit, Prez. She fucking liked it, man, asked for it all the time by wearing those tight shirts and pants. You know you've done the same, Mason. I've seen you time and time again with your hands all over her. This is bullshit, man, and you know it. You're just pussy-whipped by the bitch fucking the hockey star."

Oh man, Slate did not have a good feeling about the ending to this particular story. He watched Mason grind to a halt, turning slowly to face the former member. "You need to shut the fuck up now, Cut. I'll give you five seconds, and then I'll own you. One," he said softly.

"This is bullshit, Prez," Cut repeated, and Mason's hand reached out and closed over his throat.

"Five," he finished softly, his other hand coming up from nowhere to land one solid, crushing blow to the side of Cut's head.

He dropped the unconscious man on the grass and asked coolly, "Slate, you got someone to clear the trash tonight?"

"Yeah, Prez, Skeptics indicated they'd be happy to perform catch and release for us, unless you don't want Cut released," Slate called across the yard, waiting to hear which way the scales would tip tonight.

Mason nodded, saying only, "Release."

***

The room wasn't really big enough to accommodate an angry Slate. He held the phone to his ear, pacing back and forth along the length of the room. Last night, Mason had sent him for a sit down at the Wisconsin compound with the leaders of the Disciples, and since it was late when they finished, he'd stayed and partied with their guests. Slate had a hangover, but it wasn't bad, and wasn't what had him riled this morning.

"GeeMa, what do you mean he's gone? Did his band go on tour early?" Slate softly spoke the question into the phone as he ran an absent hand through his hair, standing it on end. He listened to the voice on the other end of the phone for a few minutes, his face gradually falling into its normal, hard lines.

"Wait up, wait up...you mean he stole money from you? Wasn't he still working?" Slate ground out. He paced up and down again, pausing to lean against the wall, tipping his head back with a thump. "No, no, I believe you, GeeMa. I don't get what he was thinking. I'll call Myron, get a wire transfer into your account tod—" He paused when she interrupted. "Yes. No...I know that's not why you called, GeeMa," he said softly with a smile in his voice, "but gotta keep some mad money in there; never know when you and GeePa will want to go off for a wild weekend."

Grinning at the response on the phone, Slate closed his eyes. "It's good to hear your voice too, GeeMa. I love you guys, ya know. Let me know if you hear from Ben, and I'll do the same. Don't worry about him. He's probably in the bus with the guys, headed to those gigs out on the west coast he was talking about a few weeks ago. I don't have a thing to say about him leaving, but we'll have words about the thievery. I'll make sure he understands, GeeMa. There's only so many times you should have to put up with his as—butt doing something like this. I got this."

There was a pause, and the grin on his face grew a little wider. "Yes, ma'am, I will. Love you, too. Bye." He disconnected the call and stood still for a minute, leaning. The backward kick, which knocked a hole in the wall behind him, combined with a violent yell of, *"FUCK,"* caused pounding at his door in seconds. "Slate, you okay man?" he heard one of the prospects asking through the door. "Yeah, man, it's all good," he muttered. "Call Woody and tell him he's got a wall job." Hearing a message of assent, he turned and sat down on the edge of the bed, forearms propped on his thighs and hands dangling loosely between his knees.

He didn't know how long he sat there like that, his mind circling and teasing at Ben's behavior, which had worsened dramatically over the past few years. His little brother started a band in his late teens, and they'd been playing in Cheyenne bars for the past few years. He'd been drinking before he was legal, but once he hit that magic age, it seemed that every picture he saw of Ben, there was booze in his hand.

A few months ago, he'd sent money out for Ben to buy some recording time in a studio, so the band could make a demo CD. It was done with the understanding that his little brother would straighten up his act. If he was serious about music as a career, then it needed to become a job, not a fucking life-long party. Susan fucked that up; she found out about the money and weaseled about half of it out of Ben's hands. She'd done what she did best, partied for days with her dealers and johns.

Ben had been so pissed at himself about trusting their mother—again—that he'd punched a wall and broken two knuckles, negating the need for use of the studio for weeks. By then, the rest of the money was gone too. Slate snorted softly. His brother had a good voice, really good, and that little fucker could make his guitar weep when he wanted to, but he didn't have any common sense in his head.

A tapping at the door drew Slate's attention. "Yeah?"

"Prez is on the horn, man, wants to chat," came through the door.

Sighing heavily, Slate stood, opening the door and holding out his hand to the prospect for the phone. "This is Slate," he said quietly, acknowledging the open line.

"Brother, we had a break-in at Tupelo's last night," Mason started. "They bypassed security, nothing on the tapes. They passed up the till, ignoring the cash. What they got was the armory, or at least part of it." Slate leaned his forearm against the doorway, listening intently. Mason said, "Skeptics were on a run, saw Cut's bike parked around the side last night. They thought it was odd enough to note, and thought that note was enough to mention, when they heard about the trouble. Bones called me a half-hour ago."

"Fuck me. Bones was sure of the ID?" Slate asked quietly.

"Yeah, the paint on that scoot is distinctive, hard to miss his tank," Mason growled.

Slate nodded silently, the fucker had replicated his ugly fucking shoulder tattoo in paint on his bike, and it would be hard to mistake. Running his tongue against the inside of his teeth, he sighed, "All right, yeah, I got this, Prez. Where do you want him delivered?"

"Just get our shit back, Slate. Call a brother to help, if you need it." There was a slight pause. "Hey," Mason started in a more upbeat tone, "did I tell you about Mica's ink?"

Slate chuckled. "Naw, what did princess get?"

Their conversation ended soon after, and the amusement slowly faded off Slate's face. Picking up his cellphone, he punched in a number from memory. "Myron, hey, man, it's Slate. I need you to wire five thousand into my grandmother's account at her bank in Wyoming. Yeah, same account information. Make sure you pull this from my account, fucker; it's me, not Rebel."

Striding through the clubhouse, he tossed the other phone across the room at the prospect standing near the bar. "Okay, Myron, can you text me when it's done, and I'll let my grandmother know?" He walked into the kitchen area, looking at the pan of scrambled something on the stove. "Sure, man, thanks." He disconnected the call, shoved the phone into his front pocket, and grabbed a plate, serving himself.

Carrying his plate back out to the bar, he pulled the phone out again, making several calls to arrange meetings in Chicago in a couple hours. They'd meet at Tupelo's, where he could look over the damage for himself. It had the benefit of being a neutral location, which meant he was able to ask Skeptics and Dominos to show too.

Two nights later, Slate was standing in the back room of a Skeptics' clubhouse in St. Louis, looking down at the battered piece of meat that was once Tucker. "Franks, get me a bottle of water, would ya?" he called over his shoulder at the doorway.

Holding out a hand behind him, he accepted the water slapped into his palm, and squatted next to Tucker's head. "Cut," he started in a conversational tone, opening the bottle, "man, you don't have to go out like this. Just tell me where things are. You can still walk away." He dribbled water into the open mouth below him. "Doesn't that sound good? Doesn't it sound better than this? Being able to walk away? It's what you shoulda done to begin with, but you can still do it." Tilting his head down, he listened intently as Tucker responded. "There now, that wasn't so hard, was it? We'll check it out, and I'll be right back."

Standing, he turned and walked out, closing and locking the door behind him. Taking a deep drink from the bottle, he spoke, "It's in a storage locker across the river in East St. Louis. You got someone we can call to check it out?"

Franks nodded, pulling out a phone. Slate gave him the information, and took another drink of water. While they waited for confirmation that the stolen merchandise had been recovered, Franks asked him, "Mason give you the nod to let this fucker go?"

Slate tipped his head to one side, cutting a look at the man. "Yeah, my call, and my call is that we're gonna brand the fucker's colors off, but he gets to live. Consider it...a lesson to others who might think about fucking with Rebel property of any kind. My brothers expect no less."

Franks blanched, taking in a shallow breath. "I'll call Doc. We'll make sure he keeps breathing until you are ready to turn him loose."

Slate tilted his head again, seeing the look of fear and respect on Franks' face. "That'd be good. You do that, man. Much obliged for use of the clubhouse. Sorry for the bother, but appreciative of the assistance."

Later, when the sounds of screaming and the smell of burning flesh had both faded from the air, Slate stood in the bathroom for a long time. Knuckles white against the edges of the countertop, he studied his own face in the mirror, not liking what he saw there.

***

Hanging around at Mica's office for so long while on babysitter duty had given Slate insight into some of her clients, and he'd found a juicy squeeze in Donnelly, the one who he'd taken Mica to see, when he'd been pawed at by Daniel's ex. Part of a family long entrenched in the shady side of Chi-town, it hadn't been hard to find details to use against him. Then, it hadn't taken much use of that leverage to convince him to throw more work Mica's way once she came home and got settled back into her business.

Slate'd been so successful in his campaign that Mica had expanded her business, hiring additional full-time employees and taking on new clients. To celebrate, she'd had a grand re-opening tonight, and from reports, the party at her offices had been successful.

Standing behind the bar in Jackson's, Slate looked around at the crowd, pleased. This was where the real party was, after that fancy pants shindig in the offices earlier. For a private party, there were a lot of people here, Slate estimated over a hundred in the bar now, and not everyone had shown up yet. Of course, since it was a party for Mica, it shouldn't be a surprise it was well attended. Everyone loved her, and there'd been quite a few here tonight who felt like they had a hand in her triumph.

Slate had been stuck down in Memphis for a few weeks, and had gotten back in town just today. The Rebels were in the middle of chartering a new chapter there; it made a secondary mid-point between Chicago and Houston, taking some of the strain off the Little Rock members.

While they did not yet have a charter in Texas, there was a big push from some of the smaller clubs they'd run into there. Those clubs all wanted affiliation with the Rebels, but it wasn't good business to have too much room between club chapters, so they had some things they needed to get into play first. Memphis was a good fit, and he'd settled a lot of details, including locating a couple of good revenue streams they could snap up easily.

He liked that part of the club life; he enjoyed finding puzzles that needed solutions, and then sourcing the right answer. That business side of things gave him a lot of satisfaction, because he knew he was helping support his brothers and their families. Everything came down to the brotherhood, this family he'd chosen, and the loyalties he felt for and with them. His face hardened. He might not relish—fuck that...he fucking *hated* the enforcement portion of his position within the club, but he knew it was important, too.

Mason had seen how much the business in St. Louis had taken out of him. He'd been sympathetic when he heard the decision Slate made, the discipline enforced on Cut, but they both understood it was necessary. You couldn't let anything slide; if someone fucked you or the club, you had to fuck them back in order to ensure no one else thought they could take advantage of the club. He mouthed, *God forgives; Rebels don't.*

The Rebels couldn't let Cut run around with the club tattoo on his back either, so the actions served two needs, but *God*, it had been a hard task, and Slate still woke up in a cold sweat from nightmares of the man's screams.

Slate rolled his shoulders, consciously releasing the tension that came when he thought about St. Louis for too long. He hooked his thumbs through the belt loops of his jeans, leaning his shoulders back against the wall.

Scanning the crowd, he started mentally marking a number of the people already here. There were four different patches on cuts, arrayed alongside Armani suits; rough hockey players bumped glass rims in toasts with lawyers and judges. Mica's area of influence had spread wide in the years she'd spent in Chicago, and the attendees tonight reflected that.

His phone buzzed in his pocket, and he pulled it out to read a text from Road Runner. Seemed he needed someone to set up some tables in the bar for food, because he was finally on his way. He raised a hand, pointing to and calling three prospects to his side. He gave them orders to pull tables from one of the private rooms and line them up along the front wall of the bar, and then to go outside and watch for the van with the food.

Satisfied they'd get things ready, he strolled over to talk to Bingo. His next trip would be down to Fort Wayne, and the chapter president was a good source of information. They were deep in conversation when Slate felt the atmosphere in the bar change, the hair lifting on the back of his neck. He lifted his head, glanced around, and froze in place.

Across the room, barely inside the door, was a beautiful woman with shiny, dark hair, and she was looking right at him. He felt a smile break slowly across his face, and he turned and walked away from Bingo without another word. "Little girl," he breathed as he got closer to her, "I didn't know you were in town. God, you look good, baby." He reached out a hand, tucking a strand of her hair behind the curve of her ear, trailing his fingers down the side of her neck to her collarbone. His mouth tipped up on one side, and he grinned at the shiver she tried to hide.

"Come here, baby; give us a hug," he said, cupping one hand on her shoulder, his other going to her waist as he pulled her in close for a hug. Her hands slid up his back, and she turned her face into his neck, nuzzling into his chest. "Baby?" he questioned, "do you know how much I've missed you?" He felt the lifting of her cheeks into a smile, and heard her deep sigh, but she still hadn't said anything.

Slate felt a buzz of concern thrill through him, and pulled back to look into her face. She was smiling slightly, eyes opening slowly, and she tipped her chin up, looking in his eyes. "Hey, Slate," she murmured, "I've missed you too."

He kissed her softly, gently covering her lips with his own. He stepped back, sliding a hand down her arm, winding his fingers in-between hers. Tugging, he pulled her with him, returning to where Bingo was standing, watching them with a curious gaze. After making introductions, he picked up the conversation with Bingo where he'd left off, keeping her close by his side. Throughout the rest of the party, he kept her beside him, openly advertising her position in his life with constant touches and strokes of her skin.

Not a single club member in the room missed his silent declaration, and he saw Mason frown at him several times. Fortunately, he was busy behind the bar with the crowd. Slate knew they'd have to talk soon, but not right now, not when Essa had just walked back into his life. "Introduce me, my friend," he heard from behind him, and turned with Essa tucked tight into his body.

"Bones," he said with a friendly smile, releasing her for a minute so he could thump the Skeptics president on the back. Wrapping his fingers around her hip, he pulled her close to his side and splayed his hand across her lower belly as he said, "Brother, this is Essa; she's Mica's cousin."

Bones held out a hand, and she placed her tiny one in his. He lifted it to his lips, softly kissing the backs of her fingers as Slate stiffened. "Essa," Bones said smoothly, "a friend of Slate is a friend of mine. This is a powerful man you've aligned yourself with, and your presence at his side reinforces my belief in both his intelligence and good taste. It's good to meet you. I've known your cousin for a long time, and am thrilled to see your beauty challenges her own."

Essa raised her eyes to Slate's, blushing as she responded quietly, "Thank you, it's good to meet you too." The men talked for a few minutes about Mica and her success, and Bones asked Essa several direct questions, which she answered as briefly as possible.

Her discomfort was clear to Slate, and he pulled her away as soon as he could, wanting to understand the problem. Taking her into the back room, he closed the door behind them. He smiled, thinking about when he had first come to Chicago, and Jackson's, and steered her down the hallway and into the room that'd been his home for several months before he got his own place.

Kicking the door closed behind them, he pulled her body flush against his front, reaching down to cup her ass through her jeans. Walking her backward to the bed, he stopped when the backs of her legs bumped against the mattress, only pausing as she stiffened. "Baby," he murmured, his lips moving along her cheek. He turned, sat on the edge of the bed, and pulled her down onto his lap. "I just want to hold you for a minute," he whispered, lips pressed to the side of her head. Slate looked down into the deep, brown eyes of the woman in his arms, trailing kisses along her temple, down to the corner of her mouth.

"Slate," she said, pulling back and sliding herself off him to sit next to him, "can you slow down a minute? I'm not sure what's happening here tonight."

Tipping his head sideways, he looked quizzically at her. "What do you mean, baby?"

"Why did most of those men ignore me? And, what was up with that last guy, the one with the bizarre tattoos on his head? It was like he wanted to scare me, like he was trying to be frightening. I don't understand what any of it means, and the conversation with that guy was just weird." She laughed, asking, "Why did you tell them that I was *with* you? Is that like being your girlfriend?"

Slate frowned. "I wanted to introduce you to my brothers, little girl. This is my family, even if not by blood. They're important to me, and I wanted them to meet you. They were all respectful of you, weren't they? That's why I told them you were with me; it establishes that you aren't open for invitation, that you are in a relationship."

"With you, you mean? In a relationship with you?" she questioned. "But I haven't seen you in months. Why would you tell them that? We're friends; I wanted to hang out with you tonight, and I thought that's what we were doing."

At that, Slate moved slightly away, separating from her and getting some space between them. He dropped his hands, letting them lie on the top of his thighs. He had a sick sensation in his chest; it felt like something was breaking apart. He carefully schooled his face to show nothing of the dismayed emotions he was feeling. *She didn't...she wasn't interested anymore, maybe not ever. Fuck,* she was just a little girl; she didn't know what he'd wanted. At least he'd never fucked her. She'd only wanted to hang out, and he'd made a statement out of introducing her.

He abruptly jackknifed to his feet, reaching down to pull her up. Striding swiftly, he tugged her into the hallway and leaned forward to kiss her temple gently. "I got shit I need to do, little girl," he said, avoiding her eyes. "Good to see you."

"Slate," she started, and he waved her words off with a quick hand motion. "Tell Mason I had to leave; he'll watch out for you," he said. Leaving her standing in the back hall of the bar, he went to the exit, letting himself out and closing the door softly.

He got on his motorcycle, starting the engine with a kick. He sat for a second, listening to the pipes rumbling, eyes unfocused and hands loose on the handlebars. "Fuck me," he muttered, opening the throttle and pulling out into the street.

17 -   Alone

Working with the Rebel chapter in Fort Wayne had turned out to be a welcome reprieve from constantly thinking about Essa. Slate had come down to learn about the chapter and brothers, hoping to clear up some of the business issues he and Bingo had identified. There was a ton of work to do, and most nights, Slate fell into his bed in the clubhouse late, falling asleep before undressing sometimes. As long as he could keep busy, he could keep his mind away from her.

One of the first things he'd changed was to implement regular sweeps of the blocks surrounding the chapter clubhouse. On their first run, he'd found drug dealers openly selling within two blocks of the chapter's home base, and that shit needed severe discouragement.

They'd rousted most of them, chasing them off with a message to not return. A few days in, Slate ordered one of the most persistent dealers to be picked up and brought to the backroom of the clubhouse. He'd sat on a chair in the middle of the room, slouching and insolent. Slate stepped into the room, standing just inside the door and gazing consideringly at the man. "You know where you are, man?" he asked casually, leaning back against the wall and pushing his hands deep into the pockets of his jeans.

"Man, you don't know who you are messing with," responded the slightly built man. "You let me go now, Tony'll go easy on you."

"I asked you if you were aware of where you are—the location. Do you know where you are?" Slate asked again, slightly differently. "It's okay to say no, man. I want to start this conversation with you knowing exactly how fucked you are."

"I done tol' you, *man*...you don't know who the fuck you messin' with," the man hissed, the acne on his cheeks standing out in sharp relief to the pale color of his skin.

"Yeah, yeah, Tony'll go easy on me," Slate finished for him, sighing, "I heard you." Taking two steps from the wall, Slate kicked the man hard in the chest, lofting the chair over backward and knocking him airborne for a couple feet before he slid headfirst into the wall with an abruptly ended scream.

Slate strolled over to where the man lay on his back, coughing. He stood over him for a second, then squatted down beside him. Pulling his hands from his pockets, he rested them on his knees, lacing his fingers together. "Do you know where you are, piss-ant?" he asked again. "Last time I'll ask."

"Some fucking bike gang compound," the man ground out, raising one hand to the back of his neck, holding his chest with the other.

Slate stood abruptly, kicking the man in the ribs several times to emphasize each word he called out, "You. Are. On. Rebel. Property." He let that sink in to the little fucker's brain before continuing steadily, "This is the Rebel Wayfarers Fort Wayne chapter clubhouse. Our mother charter is in Chicago, and with the twenty-five chapters across the Midwest, we have more than a thousand members. This is not a *fucking bike gang compound*, and you would do well to remember to hold respect in your mouth when speaking about Rebel property to a national officer." He kicked him again, high under the arm, and winced when he heard the distinct sound of breaking ribs.

"Fuck, man, that sounded like it hurt," he said with some empathy, looking down at the asswipe keening on the floor. "I'd like to get a message to Tony." He kicked the man again, catching him on the arm just below the elbow. "Hold on, I need to do something," he said, placing his hands on the wall to balance himself as he kicked him several more times.

"There, that's better." Taking a deep breath, he continued, "I'd like to get a message to Tony Manzino. Are you the man to do that for me?" He stooped down again, squatting next to the dealer, catching his gaze and holding it. "Are you? Do you think you can manage to remember the message long enough to tell Tony?"

"Yes, yes," came out on a high-pitched squeal, and Slate nodded at him. "Alrighty then. The message is, *Fort Wayne is mine. Get the fuck out. You've got one day.*" He tilted his head, looking at the man again. "Are you motivated to carry the message?"

"He'll kill me. He'll kill me..." This was repeated frantically a few more times, the voice trailing off to silence.

"Not motivated then? Because I can kill you now, save Tony the trouble, if that's the case. Or are you gonna help me out?" Slate placed his hands on the wall again, looking down as the man tried to crawl away.

"I'm motivated. I promise. I'll tell him the message," was the breathless response.

Slate nodded. "Remember, the message is, *Fort Wayne is mine. Get the fuck out. You've got one day.* And don't paraphrase anything, that shit pisses me off." Raising his voice, he called, "Hoss, get your ass in here," as he walked back over to the wall and leaned casually against it.

The door opened, and one of the Fort Wayne members stuck his head in, glancing over at the shithead on the floor before focusing on Slate. "Yeah?" he grunted, grabbing the doorframe and slouching in the doorway.

"Get a cage, take this man down off Anthony, and drop him near our auto repair place." Slate rolled his shoulders. "Don't overtax him. He's a messenger now...got a message to deliver." He watched Hoss grab the guy by the back of the shirt, picking him up and putting him on his feet effortlessly, then holding him there as the guy's legs threatened to collapse.

Wrinkling his forehead, Slate walked into the main room of the clubhouse, taking note of the groups of members who stopped talking as he entered the room. There were several guys from Chicago who'd joined with Bingo to start the chapter, and a few dozen who had come from other chapters across the country. Those men all waited for him to approach, showing respect for his position within the club.

There was another handful who were skating the edge of disrespect, and he wasn't yet sure why. He suspected it could be the feeling of being pressured from a national officer coming in and cleaning up their messes, and with a couple of them, the possibility their behaviors weren't always in the club's best interests might be found out.

Today was gonna be all about straightening up the other businesses. Slate kept walking across the room, knocking when he came to the office door; he waited politely for Bingo's response before he opened the door. Deke, Sergeant at Arms for the Fort Wayne chapter, was sitting in a chair facing Bingo across the big desk. Slate dropped into the remaining chair, and Deke slapped the door closed behind him. "How'd it go, brother," he asked Slate.

Shrugging, he responded, "About what you'd expect. 'Oh, you are so fucked' changed into 'Whatever you want' pretty quickly. He's taking the message to Manzino, who will have a day to figure out if he wants to keep breathing or not."

He wiped his palms down the tops of his jeans, a gesture that didn't go unnoticed by Bingo. Frowning at Slate, he said, "We could have handled this, you know. Didn't need to come down to deal with the shit storm; we clocked those fuckers two weeks ago, and have been running them off the neutral since."

Without raising his head, Slate cut his eyes over and looked at Bingo. "Better if it's coming from national, man, and you know that shit. Underscores the fucking backing that you have. Plus, it keeps your family out of the line of fire, and your nieces and nephews don't need this kind of shit. It's done; we'll sort it out. I'd like to move on today to the other things we discussed."

Bingo's eyes dropped, and he nodded, "I called Doc earlier; he's headed over to the strip club. We'll have blood work back on all the girls by tomorrow."

Slate narrowed his eyes. "Call him. I want to talk to him." Deke reached out, punching a number into the phone, and put it on speaker. "Yeah?" came over the line. "Hey, Doc, Slate. You get started yet?" He slumped in the chair.

"Not yet, getting the last of the late arrivals on board with the program," Doc grumbled, and they could hear females yelling in the background.

Grinning, Slate looked up at Bingo. "Get'em in line, Doc. Do you have resources to do drug screening in addition to STDs and pregnancy?"

There was a pause. "Some...is there anything specific you looking for, Slate?"

"Blow, horse, meth, the usual," he said, rubbing his hand across his jaw.

"Yeah, I got shit for that. I'll get it all done at once," came the response. Slate nodded and Deke ended the call.

"Want to tackle the Highwaymen next, or look at the books on the shooting range?" Slate asked Bingo.

"Fuck, man, you are relentless," Deke said with a laugh.

Bingo scowled. "Shooting range. Might as well get the hard shit over with."

Slate nodded. "We'll want five or six full-patch brothers to go with. I need to know who you trust and want at your backs." He listened as Bingo and Deke named off a few people, and noticed which names didn't make the roster. He waited patiently as they carefully gathered their trusted circle, and before long, the men they'd carefully chosen were crowding into the office with them.

He let Bingo give them the rundown of what the task was about, watching the expressions on the faces of Diablo, PBJ, and Gunny. Two of them were clearly not surprised by this job, and he called them on it. Unfolding and climbing to his feet, he faced the men in the room. "Brothers, anything that's already known would be good intel to have at this point."

Gunny looked at Bingo, then back at Slate. "There's at least one private party who never made it into the books, man. I got a new piece a few weeks ago, and wanted to go drop some rounds to dial it in. Ramone was on the door and told me there was a cop group there, but when I looked at the schedule later to see when I could book some time, there wasn't no entry for that group at all. I asked him, and he said he didn't do the schedule, only showed up when told to." He looked back at Bingo. "I didn't think anything of it, Prez."

"No reason for you to, Gunny," Bingo said shaking his head. He looked over at Slate, "How the hell did you see this from Chicago, when I didn't see it from here?"

Waving a hand in dismissal, Slate reassured him, "It's easier when shit's not cluttered by the day-to-day, man. Harder for you to see it, buried as you are with hang-around attitudes in full-patch cuts." The atmosphere became arctic in the room, tension apparent in Bingo's posture.

"What the fuck are you talking about, Slate?" he ground out.

Slate leaned over the desk, not intimidated by Bingo's attitude. "You know what the fuck I'm talking about, man. Those names you *didn't* consider for this job? Those men are not my *brothers*, clear as fucking day. I walk into that room out there," Slate pointed at the door, "and they are edgy, nervous as hell, and nearly fucking disrespectful. You don't pull that shit when there's a visiting member unless you got bad blood, or unless you got something to hide. You sure as fuck don't pull shit like that when there's a fucking national officer visiting."

PBJ spoke up, "Couple of members headed out on a run as soon as you came in here, Slate. Who are you looking at for problems?"

Slate looked at him. "Rabid and Ramone are two of them."

PBJ made a face. "Both left, Slate. Sorry, man."

Waving off his apologies, Slate asked, "Do you know if they made any calls before they headed out?"

"Don't think so, brother," PBJ said.

"Okay, let's roll. Might as well get this over with," Slate sighed, running both hands through his short hair.

***

Thirty minutes later, Slate was seated on a stool just outside the shooting range office. He was listening to the noises from within the office with one ear, and to distract himself from the thuds and groans, he looked over at the member seated on the other side of the door, asking with a grin. "PBJ, how the fuck did you get saddled with a sandwich as your road name, man?"

The big man's face split with a grin, his teeth shining whitely through his full beard. "Aww, man, don't bring up painful memories."

Slate laughed. "Really, man? What the hell?"

With a huge sigh, PBJ rubbed his belly under his shirt. "I fucking love peanut butter. When I was a prospect, I'd make peanut butter sandwiches every morning and pack them in my saddlebags. I never knew when we'd get called out, or if we'd have time to stop and eat on a run, and I get hungry, bro."

He laughed. "The third or fourth time we pulled up to a stop and I snagged out a sandwich, Bingo grabbed it and took a bite. He spit it out, because it was just peanut butter, no jelly, and so I became PBJ."

Slate laughed, nodding. The door opened between them, and they stood, turning to see Bingo coming out with a thunderous look on his face. He stalked past them to the outside door, kicking it open and moving through, letting it slam behind him. "Guessing that didn't go well," Slate said, turning to look in the office.

Ramone was sitting slumped into the corner, his head lolling lax on his shoulder. His face was already swelling and bruising, and he would be hurting when he woke up. The shooting range manager, Torres, was crumpled on the floor near him, and Slate had to look hard to see his chest rising and falling.

He turned to PBJ. "Go outside and get Gunny and Diablo. Let's get a cage and get them out of here. Lock up the place on your way out, but don't take them to the clubhouse unless you get a call from me or Bingo. I gotta have a talk with Mason."

Slate waited in the doorway until the Rebels walked in, then he followed Bingo outside. In the lot, Bingo was astride his bike, smoking. He sighed as Slate walked up, and grumbled, "This is fucked up, man. We need to get Mason down here, Slate. He needs to bring Myron with him; I don't know how much these fuckers have skimmed. Rabid's in the wind; he went out the back when we came in, according to Ramone. I can't be president of this club; I need to call Mason and talk to him, and he's going to fucking tell me to step down, brother. Fuck, how did I not see this?"

Putting a hand on his shoulder, Slate squeezed hard until Bingo looked up at him. "You with me, *Brother*?" he asked. "Because I need you present, you here?"

Bingo nodded. "I'm with you."

"Okay, let's not put words in Mason's mouth, and remember—we're taking care of this shit now. Regardless of what happened last week, or the week before, we are sorting the shit, and Mason knows we can handle anything that comes down the road. That's why he agreed to this chapter, and that's why he set you as president. Let's go back to the clubhouse and call him where we have some privacy, and then we'll sit down with him tomorrow."

Bingo frowned. "I'm getting too old for this shit, man. I just want to watch my sister's kids grow up."

Slate growled, "Let's talk to Mason, and give him a chance to weigh in on this shit." Walking over to his bike, he started it and waved Bingo to pull out ahead of him.

***

"Goddammit. Are you telling me the chapter is fucked? I don't have time for this shit, man. Run it down for me; tell me what you need." Mason was pissed, and it came across the phone clearly.

Frowning at Bingo across the desk, Slate started his report, "More than half the issues are solved already, Prez. Girls are tested, and we're waiting on results. Even if we have to replace some of them, the manager there is solid. It's DeeDee, and she can deal with shit as needed, now that I've given her the authority for it."

He continued, "Tony Manzino has been notified of our intent to have him vacate the fucking town. I expect a response within a few hours. We might have to push-pull a little, but it is something the solid members here can deal with. When we came back from the shooting range, there was a noticeable difference in the population of the street rabble, so I have hopes it will be more push than pull.

"The only sticking points are the skimming from the range, and the members involved. I think we need you here for church, so all members under-fucking-stand the problems and the consequences. We have two members under lockdown, a third in the wind, and two more who don't know we're looking. We need Myron down to know what kind of total volume we're looking at on the skim."

He leaned forward. "Prez, we need to consider who to put in as manager at the range, knowing they are going to have to fucking deal with LEO. With the Highwaymen, I think we can handle that final issue while you are here, because we simply need them to get they can't rumble in here whenever they think about it. This is Rebel territory now, and has been for a few years. We had a sit-down with them a couple years ago; we can repeat if we need. That about it, Bingo?" He looked across the desk.

Bingo looked at him steadily, saying, "Just about, brother, but Mason, you need to be thinking about who can replace me as president of the Fort Wayne chapter. I didn't see any of this shit coming, and I think that's because I'm tied up in knots with my nieces and nephews. I can't let one family down at the cost of the other, man. This is tearing me up."

There was a silence on the phone for a long time, then they heard a heavy, unhappy sigh. Mason cleared his throat, then said, "Let's discuss it when I'm there. Give me five hours. I'll get Digger to put Myron in a van, because you know that fucker always wants to bring his computers and shit. They can come down tomorrow; a few hours won't matter, long as we keep the range in lockdown."

Mason sighed again. "Bingo, go ahead and put the clubhouse on lockdown and bring in families. Keep patrols to seasoned members only; I don't want to get surprised by Manzino. Keep the existence and condition of Ramone and Torres need-to-know, but put out word that Rabid needs to be found. Let's grab the other two members—who are they?"

"Choir Boy and Tampa," Bingo said.

"Okay, pick them up and lock them down. Let's contain this shit; keep it from leaking," Mason responded. "I'm leaving now; see you in five. Bingo, reconsider, brother. You know I'll respect your decision, but I'd hate like fuck to have you step out, man. See ya."

The phone call ended, and Slate leaned back in his chair, watching Bingo's face. He didn't like what he saw there; it looked very much like his decision was made. *Fuck me*, he thought. "Want me to get shit lined out, Bingo? Or want to get Deke in here, loop him in first?"

"Whichever you think, Slate. It's your call, brother." Bingo ran a hand across his face. "I need a smoke; I'm stepping outside."

Watching him walk out, Slate stood for a minute thinking, and then yelled through the open door for Deke, changing seats. "Close the door, man. Got something for you to digest."

***

His head was throbbing, eyes burning from lack of sleep. Slate ran a hand through his hair, squinting across the room as Mason walked into the clubhouse. "Fuck me, it's good to see you," he called, reaching out to thump his back.

Pulling Mason into the office, he shut the door behind them. Waiting for him to sit, he was surprised when Mason selected the chair in front of the desk, instead of the one behind it. *I got a bad feeling about this*, he thought as he walked around and sat down where Mason indicated.

"Bingo went home, Mason. I couldn't keep him here without locking him down. I sent three brothers with him, because if anyone is at risk from Manzino, it's Bingo and his family. Deke is following a rumor about Rabid; I expect to hear from him any time now. Bingo never selected a LT, so Deke is as close to second in command as they have here. I've got four brothers that need discussion in church, but I don't know if it warrants waiting to know the scope of the skim or not. To me, the skim is enough; the scope doesn't matter."

Mason sat looking at him steadily, leaning back and resting easily. Slate sighed and told him, "We found that half the girls at the strip club are either dirty or druggies. DeeDee is fully engaged; she'll have replacements by the end of business today. You had a brilliant fucking idea sending her back down here to manage Slinky's; she's good, man. He rubbed his hands across his jaw. "Fuck, I'm tired, Mason. Most members are here; a lot of them brought family into the clubhouse as a precaution, like we suggested. We can sit for church as soon as we get Bingo back, if that's what you think."

They sat there in silence for a few minutes, then Mason said, "I think I'm looking at the president for the Fort Wayne chapter, Slate. You fit well here, and you have my full support. I don't know what I'll do without you in Chicago, but I think Fort Wayne needs you, unless Bingo changes his mind. Hell, even if he does change his mind, I think the shit here needs a different eye watching it. You are more valuable here than Memphis. We can always push that off by a few months, if needed."

"Fuck me," Slate whispered, shaking his head. "You know how I feel about this, Mason. Lieutenant has been way more than enough for me; I don't fucking want any of it. I've always been about the brotherhood, and wind in our faces."

"Yeah, but I also know you understand the stability and strength of that very brotherhood come at a personal cost. You've never been one to shirk duty...don't start now, *Brother*. Oh, and you keep the fucking LT at national...can't lose you there, man."

Slate scrubbed at his face with his palms, raking his fingers through his hair and looking up at Mason. He took a deep breath, saying slowly, "You are my Brother by choice, Mason. Tell me what you need me to do, and I'm on it. Let's get Deke in here; I'd like your read on him." He paused, looking down at his hands and then back up at Mason. "I got this, Prez."

Mason grinned at him, "I know you do, Prez."

18 - Women

"You know...the last thing I wanted to do, was put myself in the same position you were with Mica. I think Essa's cured me of my issues, though. It hurt like fuck when she shut me down at Jackson's, but now, she's seldom on my mind, and it's just not...fuck...I don't know, as urgent when she is. It's like I give about half-a-fuck, but can't be bothered to give much of one.

"You put her on a horse, she's a mature, attractive woman who is desirable, knowledgeable, and passionate. I spent two weeks with that woman, wanting her. Away from that world, she's barely a kid, and that's who I ran into at Jackson's." Slate was pleasantly buzzed, sitting on a couch in the main room of the Fort Wayne clubhouse. He thought that church had gone well, and Bingo had stepped down after all. It had been handled painlessly.

Slate had been confirmed as president with a unanimous vote, which was validating as hell. His conversation with Deke about Sergeant at Arms had gone well. Then, with Deke's support and Mason's blessing, he'd tapped Hoss as Lieutenant. Now, with the chapter business taken care of, he was talking to Mason about other matters.

He tipped his bottle of beer to his lips, taking a long drink. Settling back into the chair, he looked around the room. More than forty full-patch members were scattered around the room, and half of them had their old ladies in tow. Kids were all parked in the basement; they had bunk beds there and room to play. With the thick walls, they were safe from any shit that might go down.

Club pussy kept themselves to the background, working with prospects to keep things moving. The old ladies got testy if they had to share the recreation room with the whores and house mammas, and the pecking order was pretty fucking clear.

He needed to take at least half the brothers on a run tomorrow, cycle through the club businesses. It would establish him as the new leader, and if he could get Bingo to ride too, it would reinforce that this was a bloodless change. He'd already talked to Gasman, the president of the Highwaymen out of Detroit. They'd have a sit-down in two days at some shithole neutral place up in Auburn.

Rebels needed to buy another bar in Fort Wayne, use it to create a neutral zone where they could manage relations with clubs and other folks. He'd seen how well it worked in Chicago, where some of their best alliances had been forged over scarred tables and shot glasses.

They'd also need to leave enough members at the clubhouse tomorrow, in case there was blowback from Manzino. That felt unfinished, but there'd been such a shit storm over the past couple of days he couldn't be bothered to focus on it right now.

They needed to finish the financials, do an armory inventory, clear-up some prospect timeline shit, get new girls qualified and trained for the strip club...had to find and buy a garage, too; there wasn't anywhere for the members to work on their rides, and that was not gonna fly for him.

"She's young, man. She's had to deal with shit, but it didn't mature her like it did Molly. I'm glad to hear you got her out of your system; she'd never get club life," Mason said.

Slate jerked his head around, he'd forgotten their conversation. "Yeah, I get that now." He nodded. "Is Mica pissed at me?"

"Nah, Slate, she thinks you hung the moon, brother." Mason laughed harshly. "She and Daniel are doing good, really good. If she's pissed at anyone, it will be me when I tell her you'll be spending the foreseeable future in Fort Wayne. Maybe Daniel will buy the local hockey team, then they could come visit you."

"Whoa, man, shit going sideways between you and her?" Slate looked at him with narrowed eyes.

"Not sideways, but no room to move forward...or backward. She wants things to go back to how they were before, and I find myself unable to accommodate. Sounds like that fucking pirate movie she loves so much, 'acquiesce to your request'. Shit," Mason laughed again, "she comes into Jackson's like everything is the same, but it's not. That's the place she came to *with me*...came to know me, first, in order to be with me...then with our friends, and that worked, because I had whole pieces of her life outside those brief times in the bar. Now, I don't get those other pieces, so all I get is Jackson's. That shit rubs, man."

"She's happy though, right?" Slate asked quietly.

"Yeah," Mason sighed, "she's happier than I've ever seen her. The shadows that were in her eyes are nearly all gone, and Daniel does that for her. Molly's going to stay in Chicago; I think she'd like to work at Jackson's, so Merry is gonna talk to her in the next couple of days. She needs something to hold onto until her little man comes along. It's been funny to see the Rupert brothers chasing her; both Dickie and J.J. have been in town a lot since Molly showed up. Mica just watches both of them with a frown, and Molly seems indifferent...or fucking brilliant. Then, there's the rookie goalie...he keeps sniffing around too."

* * *

"I think it is a good solution," Gasman responded to Slate's offer of creating a neutral zone in Fort Wayne. Bingo and Hoss flanked Slate at the table, and Gasman had brought his VP, so the table was fairly well balanced.

"Yeah, it's worked well in Chicago. It lets members mix without worrying who needs to keep the upper hand, most of the time anyway. Bars work better than other businesses, and we can get some neutral bouncers. That's how I got started with the Rebels, you know, working without colors at Jackson's to keep shit settled." Slate grinned. "First fight I broke up was between high ranking officers in the Dominos and Disciples. I thought I was a dead man for sure."

Gasman laughed. "I've heard the story a couple of times. Mason's always been right proud of you, man." There was a short pause, and the waitress came back to see if they wanted another round. Gasman looked shrewdly across the table. "He head back to Chicago already?"

Nodding, Slate returned, "Yeah, we finalized club business last night, and he headed back this morning. I figured with Bingo and Hoss, I could handle pretty much anything needed. If I can't, then I don't deserve this patch." He thumped the President patch sewn to his cut right over his name.

Looking around the bar, Gasman clearly noted the number of Rebel club patches sitting at tables. "I don't see Rabid or Ramone, brother. You take care of that shit?"

Slate went still on his chair, his green eyes flashing bright. "Club business, man, not something for casual fucking conversation."

Gasman nodded soberly, holding his hands out with palms down. "Sorry to overstep, but I want to offer any help needed with current situations. The Highwaymen have long held the Rebels as Brothers, and I want to see that continue."

"I hear ya, man," Slate said, deliberately not using the more formal title, "and I will reach out if there is need. Thank you."

Dropping into his bed at the clubhouse that night, Slate was fucking exhausted again. He'd done a balancing act today with Gasman, and gotten everything he wanted. Other than Manzino, all the problems were starting to get sorted. Myron said finances weren't bad at all; they'd evidently snuffed the skim early in the process.

There were a thousand and one details that needed attention, and another thousand Slate knew he should look at, but since Bingo never got overly involved in the details, he risked stepping on toes if he insisted right now. He'd talked to every member today, and spent twice as much time with the many prospect sponsors.

There were so many fucking prospects, and he needed to get a read on them fast. Right now, nobody seemed to have any ideas about strengths or skillsets. They hadn't even done basic background checks on everybody. Deke was handling that now, and he'd take over running the prospects for a while. They'd discussed some standard assignments for prospects, and at one point in the conversation Deke had gotten up to speak to a redheaded girl who scurried out of the main room as fast as she could. Slate didn't ask who it was, but she didn't seem to be Deke's property.

Pinto and Pops were two members he'd also spent a long time talking to today. They'd been members of a club in SoCal, but had relocated to Fort Wayne a few years ago, going gypsy with their club's blessing. When the Rebels decided to lay claim to the town with a chapter and clubhouse, they approached Bingo early on, wanting to know how that would change their position, and opted to patch into the Rebels.

Slate found out they'd had a lot of experience with gangs and the drug cartels out west, and were flush with ideas and information. He needed to talk to Mason, but he wanted to create a new position in the club, one that would focus on the problems that came from the fucking gangs.

He woke up in the dark room, realizing he'd been dozing. Struggling to focus, he heard his phone ringing in his pocket. Digging it out, he glanced at the display and answered in a sleep-laced voice, "Yeah, Prez?"

"Sending Chase to you for a couple weeks," Mason growled and hung up.

Rubbing a hand across his face, Slate muttered to himself, "The fuck was that?" as he fell back onto the bed. He lay there for a minute, then picked up the phone and called Mason back. "Prez...what the fuck is going on?"

"He's needing a change in scenery for a while, maybe more than a couple weeks. Found him drunk, sleeping between two club whores a little bit ago. He'll be riding down with Tug, so you should expect them both for breakfast." Mason was pissed off, that much was clear.

"All right, Mason," Slate said patiently, "I'll take him on and see what's up. How long do I get Tug?"

"He's Chase's ride, so you get Tug until my son comes home," Mason responded. "Let me know if you run into issues, or if he gives you any fucking shit. Boy's sixteen going on dead if he can't monitor his mouth."

"Yeah, boss." Slate yawned, hanging up the phone after Mason abruptly disconnected. He rolled over, toeing off his boots and curling up on his side.

***

Up the next morning, he stood in the clubhouse kitchen, looking at the women who were either working or standing idle. No old ladies in here right now, these workers looked to be club pussy, and the idle-standers were acquaintances, not even hang-arounds. He cleared his throat, and every eye in the room swung to him. "How we doing keeping up with food for the members and families during the lockdown?" he asked the room in general, taking a sip from his coffee cup.

No response came, and the girls who were doing nothing to make themselves useful resumed their conversation. He laughed to himself, *Oh yeah, this was not going to be pretty*. He dragged his gaze across the room, settling on one petite redhead, who had walked over in front of the refrigerator. He'd been seeing her around the clubhouse a lot over the past few days, and was intrigued by her. He'd seen her talking to Deke and PBJ more often than not; she seemed to have a mix of confidence and insecurity, and she was always hanging close to the Fort Wayne brothers or DeeDee.

She started pulling out food and sorting it on top of the cabinet, her head firmly ducked to avoid looking at him except for quick glances. When he had first walked in, she'd been loading the dishwasher, and it was now happily swishing and glugging along. Looked to him like she was determined to singlehandedly keep the clubhouse going. Pointing at her when she peeked up at him again, he crooked a finger, calling her wordlessly to his side.

She looked left and right, and he thought that was hilarious, so he crooked the finger again, and then pointed it at her and nodded with a grin. She walked towards him, her downcast eyes cutting left and right still, noting the responses of the other women in the room. He reached out and put a hand gently on her elbow, steering her out of the room and down the hallway to his office. Speaking to her for the first time, he said, "Ruby, sit down," thinking it was the perfect nickname for the beautiful redhead.

She sat on the edge of the chair closest to the door, seemingly poised for a quick getaway. He frowned; she was clearly nervous, and hadn't yet looked up at him. He asked, "Ruby, how many of the women in that kitchen have done any cooking or cleanup at the clubhouse?"

Eyes downcast, she paused for a long minute, and then slowly spoke in a quiet voice, "I don't know, some of them."

"Would you fucking look at me, Ruby?" Rolling his shoulders, he asked again, struggling to keep his tone patient. *Fuck*, he was tired. "Answer the question; it's not hard. Simply tell me, in your opinion, how many of the whores and hang-arounds have done a fucking thing for the club, other than fuck a member." She stayed silent, and he began to lose his temper, snapping at her, "Think you could be bothered to answer me, Ruby?" What the hell was her deal? She talked to other members, he'd seen her approach more than one; was she fucking afraid of *him*?

She swallowed distinctly, raising her panic-filled, green eyes to his for the first time, her voice nearly inaudible. "About half of them help out, the other half wait for old ladies to go home so they can be with established members. That's the hang-arounds. There's a group of party dolls who show up for events like hog roasts. They don't do anything but drink and sleep with members."

Speaking in a softer tone, he said, "Thank you. Now, was that so fucking hard?" Slate slumped back into his chair, watching her face slowly relax a little as he sat and finished drinking his coffee. Thinking hard, he stood, motioning her to walk with him, telling her, "You're in charge of housekeeping, kitchen, and provisions. Who do you want to help you with the housekeeping?"

"What?" she yelped, startled.

"Did I pick wrong? Did you not hear me, or are you fucking blonde under all that red hair? Can you, or can you not run housekeeping, kitchen, and provisions?" he asked, striding quickly back towards the kitchen.

"I can, uh...but I'm not an old lady. I can't be in charge of anything," she said frantically, trying to keep up with his long legs.

"What the fuck? Goddammit, if I say you are, then you are. So suck it up, buttercup. Help me out, baby," he told her as they turned into the kitchen. "Pour me some coffee, Ruby?" He handed her his cup.

He raised his voice and said to the room, "I asked a question in here a few minutes ago, and nobody fucking answered me. That's fucking disrespectful." He pointed at the two groups of women who had no stake in the game where the club was concerned. The hang-arounds were there for the party, booze, drugs, and sex, nothing more. "You bitches are gonna get off the pot, because your opportunity to shit has been fucking revoked," he said. He turned, calling out to the main clubhouse room, "Worm, Tank, Hurley—get your asses into the kitchen."

Taking the filled cup from Ruby, he stood there, his posture relaxed, sipping at his coffee. The prospects came into the kitchen, looking between Slate and the redhead standing just behind him. He pointed to the two groups of women, and told the prospects, "Get this shit out of here.

Make sure they get a ride off the property, but in a cage, not on the back of a member's scoot."

He swung his gaze around the room again. "Anyone else want to cut out now? If you are staying, you are working. Ruby here will be assigning jobs, and if you give her shit, she will fucking tell me. Don't fuck with her. This is the only warning anyone gets." He looked at the prospects. "That goes for prospects and members, too. *Do not fuck with Ruby*. Make it known."

He turned to leave, pausing to smooth a hand down her hair. "Don't go anywhere, Ruby. Get this shit straightened out for me, baby. I'll see you in a bit." He was amused to see a flash of rebellion in her eyes, and then disconcerted when she quickly lowered her eyes again, staring at the floor between her feet. He knew there was a story here, he just needed to find the people who knew what it was.

***

Myron was sitting in a quiet room they'd set up for him and his babies, where his electronic toys were given pride of place. "Hey, need you to set up access to one of the accounts for Ruby, the little redhead. She's going to be in charge of provisions, and she'll need a card or cash." Slate paused in the doorway, leaning against the opening.

"'K, I'll take care of it," the man said without looking up. "Hey, I should have totals for you on the skim by tonight, Prez, but it's not bad." He spun around, grabbing a folder off the table behind him. "Got a lead on a bar today for you to look at—Marie's on Main. It's been in the family for generations, but they're struggling. It's pretty perfect, and I think we can get it for half-market, if we promise to keep existing staff. The family is loyal, and that's something we can all get behind."

Slate took the folder thrust at him, thumbing through the paperwork. "This looks good, man. Nice job," he said. "Should we approach personally, or go through legal? What do you think?"

"I think they'd take a direct approach best; you should take Tug. I hear he's coming in and should be here in an hour or so." Myron laughed. "Oh, before I forget, I dropped another five thousand into your grandmother's account last night. Your brother called and explained the situation, so I didn't want to wait and hold her up."

Slate froze, keeping his voice even and calm as his hands clenched into fists. "Ben called about a situation? What situation?"

Myron turned to look at him, whispering quietly, "Oh, fuck." He waited a beat, and then continued, "Prez, man...he said she needed meds, and to pay for a hospital stay."

Slate fumbled his phone out of his front pocket, hitting a speed dial number. Holding it to the side of his head, he waited for the ringing to be answered. "GeeMa, everything okay there? Are you okay?" He paused to listen to her reply. "Okay, so no hospital?" His eyes narrowed and he sighed. "Did he take it all?" Another pause, then, "I know, GeeMa. I love you too. I'm gonna see if I can get someone to find him. Let's close that account and get a brand new one set up."

He raised an eyebrow at Myron. "I have someone who can get everything done fast." Myron nodded at him. "We'll have you sorted out by..." *Tonight,* Myron mouthed, "...tonight, GeeMa. Myron will give you a call later, and he'll have all the details."

He listened for a moment, then told her, "Yes, he is a nice young man. I don't think he's got a girlfriend, but if you know of anyone..." He waited, listening and laughing. "Talk to you soon, okay? Bye." He disconnected the call, pushing the phone back into the front pocket of his jeans.

"Myron, don't sweat it. I appreciate you taking an interest and making sure my family is taken care of. She's wanting to set you up with a girl; she said you're too nice a young man to be alone." He thumped the man on the back with a grin. "You need anything else from me? We'll want to seed that new account, so transfer another five thousand. He cleaned out the entire fucking thing, not just the money transferred yesterday, so she's got nothing right now."

Myron's forehead was wrinkled as he shook his head. "I should have known better, Prez. I'm sorry. What did he want the money for, really?"

"Recording time for his band," Slate laughed, "what a joke." He turned to walk out of the room, then looked over his shoulder. "Don't forget the card or cash for Ruby. She'll need to go shopping soon; we've got a lot of families here to feed."

Myron nodded, fingers flying over his keyboard. "Gotcha, Prez. I'm on it."

Walking back to his office, he saw Deke and called him over. "Tell me about the little redhead. She a house mamma, or family? She got a name?"

Deke looked at him oddly, asking, "Cute, short, red curls, green eyes?" Slate nodded. "She's...unique, man. Not pussy, not a house mamma, and she's not fucking tradable. Melanie is...fuck, let me get us a beer." Deke turned, walking out.

Slate sat down, surprised at the response; he hadn't expected anything other than a name, really. *Melanie*, he mouthed to himself, then shook his head, smiling and saying softly, "Ruby."

Deke came back with two bottles, setting a beer in front of Slate and closing the door. He took a drink of his, looking at Slate over the bottle. "You know how that chick in Chicago has special status, first because of her shit, and then because of her relationships with members and Mason?" he asked.

"Mica, yeah, we branded her Princess; it was a first for the Rebels. It gave her untouchable status both within, and outside of the club. Put her off limits for any blowback shit from other clubs, too." He said evenly, "Most of us watched her grow up, and she is special to all of us." He thumped his chest with a closed fist, saying, "A fucking treasure."

Deke nodded. "Melanie was best friends with Lockee, Winger's daughter. Her home life was shit, and she practically lived with Winger and DeeDee from the time she was ten years old. When Winger came to be a brother, his family came with. So, she grew up around the club, like Lockee did. She was wild and fun, always in our shit and pushing to be part of things. She and Lockee were like crazy twins, sneaking out to party, using fake IDs to get into clubs, going to college parties...shit like that. When Winger and Lockee were killed in that wreck,

DeeDee held onto that relationship with Melanie. She became a...what do you call it...a substitute?"

"A surrogate," Slate clarified.

"Yeah, she became a surrogate daughter for DeeDee. She moved into the clubhouse suite we let DeeDee keep, and she's been here nearly the whole time since, even when DeeDee was up visiting Chicago. Her status is...complicated. It's more like a little sister than anything, and she's never hooked up with a brother that I know of. To us, here in the Fort Wayne chapter, she's as much our princess as Mica is yours, but without the official approval." He drained his beer.

"A couple years ago, not long after the accident, she made herself scarce, and *fuck* we missed her. I think she'd found a boyfriend, but shit must have turned out hard, because Bingo had to go snag her, but we were simply glad she came back. But, Slate, she came back different, like she'd been beat down—not physically, or I think we'd have found and killed the fucker—but she's quiet now, never causing trouble, and she's fucking cautious with her words, as I bet you've noticed." Deke looked over at Slate.

Slate tapped the tip of the beer bottle against his bottom lip. "Is she in the clubhouse because she wants to be, or because she doesn't have anywhere else to go? What will happen to her when DeeDee moves out?" He took a long drink. "Do ya know how old she is?"

Deke pursed his lips. "I'd like to think she's here because she wants to stay close to DeeDee, but who the fuck knows what goes through a woman's mind. Now DeeDee, she knows her time here is limited, but managing Slinky's is giving her a way to make good money, so she's sticking for now. Melanie would no longer be as off-limits if she weren't staying with DeeDee, but I don't know if she realizes that. She's twenty-eight or so, I think. Lockee was only twenty-five when the accident happened, and they were the same age."

"All right, man, thanks for the background," Slate said casually, dismissing Deke.

He paused in the doorway; it looked like he was deciding whether to speak. Shaking his head, Deke finally said, "Prez, Melanie is...well, fuck...she's *ours*. You get that?" Slate nodded at him; he understood that possessive streak when it came to people the club wanted to protect. Deke gave him a chin lift, and then walked back out into the main room.

Slate took another swig from his beer, draining it and setting it on the corner of the desk. He was thinking about Ruby...Melanie. She'd awoken something in him he thought had faded. He found himself wanting to protect her, but he knew she might need protection from *him* more than anything. Or maybe he was too late to protect her, if what Deke said was right.

He licked his bottom lip, tipping his head back and remembering her mouth, her lips parted and full. His cock stirred as he thought about taking her mouth, owning her, possessing her. He imagined how her kisses would taste, wanting to sink his fingers into her hair as he held her mouth to his.

God, he was hard now, and he hadn't even gotten to the rest of her. He wanted her, but he wanted her safe more than anything. He'd talk to her, see how things shook out. Looking up, he saw Tug and Chase walking through the main room. He adjusted himself in his jeans. Fuck him, he'd greet them later. They'd be back here in a minute; he still hadn't eaten and now he had a fucking hard-on.

He walked into the kitchen area, looking around for Ruby, and saw her squatting inside one of the coolers. It looked like she was inventorying food and supplies on the bottom shelf. "Ruby, did Myron get you set up for funds yet?" he asked her, making her jump. His eyes snagged on how her pants were molded to her ass and thighs. "I told him you needed to get provisions, and he's going to get you a card, but if he can't get that in the next hour, he'll give you cash."

She was looking anywhere but at him, and that was pissing him off again. "Ruby," he said, his voice low. He stopped there, simply holding her name in his mouth.

She turned her head, looking at him out of the corner of her eye, and responded quietly, "No, I haven't talked to him yet."

"You got a list together, baby?" he asked, taking a step closer to her and squatting down behind her. She took in a quick breath as his thighs came down on either side of her ass, the insides of his legs touching her. Moving to go down on one knee, she edged away from him, and he caught a hint of vanilla and something flowery.

Slate's smile lifted one corner of his mouth as he took in a deep breath, scenting her again. He raised a hand, trailing fingertips down her back to just above the waistband of her jeans. "Well, do you?" he asked, gliding his fingers back up to her shoulder blades.

"Do I what?" she asked breathily, moving forward again, out of reach.

"Do you have a list together yet, Ruby? Are you ready to head out shopping?" he asked, giving her the gist of his question.

"Oh, no, not yet...not a full list. I don't want to spend money we don't have to, so I'm trying to get an inventory done. I've got a menu ready, so I know what we need." She spoke fast, moving sideways and further away from him, still looking down.

"Buy what you need for the menu, and we'll sort the rest out later," he laughed, "unless you are making gourmet shit that costs a truckload. If it's basic stuff, then it won't hurt to have extras." He shifted to one knee, mimicking her pose and turning to face her, and asked, "Have you ever been to the Chicago clubhouse?"

Shaking her head, she tucked her chin down and started working on her fucking inventory again. "Then you've never met our cook. He is a crazy man, that Road Runner. He's a Cordon Bleu chef, and he makes all kinds of crazy shit sometimes." He grinned. "So if he was here, I'd worry, because some of his shit costs like crazy. Who in the MC would know if the rice was flavored with saffron, for fuck's sake? But to him, it matters, so we put up with him. He works at a hotel in Chicago, and he's always trying new recipes on the brothers, and then pissing and moaning, because the only 'critique' he gets is either 'it's fucking good' or 'it tastes like shit'." Slate laughed.

Watching the side of her face, he saw her lips curving up into a smile, and responded to that. "I know, funny...right? We have some women there with special status, Mica and Jess; they're kind of like you. They are probably his best hope at improving his trade. Fucking Road Runner, he's a hoot." Her sudden stillness hadn't been lost on him; when he spoke about Mica and Jess, she'd frozen in place.

"Ruby, I know how you wound up here. I'm sorry about the pain; I know about losing people you're close to, like you did Lockee. What you did—I think it was a good thing, sticking with DeeDee. Takes a decent person to put themselves aside like that, and think about someone else who's hurting." He shifted, sitting back on his ass and leaning against the inside of the cooler door.

"All the brothers here, they look at you and see a little sister, someone who's grown up in the club, someone they'd fucking kill to protect, and someone who's earned their loyalty. I get that. I do. I understand on many levels that this is your family. It's my family too, and I'm not here to fuck that up for you. I'm not here to downgrade your status. In fact, I'd like to solidify your place in the club, as much as that's possible. I appreciate you taking on the organization of shit like you have today, and I hope I didn't piss you off, but putting you in charge of the non-old ladies makes life easier for me," he explained with a shrug.

She cut her eyes over to him again, silently. "You don't talk much, do you, Ruby?" he mused.

She shook her head again. He sat there, staring at her. They stayed like that for several long minutes until she finally shook her hair out of her face and looked over at him. Speaking softly, she said, "I don't mind organizing things. It's easy, and I already know who's good at what, so assigning jobs is easy too. Since I live here, I want to pull my weight—I've always wanted to—and I've always helped where I could. I've helped with driving cages and stuff in the past, but this feels good. It feels like it's a 'job,' you know?" She paused, moistening her lips with the tip of her pink tongue. He greedily watched it sweep across her bottom lip. "I don't know what to say to you," she whispered.

"Just say what you want, baby," he whispered back. God, he fucking loved her voice.

"Status..." she started, and stopped to swallow, "...my status is...I don't have any. I know the guys, *my* guys...I know our Fort Wayne members won't hurt me, but when there's a party, I stay in my room. It scares me sometimes, what happens in a clubhouse...what people are capable of."

Pausing in silence for a few minutes, she lowered her gaze, then said, "All these new members and the out-of-town members, they scare me, too. This job scares me, because I am nothing. I know how club business works, and if I'm going to do it...this job you gave me...I can't stay in my room like I normally would. I have to get out and make sure stuff gets done, and done right.

"We want a good reflection on the club, because it matters. That scares me—having to come out like that—because I am nothing; I don't have status. I'm not protected, because I'm not family. I'm not part of it...the club I mean. I'm not with anyone. I know if it weren't for DeeDee, I couldn't even stay here. I wouldn't have a home, couldn't live with my family."

Slate waited patiently, he wanted to be sure she was through talking. "Baby, you finished?" he asked softly. She nodded, keeping her gaze on the floor between his feet. "Okay," stretching out his legs, crossing them at the ankle, he said firmly, "look at me, Ruby."

He waited again, giving her time to lift her eyes to meet his. Smiling gently at her, he told her, "You can have status now. You choose between two things, and I'll explain the differences to you, but both give you rank. One, you can choose to be our Princess. That puts you off-limits to all Rebel members, regardless of chapter affiliation. It puts you off-limits to members of other clubs, support or not. It's an official position, and carries weight. It puts you under guard, though, because a Princess is precious. We'll fucking invade your life," he grinned, "but you will be respected by members, old ladies, club mammas...everyone. So that's the first option...Princess. We could even get you your own cut, if you like to ride. Do you like to ride?" he asked curiously.

She grinned and nodded, her face brightening with happiness. "Winger taught Lockee and me how to ride, and I have a Sportster that Gypsy and Gunny helped me rebuild." She tucked her chin and dropped her eyes. "I like to wrench."

His heart stretched a little at that smile on her face; in a bare moment, she'd gone from pretty to stunning. "Well, alrighty," he laughed, "that sounds good, baby. God, I love a woman who's not afraid of a little grease. I'd love to take a run with you one day soon." He watched as that fragile edge came back into her downcast eyes and frowned; he didn't like it.

"Second option," his voice deepened, "which I happen to like a lot better, but it's up to you," he caught her eyes with his again, "is I'd like you in my bed, Ruby. I'd like you on the back of my bike. I've never wanted to have an old lady before, but that's all I can think about since I saw you. I don't know if we'd even be a good match, but goddamn...you are all I can see. Full fucking disclosure...I left a girl in Chicago when I came here, because she didn't know what she wanted, but that's not something that would cause problems. She wasn't my old lady, not even fucking close. She showed up at the club bar, but I hadn't seen her in months, and she...disappointed me." He paused, watching closely, and he saw her pale.

Slate leaned his head back against the door; he was pretty sure he knew what she was going to pick, and it didn't make him happy. "Ruby, you can't be both, baby. You'll either be Princess, and untouchable—even by me," he told her. It wasn't the complete truth; even though Mica was their Princess in Chicago, Mason had hooked up with her; he'd loved her. If Slate wanted her, he could have her. He just wanted to see what Ruby would choose though, wanted to see if she felt what he did whenever he was around her. He wanted her to choose *him*. "Or you can be my old lady, and have greater status with my patch on your back. How things are right now aren't working...for all the reasons you listed. You aren't safe in the clubhouse if you don't have rank, and baby, you don't have any right now. You are dead-fucking-right about that." He took a breath. "So which is it, Ruby? Which path will you choose? Or do you even want to remain here? Maybe I read you wrong, and you'd rather lean away from the club entirely?"

She shook her head quickly at that. "I don't want to leave, Prez. This is my family," she said simply, "and this is my home."

"So, I'm 'Prez' now, huh?" He laughed a little bitterly, then asked insistently, "Which path, baby?"

"What would be my job as Princess?" she asked.

"Is that your pick then?" *God,* he was frustrated, frowning at her; he could already see her sliding away.

She nodded, whispering, "Yes."

"The job is the same until it changes," he said curtly, standing and looking down at the top of her head. She'd fucking turned him down flat. "I'll call Chicago and make it official, and then I'll announce it in church tonight to the members. I won't lie. I wish like hell you'd picked differently—no fucking bones about that—but as Princess, you are precious and un-fucking-touchable," he repeated.

He took a deep breath in, saying harshly, all the soft gone from his voice, "You will take two prospects to the store with you. I want you gone within the hour so you can make sure to be back in plenty of time for supper to get made." He turned and walked out without another word, leaving the door ajar behind him, and Ruby sitting on the floor.

***

"You sure you want it to go down this way, Chase?" Slate asked, stepping out of range of another swing. He took two steps to the side, and kicked the kid's feet out from under him. Chase fell flat on his back, gasping for breath. "Seriously, kid, you want it this bad?" Slate asked again, standing now with his arms crossed over his chest.

"What the hell, Slate? Yes, I want to learn how to fight, motherfucker," Chase huffed, rolling to his hands and knees, climbing slowly to his feet. "Get me a teacher, man. I'm tired of Dad telling me no, and I fucking want to prospect in as soon as I'm eighteen. I have to be able to hold my own; I know that. Being who my dad is, it's more important than anything." He imitated Mason's voice, "'Remember, no dead weight'. I've heard that a thousand times." He brushed sweat-wet hair out of his face.

"Here's my read, kiddo; take it for what it's worth. You're too impatient; you need to wait for openings, not try to always create them. You lack accuracy; your swings are wild, with no real target. You think about only one thing at a time, instead of planning for the sequence of events. You are weak; you'll break your wrists if you do happen to connect the way you hit. You don't protect yourself at all; it's hard to take care of shit if you can't keep fists from your body or face. You lack stamina; it's like you've done nothing hard your whole life, and you are young, lacking weight, reach, and height," Slate drawled, watching the kid's face for anger or some other emotion, and seeing only attentiveness.

He continued, pleased at reading willingness instead of defensiveness in Chase's stance, "So here's the flip side of all that. You are young, and can be trained. You lack stamina, but that can be built. You don't protect yourself, because you've never had to. You are weak, but that's easier to fix than stamina. You think about one isolated movement at a time, but once you see the flow of the sequence, you'll understand how to combine efforts to better effectiveness. You lack accuracy, but practice can fix that. The only real problem I see is your impatience, but if we focus on the rest, then patience will come."

He reached out, grabbed Chase's wrist, and pulled him into a one-armed hug. "I'm not a good teacher, kid, but

Deke knows someone with a good reputation. We'll get you lined out with lessons, and how quickly you improve will be entirely in your hands."

Chase thumped him on the back. "Thanks, Slate, that's awesome. When can I start?"

"Probably by the end of the week. You'll be living here in the clubhouse until I get a house, but I've no idea how long that will be. No driving—you'll be with a patch brother when you leave the clubhouse. No arguments about that, motherfucker." Slate grinned. "Once we get shit straight here, we'll see about changing your driver status, but I want zero mouth out of you until then."

"You got it, Slate. No shit, no how, no way," he swore. "What about school?"

"We gotta go the homeschool route, and I've got that covered too. There's a couple of women who live here in the clubhouse who've offered to help out." He saw the look on Chase's face. "Not whores, man, wipe that look off your fucking face. DeeDee's old man died a few years ago, and she and her adopted daughter still live here and are willing to help your ass out. Ruby is our Princess, so respect, man. Don't let me hear about any shit there, either."

"No way, Slate. I didn't know you were talking about Ruby, she'd kick my ass before she let me disrespect her. I saw her take one of the prospects to town the other day for not clearing trash from the main room. She's fierce when she wants to be," Chase said seriously.

Tug was leaning against the wall near the door and he straightened up, nodding his head at Slate. "Nice job, Prez. If you're done playing nursemaid, Ruby assigned shithead here a permanent room, so I'll get the kid set up downstairs, and remind him where showers, chow, and crappers are."

Slate watched them walk out of the gym, setting his shoulders before he followed them. In the main room, he sat down on a stool, accepting a beer from the prospect manning the bar. He looked around, seeing pleasing changes from Ruby's efforts over the past few days. From what Chase said, it sounded like she had settled into her new role in the club just fine. *Not my choice*, he thought, but had to respect her for diving in like she had.

Hoss sat down next to him. "Prez." He nodded, agreeably.

"Brother," Slate greeted him back.

"Great call on that bar; it's perfect. The location is good, puts us deep downtown," Hoss said. "I think the staff will stay too."

Slate grinned. "Myron's the one who found it, but I'm glad it's as advertised. That family is managing it now, but they won't come with. Who do you see handling it day-to-day?"

"I think Gypsy would do a good job. He's originally Chicago, so he's seen how the neutral places are supposed to work. He won't have a fucking chip on his shoulder and be looking for a fight every time colors come through the door." Hoss rubbed his arm restlessly.

"Do you think the FW chapter will care he's originally from Chicago?" Slate asked.

Hoss shook his head. "Nah, he's been here since the beginning, so he's a FW founder. He's got better status here than in Chicago by now."

"Sounds good. Did we make an offer on the property yet? I'd like to get this handled, get our people in there. You think Gypsy will need Myron or DeeDee to help for a bit, until he gets a handle on the business side?" Slate asked.

"Nope, he's got a Master's in business. As long as Myron and DeeDee are available as needed, he'll do okay. Offer tendered and accepted this morning, we set closing for two weeks out." Hoss yawned. "It's been a long fucking day, Prez. Any thoughts on lifting the lockdown yet?"

Slate shook his head. "Play stays the same. Manzino is still in the wind; he's not popped his head up yet. Until I hear about him showing up somewhere other than here, then our notion he's around helps keep the club on their toes. Everything else is coming together, though. Slinky's is in training mode, so within a couple weeks, we'll be fully staffed there with clean girls."

"I'm worried about Down Range; any ideas on when we want to open that bitch back up? I get the chills when I think of PBJ having to deal with LEO every day." Hoss shivered dramatically.

Slate laughed. "Naw, man, Diablo won the toss for the range job. PBJ wants on Princess duty for now, so I told him okay. Ruby likes him well enough, and he's good with the prospects. Babysitting duty is good for them, and he's always pulling in two or three when Ruby wants to go somewhere. She's not shy about bossing them around either, which is good for 'em."

Hoss cut his eyes over at Slate. "Saw the cut, Prez. She looks good in it. I thought she was too quiet, it's good to hear she's cutting up a little; are you sure she understands being Rebel property? She's okay with the escort and interference?"

"Yeah, she gets it. I'm glad the brothers were good with it; she's making a difference around here already. It gives the members something specific to be proud of and protect." Slate stretched. "I had a couple of the boys go on a run to give notice to the Highwaymen and other local clubs, letting them know her status and what it means. We need her safe, man; she's precious to us all."

Hearing something behind him, he turned and saw a mane of red curls escaping around the corner. He grinned to himself. She'd been skirting close to him since she made her choice, he was always seeing her out of the corner of his eye or like today, darting around a corner. He wasn't sure why, and thought she might be worried about her 'job', but maybe she was keeping tabs on him. He liked that. He liked her...a lot. He still fucking wanted her, but she'd made the wrong choice for that. He'd given her an ultimatum, and she'd picked the wrong answer.

19 - Brothers

A month later

Walking in the hallway from the supply room at Marie's, Slate was carrying a case of beer for the cooler. They had a special event tonight; a band named *Occupy Yourself* was coming in. He grinned, because when he finally got to talk to Ben a couple of weeks ago, he'd mentioned this band, and Ben got all excited. He needed to see if he could get something signed tonight, mail it to GeeMa to keep for when Ben finally went home. He was still pissed at his brother, but he loved him, and would always do small things that could bring a little joy to his life.

He pushed the door open, turning sideways to move through it. Before the door closed, he thought he heard a voice call his name, so he pushed the door open again and looked back up the hallway. There was a young man standing there in dark shades, his sandy blond hair covered with a black fedora hat. Carrying an acoustic guitar over his shoulder on a strap, he looked oddly familiar.

"Hey, man," Slate asked, "are you with the band?" Nodding, the man clapped him on the shoulder as he walked past. The dude stank of whisky; evidently, he'd already been drinking hard tonight. Walking with him, Slate decided to ask for that autograph. "My little brother is a big fan. Is there any way I could get you to sign something for him?" Feeling smooth, he snagged a napkin from a table and pulled a pen from his pants pocket. Nodding, the guy reached for the napkin, and then slid the sunglasses down his nose halfway, his icy blue eyes looking into Slate's face, the corners of his mouth tipping up into a grin.

Slate's heart rose to his throat. "Fuck me," he breathed, reaching out and grabbing the guy into a tight embrace, pounding his back. "Baby brother, what the hell are you doing in Fort Wayne? Ben...Benny, oh man, it's good to see you, shrimp. God, it's good to see you. How long have you been here?"

Ben was laughing, hugging him tightly. "Andy, I've missed you. You're a fucking president, man? That's hardcore," he said, looking at his patch.

Setting him apart with a little shake, Slate asked seriously, "Does GeeMa know where you are?"

Ben nodded, pushing his sunglasses onto the top of his head. "She's the one who told me about you being in Fort Wayne, where to find you. I started looking for gigs out this way, and then heard about this place." Slate pulled him into another hard hug, closing his eyes for a moment as they embraced. Ben pulled back first, looking at him and smiling. "I gotta get to the stage, man. You gonna come watch us?"

Slate frowned. "What the fuck you mean, 'get to the stage'?"

Cocking his head sideways, Ben asked, "You really didn't know, bro? Even after I talked to you on the phone, you never, like, Googled the band to listen to some of the music?"

"Know what? What don't I know? What's going on, Benny?" he asked slowly.

"Andy, *Occupy Yourself* is my band; we're playing here at Marie's for the next week. Enough talking for now—I need to get to the stage," he paused to listen, cocking his head to one side, "because the crowd is getting restless, and believe me when I say drunk, pissed off people can get really ugly." Ben laid his hand on Slate's arm. "We'll talk after the show, Andy. Okay?"

He nodded, dumbfounded, saying, "Slate...that's what everyone calls me now—Slate, not Andy."

"What the fuck ever, bro, just come listen." Ben laughed.

He stood in the back of the bar for the next hour-and-a-half, watching as Ben and the guys in the band first captured the crowd, and then held them enthralled with their music. They were good, and for the music they played, Ben's voice was perfect, full of gravel, angst, and whisky-soaked tones.

Ben had started the set out by roaring questions at the crowd, and they'd responded in kind as the energy in the room ramped up. The band seemed to have local fans, and Slate realized the crowd was often singing along with at least the chorus, and frequently the entire song.

All the guys in the band had booze or beer near them, and they'd been drinking liberally as they played, but none of them seemed overly drunk, except Ben. He'd started stumbling about halfway through the set, so the bass player had hemmed him into a small section at the front of the stage. That, at least, kept Ben from striding side-to-side and running into equipment.

Slate heard Ben call out, slurring his words slightly, and mixing some up, "We are *Occupy Yourself,* and this is our last song of the evening, folks. You have an awesome crowd been, we want to rock you for thanking out with us tonight. We'll be here all week, so come back and party with *Occupy Yourself* again tomorrow!" He turned and made a hand motion to the drummer, who counted them off into the next song.

"Fucker is hammered," came a voice from behind Slate. He turned to see a woman standing behind him, staring at the band with a frown on her face. She was dressed for business, in slacks and a jacket, but it was her face that caught his attention. "Benita Owens?" he asked as quietly as he could, given the volume at which the music was being played.

She looked him up and down dismissively. "Yes?" her voice lilted up questioningly.

He stuck his hand out. "Andy Jones, I knew your father, Darren Owens, back in Enoch."

Her face stilled as they shook, and she said flatly, "You're Ben's brother."

Slate stood waiting for her to continue, but that was evidently all she intended to say. "Yes, I haven't seen him for a while, so watching them tonight has been fun. The band sounds good too. Do you travel with them often?" he asked her, trying to be polite.

"Yes, but I don't just travel with them; I'm the band manager," she said with a sigh. "Not that it's an easy job, at least not anymore, with all the partying they do."

They turned to watch the band again, seeing Ben stumble around the small part of the stage the bass player allowed him. Slate frowned. "How much does he drink during shows?"

Benita shook her head slowly. "It's not just during shows, Andy; he's plastered nearly all the time. We had a terrible time getting good tracks laid down in our last studio sessions; we ran out of money, and had to stop recording for a while. Thank goodness, Ben found an investor, and we were able to finish the tracks and pay for production. Before that, the band was considering dropping Ben. After he showed up with cash in-hand, they stopped talking about it. There was even enough money left over to start this tour, and we've made pretty good book at our stops so far."

"Where are you staying while you're in town?" Slate asked.

"We've got a couple of suites booked at a hotel. We'll check-in after the show tonight," she said, pushing her hair away from her face tiredly. "I've got to get the merch table set up. Good talking to you, Andy."

"Let me know if you need anything, Benita. It's good to see you again." Slate reached out and touched her shoulder before she moved away.

It worried him that Benny was drinking as much as Benita had indicated. Knowing how far his mother had fallen, and how quickly, he wondered if Benny might be in more trouble than he could recognize on his own. It had been eleven years since Slate left Enoch in his dust, and after all this time, he didn't feel like he Ben would listen to any advice he'd give him. If the roles were switched, he sure as hell wouldn't pay attention to anything his brother said, after he'd been gone from his life for so long.

The crowd's applause brought his attention back to the stage, where the band had finally finished their last song. He heard gasps from the audience as Ben tipped slowly forward, falling off the stage. Before his body hit the floor, Slate was running forward, shoving patrons out of the way. He saw the bass player throw his head back and caught his screamed, *"FUCK,"* as he stood on the stage with fists clenched.

Crouching next to Ben on the floor, Slate saw the blood pooling underneath his brother's head. Resisting the urge to roll him over, he made sure Ben was breathing as he heard footsteps approaching from behind. He pulled his phone from his jeans' pocket and dialed 911, speaking briefly. He gave the operator the address and situation, and then disconnected the call.

Looking over his shoulder, he saw Hurley, one of the club prospects. Motioning him over, Slate said quietly, "Pros, lock shit down; tell the brothers a bus is coming. Get these fuckers out of here to give them room to get a gurney in." Turning back to Ben's still form, he heard a sound of assent from Hurley. Reaching out a hand, he gently brushed Ben's hair back from his face, whispering, "I got you, shrimp. I got you."

Things got hectic once the EMTs were there, but Slate was glad to see Goose was one of the responders. He'd been a Rebel for years, and was solid. It made him feel better right away when Goose looked at Ben and then at Slate, asking, "This a relative, Prez?" If he could still see the likeness the brothers shared under all the swelling and blood, then he was paying attention.

"This is Ben Jones, my baby brother, Goose. He's hammered, been drinking all night while they performed. Passed out on his feet, and he fell face first into the floor. I didn't move him, just made sure he was breathing," Slate reported evenly.

"Good fucking deal, Prez. We'll take it from here. St. Joe's is closest, but I think we probably need to do Lutheran, in case he needs some aftercare," he said. "You want to ride in the bus, or follow us?"

"I'll follow, and I'll get out of your way now," Slate said, standing and walking away. What the fuck was Ben thinking? How often had this kind of shit happened in the past? The band had started breaking down the equipment, not even coming over to see if his brother was okay. He jumped onto the stage, walking over to the bass player.

Tucking his thumbs in his front pockets, he said, "You know you can leave the set-up as-is if you want. You're here the rest of the week. Let me know if you guys need help with anything. They're taking him to a local hospital. Who should I call with updates?"

"Not me, man. That fucker just drank himself out of the band, as far as I'm concerned. He has family in town; that's the only reason we came this far east. Maybe Nita knows the contact info for them. She's our manager." This was all said as he continued unscrewing equipment and tucking it into padded boxes arranged on the stage. "Breaking down is a habit; we take our gear with us when we go, but thanks."

"He been like this long?" Slate asked.

"Fuck yeah, he's been messed up for a long time. He's an excellent musician and talented vocalist when he's straight and on his game, but when he's drinking and using, he's useless." The guy looked up finally, and then did a double-take and sighed. "You're the brother, aren't you?" he asked resignedly.

"Yeah, I'm his brother," Slate said wryly.

Standing, the guy thrust out his hand. "I'm Danny Schraff. I play bass." He pointed over his shoulder at the drummer. "That's Blake Downey; he's the drummer, and the guy over there who plays keyboard and guitar, that's Dmitri Glass." He looked ashamed. "Sorry about Ben getting hurt. We all appreciated you investing in the band. We really needed that infusion of cash a few weeks ago."

That was the second mention of an investment, and he assumed that's what Benny told everybody about the money, instead of saying he'd stolen it from his grandmother. Investor sounded much better than 'I'm a thief', for sure. Slate shook Danny's hand, and waved at the other band members. "Do you have Benita's number? I can call her and let her know how Ben is doing. Will you guys finish out the week here, or have to cancel?" he asked.

Danny shook his head. "We won't cancel on you, man. Dmitri and I can handle the vocals, no problem. Ben's been so fucked up we've not been allowing him to play much, so we all cover his instrument portion, even if he's onstage. Plus, Ben's been in trouble in nearly every town we go through, so lately, if he's not hammered off his ass, he's been too beat-up to play. We're tired of it, man. I'm really sorry; I know he's your brother, but he's screwed up." He dug a card out of his pocket. "The number on there is Nita's cell."

"Thanks, Danny. I'll see you here tomorrow night, okay? Have Benita see Gypsy at the bar for your portion of the take from tonight, and I'll make sure he knows who to look for." Slate turned, heading over to the bar.

He talked to Gypsy, explained who Ben was, and pointed out Benita, who was manning sales at the merchandise table she'd set up in the back of the bar. "I'm headed to Lutheran. Call me if you need me, Brother." He grasped Gypsy's forearm in a shake.

"Prez, let me know if you need anything. I'll let Ruby know where you are," Gypsy called after him as Slate walked away. He winced a little at that last part; he and Ruby had become good friends over the past few weeks, but they were only friends, as he'd promised.

Arriving at the hospital, he saw Ben was still out, but restrained to the gurney, and he looked at Goose with eyebrows raised. "Sorry, Prez, he woke up in the bus and tore out his IV twice. Had a helluva time getting him secured so he couldn't hurt himself." Goose seemed abashed.

"He always was a stubborn fucker," Slate muttered. "Any update on how he's doin'?"

"Doc's been in; they are gonna do a CT scan of his head to make sure he doesn't have a concussion, but likely, he's just got a broken nose from face-planting on the floor." Here, Goose paused, looking at Slate. "His blood alcohol level was off the charts, Prez. Even if he doesn't have a concussion, they are going to want to keep him for that alone."

There was a groaning sound from the gurney, and they turned to see Ben moving his head helplessly, trying to not vomit on himself. Goose grabbed a basin and held it in place, letting Ben purge himself of as much alcohol as his stomach would allow. Ben rolled his eyes up at Slate, his hair sticking to his sweat-dampened face. "Andy, I don't feel—" he started, and then his body stiffened, shaking.

"Is he having a seizure?" Slate asked, trying to stay calm as his forehead wrinkled in worry.

Goose called up the hallway to the nurse's station, "Little help down here?" as he unstrapped Benny, rolling him over onto his side. Hurrying feet slapped the linoleum, and Slate stepped back as several medical personnel surrounded the gurney. Goose called out, "Alcohol poisoning—he's vomiting, seizing, clammy, and sweating. Did someone call Doc?"

Hours later, Slate felt like his ass had molded to the uncomfortable seat. He hadn't wanted to stay in the waiting room, so he'd pulled a chair into the hallway outside Benny's room, leaning it against the wall. He heard a short noise from the room, and walked in to find Ben awake, looking at the straps that held his wrists to the frame of the bed.

"Hey," Slate said quietly. "How ya feelin', shrimp?" Ben had a stricken look on his face, his blond hair hanging down, stringy and greasy-looking; his face was covered with stubble, giving him a further unkempt look. Dressed in a hospital gown, Ben pulled his shoulders up to his ears, sinking down into the bed. "How the fuck do you think I feel? I feel like shit," he growled, his voice hoarse. He rolled his arm, looking at the IV that was attached at his elbow. "I hate needles," he scrunched up his face and winced with pain, "and my face hurts," he shifted in the bed, "and I think I peed the bed."

"You remember anything from last night, shrimp?" Slate questioned. "You were wasted, man, totally hammered."

"I remember seeing you at the bar," Ben said, "but that's pretty much it."

Slate was surprised; Ben had sung for over an hour, and had finished the complete set before passing out. "You got drunk, passed out on your feet, and fell off the stage onto your face." Slate pulled up a chair and turned it around, resting his ass on the back of it. "From what I hear, this is pretty normal for you," he continued, watching Ben's eyes.

"I drink to loosen up for the show, An—" he started, and Slate interrupted him. "Guess what your blood alcohol level was, Ben. Go ahead, guess."

Ben tipped up one corner of his mouth. "Point-oh-eight?"

"Nope," Slate said, popping on the 'P,' "Benny, you tested at point-*three*-eight. You listening? People die at point-three-oh, and you were at point-three-eight. That was not drinking to loosen up for the show. That's drunk because you don't have the common sense God gave a goose. What the fuck were you thinking?"

"Holy shit, I've never gone above point-two-seven before. That's like a record or something." Ben laughed, and Slate was so fucking angry it washed over him in waves.

He felt his face twist as he asked, "You tryin' to die, boy? Because I have much more reliable ways to handle that wish if it's where you're going. There's no reason, no logical reason, shrimp." Slate ran both his hands through his hair. "I swear to fucking God, I'll take you out myself, rather than watch you go the road Mom walked," Slate growled out, leaning over Ben's face. "I'm not fucking kidding. I won't sit around and watch that again. You have no idea what she was like."

Ben looked up at him, his face slowly turning gray. "Andy, I'm not her. Don't say shit like that, man. I know she put you through the wringer, but she's sober now, attends meetings and everything, but I'm not her. I'd never do that to you."

Slate turned away, and then looked back at Ben over his shoulder as he walked to the door. "I won't let you, shrimp. Not happening."

***

"Benita, tell me what the problem is, hun. Let me help fix Benny's fuckups." Slate was getting tired of this bitch talking around the issues, never giving him a direct answer. If she didn't tell him what he needed to know soon, he just might turn Ruby loose on her, she could turn her attitude towards the prospects in the club onto Benita.

Benita twisted on the stool across the bar from Slate, not looking at his face. "Ben owes some people money, Andy. They've started calling me now, and I'm getting scared. They sound pretty bad, and I don't know how much he owes." She cut her eyes up to him. "They caught up with him in Denver a couple months ago, and they beat him up pretty badly."

"You got a name, Benita? Do you know who it is?" Without a name, there wasn't a lot Slate could do. Benny was in the hospital still; he was past the detox stage, but they were trying some bullshit kind of therapy on him, trying to find out 'why he drank enough to kill himself'. Slate snorted quietly, grimly amused. Benny drank, because that's what he knew from a young age. He drank, because it numbed the pain of being left behind. He drank, because it made him forget for a while. Didn't take a degree to recognize that shit.

Like he'd called it to life, her phone started ringing where it sat on the bar between them. She looked down at the display, and her face paled. "It's them, Andy."

He grunted, sweeping the phone off the bar and to his ear, connecting the call as he did so. He held the phone without speaking, waiting for the caller to start. "Beeneeta, baby, have you thought about our offer? We would surely looove to come to an arrangement with you." The voice sounded vaguely Hispanic, something about the accents on the words. "Heeeeyyy baaabe, Beenneeta. Come on, baby, talk to me."

Slate pulled the phone away from his ear, looking at the display. It was a New Mexico area code. Listening to the phone again, he heard the change in tone as the caller began to get angry. "Beneeeta, you got an answer for me, bitch? That was a one-time offer—your slut-puppy boyfriend's life for your pussy. You don't want to go there, then we can hit up the hospital right now. But you know, if you don't go there with us, then you've killed him. He doesn't get to fuck with the Machos and live a long life, not without something in trade," the voice said confidently. "So what will it be, baby? Me fucking you, or your boyfriend dead?" Slate curled his lip, snarling silently at the phone. He cleared his throat, catching the caller off-guard, and an angry, "Who the fuck is this?" came across the call.

"You tell Estavez that Andrew Jones is calling in the Carmela marker. Have him call me back at this number in fifteen minutes, or the Rebels will be going to war with the Machos." Slate waited a second, hearing the fumbling of the phone as it was transferred from one person to another.

"Repeat that, motherfucker," a different voice came across the phone, sounding American, and pissed.

"I said," Slate spoke deliberately, "tell Estavez that Andrew Jones is calling in the Carmela marker. I want a call in fifteen at this number. If I don't get a call, then his word is worth shit, and Rebels go to war. You feel me?"

"Fifteen, got it," the man answered, and the call disconnected.

Benita was looking at Slate with fear on her face, and he shook his head in disgust at her, and at the thought of

Benny owing the kind of money the Machos would not forgive. "What now?" she asked.

Slate shrugged, saying simply, "We wait."

A few minutes later, the phone rang again. Slate answered it on the second ring, putting the phone to his ear and waiting. "Andrew Jones," came a heavily accented voice, one he recognized, "I was told you wanted to speak to me."

"Estavez, what can you tell me about Ben Jones' debt to the Machos?" Slate asked evenly.

He heard a heavy sigh on the other end of the phone. "Is this family to you, this *estúpido pendejo*?"

"Yeah, Ben Jones is my blood brother," Slate informed him. "Now that we have that out of the way, what can you tell me about his debt?"

"Andrew Jones, I do not know if I can forgive your brother his indiscretions. He has stolen nearly two hundred and fifty thousand dollars—a quarter-million of your US dollars. This is his debt to the Machos." There was an apologetic tone to Estavez's voice.

"Fuck me," Slate whispered. He paused, and then raised his voice. "No way does he have that money. Do you have any idea what he could have done with it after he took it?" He thought to himself that it was a little odd he never questioned that Benny could, or would steal from the Mexican motorcycle club. He was sure Estavez was correct, and Benny had been stupid enough to steal from them.

"He met with a group of men in Denver, and we believe he passed them the money. If you can find out who they were, I can try and take it from there, and your brother might yet live." The man sighed. "It grieves me that I cannot simply wipe the debt clean."

"Let me see what I can do. Is this a good number to call you at?" Slate's mind was racing; he needed to get Benny to talk to him, or the Machos would make good on their threat to end him in the hospital. Hearing an affirmation, he hung up without parting words. He carefully put the phone in his pocket, and then picked up a chair and threw it across the room with a yell.

Tequila stalked into the room. "All okay, Prez?" he asked, quickly. Slate silently looked at him, willing him to go away. "Um, Prez, I got a wanderer in the box."

Slate tipped his head back, speaking to the ceiling, "What the fuck will be next? Any ideas?"

"Prez, it's Tony Manzino. He wants a sit-down," Tequila rubbed the back of his neck, "so I put him in the box and set Diablo outside the door. Thought you'd want to have a convo with him, given the ongoing situation. Am I wrong?"

"Not wrong, brother, just a lot going on right now. Gimme five and I'll be in there." Slated nodded dismissively. He turned to Benita again and demanded, "Tell me about Denver."

She drew in a quick breath, and then tried to dissemble by asking, "What do you mean?"

Slate snarled at her, "You know what I mean, goddammit. Tell me what the fuck went down in Denver with Benny."

Swallowing hard, her eyes cut first one way, then the other. "Ben said he had a business opportunity. He was going to invest in a record company, one out on the west coast. He met some men at the airport, came back, and then we all got in the van to come here. That's it; I don't know anything else. I swear."

"You'll fucking swear to anything, won't you? Now, why don't you start over, telling me *the truth*, Benita. Tell me about fucking Denver." Slate stared hard into her face, waiting for her to look away again, but she kept her eyes on him steadily for nearly a minute, not speaking. He saw her face begin to glisten with sweat before she cut her eyes away and down, submitting finally.

"In the van. It's in the van...a shit ton of heroin. Ben bought it in Denver. He heard about you becoming president of a bike club, and said you'd help him sell it. That was his golden plan. Then he got here, and found out from some of the men that you don't touch drugs." She took a breath. "So, he made a local contact who can take some of the drugs off his hands, but it won't be anywhere near all of it."

He was pretty sure he knew why Tony was in his clubhouse now; this cluster got bigger and sloppier with every passing minute. "You know he's in a deep fucking hole of trouble, right?" he asked Benita. She nodded. He pulled his phone out of his front pocket, hitting a speed dial number. "Deke, need you at Marie's, brother." He listened for a minute, and then disconnected.

Yelling up the hallway for Tequila, he waited until the big man stood beside him. "Need you to put Benita and the band members in the other box, man. We've got some housekeeping to take care of, and I don't want them to wander into places they don't need to be." He inclined his head to Benita. "It's not the most comfortable accommodations, sorry."

Tequila put his hands out, herding her backwards into the hallway. "Second door on the left," his voice rumbled in his chest. Slate heard the muted thunder of a bike's pipes and waited for Deke to walk in.

"Band's van needs to go into the garage. Gotta clean it of some H. There's probably more than a little, so you might want to go ahead and see about storage. I don't know; I'll leave that to you. When you're done, let me know how much we're sitting on. Keep this need-to-know among the brothers; I don't want unneeded shit started." He cut a glance over at Deke.

"I got you, Prez," was all Deke said before turning to walk back outside. One of the prospects came through the room, headed back to where Tequila was standing in the hallway. Another prospect followed, bringing two of the band members with him.

20 - Benny

Walking into the secure room they called 'the box', he took a good look at Fort Wayne's biggest drug dealer, Tony Manzino. He remembered the fear the transport guys had for this man, and the bloody evidence left for blocks around the clubhouse before the Rebels started keeping a perimeter. He wasn't a big man, and he looked soft, like it had been a long time since he'd had to do his own tidying up.

Standing in front of the door, Slate folded his arms across his chest, waiting on the other man to become tired of the silence. Slate stood unmoving for several minutes, knowing it would eventually wear on the patience of Manzino.

"Your brother is a problem for me," the smaller man finally said in a level tone of voice. Slate lifted one eyebrow, looking at him. "He's managed to piss off a lot of people in a short period of time," Manzino continued, "Mexican drug cartel, Mexican motor club, and me."

Slate snorted. "Drug cartel is a new one. What did he do there?"

"You think this is fucking funny, man? You are warped," Manzino murmured. "He ruined some product in a warehouse. If it was only a few stacks, I think they'd be okay, but it wasn't. It was a lot of product, and they want to recoup their losses." Shaking his head, Manzino looked up at Slate.

This day just kept getting better and better. Slate ran his hand through his hair, looking down at Manzino. "Why is he a problem for you?" he asked.

The drug dealer barked a harsh laugh. "I think he's one of those men who draw attention and danger, and eventually anger from those around them. Having him here, in Fort Wayne, brings unwanted attention and visitors. People I'd rather not see here in my town."

"So why are you here, in my house? Why would you deliver yourself into my hands like this, knowing we've been looking to put you to ground if needed?" Slate didn't pull any punches, letting this ass-wipe have a minute to think.

"Because I can help keep your brother alive, and we can do some business at the same time," Manzino said. "I can move the product he has on hand, which buys you some time. I make a profit, and your brother pays his debt to the bikers. That only leaves the cartel, but we can work together to keep his head off their fence. I see this as a win-nearly-win, which is a fuck-of-a-lot better than what you walked in here with." He shrugged.

"We," Slate wagged his finger back and forth between them, "don't do business. You kill families, neighborhoods, businesses, and people with your 'product', and we," he wagged his finger again, "aren't the same. We," the finger wagged one last time, "don't do business."

"If I distribute away from Fort Wayne, does that make this a more palatable decision?" Manzino asked. "Is it only the hometown aspect that bugs you, or is it the drugs themselves?"

"Distributing away from Fort Wayne? How far can you go, motherfucker? Columbia? Brazil? That might be far enough," Slate sneered.

"God, you are a hard-ass son of a bitch. I'm handing you a win here, man." Manzino shook his head, slowly unfolding from the chair.

"What did he do to get on *your* bad side?" Slate asked, reaching out a hand and shoving Manzino back down into the chair hard.

"Bah, he's not really. I was just yankin' your chain." Manzino's lips curved into a humorless smile.

Looking down at Manzino, Slate's mind was searching for a better solution than the one being offered, but he couldn't seem to find another way for Benny to *maybe* come out of this alive. He reached out for a chair, turning it to face Manzino and sat down, folding his arms across the back of it. "What's the value on the product?" Slate asked.

"Easy quarter-mill, probably more, unless your brother did something stupid," came the response.

Slate sat there for a minute, running scenarios through his head. He stood, shoving the chair back against the wall. Turning to the door, he pulled the phone from his front pocket and dialed. "Estavez," he said as he walked away, hearing Manzino's shout of disbelief behind him. Kicking the door closed on the box, he continued speaking, "I have answers, but we have to come to an understanding before we can move forward."

"Andrew, is there honor for us both in your answers and understanding?" Estavez questioned. "Because if there is, then we will grasp it like drowning men."

"Yeah, I think there is. My brother bought high-dollar drugs with the money from the people in Denver. Those people are remnants of your brother's business, the cartel. I have the product, and someone who can sell it, but using this asshole gives me a bad taste in my mouth. If we could move the distribution away from where I live, I'd be better with it." Slate paused to take in a silent, deep breath.

He continued speaking into the phone, "So here's what I think; you can finish up the clean-up you evidently missed out west by luring them with the product. You get personal satisfaction in knowing you've terminated another fragment of the business that took your daughter. I can either give you the product, and you accept the risk versus reward of converting it to cash, or we can have my guy handle distribution, and pass you back the payoff for the borrow. One way, you keep all the money; the other, you get back exactly what you are owed. Either way, the cartel is short a few heads by tomorrow morning."

"And the understanding, Andrew? Where does that come in?" His voice was low.

"You never fucking do business with my family again, Estavez. No matter the ask from my baby brother. He would become invisible to you, and his debt would be repaid, not forgiven, so you lose no honor."

Slate held his breath for a second, waiting, then gasped it out shakily when he heard, "This is a good answer, Andrew. I accept the risk, and can take possession within the hour," from Estavez.

"I'll call you back within thirty minutes; set up the meet," Slate told him. "I'll be in touch." Disconnecting the call, he walked into the area where the van had been pulled, and saw the stacks of wrapped packages covering the floor near one wall. "Deke," he called, looking around.

"Yo," came the response from within the van's cargo space, "I'm getting the last bits and pieces. There was a fuck-ton of shit, Prez. Doesn't look like it's been tampered with; the lab seals are all still on the wrapping. What the hell are we doing with all this in the building?"

"I have Machos gonna pick it up in a bit, but I wanted to make sure how much there was before I gave them the final call." Slate rolled his shoulders as Deke's face appeared around the back of the van.

"Machos?" he questioned with a puzzled look on his face.

"Yeah, that's who my brother 'borrowed' the money from to buy the drugs. They want the drugs and will take responsibility for turning it back into cash, and they won't do it in Fort Wayne. It also gives their president the opportunity to manage a business problem out west, which is...satisfying to him." Slate shook his head. "I lost a valuable fucking marker on the Machos, but get to keep my brother on the sunny side of the divide." He ran his hand through his hair.

Working together, they counted and stacked the packages into empty beer boxes, creating a tidy stack of nondescript, brown rectangles along the wall. Deke went back into the van with his tools, and verified they'd removed everything.

Slate pulled out the phone, redialing the last number. "Anytime, Estavez, I'm ready. Marie's on Main," he told him, and he hung up the phone. "Hang a minute, Deke; let's get this transfer and meet done with. Then, we can decide what to do with Manzino." He ran his hand back through his hair.

Deke looked at him out of the corner of one eye, repeating in a questioning tone, "What to do with Manzino?"

"Yeah, motherfucker showed up, just walked in, so Tequila put him in the box. We've had a chat, but he's still breathing. I want to know what you think we should do with him. Then we'll talk to Hoss, lay it out, and get everyone on the same fucking page."

About twenty minutes later, Slate heard a noise from outside. "They're here," he said flatly, and then three sharp knocks came from the cargo door, rattling it in the frame. Deke strode over and swung the regular door outward, stepping back and away from the opening. Estavez was the first man through the door, and he walked confidently towards Slate, holding out a hand in greeting. Slate allowed a hard smile to bend the corners of his lips upward, taking the hand and pulling him into a one-armed embrace. Thumping each other on the back, the men moved apart, sizing up the changes in appearance since they'd seen the other last. "Estavez, it's good to see you looking well," Slate spoke first.

"And good to see you too, Andrew Jones...Slate," he responded with an open smile. "You're doing well for yourself, President."

"Mason's a slave driver; wasn't no way he was gonna let me slough responsibility for something indefinitely. Might as well be a strong, vital chapter like Fort Wayne," Slate said proudly, putting his hands on his hips. "I'm more than happy with the club here; we've got a good set of brothers," he pointed at Deke, "like Deke here, my Sergeant at Arms."

Stepping back again, he moved towards the back wall, where the boxes were stacked. "Product is here, brother. Do you want to pull your van in to transfer?" he asked, flipping open the flaps on one of the boxes so Estavez could see the packages inside.

The Machos' President leaned over, not touching the box, and looked at the contents. He rocked back on his heels a little, running his gaze over the entire stack. "Are all the boxes full?" he asked finally.

"Yeah, they're full, and the packaging is undisturbed. They've not been opened or unsealed," Slate answered, flipping open the flaps on another two boxes to show Estavez.

"There's a good deal more here than I expected," Estavez murmured to Slate. "This is worth at least a half-million dollars, Slate. Are you still certain about the deal?"

"Abso-fucking-lutely, brother. You pack this shit up, take it far from my hometown, and deal with your brother's business problems...I'm good with the deal as long as the portion regarding the continued health of my baby brother is still in play." Slate nodded.

"I think that is no longer a problem, and I'm happy to have the opportunity to finalize aspects of my own brother's business...but I will not take advantage of you in this way. I will contact you regarding the remainder of the money, once we have everything taken care of. I will accept no other deal," Estavez said sternly and Slate laughed.

"Deke, move the van; let's get this shit shifted," Slate called across the room.

***

Brushing the hair back from Benny's forehead, Slate leaned forward and looked him in the eye. "I need you to listen to me, Benny. You with me?" he asked quietly.

Benny's eyes drifted closed, and then opened again, focusing slowly on Slate's face. "Yeah, Andy, I'm with you."

"Benny, shrimp...you fucked up, as in a *colossal* fuck up. You crossed some fucking assholes, and your band and manager were about to pay the price. If they hadn't paid, then you were never getting out of here. You got me? You understand?" he asked Benny for confirmation.

"What do you mean they were going to pay the price?" Benny's eyebrows furrowed in confusion.

"Benita was trying to negotiate on your behalf, which only brought her to their attention, and she was scared, which meant no good decisions were being made. You were nearly at the point where you weren't going to walk out of this room, Benny, but I fixed it." Slate shook his head.

Still confused, Benny tilted his head to one side, letting his hair fall across his forehead carelessly. "Andy, what did you do?" There was a tone of fear in his brother's voice.

"I have some pull in certain circles. I let it be known you're my blood brother, and that damage to you was unwise. The loan is covered, Benny. The 'product' is managed, you have a cleared marker," he bared his teeth grimly, "and then I killed your loan opportunities for the future, to ensure you continue to stay healthy and can't ever fuck yourself in the ass like this again."

The color faded from Benny's face as Slate spoke, and his head fell back against the thin hospital pillow. "How the hell did you fix this, Andy? That was a lot of money. Are you sure it's okay? Are you in danger now?" Benny asked cautiously.

"Nah, I got this. It's what I do, man." Slate shrugged. "So that's one problem handled, well...two...MC and cartel, but who's counting. That leaves us with your addicted ass. Listen, I need you to get me on this, because here's what's about to happen. In a few minutes, a couple of men are going to come in here and we are going to take you to the airport. You're getting on a plane and heading to Phoenix, and you'll be checked into a rehab facility there for a minimum of ninety days. You fuck up, and that ninety day timer starts over.

"You stay the course, you get out in ninety days, and you can come back to the band with a sober companion. If after an additional six months of sobriety things are still good, we can dispense with the companion. If not, then we reevaluate. I'm on your ass every step of the way, Ben. This is not a cake walk. I guaran-damn-tee you this is gonna be a lot of fucking work, but this is your life, Benny.

It's your *fucking life*, and I will not let you go the way of Mom." Slate reached out and grabbed Ben's hand tightly.

They sat in silence for a minute, Ben's eyes downcast at the blanket covering his lap. "What did you tell GeeMa?" Benny asked quietly.

"Truth. I told her the truth, that you won't be coming back to Enoch ever, and you're going to fucking pay back every penny you stole from her. I told her you needed this...you need to get sober, because you are killing yourself as things stand now." Slate shrugged again. "She gets it; she understands the score."

Cutting his eyes up at Slate's face, Ben asked, "Can you come with me? I just found you, and then I fucked it all up like this." Ben shook his head, tears slipping down his cheeks. "I'm sorry."

"Naw, shrimp, this is a you kinda thing. Time to pony up and clear the catchpen. But, you know what?" he paused, shaking their joined hands and looking into Benny's face. "I got confidence in you. You got this. It's what we Jones' men do."

***

After riding to the airport with his brother and seeing him through security, Slate had gone back to the bar to deal with Manzino. He and Hoss had decided to let the fucker go, but make a statement that he needed to move on from town. The little man took the beat-down in stride, arrogantly flinging blood off his face with a swipe of his fingers.

"I understand the Rebels' expectations, man," he said through swollen and split lips. Slate nodded without saying anything and stepped back, letting Tequila muscle the man into the trunk of a car. They'd drop him right outside the house in which his children lived, driving home the fact that they knew a lot about him, probably more than made him comfortable.

21 - Ruby

A month later

Backing his bike into his parking space in the clubhouse lot, Slate toed the kickstand out, but remained straddling the bike for a few minutes. With his hands balled loosely on his thighs, he was still, except for the quiet rise and fall of his breathing. Eyes sweeping the compound, he noted the bikes already parked there, and listened to the thump of music coming from the building behind him. The prospect manning the compound gate closed it softly and moved back to his stool in the shadows.

The sound of the door behind him startled him from his thoughts, and he turned his head to see Ruby walking quickly towards him. He groaned silently, *Why the hell did she come to him tonight*? He wished he could wrap his arms around her, holding her as he mourned the change in his brother. He needed that closeness tonight more than ever, but couldn't allow it.

"Ruby, now's not a good time, babe," he began, interrupted when with a little leap, she hitched her ass sideways across his tank, draping her legs across one of his and sliding her arms around his chest underneath his cut. Her scent enveloped him, vanilla and a floral she'd said was Lily of the Valley. To him, it was her signature as sure as anything; he fucking loved that smell.

She snuggled into his chest, her arms tightening around him as he lifted one hand from a thigh to try and push her backward. "Ruby," he said quietly, "what's wrong, baby? Talk to me."

The only response was her hips shifting closer to him, plastering their torsos together firmly and bringing her in contact with his hard cock straining at his jeans. She'd done this a few times in the past few weeks, reaching out to him for reassurance or comfort.

Slate raised a hand to her hair, smoothing it down her back. He tucked one arm around her waist, holding onto her hip with that hand. Fingers splayed halfway across her belly, he tightened his arm, holding her close. "Shhhhhh, baby, I got you. Talk when you are ready, Ruby. I got you." Slate laid his cheek against the top of her head, still caressing her hair soothingly.

He felt her frame hitch, and realized she was trying hard not to cry. Rocking back on his ass, he lifted his left leg over the bike's tank, keeping her securely in his lap. Slipping one arm underneath her legs, he lifted her and walked towards the clubhouse, feeling as she turned her face to bury it deeper underneath his cut and against his chest. The prospect jumped up and opened the door for him, and as their eyes met over the top of her head, the pros was shaking his head with wide eyes; he didn't know what was wrong.

Slate took the stairs two at a time, heading towards the suite Ruby shared with DeeDee until he felt her go rigid in his arms. "Okay. Not your rooms then, baby. Okay. It's okay, I got you," he whispered, and he turned down the hallway towards his room. The door was ajar, and he softly bumped it with his hip to open it wider. Stepping into the room, he kicked it closed behind him. Toeing off his boots, with her still in his arms, he crawled up the bed to lean back against the headboard, carefully arranging her on his lap.

Closing his eyes, he leaned his head back against the wood, taking in a deep breath and releasing it in a hard sigh. His fingers wrapped around her hair, sweeping it out of her face so he could use his knuckles in a gentle and slow stroke across her cheek. They sat there for a long time not speaking as Slate's eyes grew heavy. He scooted down in the bed a little, thrusting a pillow behind his head and draping her across his body so he could keep his arms tightly around her.

He lifted his eyes as he felt her move, but she was merely raising her head to look as she kicked off her boots. She put her head back down on his chest, but one small hand now curled in the shirt underneath his cut, flexing against the material slowly. He wished for the hundredth time he knew what had happened to her. The stories the older members told about the younger, wild Melanie really didn't match up against this woman who seemed afraid of everything, even her own voice.

"Gonna tell me what's wrong, beautiful?" he asked without opening his eyes. Waiting her out had become second nature to him over the time he'd known her, and he knew if he gave her an opening without pressure, she'd eventually talk to him. They lay like that for long minutes, deep breaths synchronizing as she slowly calmed down.

"DeeDee has someone over. It made me sad," she said simply, that hand beginning its twist and curl into the fabric of his shirt again. Her voice was somewhat muffled; it sounded like she had her other hand over her mouth, trying to hold back the emotions she was feeling. "You missing Winger and Lockee?" he asked, and felt her head move in agreement.

He thought that was the end of it; she was sad, because her 'Mom' had a boyfriend, and Ruby was still missing the people who had left their lives too soon, so he was surprised when she continued. "I miss them, but...I want...I can't have...I can't have what DeeDee has," she finished in a rush.

Slate stilled, waiting. He was laying on the bed, suddenly very aware of her hip pressing into his lower belly and her breasts wedged in tight against his chest. Her breath hitched as she finally said, "I want that."

Slate asked softly, "What do you want, Ruby?"

Before she could respond, there was a commotion from downstairs in the main room, and Slate jackknifed up off the bed, setting her aside quickly but carefully. "Stay here, Ruby. I need to make sure that's not blowback from today's shit." He stepped into his boots, forcing them onto his heels hard. He turned and looked at her again. "Wait for me. I want you in my bed so we can finish this conversation, baby."

He made sure his gun was tucked into the holster in the back waistband of his jeans, and strode quickly down the hallway and stairs, looking over the group arrayed across the main room. He took a deep breath when he saw it was Estavez and two Machos, and then the tight band around his chest eased when he saw a wide smile on the man's face. "Estavez," he greeted him, receiving a small nod in response.

"May we speak in private, Slate? I have a personal matter to discuss with you." Estavez waited quietly, his face impassive. Slate pointed to his office door, behind the bar. "In there. Want something to drink?"

"A beer would be good, my friend," came the response, and Slate relaxed a little more, nodding at the prospect behind the bar. They took their beers into the office and closed the door. "Slate...Andrew Jones...I have a debt to you, again. Two of the men in Denver were ones I had been looking very hard for; they were responsible for a number of things, including the kidnapping of my daughter. I appreciate the chance to clear the past, and for that I owe you.

"Also, the value of the product was significantly more than I estimated," Estavez said, reaching into an inside pocket of his cut and pulling out an envelope. "In this envelope, there is a locker key and an address. Inside that locker is a bag with a great deal of money. I will not return to the locker, so you must retrieve it, or you can allow it to go to some anonymous person if it is discovered."

Slate slowly took the envelope from the outstretched hand. He nodded, not saying anything, and folded the envelope to fit into his pants pocket. Estavez smiled at him, and then the look on his face sobered. "If I could ask but one thing of you, Slate?"

Raising an eyebrow questioningly, Slate responded, "What's that, brother?"

Estavez stood. "Please, do not call it the 'Carmela marker' again. Your name is sufficient in any form."

Slate stood and clasped forearms with the man. "Never again, brother. My word."

An hour later, Slate stood looking into his room at the empty bed. Sighing deeply, he shook his head as he moved into the room, removing his boots again. Ruby had run from him again, and he was reasonably sure they had been about to have a fine-tuning of their relationship before the interruption.

"Fuck me," he muttered tiredly, sitting on the edge of the bed and roughly rubbing his face before lying back. He was asleep in minutes, and his dreams were filled with silent smiles, unruly red hair, and soft curves.

***

Slate walked into the clubhouse kitchen, rubbing his neck with one hand and rolling the early morning kinks out of his shoulders. A warming lid on the stove covered a pan of scrambled eggs, with sausage and bacon nearby. He stood and stretched for a minute, then went over to the cabinet. He felt fingers tug at his belt loops, and turned around to see Ruby standing behind him a little closer than necessary, his cock immediately starting to thicken.

He took a step back, reaching down with one hand to clasp it loosely around her slender wrist, pulling her hand off him. "Ruby," he greeted her cautiously, turning back to the cabinet and grabbing a plate. He scooped eggs and breakfast meat onto his plate, grabbing a fork as he walked out of the room and away from her. She'd been the one to run from his bed last night, and damnit if he was going to forget it so easily.

He didn't turn and look behind him, but he could feel the weight of her gaze on his back all the way down the hall. Sitting on a stool at the bar in the main room, he motioned to the prospect for a cup of coffee, and thanked him when the mug was set in front of him. Slate felt his skin prickle, and knew Ruby had followed him. Without moving his head, he used the mirror to find her in the room, and saw she was steadily looking at him.

"Ruby," he called out, watching her stiffen and catch his eyes in the mirror, "get your leathers; let's take a run." A brilliant smile spread across her face, and his heart stuttered in his chest. *Fuck me*, he thought, *she's so goddamn beautiful*.

PBJ had heard him, and yelled from the next room, "Who's on escort, motherfuckers?"

Slate shook his head, calling, "I got this one, brother." Looking in the mirror again, he saw Ruby had disappeared, probably to get her cut and gloves. He finished his breakfast and coffee, sliding the dirty dishes across the bar for the prospect to deal with as Hoss walked up.

"Hey, Prez, Highwaymen reported some issues with non-patched assholes up north. You sure you don't want a couple brothers on your six?"

"Nah, we won't go far; I just want to get the cobwebs out of my head with some wind. There's been a lot of shit rolling around for days; things are finally starting to settle down. Want to get it out of my head for a while, and I thought Ruby could use a break too," Slate said.

Hoss nodded, and then asked, "You heard Manzino vacated?" Slate gave him a chin lift. Hoss rubbed a hand down his belly. "I don't trust it. It was too easy after all the shit we went through."

Slate agreed, "I know; I'm not feelin' it either. We put a hurtin' on his business, though, so he has to relocate in order to make his bank back. It could be as simple as that. We'll sort that shit out over the next couple of weeks. Today, I want to take a run."

He again felt a tug at the back of his pants, and reached back to take hold of Ruby's wrist, pulling her around beside him. "Ruby, you feel safe enough with only me, or want to bring PBJ?" He decided to let her make the call. She leaned into his side, tucking her head into his shoulder and resting her cheek on the leather covering his chest.

Standing still, he waited for her response, giving her a few moments to find her voice. "I'm always safe with you, Prez," she said quietly, and his chest swelled. She trusted him to keep her safe, and he was going to protect that trust.

"Then let's roll, baby." He wound his fingers through hers, pulling her towards the door. Slate squeezed her hand softly, and released her as they went to their bikes.

He pulled up to the gate, waiting for the prospect to pull it back, and he smiled as Ruby rolled up on his right, dropping her feet and keeping her front wheel even with his back one. He leaned over, telling her, "Once we get on the highway, ride beside so I can keep an eye on you."

Watching until she nodded, he grinned at her and pulled out into the street.

Within fifteen minutes, they were on the highway headed east into Ohio. Ruby was a steady driver, keeping her bike within inches of the painted fog line unless there was debris to avoid. The further they rode, the more relaxed Slate became. This was something he'd been missing—the caress of the wind on his face, that low, underhand wave towards other bikers on the road...no decisions, no problems to fix, no puzzles to put together, just the ride.

He cut his eyes over to Ruby, and saw her face looked as peaceful as his felt. For all she'd said she wanted a job in the clubhouse, maybe what he'd asked her to take on was too much. He hadn't realized how much stress she'd been carrying until now, when it was gone. She caught him looking at her and raised an eyebrow quizzically. He gave her a thumbs-up, which she returned, and they rode on.

Idling into the parking lot of a bar in Toledo a couple hours later, Slate laughed at himself. He hadn't expected them to ride so far, but it had been such a good run he'd decided simply returning would be anticlimactic. So they'd eat lunch here before they headed back home.

Home. As he backed into a parking space, he realized he'd thought of Fort Wayne as home for the first time. Not the clubhouse, because he would be moving out and into a house soon—his room there was merely transient, and didn't matter—but the club, and his brothers...they had become home to him over the past few months. Looking over at her, he realized Ruby was his home too.

Waiting for her to settle her bike, he sat still for a minute. Theirs were the only bikes in the lot; not wanting any issues about wearing their colors, he'd picked a neighborhood bar near the hockey arena downtown, instead of one of the biker bars.

He strolled in ahead of Ruby, picking out a booth near the back and guiding her towards it. She slid across the bench with her back to the wall, and he sat down beside her. He ordered them a draft beer each, along with burgers and fries. Like normal with Ruby, he carried the conversation, telling her stories about the Mallets players who frequented Jackson's back in Chicago.

If he hadn't been paying close attention, he would have missed the look that flitted across her face when he talked about his friends and their experiences. He was at a loss for what would have caused it, but knew asking her directly was a mistake, and would cause her to close off.

"...then Jason was holding Daniel in a headlock, shoving marshmallow cereal into his mouth and shouting about him being a fucking lucky charm." Slate laughed. "It didn't end well for Jason; that's for sure. He never knew cereal could cause that bad a rash if it was shoved into tender bits." *There it was; that was the look again.*

"I think DeeDee met Jason; you should ask her about his crazy shit," Slate continued, watching the look flash across her face again. Yeah, DeeDee was on her mind; she was probably worried about the hookup last night. He'd seen Jason leaving early this morning. "I'd like to take you to Chicago someday soon, so you can meet my friends and brothers there. I know a lot of them have been to Fort Wayne already, but I've kept them so busy you haven't really gotten to know them." He picked up his burger, taking a bite and letting silence settle on the table. "Why'd you run last night, Ruby?" he asked softly.

After a few minutes, Ruby cleared her throat and he looked down at her, then went back to eating. He saw the tip of her tongue dart out, moistening across her bottom lip as he groaned silently, feeling his cock twitch and begin to swell. She ducked her head, saying softly, "Sorry."

"For what, baby?" Slate asked, confused and turning to face her in the booth.

"You're mad," she said quietly.

His head jerked back in surprise. "What? No, I'm not, Ruby. Why do you think I'm angry?"

She raised her eyes to his. "When you are mad, there's this muscle that twitches in your jaw. That's how I know."

He sat for a moment, then shook his head. "That might be, but I'm not right now." He watched her face, "I'm fucking hard, baby. I want you. You licked your lips, and all I can think of is you in my bed with your mouth wrapped around my cock. I'm not angry...I fucking want you."

Her breath caught, her body going very still. She clearly wasn't thinking when she pulled her bottom lip in-between her teeth, biting on it softly. Slate groaned out loud this time, reaching over to tug it gently out of her mouth with one fingertip. "And now, I want to bite that lip," he said softly, bringing his mouth near her ear to whisper, "and lick it and kiss you...because I want to taste you, baby, but you gotta give me some indication of what you're thinking, Ruby.

"I've been shutting myself down for months now, but I still fucking want you, seems like more and stronger every day, but I won't go there unless you tell me to. I need to hear it from you so I know if you are leaning the same way. If you want...me. I'm not a hearts and flowers guy, but you have to know you are killing me."

A slow smile spread across her face, lighting it from within. She ducked her head, and then looked up at him again. "Yeah?" she questioned.

"Yes, baby," he reassured her, struggling to remain still as he sat beside her. He felt her hand come to rest on his thigh as she bit her bottom lip again.

Slate reached down, plucking her fingers from his leg, and brought her hand to his mouth, running his lips across the backs of her knuckles. He nipped at them, and then kissed each finger in turn. She twisted her hand in his, cupping his jaw in her palm. "Slate, I want to ask you something," she said, still looking at him with that smile on her lips.

He looked at her, waiting patiently as he brought her palm to his mouth, softly kissing it. He opened his lips, dragging his tongue across her palm, sliding her thumb into his mouth, biting and sucking gently. He smiled at her as she gasped softly, still waiting for her to continue. "I would like to have my own room," she finally said.

Surprised, that wasn't what he expected. Stalling, he murmured against her skin, "Your own room?" and continued his assault on her palm and digits. She squirmed a little in the seat as he softly bit the pad of her thumb.

She took in a breath, whispering, "Yeah," and pulled against him, trying to free her hand. In a rush, she said, "You are almost ready to move into your apartment, DeeDee will be moving out of the clubhouse soon, and I don't want the suite...it's too big. I'd like to have my own room, so I can keep my stuff in one place." She stared at him, a look of fear chasing across her features when he didn't immediately respond. "Slate, you aren't going to make me move out when DeeDee does, are you? Do you want me to leave?"

He watched as her breath came faster, not sure why she was nearly panicking. "No, baby, you don't have to leave. Fuck, you are in charge of assigning rooms, so just give yourself whichever room you want. Get a prospect to help you set up furniture, and buy anything we don't have in storage you need."

He stared at her, waiting for her breath to even out, thinking to himself, *Fuck it—she'll never know if I don't tell her plainly.* Speaking evenly, Slate told her, "But, baby...what I want is you in my bed. I want nothing more than you in my room until I move out, and then you with me in my house...our house. I want to come home to you; I want to make love to you...I simply want *you.*"

He placed her hand back on top of his thigh, finger and thumb encircling her wrist and stroking slowly upwards, then back down. Releasing her, Slate reached for his burger and began eating again. He nearly choked when Ruby raised her chin, looking him in the eye as she said, "I want that too, Slate."

A slow smile broke over his face, lifting the edges of his mouth and crinkling the corners of his eyes. "I'm going to kiss you now, Ruby," he warned her, moving towards her.

"Okay," was all she said as she leaned into him, tilting her face to meet his. Slate fit his mouth over hers, kissing her softly and slowly. His tongue teased along her bottom lip, seeking entrance; she opened to him, and his tongue slid along hers as he tasted and explored her mouth. Slanting his mouth across hers again, he reached a hand up and tangled his fingers into the curly hair at the back of her head, using that grip to hold and guide her responses. Slate ate at her mouth, trying to get his fill of touching her, kissing her, savoring her...after wanting her for so long. *Fuck*, he had to slow down before he scared her.

God, she tasted good, a little citrusy, a little spicy, and hot as hell. He was having a hard time catching his breath, so he broke off the kiss, resting his forehead against hers, struggling for control. Running his nose along the edge of her jaw, he licked and nibbled the column of her throat, softly kissing just below her ear. "Slate," she murmured.

Like him, her breathing sounded like she'd just run up a flight of stairs. Her hand slid up his thigh, and he growled low in his throat, freezing her movement. His lips moved against her skin as he said, "Baby, unless you want me to bend you over this table and fuck you, you won't move that hand again."

He brought up his hand, splaying his fingers across her throat and cheek. He wrapped his thumb around the underside of her jaw, tilting her head for another kiss. This was softer and sweeter than the desperate ones that had gone on before; there was more give and less take, but he boldly possessed her mouth with his.

His heart jerked and stuttered when she took his bottom lip between her teeth; she tugged gently as she mock-growled at him. His eyes flashed open to find her green ones staring into him, humor tilting the corners as she smiled around his lip still gripped in her teeth. Slate's hand tightened on her jaw, and he saw those eyes darken with arousal, her mouth opening as he felt her small hand slowly stroking up his chest.

"Ruby, baby, slow now. Goddamn...slow...down. I don't want to rush this; I want you in my bed, where you feel safe, where I can take my time. Not taking you for the first time in an alley in fucking Toledo," he ground out, settling back away from her by only a few inches, "and I'm not looking for casual, baby. We do this, then you are mine..." he paused, his thumb stroking her throat up and down, "...mine, baby."

She nodded at him, never breaking her gaze from his. "So no room," she agreed, and kissed him back.

After the two hour ride back to the clubhouse filled with heated glances, he stood and watched Ruby back her bike in beside his, her eyes holding his gaze as she took off her cut and stored it in her saddlebag. Taking the two steps to her, he lifted her off the bike, sliding one palm under her ass, and the other around her back as she wrapped her legs around his waist.

Kissing her deeply, he paid little attention to the prospect opening the door for them. Slate strode through the clubhouse, ignoring the dozen members arrayed around the room. He was focused entirely on Ruby, her cheek tight against his face as she moaned, running her fingers through his hair. She used her grip to pull his head closer and flexed her hips against him, her heat searing his rigid cock behind the fly of his jeans, seemingly as desperate as he was to get closer.

Taking the stairs two at a time, he retraced his steps from the night before, going to his room and closing the door behind them. Slate stopped in the middle of the room, realizing he wanted to simultaneously keep holding her like this and strip off their clothes, and he laughed softly against her throat. "Baby, I'm going to put you down, but you don't get to leave this room. No more running," he whispered. "I want to see you."

He loosened his hold, allowing her to slide slowly down his front, her shirt rucking up in the front as it caught on his belt buckle. Slate reached down to grab the hem, pulling it over her head and tossing it on the dresser. Ruby ran her hands down his cut, slipping underneath to shift it off his shoulders. He caught it in one hand and draped it across the chair that stood next to the bed.

Reaching one hand behind his head, he grabbed the collar of his shirt and tugged it off, then reached down to her jeans, unsnapping the waistband with the fingers of one hand. Ruby smiled up at him, saying softly, "Boots," as she settled to her knees in front of him. Her small hands helped him remove his boots and socks, and then she was laughing as she tipped over backward to pull her own boots off.

He groaned out loud as she tilted her face up at him, one hand raised for his assistance as her hair cascaded down her bare back. He took in the sight of her—breasts barely contained by a lacy white bra, belly exposed where her jeans gaped open, teasing him with a glimpse of white lace panties, her feet bare, and that mane of red curls wild around her face.

"God, baby," he ground out as he reached down for that outstretched hand, pulling her to her feet and up against him. Her hands were working at his jeans, and she gave a little shimmy as her own slid down her legs to the floor. Unselfconsciously, she stepped on the hem to pull them off her legs all the way, pushing the denim fabric of his down his legs at the same time. His cock slid into view, turgid and hard, slapping against his belly as it sprung free, and she reached for him.

Slate gathered both her hands into one of his, stopping her. "I won't last, baby, not if your hands are on me right now. When I come, I want to be buried deep inside you." She gave a gasp as he growled the words into her ear. "Get on the bed, Ruby," he said, releasing her. He eyed her as she sat and then moved up the bed on her ass using her heels and hands; she watched him as he stepped out of his jeans.

"Ruby," he said softly, putting one knee on the bed and crawling up to stretch out beside her; he wrapped an arm around her to drag her to his side. "Baby, I need you to know I'm not fucking around here." He draped her over his chest, tipping her chin up with one finger so he could see her face. "I don't do casual. I won't do public, and I will not fucking share. I want you bare too, because that's reserved for my woman. I need to hear you say what you want, because if we aren't on the same page, this ain't happening." Her eyes grew big and round, and she rested her forehead against his chest, nodding. "No, baby, not good enough. I need the words, Ruby. This means something to me, and you have to fucking know that."

He heard her throat click as she swallowed, and he watched her lick her lips before speaking in her low voice, "It's not casual for me either, Slate. I've never felt anything like this before. I want you. I've wanted you since the first time you came to Fort Wayne. I've never been with a club member, and I'm clean. I haven't had sex for nearly three years. I want to be with you, and I don't share either," her voice went soft, "but I'm not on birth control."

His arms tightened around her as he asked, "Do you want babies?"

She flinched, but said, "Well...yes, someday."

He nodded and kissed the top of her head. "I want to see my babies growing in your belly. I want to watch you become ripe and round, and I want to hold our children. If you get pregnant, I'll be far from upset, baby. From your belly to the breakfast table, I want that."

Slate ran his hands down her back and side, shifting her off him as he sat up to tug her panties down her legs and toss them aside. Unfastening her bra, he slid the straps down her arms and discarded it as well. Rising over her on one elbow, he captured her face in his hand, pulling her effortlessly into another kiss. Stroking her tongue with his, he ravished her mouth, biting and sucking on her lips until they were puffy and sensitive as her hand clutched at his bicep.

Pulling back, he watched his fingertips trail down her throat and across her chest, stroking the sides and bottom of her breasts with his knuckles. She was so soft her skin felt like silk against his fingers. Palming her breasts, he rolled one of them in his hand, feeling the nipple pebble and tighten against his skin. *I could eat her up*, he thought.

Lowering his head, he slowly licked across a nipple, then blew on it, the chill from his breath making it harden even more. Tweaking the peak with his rough fingertips, he pinched softly, listening as her breathing became erratic.

Moving his attention to her other breast, he sucked her deep within his mouth, feeling her hands wrap around his head, cradling him there. Ruby arched her back, pressing up into him, and he smiled against her skin, nipping with his lips and teeth just to hear that catch in her breath again.

He slipped one hard thigh between her legs, pressing firmly against her soft, red curls, and he felt her shudder beneath him. Her hand curled around his shoulder, touching him as her head pressed back into the pillow; she made a soft noise in the back of her throat as her hips moved against him involuntarily. Slate smiled against her skin again, moving his mouth down across her belly, slowly licking and kissing from side to side, shifting his mouth down bare inches at a time.

He paused for a moment, surprised by the ink on her ribs. He hadn't known she had a tattoo. It was a small piece, but she had memorialized her best friend with their names twined in ribbon, 'Lockee & Melanie' with the word 'Sisters' connecting and binding everything together. "Beautiful, baby, that's beautiful. I love that you care so fucking much," he whispered against her skin, tracing the ribbon and words with his tongue and fingertips.

"Scooch up a bit, Ruby," he said, moving down further in the bed. His hands captured her hips as she moved at his instruction, and he trailed his tongue across her belly, hipbone to hipbone, and back again. Moving between her legs, he pushed his hands underneath her ass, lifting her to his mouth as he spread her labia wide with his thumbs. Pressing his nose into her curls, he took in a deep breath, savoring the scent of her arousal. "God, so fucking pretty, baby," he murmured, his lips against her inner thigh.

Beginning with the tight little rosebud between her cheeks, he licked and laved every inch of her with his tongue, dipping inside her pussy before swirling back around her opening. He wanted this to be slow and smooth, teasing her with the sensation of his mouth and hands on her.

Dragging the flat of his tongue up to her clit, he lavished attention on that sensitive bud of nerves, using his hands under her ass to hold her firmly against his mouth as she bucked and tried to move away. Sucking her clit into his mouth, he pressed against it with his teeth and tongue over and over, stimulating her ruthlessly. Looking up her body as she moved on the bed, his eyes fixed on her face, watching as she pressed her lips between her teeth to hold back her passion. Slate felt her muscles begin to tense and release, and knew she was close to coming. "Let go," he whispered.

He slowly slid his hands out from under her, following her down into the bed with his mouth. Pushing her legs wider, he continued to eat at her, teasing and licking her up and down as he positioned his hands. "God, you are so fucking beautiful, baby," he muttered, "so hot and wet. Fuck. You are soaked for me, so fucking wet." His fingers were slick with her, and he smiled at her moan as he grazed her clit with his tongue.

"Let go," he said again, his mouth on her. Pulling her clit into his mouth, he brushed and sucked it as he plunged two thick fingers deep into her, scissoring them against her tight inner walls and thrusting them in and out of her. "Come for me, baby. Come on my mouth, Ruby. Let me feel you. Give yourself to me."

Her climax came hard, not as a wave or build-up, but as an explosion, and she said his name on a single breathy gasp deep in her throat as she tensed and arched up from the bed. "God, Slate. Oh God." He was relentlessly pumping his fingers into her, but gradually moved them more deliberately, and he gentled his assault on her with his mouth, slowly allowing her to relax.

After one final lick, bottom-to-top, feeling her try to squirm away from his mouth, he moved up beside her in the bed. Wrapping her in his arms, he pulled her tight to his side. "Beautiful. Fucking beautiful. Love watching you. Can't get enough, baby. Let me know when you are ready," he whispered into her ear, softly kissing her temple. His hands moved restlessly, stroking and plumping her breasts, then trailing fingertips across her belly and into the indent of her bellybutton, garnering a giggle from her, which quickly silenced as she tensed up again.

"Slate?" she said questioningly.

"Hmm?" was his response, and when she didn't say anything else, he lifted his head to look down at her face, his hands still roaming her body. "What is it, baby?" he asked.

She bit her bottom lip, and he rescued it, sucking it into his mouth and then kissing her hard. "Slate," she started again, and tucked her chin down, hiding her face from scrutiny. He sighed, settling back beside her and waiting, quiet and still. He could tell she was scrunching her face up and thought he knew what was wrong, but needed her to tell him so he'd know for sure. One corner of his mouth lifted into a smile, thinking, *God, she's a lot of work, but worth it*. Taking in a quick breath and blowing it out, she asked, "Slate, you didn't...um...don't you want me?"

He smiled wide at that, pulling her closer; he took one of her hands and brought it down to his rock-hard cock. He wrapped her fingers around it, and dragged her hand up and down several times, letting her feel the evidence of his desire for her. "Baby, I want you so fucking much it's physically painful. I want to be inside you. I want to own you, to possess you, but this is about more than simple pleasure, and I want you to always know that. This is about us—me and you, and being here together. Fucking is quick, but I want this...I want us to last forever. I will wait until you are ready to have me buried inside you, and fight really hard to not rush you too much."

He could almost see the gears moving in her head as she digested that. "Forever?" was the word she latched onto, and he nodded. "For-fucking-ever, baby."

Her hand moved on his cock again, and she said quietly, "I want you inside me, Slate."

He felt his cock twitch, and grinned against the side of her head as he slid his hips between her legs and she opened to cradle him. "About fucking time. I want you to wrap those beautiful legs around me, Ruby."

Reaching down between their bodies to position himself, Slate kissed her hard and deep, holding still with the tip of his cock barely inside her. She'd been so tight on his fingers he knew he had to go slow to keep from hurting her. "God, you are so hot, baby," he groaned as his hips moved and he slowly slipped into her. "So hot and fucking tight, you're like a glove wrapped around me; I can feel every breath you take like a caress on my cock. Beautiful."

He felt her shudder underneath him, and stilled. "Fuck, baby....fuck, that was like a ripple, tightening around me. I don't know how much I can take. Every breath you take...so tight. Be still, shhhh a minute. Be still..." he was panting, trying to hold onto his control. Mentally trying to push back the tingles and tightness in his balls, he took a harsh breath and was lost to her scent—vanilla and flowers. "God," he growled as he pushed deep into her, then held her tightly, unmoving, "you smell so fucking good. I want to eat you up. I could fuck you all day and never get enough of you. Every breath is mine. Mine."

She'd inhaled deeply when he thrust into her, and then panted underneath him as they lay still, joined. Using her heels as leverage, she pushed up hard against him, seating him the last inch he hadn't even realized was waiting. "So fucking deep, baby. Fuck. Be still, just...be still. Be. Still. God, tight. Mine." He adjusted his arms, pulling the pillow out and caging her head in with his forearms. Kissing her deeply, he slid his tongue along hers again, breathing in deep gasps against her mouth.

"Baby. Ruby, baby, this won't...I can't...I'm not gonna last. God, you feel so good. I've waited so long for this. I fucking love you, baby. I love you," he said as he began to move finally. His declaration continued with every hard thrust, "I. Love. You. Baby. *Fuck.*" He drew in a deep breath, muttering through clenched teeth, "Fucking. Love. You. *God.*"

He kissed her again, and then buried his face in her neck, slipping one hand down her back and cupping her ass, lifting her against his strokes. Sliding his fingers between her ass cheeks, he groaned in her ear, "Fucking wet for me, baby. Fucking drenched. Love fucking you."

With his fingers, he spread the slippery wetness around her tight opening, slipping his little finger inside her ass. "I want this ass. One day, baby, I want all of you. You are mine," he told her, and he felt her begin to go over the edge. "Yeah, baby, come for me. God, yes, *fuck*...come for me, baby. Ruby," he groaned as she fell into her orgasm, her inner walls tightening down on his cock hard, pulsing with her climax.

A handful of hard thrusts later and he was with her, shouting her name and biting down on her shoulder as he came apart inside her. Pushing deep and holding there as his cock throbbed and spurted, coating her inner walls with his semen, he felt her begin to slow and loosen. He thrust deep one last time to the root, hearing her catch her breath, and he felt her legs tighten around him again. "God, baby, so good," he murmured against the side of her head, shifting his arms to take most of his weight off her.

"Baby?" he asked, stroking her hair back away from her face, laughing to see the satisfied look on her features, and then laughing again as she made a pout of displeasure when he slipped out of her. "Are you good, Ruby?" he asked.

Smiling, she tilted her face up for a kiss, running her hands up and down his back. "Yes, Slate, I'm good."

He tucked his face into her neck again, smiling. "Me too, baby."

Waking the next morning, Slate knew without looking that Ruby was still in his bed. She was tucked in beside him, the warmth of her back to his front, and her face snuggled into the crook of his arm. Eyes still closed, Slate allowed the memory of what they'd done the night before to run through his head. He felt her move slightly, and realized she was awake.

"Hey, baby, good morning," he whispered, softly kissing behind her ear, reaching up to sweep the hair from her face. He felt her face move against his arm, and knew she was smiling. "Are you hungry, Ruby?" he asked, sliding one hand up and across her side to her chin, tipping her face to meet his, and then covering her mouth in a fierce, possessive kiss.

She kissed him in return, twisting in his arms so she was on her back, threading her fingers through his hair and holding him tightly. Slate slanted his mouth across hers, hard and hungry, feeling her hips begin to move. He dragged his fingertips down her belly and cupped her mound, slipping his middle finger between the folds and into her, pushing in deep.

"Baby," he said as she tried to cover a wince, "you're sore." It was a statement, not a question, but she still shook her head negatively. He smiled down at her. "No, Ruby, don't do that. I won't hurt you, not for my pleasure. We have a long time to get to know each other, and I won't have pain in our bed."

"Slate, it's okay," she said softly, reaching up to cup his cheek.

"Baby, no, it's not," he told her just as softly, sliding down in the bed. He covered her belly in kisses, making her giggle with his nibbling and licks. Settling between her legs, he stroked the sensitive skin with his thumbs, slowly parting her lips. "Oh baby, you are swollen," he moaned apologetically, kissing her pussy softly. "That's something you need to tell me in the future. Don't try to make decisions for me, Ruby." He kissed her again, gently licking alongside her clit. "Don't assume what I want. You need to ask me."

Ruby's fingers twined in his hair again, and she tugged his face up, saying, "Slate, you don't have to do this."

He grinned up at her. "Baby, mmmm, I know I don't *have* to. What you don't get is that I *want* to. This is something I'm allowed to do now, because you are mine." Running his nose along the skin between her thigh and labia, he kissed and licked his way across to her other leg, and then down.

"Mine," he repeated, dragging a calloused fingertip across her clit, listening to the catch in her breath. "Mine," he said once again, following that with a soft laving of his tongue. "Mine," he told her with a soft kiss one last time, before he made it his mission to have her breathless and breaking apart on his fingers and mouth.

About an hour later, strolling into the main room of the clubhouse with Ruby tucked underneath his arm and walking at his side, Slate was prepared for shit from his brothers. He knew they all held Ruby in high regard; she was precious, their Princess. He would simply have to make sure they knew this was Ruby's decision. He'd given her all the power, and she'd picked him.

What he wasn't prepared for was a room full of men all staring at them with hard eyes and bunched muscles.

Ruby tensed and went to slide away, but he stopped her with his hand cupping her shoulder, keeping her at his side. She put a hand on his stomach, clutching at his shirt, and her other hand wound in the belt loops at the back of his jeans.

The two of them had stood there for a minute, two strides into the room, before the men broke into smiles, with applause and catcalls starting in the back of the crowd. "About fucking time," PBJ said from beside him, reaching out to stroke Ruby's cheek. Slate smiled and swatted his hand away, growling, "Mine," at him as PBJ laughed aloud.

He looked down and saw Ruby's face was bright red, her eyes cutting from one member to another as the clapping died down. "All right, fuckers, you've had your fun," Slate called. "Stop embarrassing Ruby." He pulled her along with him as he moved towards the bar. "Is there food, or y'all slackin'?"

***

Sitting in his office, Slate was going over the reports Myron had provided on the existing businesses the Rebels had in Fort Wayne. Everything had settled down over the past couple of months, and the financials showed it. Even Marie's, the most recent acquisition for them, was turning a profit. At this rate, they'd be able to pay off the loan Chicago gave Bingo to start up the chapter.

That prompted him to remember the duffle sitting in a locker somewhere, and he opened a desk drawer, pulling out the envelope Estavez had given him days ago. Without looking up, he yelled for Deke, motioning him to close the door when he stepped inside.

"Who do we have that's tight with LEO?" he asked. "I have a pickup that has potential for eyes, and I'd like someone who won't get tagged in case FWPD is around."

Deke grinned at him. "Probably your best bet is me then, Prez."

"How so, Deke?" he asked, puzzled.

"My brother is on the force, man," Deke said. "I'm as close to an inside guy as you're going to find."

"Fuck me...how did I not know this? Well, alrighty then, here's the deal," Slate said, and then explained about the locker and cash.

Deke swallowed and paled. "Holy fuck, Prez, you telling me you've left what could be a quarter-million dollars sitting in an unguarded locker for more than a week?" He shook his head. "Are you fucking insane?"

"Nah, man, just had more important things to take care of." Slate grinned, thinking about the past several nights with Ruby in his bed.

Deke shook his head. "I'll go now; call you when I'm out with the bag," he muttered. "Fucking shit, man, you are crazy."

Slate went back to the reports until there was a knock at the door. Looking up, he saw DeeDee standing in the doorway looking unsure of herself. "Hey, DeeDee," he said pleasantly. "What's up?"

"Hey, Prez, can I talk to you for a minute?" she asked nervously.

"Sure, anytime," he smiled at her, and then the smile fell away as she came in and closed the door. "What's up?" he repeated, wondering if this was about Jason, her suite in the clubhouse, or Ruby.

"I wanted to talk to you about Melanie. There're things in her past I don't know if she'll be able to talk about, but I really think you need to know, Prez." She smiled at him then. "I haven't seen her this bright in a long, long time, and I want to make sure you have the knowledge you need to keep those smiles on her face," she said, then asked, "Has she talked to you very much about Michigan?"

Settling back in his chair, Slate tipped his head. "Nada. What happened in Michigan?"

Taking a deep breath, DeeDee shook her head. "I was afraid of that. *Shit*." She rubbed her forehead with her thumb and forefinger. "Shit. Shit. Shit. Okay." She shook her hands out as if she was readying for a fight. "Right after the accident, Melanie went a little off the rails. She had always been a willful child, and when you put her and my Lockee together, the sparks could fill a room, but this was different, because she was hurting. I didn't see it until too late, but there was so much going on then I don't even know if I could have done anything differently if I'd known."

She looked up at him. "You've heard of the Devil's Sins, right? They are a Michigan MC from up past Mackinac; they've got a few chapters spread across the upper peninsula of Michigan, and over in Minnesota. One of their officers was down here for a sit down, and he saw her. When he left, she had gone with him on the back of his bike.

"It was willing, at least as far as we could tell. She was too old for me to tell her no, but something felt off. We didn't see her for more than half a year, and when we got her back, she wasn't the same, Slate. I only know what she's shared with me, but he ruined her in ways that are still apparent." She used her thumbs to wipe tears from her cheeks.

"How did you get her back?" Slate asked quietly, his eyes fixed on DeeDee's face. He felt pain in his chest and couldn't take in a breath; he'd known there was shit in Ruby's past, but didn't know what to expect. This was painful to listen to, but he suspected it was gonna get worse.

"She called me and asked if she could come home, if she could come back...and I begged Bingo. He took a half-dozen Rebels to Chicago and got Mason's okay, and then they went through Wisconsin into the UP to get her. She was waiting at the gate of a compound there; they'd locked her out and left her. By the time he got there, she'd been standing in the snow for nearly three days," she said, watching his reactions.

"Was she this officer's old lady?" he asked tightly, eyes down; this was shit he should have been learning from Ruby, not DeeDee.

"No, not at all. We think he took her to make a point with the Rebels, but then found out she wasn't leverage. So then she was just...well, you know how devalued women are in some clubs." She lowered her head.

"She told me she'd only ever had sex with two men," Slate said. "Do you think that's true?"

Her head came up. "Yes, Demon kept her for himself—that I know."

Slate took in a deep, slow breath. "Demon? The Devil's Sins' president? That's the fucker responsible for Ruby's fear?"

DeeDee nodded. "For years now, I've watched her live with what he did to her. Slow to trust, quick to push away, she's kept herself alone, even when surrounded by people who care about her. The brothers have tiptoed around her for a long time, and she was...*is* so fragile. I don't know how you got close, but I've liked seeing the smile on her face over the past week. I like seeing how she looks at you, even when you can't see her."

"DeeDee, tell me what he did. I want to know; hell, I *have* to know. She's...important to me, and I've made promises to her. I want to make sure I can keep those promises, but I have to know what happened," he told her, leaning forward and laying his arms on the desk.

She nodded, gathering herself visibly, and Slate wondered how he could stand to hear this, if it was that bad. "He kept her in a closed room, no window. She said he'd feed her when he remembered, usually after fucking her. Sometimes he'd gag her; she told me he kept her gagged for nearly two weeks one time, only taking it off when he wanted her mouth, or sometimes to let her eat the food he threw on the floor.

"He kept her naked, and blindfolded her a lot. That way, she'd never know where the next hit or touch would come from. If she backed away, he'd beat her. If she flinched, he'd beat her. If she said anything, he'd beat her.

Taking a deep breath, she continued, "That was her life; he fucking broke her, Prez. She still has nightmares about it, and she is still so strongly affected by the experience that in some situations, her fear rolls off her in waves. You are the only one she's let get close and...I love her like my own flesh and blood, Prez. I can't bear to see her hurt again. I couldn't stand it."

As she talked, Slate's jaw clenched tighter and tighter until he was surprised his teeth weren't splintering under the pressure. The fucker had conditioned her in a low-sensory environment, where she was entirely dependent on him for her life. He'd taught her that fear was normal, touch was abhorrent, and pain was expected. Straining to keep his voice even, he asked, "Why did he turn her loose?"

DeeDee clasped her hands in her lap, looking down. "She got pregnant."

Slate suddenly comprehended he was looking down at DeeDee, and she had a panicked look on her face. He was standing over her; he'd rounded the desk without even realizing it. She was saying something, apparently answering a question he'd asked. Unclenching his fists, he stepped back, put his shoulders to the wall, and took a deep breath. "Hold a minute, DeeDee. Sorry, honey, say that again."

She covered her mouth with her hand to hold back a sob. Looking up at him, she tore his heart in two when she replied, "He'd given her something to make her miscarry before they locked her out of the clubhouse. It happened on the first day she was waiting. By the time Bingo got to her, it was done."

"Fuck me. He turned her out and then took her child? Anything else I need to know, DeeDee? Fucking *shit.*" DeeDee shook her head. He rubbed his face with both hands, remembering Ruby's flinch when he asked her about kids. "God, this is fucked up. I've met Demon, back in Chicago." Running his hands through his hair, Slate felt like murdering the motherfucker. "DeeDee, she's got to be one of the strongest women I have ever met. I feel so...God, I cherish her, and she's giving her trust to me. After he did that shit to her, she's giving herself to me. *Fuck.*" He took in a breath. "Who else knows this, Dee?"

DeeDee stood, took a step closer to him, and laid a hand on his arm. "No one...I've told no one. There was no reason to before; she kept everyone at arm's length. The members who rode to bring her back knew she was bloody and bruised, but no one knows the whole story. You are helping her heal though, and I think you are amazing, Prez."

He pulled her into a hug, kissing the top of her head. "Call me Slate, would ya?" Pulling back, he moved back to the chair and sat down. "I have a question for you," he started, and she tilted her head at him, raising one eyebrow quizzically. "Were you going to tell me Jason was in town?" He grinned at the surprised look on her face. "DeeDee," he chastised her jokingly, "I saw the fucker slinking out of here a few mornings ago," here his face and tone got serious, "but, honey, you know better than to bring him back to the clubhouse, even if this is where you live. You go to him, or find a neutral place; I don't want to see him here without my invitation again."

She nodded. "I didn't mean for it to happen; he tracked me down here, and we went upstairs to talk. I didn't invite him, Slate...Prez. I wouldn't do that." She took in a breath. "I've found an apartment. It's nice, and it's near Slinky's, so I can keep on there if you want. I was going to tell you soon, and now seems like the right time."

"Glad to hear you're willing to stay managing Slinky's, DeeDee. You're doing a good job. It's good you're finding your own place too. That's a big step, and we all know it, but you know you're always welcome here. You'll always be Winger's old lady, and we love you." He smiled at her, but stayed sitting. He wanted this conversation to be over; he was having a hard time keeping it together, and the urge to destroy something was still running strongly through him.

She smiled and reached for the door. "Close it behind you, DeeDee? Thanks," he said, reaching for his phone. Hearing the click as the door shut, he hit a button on the phone, waiting only a moment for the call to connect. "Mason, *Brother*," his throat was closing, "I don't know what to do, man. This is so fucked up."

"Slate, talk to me," Mason said quietly, and the strength of their friendship was in the words he said, offering support without question, and Slate grabbed that like a lifeline.

***

"I have something I want to show you. Want to take a ride with me, baby?" Slate asked Ruby, coming up behind her in the clubhouse kitchen a few days later. He rubbed his hands up her arms to her shoulders, wrapping them around and pulling her back tight against his chest. She tilted her face up for a kiss, and he captured her lips with his, watching her eyes close slowly as the heat rose within the both of them. Slowly stroking her bottom lip with his tongue, he pulled back, ending with two soft kisses. "Ride with me?" he asked again, and she nodded.

He picked her up, turning her in his arms to face him, and she wrapped her legs around his waist. Punctuating each word with a kiss, he told her, "Go. Get. Your. Leathers. Baby," and she giggled, placing her hands on his shoulders and pushing back.

Breathlessly, she told him, "You gotta put me down, babe."

The casual endearment took his breath, and he stroked her cheek with the backs of his knuckles. Relaxing his arms, he let her slide down his front, kissing her again as she settled her feet on the floor. "I'm going to make us some sandwiches, baby. Any preferences?" he asked her, releasing his hold.

Ruby looked up at him with a question in her eyes, but said, "There's lunchmeat and cheese in the cooler. I'm not picky, Slate."

He kissed her again, watching her turn and walk from the kitchen. Busying himself with their lunch, he had packed and cleaned up by the time she returned. "Ready to go, baby?" he asked, grabbing her hand and twining his fingers with hers. She nodded, and they went through the main room into the lot.

Slate smiled to himself as she straddled the bike behind him, lacing her arms around his waist and tucking her legs up around his ass. *God, this feels good.* He could get used to her heat wrapping around him like this. Throttling out slowly to let the prospect open the gate, he turned to go downtown. They were headed to his new apartment...their new home.

Pulling into the underground parking, he located his assigned spaces and backed into one of them. Toeing down the kickstand, he settled the bike and raised his hand to assist Ruby off. "Slate, what are we doing here?" she asked quietly, sweeping her hair back off her face with one hand. Grabbing their lunch from the saddlebags, he reached down for her and was thrilled when she beat him to it, taking his hand with both of hers and looking up at him.

"Checking on the renovations," he said cryptically, and then grinned. She scrunched her nose up at him, and swung into place, walking at his side to the elevator. At the door to the apartment, he paused, handing her the food and drinks. Using his key, he opened the door, and then startling laughter from her, he swept her into his arms to carry her inside.

"What are you doing, babe?" she asked, the laughter still present in her voice.

He felt his heart swell that she was becoming so comfortable with him, and hoped today didn't change anything. "I'm carrying my woman into our home," he mock-growled into her neck, nipping at her shoulder.

She grew still, and he pulled back to see a wide-eyed look on her face; it was not quite panic, but close. "Ruby, baby, it's okay. This is the apartment I've been working on. Remember? I want you here when I move in?" He soothed her, "It's okay." Holding her tightly against his chest, he walked into the kitchen and set her on top of one of the counters.

Looking around, he was pleased with the work so far. It looked like it was nearly ready to move furniture in, and that was easy enough to schedule. "Ready for the tour, baby?" he asked, stepping between her knees, pressing them apart as he pulled her to the edge of the counter and against him.

She nodded, twisting to set the food and drinks on the counter, and then slipped off to stand beside him. He waited a moment, and she finally reached out to take his hand with hers, winding their fingers together again. "God, I love when you touch me," he whispered, leaning down to kiss the top of her head.

Walking through the arched doorway, he led her into the main downstairs room. "This is the living area; I liked the view of the downtown skyline, and I heard we could see fireworks from the Tincaps' games from here." He pointed to the large windows on the west wall. Pulling her along with him, they returned to the kitchen, which was outfitted with stainless steel appliances. "If you like to cook, you'll love this kitchen." He showed her some of the hidden things, like the knife drawer and the tip-out cabinets for bulk vegetables.

Pointing up the short hallway, he said, "Half-bath, then a guest room with its own full bath." Walking back through the kitchen, he grabbed their lunch, pulling her towards the stairs. They were headed to the only furnished room in the apartment, and where he intended to spend the rest of the day. With a smile, he scooted her up the stairs ahead of him, watching her face as she saw the wide, open loft for the first time. There was a huge cherry wood bed set, with mocha-colored bedding.

"Bedroom," he said unnecessarily, and then led her to the far side of the room, opening the two sets of doors there. "Closet," he closed that door, then "bathroom," and walked inside with her. The tile shower had been enlarged, but still left room for a deep tub alongside it. He saw a brief smile on her face, and then she turned to him. Biting her bottom lip, Ruby looked up at him for a long minute while he waited. He finally reached out and rescued her lip with a fingertip, tracing her mouth slowly. "Baby?" he prompted.

"Ours?" she asked quietly.

A smile broke out over his face. "Yeah, baby. Ours. I wanted you to see it now before everything is final, so you can tell me if you like or don't like something and we can change it." He repeated, "Ours. Let me show you something else."

Pulling her into the short hallway that led past the loft's far wall, he opened another door. "It's not very big, not big enough for a bedroom, but this can be whatever you want it to be, baby—an office, so you can keep the accounts for the clubhouse straight without having to be there all the time, a fucking craft room, if you are into that. Are you into that?" he asked, and she shook her head. "Thank God, I don't even know what a craft room is, but the guy who did the painting mentioned it."

He paused, and then said what he'd been leading up to, "It could also be a nursery. It's the right size—" She dragged in a deep breath, opened her mouth, and then closed it. "No rush, baby, but something to keep in mind," he said as he shut the door, moving back to the bedroom.

Scooping her up and setting her on the edge of the tall bed, he asked, "So what do you think, Ruby? Anything you want to change about our home before we get furniture in here?"

She shook her head with a soft smile, reaching up to cup his cheek with her palm. "I think it's good as-is, babe. Still getting used to the 'ours' part of this," she said, stretching up to kiss his lips softly.

They camped out for a couple hours on the bed, eating lunch and talking about the apartment and the finishing steps that still needed to happen before they moved in. Slate expected them to be installed within a couple of weeks, but he told her they would keep his room at the clubhouse for lockdowns and parties.

He asked her dozens of questions about her preferences in things like kitchen storage, small appliance brands, thread count on sheets. He asked her anything he could think of, because he needed her to talk freely with him, needed to hear her voice like it was a drug he'd been denied for far too long.

Leaning against the headboard, he held her in his arms, draping her legs across his lap and pulling her close. "You got questions for me, Ruby? Ask me anything, baby. I'm an open book for you," he prompted her, resting his cheek on top of her head.

She was quiet for a minute, and then surprised him by asking, "Will you tell me about your childhood?"

"Aww, baby, that's so long ago. Lemme see...I was born and raised in Wyoming on a working ranch. My daddy died when I was a teenager, and we moved to town to live with my grandparents. I have a little brother, but you know that; you heard about Benny's shit a few weeks ago." He tilted his head back, looking up at the ceiling fan.

"Your family?" she asked, encouraging him to continue.

"My grandparents are still in Wyoming; GeeMa's a kickass woman. God, I love her. I phone her at least once a week, more often if I can. She keeps trying to set Myron up with some sweet girl from her church," he laughed, "and I think he calls GeeMa as much as I do; they could talk for days."

"Your mom?" she asked softly. She tipped her face up to look at his face, and he caught her lips with his for a quick kiss. "She lives in Denver," he clipped. Her eyes found his, and he saw she was puzzled at his short answer, but he really didn't want to talk about his mother right now. She'd fucked up enough shit for two lifetimes for him, and he didn't want her in his head or his life. "Any other questions, baby?" he offered, sliding a hand slowly up and down her back, shoulder to hip and back again.

She tucked her chin down, a sure sign she was uncomfortable. Mumbling a little, she asked him softly, "Have you ever been in love?"

He nodded his head. "Hard questions, that's good, baby. You mean before you, right?" he asked, and he was rewarded with one of her smiles. "There was a woman I could have loved, but she needed something other than me. I helped her find what she needed, and then got back in the wind. See this?" He pointed to the inside of his left forearm, where the compass was. "This is the lesson she taught me— 'Never let your fear decide your fate'. Lottie was fearless; she simply had to find it inside herself again."

He looked down at her. "Remember the girl I told you I left in Chicago?" She nodded. "I was infatuated with one aspect of her, but when I saw the whole person, there was nothing there for me," he said softly. "She didn't fit me, not like you do, baby. She wasn't you."

Ruby relaxed into him, and he continued stroking her back softly, slowly. "Actually, there is someone I loved." He pointed to his right forearm. "This was her lesson to me—'We live with the scars we choose'."

Ruby had tensed up again, and traced the tattoo with one fingertip, asking softly, "You loved her?"

He nodded. "Yep, still do. Carmela is easy to love. She is a gorgeous thing."

Hearing her breath catch in her throat, he decided he couldn't tease her like that. "She was also a child in a terrible situation, and I helped rescue her. The tat reminds me how we choose to live can be because of—or in spite of—our experiences."

Pulling back to look up into his face, she asked, "A child?"

He nodded. "Yeah, we grabbed her from a situation in Juarez, Mexico. I was hanging with the Southern Soldiers from Las Cruces then, trying to find my place. We set off a cartel war that wound up in my favor, oddly enough. Estavez, president of the Machos, you've heard of him?"

"Yes, he was at the clubhouse a couple weeks ago," she whispered.

"Well, it turned out Maria Luisa Carmela Estavez is his daughter," he said quietly, "and he would do anything in his power to ensure she stays safe for the rest of her life, including helping me save my brother's life and owing me a marker."

Ruby slowly relaxed again; he could feel the trust she gave him seeping into his bones like the warmth of the summer sun. Slate gave her another, final chance at questions. "Anything else, lover? Any other questions for me?" He saw a quick smile cross her face, and she shook her head.

"Okay, baby, now it's my turn, but you can still ask me anything, anytime," he whispered into the hair on the side of her head. "What do you want me to call you?" he began with what he hoped was an easy question.

"Ruby," she responded quickly, "that's your name for me, and it means something."

He nodded. "How long have you been around the club?" He already knew the answer to this, but it was a good lead-in to what he really wanted to know.

"Around *a* club since I was about ten, I think. Lockee and I went to school together, and my folks were...inattentive at best. She'd invite me over, and we'd play under her dad's desk. Then, when Bingo came to Fort Wayne, Winger decided to merge his club into the Rebels. I've been around the chapter since the beginning." She shrugged. "I've known some of the guys all my life, it feels like. They're my family."

"I know what you mean, baby. I have my blood brother, but never felt like I was part of something real until Mason pulled me into the Rebels in Chicago. I'd been riding around the country for a few years, working and staying a while in one place, then pulling up stakes and riding again. Met some interesting people, but I always seemed to gravitate towards the clubs, where they acted like brothers...like family," he closed his eyes, talking slowly.

"When I met Mason, I was looking for a job. I'd been sent to this bar in Chicago by a friend, because he knew Mason. Watcher, President of the Soldiers, was one of the guys who helped save Carmela. We're tight, and I still talk to him several times a year. So, get this...the first job Mason gave me was to break up a fight outside one of our neutral bars, Jackson's. What he didn't tell me—until I'd already stepped into the middle—was that the fight was between two high-ranking officers of rival MCs. I thought I was fucking dead, right then," he laughed, "but Mason had my back...then, and now. He's my brother by choice, you know?"

She nodded against his chest. "The club will always be with you. They're your family."

"Yeah, baby, you get it. I knew you did." He grinned.

"So, next question...have you ever lived outside of Fort Wayne?" he asked lightly.

She paused, then answered slowly, "Yes, I lived in Michigan for a few months."

"What made you move, baby?" he pushed her.

She tucked her chin down again. "I met someone after Lockee died...thought he was special."

Waiting patiently, after a couple minutes, he realized she was done talking. "What happened?" he pushed again.

She'd grown stiff, her muscles tightening and tensing, hands clasped in her lap with fingers wound tightly together. Slate kept up the unhurried strokes from her shoulder to hip and back again, pretending he didn't notice her anxiety. "He wasn't," she said finally, "special, I mean." Deliberately stroking up and down, he reached his hand up and cradled the back of her head, pulling her tighter against his chest. "What happened, Ruby?" he whispered softly in her ear.

She'd become so motionless he had to focus to see the rise and fall of her breath. Seemingly drawn down into memories, she was quiet, sitting with her eyes closed. Slate thought he could almost see her considering and discarding words and phrases, and he waited on her. He waited on her to trust him, to believe in herself. He'd wait on her forever, if she needed that long, but she had to tell him what happened, so they could get past it. This was tearing him up inside, and even knowing it was a selfish thing to make her relive this, he still needed to know, needed her to have enough confidence in what they were building to tell him.

Taking in a deep breath through her nose, she opened her mouth, and then closed it again. Shaking her head, she blew out the breath and started, "Why do I think you already know?" He continued sitting with her in his lap, waiting.

She shook her head again. "Demon...he told me I'd be his old lady. I was stupid and young. What did it matter to be the old lady of an MC president? But he seemed sweet and twisted me up inside. I missed Lockee so much, missed Winger. He said the things I wanted to hear, so I went with him, but when we got to their clubhouse, he only wanted to know whatever secrets I knew about Rebel operations. I didn't know anything, but he didn't believe that. He never quit thinking I'd pulled something on him, that I was hiding something, that I knew something...anything.

"He'd used up a lot of trust in his club by taking me, and once he knew I couldn't help him, he found it was better to keep me out of sight. I was isolated from the members, not allowed to go or do anything by myself, and after a while, not even *with* anyone. He told me things, threatened me, accused me of terrible things. By the time he was done with me, he'd convinced me of everything he had said." She shuddered. "If you hear something often enough, for long enough, it can become a truth. You begin to believe it, you know?" she queried, and he shook his head.

She forced a laugh. "No, you wouldn't know. You've never been that weak, never allowed someone that level of control over you, but I believed him. I was fat. I was ugly. I was old. I was useless. I couldn't cook. I was a whore. I couldn't fuck. I couldn't do anything right. I *believed him.*" She shuddered again, the movement roiling through her body.

She turned her head, pulling against his hand, her gaze sweeping the loft. "The room he kept me in was about as big as the dresser over there, more like a closet. It was small, and after a time, I knew the walls like the back of my hand. When he didn't tie me up, I would walk the edges all day long. I still dream about it. Fingers against the wall, it was one step, three steps, one step, touch the doorframe, three steps.

"Sometimes, I'd lay down on the floor and try to see underneath the door. One time, there another woman looking back at me, and I got excited. I realized that the eye I could see wasn't blinking, and then I understood she was dead."

Slate held himself still; the only movement was his hand as he continued to slowly caress her. Ruby's face slowly swung back to him, and he cupped her head, holding her close again. "There was this one day...I knew something was wrong. Things were off, and Demon was beside himself. He punished me for a million reasons. I didn't know how long I'd been there, because I'd lost track of time along the way; by that point, I didn't care about much of anything. He brought in a man, and they drew some blood from my arm. I was afraid of the man, because I hadn't seen anyone other than Demon for a very long time."

Ruby took in a deep breath. "Demon came in the next day with two members. They held me while he poured something down my throat until I thought I was going to suffocate. I was given clothes and told to dress, then was handed a phone and told to call a ride. I called DeeDee; that was the only number I could remember. I didn't even know where I was, only the general area from when we had arrived months earlier. They set me outside and left. Bingo came and got me."

She was shaking now, trembling all over, but seemed determined to see it through. "I didn't know." She lifted her eyes to his. "I swear I didn't know." Tears were streaking down her cheeks. "I didn't know," she repeated. "I was pregnant, but lost the baby." Her hands wound into his shirt, and she pushed her face into his chest, sobbing.

"Baby, I love you. Do you hear me, Ruby? I love you," Slate murmured softly. "I'm so sorry that happened to you, baby, so, so sorry. Did he hit you?"

Her head nodded. "A lot."

"And he took your baby. That's what he made you drink, right? Something to take your baby?" Slate hated asking these questions.

Her breath hitched, and on a breath, she said, "Yes, he made me miscarry."

"Ruby, did he share you?" He held his breath, waiting on her answer.

"No, it was only him," she said, scrubbing her face back and forth on his shirt.

"You are beautiful, baby, so fucking strong and brave. I love you," he reassured her again, trying to make sure she understood him, that she really heard what he was saying.

With her face against his chest, she whispered, "For a long time, I felt like I was on my own. In my head, you know? Alone. I've been afraid for so long, but you took that and you smushed it, pulling me into you. I was freefalling for a long time, but you caught me. I know you love me, Slate. I feel it, the connection we have. I've felt it since the first time I saw you, the first time you touched me...the first time you spoke to me. You didn't know it, but I was chasing you for months after you made me choose." She tipped her face up to him, and he saw her eyes were still swimming in tears. "You made me want to *be* again. I love you too, Slate."

They held each other tenderly as dusk settled down on the city, shadows edging into the room, but not daring to touch them as they lay together on their bed.

22 -   Unprepared

"Baby," he murmured, feeling her slide from the bed in their room at the clubhouse, "where you headed?" His eyes still closed, he heard her moving around the room, gathering her clothes.

"I need to go to the store, and I want to finish there before they're too crazy with people," she told him, leaning close and dropping a sweet kiss on his mouth. "Slate, we're still meeting at Clara's for lunch, right? I love that place, with the swings at the tables." She leaned in again, kissing him a second time.

"Yeah, Ruby," he said, eyes still closed, "pizza for lunch sounds good, but why are we meeting there and not here?"

Ruby laughed. "Because I'm going to the apartment from lunch, and you have to head to Slinky's."

"Mmm, yeah, that's right." He took in a deep breath. "I should get up now, yeah? Kiss you properly before you go on your spree."

"It's not a spree; we need nearly everything for the kitchen still," she laughed, "and you should go back to sleep, take a little time. It's all good, babe. I love you." With that, she kissed him a final time and darted out the door.

He called after her, "Take someone with you, Ruby," hearing her laughter come back up the hallway with a snotty, "Yeah, yeah."

Slate dozed in and out for a short time, and then decided it was time to wake up, running a hand through his hair. In the weeks since he forced Ruby to talk to him, things had been good between them. She was excited about their apartment, and had even helped DeeDee move out last weekend with no tears. Slate'd enjoyed introducing her to Jason, watching the carefully-circling interaction between them as they each sized up someone they knew was important to DeeDee.

Strolling into the main room, he was surprised to see all three prospects behind the bar; at least one of them was usually on babysitting duty. Looking around, he spotted PBJ sitting at a table along the wall, and he walked over. "Hey, brother, who went with Ruby to the store?" he asked.

Cutting his eyes up to Slate, PBJ shook his head and stood. "I didn't know she was gone, Prez. How long ago?" he asked, looking worried.

"Fuck me," Slate said softly, "probably an hour now. She wanted to get to the store early. I'm gonna text her, hang on." Pulling out his phone, he sent, **Ruby, where are you?** and waited impatiently.

In a few seconds, he received an answer, *Still at the store. You need something?*

He typed a quick, *You at Jefferson?* and waited.

Yes, Bed Bath and Beyond now. Kohl's soon.

Tightening his mouth, Slate typed, *Who's with you?* This time, the wait for a response was longer...quite a bit longer. He was proud of his girl though, when she didn't shy away from the hard stuff, texting back, *Everyone was asleep, but I'm fine*.

Gripping the phone tightly, he sent, *I'll be there in 10. Stay at BBB*, and shoved the device into his pocket. "She's at Jefferson; I'm headed over there now. Why the hell would she do this, PBJ? Has she been complaining about the security again?" Slate was pissed; Ruby may have put herself in harm's way without realizing it.

"I'm coming with you," PBJ growled, knifing to his feet, then yelled, "Tank, let's go, brother," and saw a prospect round the end of the bar to open the outside door. Slate felt his phone vibrate in his pocket, but figured it was Ruby telling him not to bother, and since he wasn't going to listen to her anyway, he ignored it.

"She planned on shopping, then lunch, then the apartment," he told them Ruby's agenda for the day, and watched as Tank nodded. He finished with, "She took the Civic, since she was shopping."

"Got it, Prez," the prospect said, starting his bike with a kick, waiting on Slate and PBJ to pull out, leaving him in the six position.

At the outdoor mall, they rolled through the parking lots near the store she'd mentioned, finally seeing the club car parked in an edge lot away from the building. Slate pulled up beside the driver's door, expecting to see an irritated Ruby waiting for him, but the car was empty. Balancing the bike, he dug the phone out of his pocket, looking at her last return text, **Argh. Fine**.

"PBJ," he called, "she should be here, man." He texted her back, **Where are you? At car, no you,** and waited. Nothing came in response. *Shit,* he thought, *shit, shit, shit...where the fuck is she?*

Tank yelled, "Shopping bags are in the car, Prez." Slate killed his bike, putting down the kickstand and dismounting in a hurry. He cupped his hands to look through the back windows and saw Tank was right; there was a pile of bags stacked carefully in the backseat. He resent his last text, and waited again, his heart seizing in his chest with fear.

Opening the car door, PBJ picked up something from the front seat, and turned it so Slate could see. It was Ruby's phone lit up with his most recent texts. Clasping one hand over his mouth, he started shaking and felt a chill settle into his stomach; he couldn't catch his breath. "Fuck me," he choked out, shaking his head hard. "Where the fuck *is* she?"

Taking in a deep breath and trying desperately to control himself, he clipped, "Tank, go to the store; have them page her." Eyes wide, he looked at his friends. "PBJ, stay with me; you clock anything, you tell me right the fuck now." The prospect took off at a run towards the store, and Slate spun in a slow, deliberate circle, looking hard at the vehicles parked within sight, but saw nothing suspicious.

"Anything?" he barked at PBJ, receiving a, "Nothing, man," in response. Running his hands through his hair, Slate strode to the car, wrenching open the door and looking inside for anything out of place. Behind him, he heard PBJ say, "Thank fuck," at the same time he heard Tank call, "Prez," and turning on his heel, he saw Ruby walking across the parking lot with Tank at her side.

Taking in a deep breath, Slate let it out in a series of gasps, feeling lightheaded. "Holy shit, she's okay," he breathed. "She's okay. Oh, fuck me, she's okay," he repeated to himself until she walked into his arms. Holding her tightly, he kissed her hair and cheek fiercely over and over. "Baby, oh, thank fuck."

"Slate, babe...what's wrong?" she asked into his chest; he had her trapped immobile against him.

"Ruby, you weren't in the car, but your phone was. Baby, you didn't take anyone with you, and I didn't know where you were," he whispered. "Thank fuck you are all right, baby."

"I'm right here, babe," she murmured. "I'm right here."

He held her until his heart slowed and the pressure eased in his throat. When he finally regained his composure, he cleared his throat, pressed his lips against the side of her head again, and asked, "You still want lunch, baby?"

The four of them sat on the upper level at Clara's Pizza King, taking up residence at one of the tables that had a porch swing on one side instead of a bench. Slate and

Ruby had claimed the swing, and she had her feet tucked up on the seat; one arm around her knees, she was leaning into his side as they ate their pizza.

"I love this place," she said. Pointing at the wall behind the two men across from them, she said, "That stained glass window is beautiful; it makes this place unique."

"Me? I just like the pizza," said PBJ, rubbing his belly lightly and laughing.

"After this, you can head out to Slinky's," Slate said. "I'll follow Ruby to the apartment, make sure she gets inside okay, then I can meet you at the club."

PBJ shook his head. "I'd feel better if we rode with you, Prez. Highwaymen are still reporting shit from up north, and you know the success we're seeing here in the Fort makes you a target."

Slate shook his head. "Nah, it's a short run. I'll meet you at Slinky's, man. It's all good."

**

"Holy fuck," said a voice, and a different one responded, "No shit." Slate wanted to tell them to keep it down to a mild roar; he hadn't suffered from a hangover this bad...ever. *Fuck*, he felt like his head was nearly detached from his fucking body. Good goddamn, it hurt...oh no; goddammit, he was gonna puke. Fuck, he *hated* throwing up.

"He's vomiting; roll him," he recognized Goose's practical-sounding voice, and then hands roughly pushed him around so he didn't puke all over himself. Nice of them, but they could have been easier with it; his head fucking hurt. "What the fuck is that smell?" was asked from somewhere near his feet. "Ether, I think," he heard, as he started slowly regaining control.

"Fuck me," he muttered. "What the fuck...?" He raised one hand to clutch at his forehead, knowing he was going to puke again.

"Welcome back, Prez." That was Goose again. There was a wheeze, and without opening his eyes, he knew someone was down in his face.

Sure enough, he heard Hoss' voice from right in front of him. "Prez, where's Ruby?"

With that single question, Slate was pulled from the fuzziness that still surrounded him, and propelled into the present, complete with debilitating pain. He opened his eyes to see he was lying in front of the elevator in the parking garage. Twisting his body, he saw the Civic parked behind him, the doors all tidily closed.

"She was standing with me, here," he said. "Ruby was right here." Turning to scan the garage, he didn't see that mane of red curls anywhere. "She was right here," he said again, puzzled. There was a flurry of activity as Hoss called out orders to the brothers gathered in the apartment's garage. Men were pulling out phones, scattering towards their rides, which were randomly parked like pick-up-sticks across the area near the elevator.

"Is she in the apartment?" Slate asked rolling to his hands and knees, trying to get his feet underneath him so he could stand. "Prez, hold on; you've got a nasty head wound," Goose said soothingly. "Let me help you up, man."

Slate glared at him, shouting, *"Is she in the fucking apartment?"* He clutched at his head again as the pain ratcheted up about fifteen degrees.

Hoss looked at him steadily. "She's not in the apartment, and her phone is turned off; it's going straight to voicemail. We can't track it. No one has seen her since you guys left the pizza place."

Slate bent over, hands on his knees, puking again. He stayed there for a minute, thinking there was something important he needed to remember about the garage. Straightening up and wiping at his mouth with the back of a hand, he said, "Security cameras...there are security cameras here. Make the call Hoss; let's get the footage. Lock us down too, man."

After searching the apartment himself, Slate rode his bike back to the clubhouse; he knew he wasn't any use right now out searching, but he'd be damned if he would simply sit around. He'd uploaded the security footage, and then called Myron. By the time they got there, he would have the video sorted, and they'd see what happened.

Slate pulled out and checked his phone again, looking for any new texts or calls he might have missed. Whoever took Ruby had to want something, and he was ready to trade anything to get her back. He simply had to be ready when they contacted him. He couldn't get a handle on who would have vanished her, but his money was on the fucking douche canoe Manzino. That fucker had released his territory way too easily, and he'd known it felt wrong. Now, he'd touched Ruby, and he was going to pay...and pay...and pay.

Slinging himself off the bike, he hurried into the clubhouse and into Myron's office. "Tell me you found something," he barked. "Fucking tell me something is on the footage."

Nodding, Myron said, "We have it on the camera, Prez. It's cued up and ready. Tell me when, man."

"All right...roll that shit," he told Myron, turning to look at the computer monitor. He saw the car and bike pull in, and saw them park beside each other. Slate watched as the two figures on the screen came together in what was clearly a passionate kiss, Ruby stretching up on her toes to meet his mouth. He saw as they turned towards the elevator, facing the camera, then figures came into frame from the sides and he stopped breathing.

There was no fighting; they'd dropped him within seconds, holding a cloth over his mouth and nose. Ruby struggled in the grip of one big guy; they could see she was screaming, her mouth open wide. Another figure walked into frame and kicked Slate in the head; Ruby sagged in the big man's grip, still screaming. The figure moved towards her, reaching out one hand to cup her face and she stilled; they saw her knees buckle.

Turning around, heedless of the camera, the figure walked out of range of the camera as the big guy dragged Ruby along. One look at the face was all Slate needed to identify the motherfucker. It wasn't Manzino, as much as he'd rather it be. The man who took Ruby was Demon, President of the Devil's Sins, and Ruby's personal nightmare.

***

He'd always been good at putting puzzles together, whether it was a job, run, or business. Slate's gift was bringing the right people to the table to pull off whatever was being planned. He needed to tap into that talent, stir that skill, and right now, it was like his brain was frozen. He couldn't think of anything except how Ruby had collapsed when Demon touched her face.

He knew he needed to pull it together. This was no different from dozens of other plans he'd laid over the past years. If he could simply get an outline going in his head, he could figure it out. Ruby'd screamed and fought when they took him down; she'd tried to get to him. He had to find her. Had to...

Staring at the floor between his boots, Slate sat on the edge of his desk with the door open so he could hear the comings and goings in the main room. He'd come in here to plug in his phone, not wanting to risk it going dead. She could be calling him soon, any time now.

One of the prospects had turned on music; Slate heard *Just Save Me* from Like A Storm, which was one of Ruby's favorite songs. One night last week, she'd told him it was her song for him; as he'd thrust into her, she whispered between moans into his ear that it was because he'd saved her.

"Fuck me," he breathed, "pull your shit together, man. You got this." He called out to the main room, "Hoss, to me, man."

His brother strode into his office. "Yeah, Prez?"

"You call Mason yet?" he questioned, and swore again when Hoss shook his head. "All right, how many brothers do we have available in the Fort?" He was making quick lists in his head.

"We have over fifty, Slate," Hoss told him. "Did you put the chapter in lockdown? We got families coming in?" He needed to know, so he could plan on the clubhouse's defense if needed.

"Yeah, you called that back at the garage." Hoss looked at him quizzically.

"Okay. Get DeeDee in here if she's not already on the way, man. I'm gonna make some calls. I want to talk to you, Bear, Gypsy, Tequila, and Deke in five minutes." Slate ran his hands through his hair, leaving it standing up in all directions.

Hitting a number on his phone, he waited for the call to connect, cutting off Mason's greeting harshly. "Prez, Ruby's been taken. I'm going to war with Devil's Sins. Motherfucker took her from my side, man. She was at my fucking side and wasn't safe from him. I'm leaving Hoss here and taking twenty men. I think I know where they are; Bingo told me Sins had a clubhouse here in town. We'll go there first, looks most promising."

Listening to Mason's crude response to the news, and relieved he gave full support of whatever it took to get Ruby back, Slate's muscles unknotted a little bit. In response to Mason's offer to come down, Slate said, "Nah, Prez, I got this. If he's in the Fort, I got this. If he's in the UP, I'll need you where you are. Someone will update you every couple hours; I'll see to that."

They hung up after Mason told him, "I know this is shit, Slate, but you didn't find her only to lose her. She's your fucking always, man...not happening."

Walking out into the main room, Slate shook his head at the offer of a beer; he wanted his mind clear for this. The men he'd asked for were waiting for him, and he strode over to where they stood. "Devil's Sins had a clubhouse down on Wayne a few years ago. We're going down and taking it. I've got Mason's approval—any force necessary to get Ruby back. Fucking war, man. He's calling the national president for the Sins now, but since that's the same fucker who took Ruby, we don't hold out any hope he'll be reasonable," he laid out the beginning of his plan.

"We need twenty members. Hoss, you aren't going, man. You are second, and need to stay here, just in case. Tequila, Bear, and Gypsy, I need you to pick six members each, get them armed and ready to ride in ten minutes. Serious as fuck, man, I'm out the gate in ten fucking minutes, and it's taking everything I have to wait that long. You don't know the history between this motherfucker and Ruby, but every minute she's in his control is sixty seconds too fucking long."

"Pick your men, and assign them front or back for the entry. Gunny's my pick; he'll be on point from the back. She's probably in the basement, which is accessed through the backyard, as well as through the house. Make your list, give it to Myron. He's going to text building layout and the address to everyone." He looked from face to face, making sure they all understood what was going down.

"Hoss, call Gasman and bring him up to speed. You need to call Mason in two hours; tell him what you know at the time. Rinse, repeat, Brother, as long as it takes. Deke, I need you to call your brother, man; warn LEO to stay the fuck out of my way." His face turned grim. "I can guaran-damn-tee you there will be casualties today, Rebels. Pick your men wisely; let's not leave babies fatherless if we can help it."

Stepping back from the group, he yelled across the room, "Goose, come here." Turning to walk back into his office, he waited for Goose to enter and shut the door. "Check me, man. Make sure I'm not putting anyone at risk; my fucking head hurts like shit, and I'm still trying to sick up."

While Goose checked him over, Slate kept talking. "The motherfucker who took Ruby had her for six months a few years ago. He beat her bad, raped her over and over, and poured something down her throat that made her miscarry a baby. I want you with us, but hanging back. Only after we go in and find her do you breach a fucking door, but I need you there, man."

He watched Goose's hands pause as they moved over his head, and then saw them start to shake as the full import of what he'd said sunk in. "Not a fucker here knows this except me, and now you. That's as Ruby wants it, but she's going to need all of us, man. You are the only one I trust her with if he's been at her again." Slate tipped his head down in response to pressure on the back of his head.

"The stitches I put in are holding fine, and you don't really show any signs of a concussion except the nausea. I think you are as o-fucking-kay as you are going to be right now, Prez." Goose paused a second, then said, "I'll pack a bag to take on my bike. She have clothes in your room?" Slate nodded, and Goose left the room at a run.

Outside, sitting astride his bike at the edge of the compound driveway, Slate looked at his phone to see the time. It was nearly eight minutes after he told them to roll, and there were more than twenty men sitting alongside and behind him. His brothers were ready to ride with him, no matter what the outcome. Lifting his hand and motioning, he roared into the street, headed towards where he hoped and prayed Ruby was.

They pulled into the parking lot of a store located a half-block from the house, idling as softly as possible when there were this many powerful bikes in one place. Standing in a circle of his brothers, Slate looked around, noting each face.

"You should all have the house layout. We think she's probably in the basement. Gunny, you are my pick for point to go into the basement from the backyard. I'll be inside in the back, and will go down the stairs there. We run this to the end of the line, brothers. If she's in there, then no one in that building is innocent." He saw a couple of the men pale at that.

"This is Rebel business. Ruby is Rebel, was claimed months ago as our property. Now, she's my old lady, and these motherfuckers took her from my side. For me, this is personal. Fuck, for all of us, this is personal, because we are Rebels. Rebel Wayfarers forever," he said, and heard the echoes from around him, "forever Rebels."

Running up the alley behind the houses, Slate followed Gunny; half-bent over in a crouch, they took advantage of what cover was available. He heard soft footfalls behind him, and saw shadows moving up the street that ran parallel. This was near a historic district, and some of the houses looked old and well kept. If the owners looked outside, they'd get a shock at nearly twenty-five badass bikers in leather and denim traveling at a soundless dead run.

Gunny pulled up and indicated they were at the right address. Slate verified and nodded at him. He texted Bear they were going in, and they swarmed through the backyard, half of the men going towards what looked like barn doors mounted in cement against the house, and half heading towards the screened-in entryway porch.

Slate and Tequila were side-by-side in the hallway when they heard the first gunshots from the basement. They rounded the corner into what looked like a huge farmhouse kitchen, seeing a narrow door in a nearby hallway. There were two men in the kitchen, and they seemed frozen with indecision. Slate took care of that for them, clocking them in the head with the butt of his gun as he ran past, making sure they were unconscious when they hit the floor.

The door slammed open, and a big man stepped up from the basement stairs. He looked startled to see them in the house, and his running momentum had him half turned around before Tequila could grab him. He slammed Tequila against the wall, but Pinto got behind him, whipping his pistol against the side of the man's head until he slumped against the bottom of the wall near the doorway.

Another gunshot from the basement had Slate moving down the stairs as fast as he could go, his eyes sweeping the open, unfinished, empty room. He recognized Bear's voice upstairs roaring at someone, and heard running feet on the floorboards over his head.

There was blood on the floor in the next room in the basement, and Slate caught himself on the doorframe as he took in the scene. Two men were motionless on the floor, and Gunny had his handgun pointed at a man kneeling in the center of the room. Ruby was bound to a bare metal bedframe in the corner. She was naked, and wasn't moving.

Tug was next to the bed fiddling with something, swearing and jerking his hands back before reaching forward again. He looked up at Slate, yelling, "Don't touch her; the bed is hot. Give me a second, Prez. Don't touch her."

He took a shaky step towards her, and then another, and was at her side in two more strides. He heard Tug, but didn't understand. "Prez, give me a minute, fuck. Hold, man. Hold." Reaching out his hand, there was a sharp spark between Slate's fingertips and her face as Tug yelled, "Got it."

Cupping her chilled face in his palm, he couldn't feel her breath on his skin. Pulling out his knife, he sliced through the leather that bound her to the bed, hollering, "Get Goose! Someone get Goose." Slate pulled her body into his lap; she draped over his legs and arms loosely, her joints bending in ways they shouldn't.

Goose was there a moment later, pulling her from his arms. "Give her to me, Slate. Let me help her, man." He positioned her on the floor and quickly checked her, then started pressing on her chest. "Slate, call a bus. Tug, count for me. Somebody find a blanket; we need something to cover her," Goose barked as Slate sagged to his knees next to Ruby on the floor.

"Nine-one-one, what is your emergency?" he heard over the phone, then gave them the address and nothing else before ending the call. "Hoss," he started as his next call connected, "we have her, but she's bad." He terminated that call, too, still watching Goose work with Ruby.

He heard Tequila and Bear yelling upstairs; there were two more gunshots, and then silence from the house above them. His eyes were focused on Goose, who was counting along with Tug. Turning his head, he looked into the face of the man Gunny had at the end of his barrel, and saw it was Rabid. The man had once been a brother, a Rebel, and he was in the same room as his Ruby.

Tug called, "Gunny, secure the motherfucker. Get a blanket." Slate kept staring at Rabid for a minute, clenching his teeth. Deliberately turning back to Ruby, he leaned down and put his lips next to her ear, whispering, "Come back to me, baby. Come home, Ruby. Love me, baby? Love me enough? Come back; I want you here with me. Love you, sweetness. My lover, my life, you are my breath. I'm here, baby. Right here, see me?"

He heard a noise, and saw a blanket settle over her belly and legs. Turning his head, he saw the car battery sitting on the table near the bed, and realized what had happened to Ruby...what they had done. He reached out his hand and cupped her cheek; it was cold to the touch, and he jerked back. "Goose?" he snapped, asking his question without any more words.

"It was constant current, body-wide, and she's dry. We have to get her heart to beat normally; it's all over the place right now, Prez," Goose gasped out between compressions. "You keep talking to her, man. Keep her engaged; she's in there. I know she is. She's still here, brother." Slate nodded, reached out again, and touched her face unflinchingly. Lowering his face to hers again, he whispered in her ear.

There was a commotion upstairs, and he realized he'd been hearing sirens getting closer. There was a clatter of feet, and two men in EMT uniforms came into view, stopping beside one of the men on the floor. Slate stood with a shout that got them moving, "Get the fuck in here. *Help her.*"

Goose turned her over to one of the men, who put his hands on Ruby's chest. Slate winced at him touching her, but put his mouth back down by her head, continuing to whisper to her, "I'm here, baby. I love you. Come back to me, lover. Come home, baby. Ruby, I need you. Come back, come home."

The second man affixed sticky patches to her ribs and chest, then they moved back, telling Slate, "Move back for a second, clear." Ruby's body moved slightly on the floor, but Slate didn't pay attention to that; he watched avidly as her mouth moved, lips opening in a cough. "Thank fuck," he whispered.

Both EMTs swooped down on her, rattling off medical terms and using various pieces of equipment they'd brought with them in a toolbox. One of them looked up at Goose. "We need the gurney," he told him, and Goose stood, turning to go to the doors opening into the backyard, asking as he went, "Bus in front?" and receiving an affirmative response.

Slate levered himself to his feet and looked over at Gunny and Tug. "Get shit tidied, Brothers. Did we find the one who started this?"

They nodded at him, Tug telling him, "That one is on the main floor, Prez. I'm on it; stay with Ruby." Tug turned, calling orders as he ran upstairs. Within a couple of minutes, the men who had been unconscious on the floor were gone, taken into the backyard and carted off in a van brought for this purpose.

Deke came downstairs, took a look inside the room, and his face tightened as he took a step backward, yelling, "They had her on that bedframe, man? They fucking electrocuted her? What was the fucking point?" At that, one of the EMTs turned and looked, and his face tensed. He grabbed the mic on his shoulder, telling dispatch or the hospital they had an electrocution victim incoming, rattling off a bunch of numbers and acronyms.

"What hospital?" Slate asked, hearing the response, "St. Joe's," and he nodded. Dialing, he said softly, "Taking her to St. Joe's. You've got some packages coming, brother. Box those leftovers up for me, and keep them." He hung up, sliding the phone into his pocket.

They transferred her to the gurney Goose brought in; he'd moved the bus to the back alley to make it easier to get her out of the house. Slate looked around. "Deke, with me, man. Tequila, call PBJ; have him come to the hospital. Take the rest of the brothers home. This shit could fracture the club...fucking Rabid. Goddammit."

* * *

Hours later, Slate was sitting on the edge of Ruby's bed. She was exhausted from the tests and medication, and he hoped she'd be able to rest for a while. She'd been confused when he was finally allowed to see her, unsure of what was going on. Totally focused on watching her face as she slept, he was startled when he heard Mason's voice from behind him. "She's going to be okay, Slate. You got her, man. You got her back."

Turning to look behind him, Slate stood, stepped towards Mason, and pulled him close in a one-armed embrace. "I didn't know you were coming, but it's good to see you, brother," he ground out through sudden, harsh tears. "We won't know for a few days if everything is okay, but they said the swelling in her brain is nearly gone. Now they're waiting to see if there's organ damage."

He shook his head. "This shit is so fucked up. I feel useless, Mason. I can't do anything to help her." He wiped at his eyes with the backs of his hands. "They stole her from my side, man. She was by my fucking side, and I couldn't keep her safe. It was touch and go too. She nearly died in that basement, because I couldn't keep her safe. She wasn't fucking breathing for the longest time; Goose saved her life." He swept his arm towards her. "Look at her, Mason; look at where she is...what she's gone through. This shit is because of me, because of us. It hurts so fucking bad, man. How can I do this?"

Mason looked at him for a long minute, then reaching out one hand to grip his bicep, he asked, "How can you not, brother?"

They stood in silence watching Ruby for several minutes, then Mason stirred. "I'm not staying, just needed to stop in on my way to the clubhouse to see for myself how she's doing. I'm taking care of these fuckers tonight, Slate. You stay here and be with your lady. Our brothers and I have this under control, and we will handle things as needed. The hard shit's *here*, man; I don't envy your path," Mason pulled him close again, whispering in his ear, "but she is fucking *worth it*. Like Mica would say— she's your always, man. You are one lucky motherfucker; not all of us find ours."

After Mason had left, Slate moved back to the bed, perched on the edge, and leaned close to hold Ruby's hand. He didn't even know he was dozing until her hand shook his shoulder. "Babe, wake up. You're about to fall off the bed."

Straightening his torso, he stretched a little and looked down at her, a smile quirking his lips. "Hey, you," he said softly. "How are you feeling, baby?"

Ruby closed her eyes and sighed. "Like a bus ran over me, backed up, and ran over me again." She tipped her head back, slowly opening her eyes. "Climb in here, babe," she told him. "I can't sleep without you."

Grinning, Slate didn't wait for a second invitation, toeing off his boots and crawling into bed beside her. He arranged himself next to her, carefully wrapping one arm around her waist and pulling her in tightly to his side while watching out for the various lines and wires attached to her. "Can you sleep now, baby?" he asked quietly.

"Mmm hmmm," she murmured into his chest, "I love you, Slate."

He felt her smile on his skin and had to tighten his lips to hold back a sudden sob. "I love you too, Ruby," he whispered against the top of her head, "more than I can tell you. Baby, you are my everything, my...always. You're not getting away from me, you know that? I love you, and this is forever."

From her even, slow breathing, he knew she'd gone to sleep, but just as he'd carried on a one-sided conversation while Goose and the EMTs worked on her, he talked to her now. He told her about his family in Wyoming, and how things had changed after his dad died. He hit the high points of his years spent wandering, telling her the story about the shortest-lived job he'd ever had, and how he'd fallen into the sheep dip.

Slate gave her every significant detail about his life, all the things that made him the man he was today, including Lottie and Edith; he didn't hold anything back. He told her about Mason, and how the job in Chicago had gotten him focused. By the time he finished talking, his voice was raspy and sore-sounding, and Ruby had been awake and listening for a long time.

She reached up, tracing his nose with her fingertips, down to his lips. "You are amazing, did you know that? I'm so in awe of everything you've done and accomplished, babe, so proud of you, and blown away that out of the whole world, you picked me. Slate, I love you—never doubt it."

23 - Home

"No, seriously, get your ass in here and talk to me, Slate," Ruby yelled from the bedroom.

Pulling on his jacket, he walked up the stairs. "What do you need, baby? I gotta get to the clubhouse; there's still a shit-ton of fallout that needs to be handled before I go. Gasman is coming in for a sit-down, then I'll be going to Marie's about six o'clock if you wanted to come down for dinner." He stopped and cocked an ear towards her phone where she had music playing, listening to the words with sudden intent. "What song is that, baby?"

Ruby smiled at him. "It's *Love Don't Die*. Do ya like it?"

Grinning, he laughed at her. "Baby, that's your song. Holy shit! They pegged you! 'You don't say much...but you know I listen when you do'...and sweetness, they will never be able to take me from you. God, that song is fucking perfect. Who is it?"

Laughing, she walked over to him and slipped her arms around his waist. "The Fray...I can't believe you like it."

"It's perfect," he said, punctuating each word with a kiss, "Just. Like. You." She'd come home from the hospital three months ago, and things had slowly swung back towards a semblance of normal. Now, Mason had asked him to take a ride and visit some problem chapters, putting his skills to use to suss out what the issues were without an official inquiry.

"Such a goof off," she chastised him, laughing. Pulling his face back down to hers, she kissed him soft and slow, her tongue demanding entrance into his mouth and then sliding across his, her fingers twisting in the hair at the back of his head.

"Mmmm," he said into her mouth, "nice, I like it when you take what you want, baby."

Resting her head against his chest, she asked him one last time, "You sure you don't want me to come with on your run, babe?"

"Ruby, we talked this through. I'm headed to a full-dozen chapter clubhouses, then dropping into New Mexico to see Watcher. I'll be home in three weeks max," he reassured her. "This is not a run for you, not in your condition."

"I don't like that you aren't taking anyone with you, Slate." She picked up her head, looking into his eyes. "Things can change so fast, get sideways and messed up. We know that more than most people. I'd be happier if you'd take someone with you."

"It's not happening, so you might as well give up the fight." He shook his head at her. "I go alone, or I take thirty brothers. After the shit we've dealt with, there's no middle ground. Either I'm confident enough to trust the chapters, or I ride in looking for war."

He continued, "I don't want war. I don't want fucking shit every time I turn around. I want you safe, and I want our baby safe." He reached out and put his palm across her low belly. Ruby smiled up at him, and he watched the joy flow across her face. "I'll be back before you even know I'm gone." He leaned in and kissed her.

She scoffed. "I doubt that, but I get it. I do. Full support, I'm on board." She laid her cheek against his chest. "It won't be long and we'll have a bump between us when we stand like this." She giggled. "Who'da thunk it three months ago, yeah?"

Holding her tightly, Slate couldn't suppress a shudder, and he softly echoed her words, "Yeah, who'da thunk it?"

***

Rolling the muscles in his neck and shoulders, Slate tried unsuccessfully to relieve the tightness he felt there. He was standing in a poor excuse for a clubhouse, trying to decide how long it would take him to clean up this shit. He was already a week overdue back in Fort Wayne, and he hadn't even gotten out west yet.

Pulling out his phone, he called Mason. "Prez, this is bullshit, man. Weak officers, defenseless clubhouse, shit for finances...this chapter is a disaster. How the hell did Memphis go so fucking wrong? We laid out a good plan, but this," he scoffed, "this is shit."

"How long, Slate," Mason asked, "and fuck...does it have to be you? Can't I send down Tug?"

Slate frowned at the wall for a second, puzzled, and then started laughing. "She fucking called you, didn't she? Goddammit, Prez, you listening to Ruby now?"

Mason laughed with him. "Busted. Slate...she misses you, man. There's an appointment in three weeks that she wants you there for—if you intend on keeping your balls where they are now."

Slate shook his head, chuckling. "Yeah, she's excited to find out the baby's sex. Fuck, Mason, I'm having a baby. How bizarre is that?"

"Gonna put a band on that hand?" He could hear the smile in Mason's voice as he asked the question.

"Yeah, got a ring and everything, just need to find the right time to ask her. Fuck, I want to go home to her now, so goddammit, Mason," he half-yelled, "send Tug. I'll get shit started, but he can put all the pieces together when he gets here. I'll be out of here in the morning, so make the fucking call, man."

"About damn time," Mason agreed. "You still going to visit the Southern Soldiers?"

"Yeah, Watcher is expecting me. Estavez is bringing Carmela up; I can't wait to see how she's grown up. Then I'll be in the wind, headed home." He smiled. "I'll call Ruby when I hang up with you. Make the call, Prez. Thanks, man."

Warmth suffused Mason's voice as he said, "Anytime, brother."

It was noon the next day before he felt comfortable leaving the chapter. Now that they knew Mason was sending someone down to sort their shit, they were running around and trying to cover, so he took control to ensure nothing important went for a walk.

Without thinking, when he pulled onto the highway, he turned east instead of west, winding around the south end of Memphis, taking a familiar exit. He drove a mile down a country road, pulling into the entrance of a well-kept cemetery. He tilted the bike over onto the kickstand and stood, turning to look out at the pastoral scene. "It's quiet here," he said to himself.

Walking into the cemetery, he started scanning the gravestones. It only took a few minutes to find what he was looking for, and he reached out, tracing the letters with his fingertips. Mouthing the words silently, he read, *Edith Khole, never alone.* He placed his palm over the blackbird etched in the stone, captured as it was bursting into flight.

"I'm sorry I didn't do more, Edith," he said quietly. "I'm a better person now; I wish you could see how you changed me." He stood still for another minute before returning to his bike, turning his face west.

***

He hadn't planned on stopping in Longview, but hated knowing he was within a few miles of Blackie and Peaches without at least trying to see them. Pulling into a truck stop, he sat on his bike and pulled out his phone. Listening to the ringing, he was surprised when instead of going to voicemail, the phone was answered by a child.

"Is Blackie there?" he asked gruffly.

There was silence, and then the voice yelled, "Daddy, telephone!" In a softer tone, he heard, "I'll take him the phone, hang on."

Slate asked, "Is this Randi?"

There was another silence, and then a cautious, "Yeess."

"Awesome, tell Blackie it's Slate…Andy," he said, holding the phone away from his ear in anticipation.

"Uncle Andy! You haven't been here in a long time. I'm a lot older now. Are you coming to see us?"

"Maybe, Randi, lemme talk to Dad, okay?" he put her off.

"Slate, my man, where the fuck are you? Randi isn't making sense," Blackie half-yelled into the phone.

"I'm sitting at the truck stop on I-20, man. Y'all got enough supper for another mouth, and a bunk for me?" Slate asked, and pulled the phone away from his ear again.

"Fucking right we have food and room for you, brother. You know it. You get your ass down here; we'll be waiting," Blackie yelled, and then disconnected the call.

Sitting around the fire pit in their backyard late into the night, he and Blackie were quiet, watching the flames dance across the logs. Several members of Blackie's club had been over earlier, but they'd left a while ago. It was good to see them again; Slate knew his life was full of friends and brothers all across the country and he felt gratified.

Peaches was inside settling the kids into bed, and he started talking to Blackie about what had gone down with Ruby. Blackie'd already heard the story secondhand, so he tried to fill in the details. As he spoke about how she'd been taken from the garage as he laid unconscious on the ground, he heard Blackie's growl clearly through the night air, and nodded. "Rabid, man...fucker skimmed from the club and then pulled a runner, leaving his Brothers to clean up his mess," he said, "blaming me, because I'd called him on his shit.

"Then, he finds a crack, a vulnerability, and decides he's not done fucking with the club and me. He'd heard stories about Winger rescuing Ruby, tracked down the one fucker who had her before, and presented him with an opportunity he couldn't turn down. Fucking Demon...hard to believe so much evil existed inside one man's skin." He leaned forward, his hands twisting and fisting. "I can't tell you what it did to me when I saw that motherfucker's face on the video. Blackie, I still can't sleep for seeing the pictures in my head."

He looked up, and saw Lottie had come out and was sitting on the arm of Blackie's chair, leaning into him and listening. "There were five of them—five, against one tiny woman. They didn't beat her, didn't fuck with her like that, but Rabid, that crazy motherfucker, he had hooked up a car battery to a bed frame. Blackie, they stripped her, strapped her to the frame, and turned it on." He rubbed his hands across his face hard, scrubbing at the memories.

"The docs figure she was in the current for more than forty-five minutes, and maybe as long as two hours—two fucking hours of low-voltage, constant electrocution. When we got her off the bed, she was like a broken doll, nothing moved the way it was supposed to. She flopped around, like her body was empty of everything...empty of her." He scrubbed at his face again, running a hand through his hair.

"She was so fucking cold, man; she felt dead, Blackie. I thought for sure she was gone when I touched her. I couldn't fucking think, couldn't speak or move. She wasn't breathing and her heart was beating wrong; she was gone. I swear, she was dead, and I was frozen, like my strings had been cut. Goose, man, he kept working on her and talking to me. We got to the hospital, and they'd brought her back; she was present...with us again.

"She's got memory problems. They said she might never get back the memories she's lost, which I think is a fucking Godsend, because she doesn't remember that day at all. Her short-term memory gives her fits sometimes though, like the one day she told me the same joke three times. That's getting better, thank fuck. There's also this phantom pain in her hands and feet, where it starts hurting and burning, but there's nothing wrong.

"I hate that she went through this, Blackie. I keep thinking I wasn't any use, because she was *right beside me*. She was right fucking *there*, and they took her from my side. How can I keep her safe if shit can come after her anywhere?

"Now, God...now, she's pregnant. We're going to have a baby, a kid. I'm so fucking scared all the time, brother. How the hell do I help her through this, man? Fuck want...how can I be what she *needs*, when I don't even know how to be in a relationship? I've never felt like this about anyone. My whole life, I was clear with the women I was with that it would never be anything other than temporary. Fuck me, man—kids are not temporary."

At his statement, Lottie snorted and laughed, agreeing, "Nope, they are with you all their lives."

"Exactly, so how the fuck do I do this?" he asked her.

Laughing, she reached up and ran a hand down the side of Blackie's face, asking, "Do you love her, Andy?"

He jerked at her use of his name; he heard it so seldom anymore. "Yeah, I fucking love her. I can't breathe if she's not sharing my air, can't sleep if she's not wound up in the sheets with me, can't relax without my hands on her. I've never...fuck me, I've never loved anyone before." He took a long look at her sitting with her man, and said, "I think I came close once, but Ruby...she is it for me."

"Then simply love her, Andy. Tell her; be honest about your fears, but you also gotta be honest about your love. She'll need to hear that, especially with everything that's happened to her in these few short years. She's going to be afraid she's not enough, because she's younger, because of the abuse, and because you have such a history...a reputation. Love her, Andy. Simply love her," Lottie told him, and then Blackie pulled her into his lap, biting and kissing her neck with resulting giggles and laughter.

He looked at Slate, saying fiercely, "When you hold your heart in your arms—your woman, your children— you can't do it wrong." He stood holding Lottie, and then walked into the house.

***

"Baby, I miss you so fucking much," Slate said softly, hearing her sigh. "I wish I'd brought you with me. It's been too long since I held you." On impulse, he told her, "Come to me. Finish this with me. You could be here in hours, baby."

Waiting on her response, the smile faded from his face as the silence on the line went on for long seconds, then he grinned wide when he heard a squeal as she shouted, "Of course, yes, yes, babe! Yes!"

"Gimme a second, baby; lemme get Dig on the phone," he said, quickly adding Digger to the call.

After explaining what they needed, they hung up, waiting on confirmation that Ruby was booked on a flight to Las Cruces, where Slate would meet her.

Leaning on his bike at the curb in front of the airport, Slate crossed and uncrossed his ankles for what seemed like the hundredth time, waiting impatiently on Ruby. He was early, but wanted to be there in case her flight got in sooner than expected. Looking through the tinted glass doors, he saw a small form moving quickly through the scattered groups of people and knew it was her. He recognized the way she moved, the shape of her body, the angle of her neck. This was his Ruby and she was headed right for him, like an arrow shot from a bow.

Opening his arms, he stayed leaning, bracing himself for her greeting. Dropping her bag on the sidewalk near his feet, she silently launched herself at him, wrapping her legs around his waist and pulling him in tightly with her arms. They stayed like that for a few minutes, wrapped up in the comfort and love of the other's embrace.

Slate slid his hand down to cup her ass, and his other up to thread into the hair at the back of her head, gripping it to pull her face out of his neck so he could capture her lips in a slow, soft kiss. "Ruby, baby, I missed you. God, I didn't know how much I needed you until I couldn't have you every day." He kissed her again, slanting his lips over hers and teasing with his tongue until she granted him entry. Sliding his tongue along hers, he deepened the kiss, eating at her, working his mouth over hers again, fingers tightening in her hair, guiding her responses.

"Ruby, I love you." He released his hold slowly, letting her slide down his front and swooping in to kiss her again when he felt the small swell of her belly between them. Slate reached into the pannier bag on the side of the bike, pulling out a small leather case. "Baby, you know me; I don't do hearts and flowers, but I've told you for a long time that we are forever, yeah?"

She nodded at him, and he saw the tears gathering in her eyes. He continued, reaching out to touch her belly, covering that precious bump with the palm of his hand, fingers stretching across her from hip to hip possessively, "Marry me, Melanie Davidson. Give me you and our kids. I want you to be my family, baby. I love you."

Opening the case, he pulled out the elegant but simple band, the red and white gemstones twinkling in the sunlight. "Rubies for your heart and heat, for my memories of you, for my love of you. My Ruby. My flame-haired beauty. Diamonds for our forever, protecting and holding our love. Baby, I love you. Marry me." He slid the ring onto her finger, tugging her in close to him again, waiting for her response.

"Yes, Andrew Jones, I will marry you," she told him solemnly, and then giggled. "Slate, babe...I love you too." Wrapping his arms around her again, he buried his face in her neck and hair, feeling complete for the first time in his life.

***

Watching Ruby with Carmela, Slate shook his head, wondering how he had never put together that they were about the same age. When the women met yesterday, they'd bonded quickly; with each knowing the other's story, there were no awkward explanations, simply a deep and mutual friendship.

Hearing footsteps coming up the path behind him, he turned to see Estavez approaching. "My friend," he said in greeting, and Estavez responded with a raised hand, eyes focused on the women sitting at a table nearby, who were laughing and talking.

"Your Ruby is a priceless find, I think," he said to Slate, turning to pin him to the chair with his eyes. "She is good for you."

Laughing, Slate agreed with him, "That she is. She keeps me in line, brother."

"My daughter is talking about coming to the wedding. Would I be welcome as well?" Estavez teased Slate.

"Of course you're invited, man; you're my brother," he responded. "Ruby wants it to be soon, so we have plenty of time before Peanut gets here."

Laughter sounded from behind him, and he saw Watcher stroll around to sit down next to him, "Peanut, man? That's a sad name for a kid."

"Shithead, you know what I mean. I can't keep calling it 'it,' so Ruby suggested Peanut. That's way better than anything I came up with." Slate chuckled. "Will you come to the wedding, Watch?" he asked, and was relieved when he got a quick nod in response.

"Fuck yeah, man. A lot of the brothers have expressed an interest too. You need to plan on a big party, Slate," he grinned, "all on your dime."

"No doubt," he responded, laughing again, "and happy to, man. Simply tell me whatcha need. I got this."

Lying in bed that night with Ruby tucked in beside him, Slate couldn't remember ever being so happy and content. He laughed when she reached up and traced her fingertips across his forehead. "What are you doing, baby?"

"You haven't frowned once since I got here, is all. I like this, being here with you and your friends," she said quietly. "Most of the guys in Fort Wayne aren't your friends; they are your responsibility, and it shows on your face there." He started to speak, but she quieted him, "Shhhhh. I get that it's your place, they are your brothers, and there *are* friends there...but I've never seen you like this, and I kinda like it." She smoothed her hands down his face, plucking at his lips with her fingertips and giggling. "You are all loose and relaxed," she told him, plucking at his lips again, "even your mouth." She leaned in for a quick kiss.

"Baby, not all of me is relaxed," he whispered, pulling her hand down to his cock, hearing her soft intake of breath as she wrapped her fingers around the hardness she found there.

Pulling her towards him as he raised up on one elbow, he angled himself over her upper body, sliding one hand up her side slowly, gathering the material of her shirt and tugging it off over her head. "I want you, baby," he whispered. "I need you. I always need you. God, I need to be inside you." Kissing her softly, he felt her hand work its way up his torso, pulling at his shoulder, her other hand slowly stroking him.

Pushing his hand down her back and underneath her panties to caress the curve of her ass, he lifted her hips to him, trapping her hand between their bodies as he pressed her against him, feeling her grind into him with a roll of her hips. "Please, babe," she murmured against his neck, licking her way along his skin.

Shifting to slide her panties down her legs, he raised her up as he moved to kneel between her legs, draping her calves over his thighs. She was open to him as he stroked up the inside of her thighs with his thumbs, his hands meeting over her pussy. He spread her open gently, watching as he touched her and his fingertips slid along her folds. Pressing the pad of one thumb over her clit, rolling and stroking, he pulled a soft gasp from her.

Slate bent forward at the waist, capturing one breast in his mouth and sucking deep. She made another soft noise, arching her back and pressing up into him, wrapping one arm around his head and cradling it to her chest. He released her nipple with a gentle kiss and shifted back to her mouth, unable to get enough of her body after being without her for so many nights.

He maintained a slow stimulation on her clit as he slid his thick middle finger inside her, biting down on her bottom lip as he felt her walls clench around him. Ruby's hands had moved to his back, and he felt the first sting of nails against his flesh, welcoming the proof of her passion. "Baby, you feel so good. I can't wait to be inside you," he murmured against her lips, adjusting his position to lift up on one arm.

"Mine," he whispered, letting his hard cock drag against her leg. Shifting, he settled between her hips, and as his tip grazed against her heat, he leaned on his elbows to raise both hands to cup her face. She reached between them, arching her head far back as she guided him to her entrance. She inhaled deeply when he rolled his hips, thrusting the head of his cock inside.

"Mine," he repeated, bringing her face back to his and kissing her fiercely. Pressing his forehead against hers, he pushed into her, tantalizing them both with the slow glide of his cock against her inner walls.

Seated inside her, his balls resting against her ass, he shifted his hips, grinding against her clit with his pelvis. "Mine," he muttered, feeling a sheen of sweat break across his back and shoulders. Holding himself still, he was waiting for the intake of breath that would tell him she was getting frustrated with the slow pace. His abdominal muscles were trembling with the strain of holding back, and he buried his head in her neck, biting her shoulder softly, and then trailing his tongue across it to take away the sting.

"Slate," she breathed, her voice scarcely loud enough to hear, "move with me, babe, please." Her breath puffed across his neck.

He smiled, knowing she wanted him as badly as he wanted her. Buried as deep as he could get inside her, it still wasn't close enough, and he wanted to possess her, to feel her hands on him, have her mouth under his. "Love you, baby," he hummed as he started to move.

Moving slowly at first, he felt the subtle drag of his engorged head as he slid in and out of her with full, long strokes. He felt her fingers cupping his ass, pulling him deeper. Adjusting his position, he began the short, deep thrusts he knew were guaranteed to push her closer to her climax.

Gasping for breath, she moved underneath him, her heels pushing restlessly at the mattress, lifting her hips up to meet him. "Slate," she whispered, and he felt the heat of her mouth as she took his earlobe between her teeth gently. Her hands were grasping at his shoulders and back, sliding up from his ass so one could cup around the back of his neck. Slate felt the sting on his back again, and knew she'd marked him; he was used to the pain from those little wounds, loved using them to gauge where she was in her intimate response.

"Come for me, baby," he called to her, moving steadily between her thighs, the sounds of their lovemaking filling the room. Kissing her again, he gasped against her mouth. "Baby...God...Ruby, please, take me with you, baby. Come for me." He increased the speed of his thrusts.

Feeling the fluttering of her inner muscles around his cock, he thrust deep and held, letting her explode around him, clenching him tightly. Her legs tensed, heels digging into the mattress again as her arms tightened around him. Her breath hitched as she moaned deep in her throat, and he knew she was there with him as he started moving again, fast and deep, wanting to share this with her.

His orgasm rode hard down on him, the tingling beginning at the base of his spine, crawling around and through his balls, drawing them up tight against his body as he came deep inside her. "Fuck, baby, now. God, I love you, Ruby. My Ruby. Mine. My wife, my life." He shuddered and thrust hard, flexing on top of her with the powerful effects of coming apart inside her. "I love you," he said as he slowly recovered from his climax, resting his head against hers again.

Long minutes later, he lay down beside her, smiling as she made that disappointed noise when he slid out of her. Pulling her close, he kissed the side of her head and neck, then laid his head down on the pillow. He was nearly asleep when he felt her move; frowning, he tightened his arm around her. "Baby, where you goin'?"

"Bathroom," she whispered, so he released her. A few minutes later, he felt the sheet being pulled back, and rolled over to find her standing above him with a warm, wet washcloth in her hands. "Let me clean you up, babe," she said softly, and gently attended to his cock, laughing quietly as he began stirring to hardness again at the ministering of her hands. She leaned over, stroking and kissing the head of his cock softly, then she spoke to it. "Not right now, mister. Mamma's kinda tired."

He laughed out loud. "Baby, you talking to my cock?" he asked, rolling his head across the pillow to look at her.

"Maybe," came her laughing response.

"Well, if you don't want 'mister' to be bothering you in a couple of minutes, you need to get your hands and mouth off him," he told her, reaching up to pull her down beside him, holding her so her head was on his chest.

He laughed again a few minutes later, the movement of his chest disturbing her until she asked sleepily, "What?"

"Just telling you now, putting it out there...you talking to my cock is cute, baby, but I'm not having a conversation with your pussy. It's going to be having my babies, and I don't want to know what it has to say." He cut his eyes down to her face, taking in her lips curving into a wide smile and her still closed eyes. "Love you, baby," he whispered, his heart growing full when he heard her respond, "I love you too, Slate...and your Mr. Cock."

***

Annoyed, Slate took a drink of his coffee, looking out across the restaurant and away from her. "No," he clipped to Ruby, still refusing to look at her.

"Slate—" she started, but he cut her off.

"I fucking said no, Ruby. Subject closed," he growled at her, slapping the palm of one hand onto the table next to his cup, making it jump. "Where's the fucking waitress?"

She sat in the seat across from him, her chin tipped up stubbornly, green eyes flashing across the table. Standing, she quickly moved and sat next to him, determinedly pressing her hip and leg against his. "I don't want to fight," she got out fast. "I love you."

He snorted. "I love you too, baby, but this is a no-go for me."

"We're nearly halfway there now," she cajoled. "I'd like to meet your mother, Slate."

Rubbing his forehead with fingers and thumb, he then pointed to his face. "See that? I'm frowning again," he told her, "and it's your fault."

"Babe," she scolded, "I know what you've told me. I know you don't have a good relationship with your mom. I'm the last person to judge, and you know that—I've told you about my parents—but you also told me she's sober now, and I want to meet her."

"Not happening, baby," he said softly, resting one palm on her thigh.

She sighed and said, "Okay, then I'll simply have to invite her to the wedding," and laughed as his head fell back and he groaned out loud.

Five hours later, Slate pulled the bike up to the curb at the address he'd gotten from GeeMa. It was a tidy looking little house, freshly painted and well cared for, sitting on a small lot in a nice neighborhood. He felt Ruby's arms loosen their hold on his waist, and turned to slip a hand around her neck, pulling her close for a quick kiss.

"Hey, baby..." he started, and heard the front door open. Sighing, he turned to look at the house again, seeing a woman walk out to stand on the front porch. He knew he hadn't seen her for more than a dozen years, but this woman didn't resemble the one he'd left behind in Wyoming at all. She looked a lot more like the one he'd known years before that, when he was a child.

Her hair was attractively styled, and her eyes were clear. There was no smile on her face, but he figured that was more to do with him dropping in on her like this than her normal personality, because she had soft smile lines next to her eyes and in her cheeks. Trim and fit, she was dressed casually in jeans, with a lightweight sweater over a t-shirt; she was barefoot, something he remembered as a thing with her when they had lived on the ranch before Daddy died.

Without saying a word, Slate held out his hand for Ruby to help her dismount the bike. Once she was firmly on the ground, he tilted the bike over onto the kickstand and swung his leg over the seat, not taking his eyes off the woman on the porch. Her arms were wrapped around her torso, fingers digging in the fabric along her sides.

He felt Ruby's fingers wind themselves into the belt loops at the back of his pants, and he smiled softly. Seeing that change of expression on his face, the woman's aspect lifted, not quite into a smile, but at least a softening of her features. "Andy," she said, and covered her mouth with one hand.

"Hey, Mom," he responded, moving around the bike and up the walk towards her, Ruby in tow behind him. Reaching around for her hand, he pulled Ruby up beside him to go up the steps. "How you doin'?" he asked softly, reaching a hand out to his mother's face; he pulled the hand away from her mouth and gripped it in his, her small hand enveloped in his much larger one. "Mom," he said, turning to look down at the red curls beside him, "this is Ruby."

They talked late into the night, long after Ruby had fallen asleep on the couch. His mother wanted to hear everything about his life, all the things she'd missed over the years, good and bad. He'd told her about the last time he'd seen her, and they'd both cried over what that had done to the Andy he was back then.

The topic of Ben came up often; she'd seen him a couple years ago when the band was in Denver for a show, but he never knew she was in the audience. "I wasn't sure what kind of reception I'd get, and I didn't want to take away from his night," she told Slate.

"He's kind of a prick most of the time." He nodded at her. "It was probably a good idea to not ambush him in public. He's different now, back with the band. His sober companion is working for now, and we recently extended the guy's contract another six months. Benny's afraid he'll slip back to how he was."

"Andy," she said, tears welling in her eyes as she reached out to cup his face with both hands, "I cannot change what I did to you. I wish I could—*God*, how I wish it—but I can't. I don't deserve forgiveness, but I have to take this opportunity to ask for it, or I'll never know. I'm so sorry for what I did, for what you witnessed, and the things you had to do. I have no excuse, but I am so sorry."

She was crying by the time she finished speaking, but refused to hide her pain by looking away, and he was unexpectedly proud of her in that moment. Raising his hands to cover hers, he sighed. "Mom, I get it. I do. I can't imagine your pain, not just at losing Daddy, but afterwards, when you realized the things you'd done. I'm amazed by your resilience and strength to come back after falling so far. Did it suck?" he asked rhetorically and nodded, pulling her hands to the table and covering them with his own. "Yeah, it sucked hard. It was a fucking hard life and changed us all, but I want you to listen to me, and *hear* me.

"I am who I am today, because of who I've been in the past. If you hold onto the fear and the pain of what's gone before, then you let that past rule you. We live with the experiences we choose to give weight and presence to in our lives, and they shape us in all the important ways. Read my fucking tattoos, Mom. It's all here. Every bit of it. Every lesson."

He stood, stripping off his shirt and tossing it onto the chair. Pointing to his left shoulder where the angel stood sentinel, he explained, "This was for Benny, my shrimp. I love my brother, and will always be there for him. You taught me family should be everything way back when Benny and I were just kids. That's stayed with me." Twisting his arm so she could see the words, he pointed to the tribal on his left bicep. "If the past is practice, then the only lesson is to not repeat the shit we do that hurts people, yeah?" She smiled up at him through her tears, nodding.

Showing her his left wrist and forearm, he read the words to her, "See this? 'Never let your fear decide your fate'—for me, that means while we might be the sum of our experiences, we can move past our fear and take control. I think that's what you did when you got sober. It had to be hard, here...by yourself, alone...but you did it.

"This one on my ribs," he pointed to his left side, "says 'The journey is the reward.' Not the destination, but the journey...because fuck, if we are traveling through life for the sake of getting where we're going, then we're stuck. We have to be constantly learning, changing, and growing...and moving forward, yeah?"

Pointing to his right forearm, he said, "This one...this is the most intense statement I've ever heard. 'We live with the scars we choose.' It's profound, because it doesn't mean physical scars. This is talking about the hard shit, the demons inside us that'll tear us apart if we let 'em. What we have to do is not give them space to fucking breathe, and only keep the things that matter, the people we love and the lessons we've learned...the things that make us *better.*"

He leaned down, cupping her cheeks in his hands like she'd done to him earlier. "I am so fucking proud of you, Mom. You didn't let the past rule or define you. You made yourself better and stronger. I love you. I'm sorry I didn't come sooner to see."

***

Rolling east out of Denver, Slate leaned back, tipping his heels on the pegs. He felt Ruby press against him, fingers tightly laced around his middle and her cheek against his back. He'd talked to his mom for hours, and then this morning, she and Ruby had gone shopping for a couple of hours, buying things for the baby, and his mom would mail them soon. She'd be coming to the wedding too, and he couldn't wait to introduce her to his brothers and friends.

Frowning, he thought to himself that he'd have to prepare Benny so there'd be no problems. Maybe he should bring her out a couple days early, so the two of them would have time to sort their shit before things got crazy.

They were approaching an exit and Ruby tapped his shoulder, so he took the ramp, pulling into a gas station. Helping her dismount the bike, he was surprised when she leaned into him. She wrapped her hands around the back of his neck and pulled his face down to hers. Sighing, she traced his jawline with the tip of her nose, and he slowly stroked her braid. "I love you," she said softly, pulling back to look into his eyes intently.

Puzzled, he responded, "I love you too, baby."

"I'm proud of you, Slate," she told him. "You are such a good man." She smiled, leaned in to kiss him, and then turned to walk into the store.

Shaking his head, he put down the kickstand and dismounted the bike to gas up, wondering what the hell that was about.

***

Sitting at the bar in Jackson's, Slate felt like he had come home. He looked over at Ruby where she sat in a booth with Mica, Molly, Jess, and Brandy. The girls were doing shooters, while Ruby and Mica were drinking the herbal tea Mason insisted would be good for the babies. Mica's look had nearly scorched the bar, but she relented when Ruby laughed, and they had both reached for the cups.

Ruby and Mica were due only a few weeks apart, and Ruby promised to come see Mica and Daniel's little boy as soon as he was born. The two women had been chatting nonstop for a couple hours now, and didn't appear to be running out of topics anytime soon.

Mason and Bones sat on stools at the bar beside Slate, and he had an odd sense that his life was coming full circle. These two men had influenced him greatly, and they would be at his wedding. *His wedding*...that still sounded odd, even when it was only in his head.

Mason laughed. "Did you hear what Daniel and Mica are going to name the baby?" Slate shook his head. "Jonathan Mason Rupert," he said proudly, then laughed again. "Mica thought the first name should be after

Daniel's dad, but he argued for *Jason*. That would have made the kid Jason Mason. I told him it sounded like a fucking serial killer."

Slate and Bones both laughed at that, and they looked up as Daniel walked in through the door. He first went to Mica, leaning down to speak to her, and then kissed her softly. Turning, he walked across the bar to the men, giving Merry a casual wave. Reaching out his hand, he pulled Slate into a brief, one-armed embrace. "How you doin', Slate?"

"I'm good, man, real good. Ruby and I are getting married in a coupla weeks. You gotta bring Mica down for the wedding," Slate laughed, "and Jess, Brandy, Molly, and her little man. Fuck, man, you'll need to rent a bus."

"I think Brandy is making the cakes," Mason said with a grin, "so you'll have to transport baked goods across state lines. You good with that, Daniel?"

"Fuck you, Mason," he laughed. "I'll get Dickie to drive; no one will be the same by the time we get there."

Slate leaned back looking at Daniel, and then across at Molly, "I heard J.J. was interested in Molly. That shit stick, or did he move on?"

Daniel rolled his eyes. "It's sickening how they are around each other. He likes her, she likes him...but neither will act on it, so there's this thick, cloying, sexual tension. He's fucked in the head because of being in the wheelchair, and she sees herself as the unwed mother. I hope they figure it out soon; that's all I'm gonna say. You decide where you're holding the ceremony and reception yet?" Daniel asked Slate, who shook his head. "Okay, if you decide you want to use the Coliseum, let me know, I know the GM for the ECHL team there, so I bet I could help."

"Fuck me, the hockey arena? I don't think we need anything that big, man," he started, and stopped when Mason and Bones laughed. "Seriously," he started again, "I don't think..." He trailed off, because they were laughing again.

Mason clapped a hand on his shoulder. "Slate, brother, I know of nearly four hundred Rebels who are going to be there, plus about a hundred Soldiers, and another couple hundred Machos. I've heard from Disciples, Dominos, Highwaymen, and Devil's Sins—now that they cleaned up their shit. Bones, man, how many Skeptics you bringing?"

Bones laughed. "About a hundred."

Daniel spoke up, "The entire Mallets team is coming, and since Jason is in Fort Wayne, he's bringing a bunch of the local players too. By my count, that's nearly a thousand guests, man. Let me know about the Coliseum."

Slate laid his head down on the bar top; he was a little dizzy. "Fuck me," he breathed, "a thousand people?"

An arm reached around him, pulling him back and depositing a plate on the bar in front of him. Twisting around, he looked to see who it was and grabbed the big man behind him in a tight hug, thumping his back hard. "Fucking Road Runner, man, I want you to meet my Ruby. I think you are part of the reason we're together. I told her so many hilarious stories about your fucked up menus."

Road Runner looked offended for half a second, and then the look fell off his face, replaced with a wide smile that split his beard. "Happy to help, motherfucker, and happy to meet the one who captured your heart." At this, he clasped his hands in front of his heart, then nearly fell over laughing.

"Fuck you," Slate chuckled at him.

"Before we go there, I want you to try this. It's pan-fried mushrooms in a reduced sake and compote sauce and I like it, but I wondered...why are you laughing?" Road Runner's face fell, and he yelled across the room, "Mica, Mason's being an asshole. So's your husband."

The women crowded around them, and Slate found his smile was stuck on his face. He introduced Ruby to everyone who came into the bar, and she tried a half-dozen dishes for Road until she finally shook her head, biting her lips between her teeth. "No more, please. I'm so stuffed." She hugged the chef, and he caught Slate's eyes over her head, grinning and nodding his head in approval.

They stayed in Slate's old room in the back of the bar. As quiet fell on the building after everyone left, he pulled her close to his side in the bed, listening to her slow breathing as she slept. "I love you, baby," he whispered, kissing the side of her head, "so much."

***

Pulling into the parking garage, Slate tensed, looking around. He'd done this every time he parked in here since Ruby was kidnapped; he just couldn't help himself. Ruby started to get off the bike and he snapped, "Wait a min," swiveling his head back and forth, looking for threats.

"Babe, it's okay; there's no one here but us," she tried to soothe him, running her hands down his back. In his head, he kept thinking, *She had been at my side when she was taken.* Every time he remembered waking up on the floor of the garage without her, it stole his breath and reminded him nothing was safe.

Inside the elevator, he took a deep breath. *I have got to get past this*, he thought, shaking his head at himself. "Glad to be home, baby?" he asked Ruby. "Ready to sleep in our bed?"

"Ohhh," she moaned, "you have no idea."

Sitting in bed that night, she had her head in his lap and he was stroking her hair. "Ruby, we need to decide where we're getting married. I was talking to Bingo, and he said there's a state park not far that might work. They've got an inn on the place we can rent for the party after. We can let folks know they can camp there; plus, we can put a couple hundred up at the clubhouse. Pokagon sounds about right to me." He leaned over to see her eyes were closed and smiled, tracing down her nose with one fingertip. "Okay, baby, you sleep. I got this."

***

"That was a fucking awesome wedding, Slate," Deke told him, clapping him on the shoulder. "I about lost it when I saw how many brothers came to honor you, man. I'm fucking proud of our club and members. This has been epic."

Slate nodded, taking a deep breath. It had been epic, and amazing, and fucking scary at times, but it was behind them now. He looked down at the plain platinum band on his finger, remembering the intense look on Ruby's face as she put it there, her pretty lips mouthing the phrase she'd had engraved on the inner surface, *'For-fucking-ever, babe'*, and he smiled.

"It was a good day, yeah?" He looked up at Deke, and then swung his gaze across the field, taking in the hundreds of people standing or sitting in large and small groupings. "I am humbled, man," he said softly. "I love these motherfuckers, and they all came here for me and Ruby."

The wedding had been casual; they'd gotten Preacher from St. Louis to do the vows, and had a small group of close friends and family to witness. The hog roast afterward had been huge. Mason had been right—there were nearly a thousand people who came, but he'd gotten help with the logistics of feeding and housing that many people, and it had gone pretty smoothly. It helped that the weather cooperated too, giving them beautiful, cloud-free days and warm nights.

He spent the next hour moving from group to group, thanking people for coming and accepting their congratulations. He knew Ruby was doing the same in a smaller way with their family, most of who were staying at the Potawatomi Inn. They had made plans to meet back at the Inn shortly, so they could get in the wind and away from everyone.

The last group he stopped at was filled with his friends: Watcher, Mason, Bones, Bingo, Mica and Daniel, Molly and J.J., Jason, Bear, Duck, Digger, Tug, Estavez and Carmela, Blackie and Lottie...so many familiar faces around him. He realized he'd been there longer than expected when he saw Ruby making her way over to him, and within minutes, he felt the familiar tug of her fingers winding their way into his belt loops.

Reaching back, he loosely clasped her wrist, pulling her up alongside him, tucking her into his side. Wrapping an arm around her waist, he covered her belly with his palm, dragging his fingertip across the waistband of her pants. Leaning down to kiss the top of her head, he said softly, "You ready to go, baby?" He felt her nod against his chest and leaned down, scooping her up into his arms as she squealed and giggled.

"I'm taking my woman away now, Brothers," he announced to the crowd. "Last one out, turn off the lights." He smiled, hearing the catcalls and laughter from around them, and turned to walk her to his bike. Slate stopped short when he saw the lines of people stretching across the field; he would have to walk between them.

"Ready, baby?" he whispered to her.

"Always ready with you, Slate; let's go," she whispered back, and he began striding between the rows of their friends. Hands were slapping him on the back and ruffling his hair, but there were also hands that reached out to drop things in Ruby's lap. He saw patches, jewelry, money clips with cash, cards...it seemed nearly everyone had something small they wanted to give, and Ruby's hands were working overtime to gather them all.

Slate leaned his forehead against the side of Ruby's head as he walked, carrying her. "I love you so much, Ruby. Love our Peanut, too." He kissed her neck.

"Love you too, babe," she told him. It took them nearly twenty minutes to transit the field, and her lap was overflowing by the time they arrived where Susan,

DeeDee, GeeMa, and Ben were standing near the bike, waiting to say goodbye.

DeeDee had a duffle in her hand, and she laughed when she saw the piles of gifts stacked and strewn across Ruby's belly and chest. "I heard there was a gift line and thought you might need something to carry it all in," she said, coming over and holding the bag open for Ruby. "Love you, baby girl," she said, leaning in to kiss first Ruby's and then Slate's cheek, " and love you too, big guy." Slate put Ruby down and watched as she hugged his family. *Fuck me*, he mouthed as his heart clenched; *she* was his family now.

Sitting astride the bike, he held out a hand to help her up onto the pegs and onto the seat behind him. "Hold on, baby," he called, and they moved slowly down the drive. Once on the highway, he opened the throttle up, feeling her fingers tighten around his waist. Tipping his chin, he pointed the bike south and put them into the wind.

***

THANK YOU FOR READING *Slate*!

This is Book #2 in a series. I hope you enjoyed and fell in love with the characters as much as I did while writing Slate's story. You can learn more about Mason, Bear, and Eddie's story in Book #3 of the Rebel Wayfarers MC book series, *Bear*, available now.

ABOUT THE AUTHOR

Raised in the south, MariaLisa deMora learned about the magic of books at an early age. Every summer, she would spend hours in the Upshur County library, devouring stacks of books in every genre. She still reads voraciously, and always has a few books going in paperback, hardback, on devices! On music, she says, "I love music of nearly any kind—jazz, country, rock, alt rock, metal, classical, bluegrass, rap, gangstergrass, hip hop—you name the type, I probably listen to it.

"I can often be seen dancing through the house in the early mornings. But what I really, REALLY love is live music. My favorite way to experience live music is seeing bands in small, dive bars [read: small, intimate venues]. If said bar [venue] has a good selection of premium tequila, then that's a definite plus! Oh, and since I'm a hand gal, drummers are my thing—yeah, Paul and Alex—you know who you are!"

ADDITIONAL SERIES AND BOOKS

Please note each book is part of a series, for the most part featuring characters from additional books in the series. If the books in a series are read out of order, you'll twig to spoilers for the other books, so going back to read the skipped titles won't have the same angsty reveals.

It is strongly recommended they be read in order.

Rebel Wayfarers MC series:

Mica, #1
A Sweet & Merry Christmas, short story #1.5
Slate, #2
Bear, #3
Jase, #4
Gunny, #5
Mason, #6
Hoss, #7
Harddrive Holidays, short story #7.5
Duck, #8
Biker Chick Campout, short story #8.5
Watcher, #9
A Kiss to Keep You, novella #9.25
Gun Totin' Annie, short story #9.5
Secret Santa, short story #9.75
Bones, #10
Gunny's Pups, novella #10.25
Never Settle, short story #10.5
Not Even A Mouse, short story #10.75
Fury, #11
Cassie, #12 (2018)
Road Runner's Ride, novella #12.5

Occupy Yourself band series:

Born Into Trouble, #1
Grace In Motion, #2 (2018)
What They Say, #3 (2018)

Neither This, Nor That series:

This Is the Route Of Twisted Pain, #1
Treading the Traitor's Path: Out Bad, #2
Trapped by Fate on Reckless Roads, #3 (2018)

Other Books:

With My Whole Heart
Alace Sweets

More information available at mldemora.com.

90699356R00276

Made in the USA
Columbia, SC
11 March 2018